DAGGER OF RED

SPIRITS OF LIANA, BOOK 1

SIMON PITTMAN

For Jensen and Mina, my prince and princess, hero and heroine.

Simon x

1

THE DAY OF DARKNESS

An ear-splitting boom echoed across the tropical island of Coryàtès, an island which sat on its own in planet Mikana's Eastern Sea. A ferocious tremble followed the amplified, drum-like noise causing everyone in the city to fall. The previously clear-blue sky above darkened, the sun blocked out by layers of descending ash. People began to desperately gasp and choke as thick, grey grit lined their throats and lungs.

Among the first to drag themselves up off the still shaking ground was the Queen as she found the ledge of a window to pull up and balance against. She gazed out across her city from the perch of the window. Despite her elevated position above the grey and dense cloud, not much of the city was visible to her as the ash continued to descend across the city rooftops. Soon the ringing in her ears from the thunderous explosion faded and was replaced with the screaming and screeching of men, women, and children alike. She looked to the south and could no longer see the rocky shoreline beneath that her castle sat upon. It was as if the castle was floating in mid-air on a dark and bespeckled cloud. She turned her gaze North, inland towards the cause of the devastation. The islands' volcano that had lay dormant for longer than any record in any manuscript in existence had erupted.

"Vivek, are you okay?" asked the Queen, turning her head to investigate the circular room she was standing in. She looked for where he had been sitting but could not see him. As she continued to look, she caught a glimpse of her slender figure in the shards of broken blue glass on the floor that had broken from its window frame. Her long and wavy jet-black hair remained largely unmoved and unblemished - unlike her soft, well-formed face that had blood trickling down the sides of her nose from a cut on her forehead.

"Vivek??" she repeated.

"I'm okay... I think," replied a weak voice as a head poked out from under a large wooden table, triangular in shape, positioned in the centre of the room.

"The mountain... it exploded," the Queen said, still trying to catch her breath.

"What do you see?" asked Vivek, seeing the Queen standing at the window.

"Low, dark grey clouds surround us. A glint of light at the top of Mount Indigo - that is where the smoke is coming from. And..." The Queen hesitated, questioning whether she should say aloud her next observation. "A rainbow also emanates from the peak of the mountain,"

"A rainbow...?" Vivek said in a perplexed tone.
The Queen nodded before continuing. "Wait... the rainbow has vanished. Gone as quickly as it appeared," She drew three deep breaths to compose herself. "Vivek, today is the day, isn't it? It's written there would be a day when the sky would fall,

and your ears would bleed, and a red river would dissolve all in its path. The sky is falling, and my ears are bleeding, but where is the red river?" the Queen questioned, turning to her closest and wisest advisor.

"Perhaps it is on the other side of the mountain, your Highness?" replied the elder man, struggling to piece his sentence together and still unable to stand from the tremble.

"But Vivek, the mines!" exclaimed the Queen. "The mines are there!" she repeated.

"Your Highness, if the mines are gone, then we have lost our biggest trade and raw material commodities," replied the clerk, still strewn across the floor. "Not to mention... other possible consequences," continued the Clerk. His voice was clear with concern, but his eyes showed fear at these other possible consequences. "Perhaps the explosion was too power-ful, too overwhelming? Perhaps this event actually means we can end that particular chapter?"

"We cannot assume anything, Vivek," replied the Queen.

"Then we must send men to scout out the mines and surrounding area, Your Highness," said the Clerk.

"If the people see us sending men to the mines rather than helping the city there will be unrest at best. They need us to show them strength and support," the Queen said thoughtfully.

"But we must know as soon as possible, your Highness. If we are to assume the worst right now, then we are in more danger than what this eruption has caused," said Clerk Vivek, who was now sitting up against the leg of a table.

A portly maid then came running into the circular room through the door, which was actually more of a hole in the wall due to the explosion as the door was barely hanging off its bottom hinge, although still standing more upright than Clerk Vivek.

"Queen Adriya! Are you okay, are you hurt?" the portly woman exclaimed.

"I'm okay, thank you Agatha" confirmed the Queen. "Agatha, find my uncle, I need to see him right away."

"But my Queen, you are wounded, and your face is covered in blood. I must tend to you and Clerk Vivek first," said the kind-voiced maid.

"Agatha, I am fine, I must speak with my uncle," repeated the Queen, forcefully.

"Of course, your Highness, I will find him right away," replied Agatha, who on her way out helped up the struggling Clerk onto a chair.

Queen Adriya drew up a chair next to the window and continued to stare out at the devastation below.

"I will send only my uncle. He can ride faster than anyone else," said the Queen decisively.

"Will you tell him? Will you tell him the truth?" questioned the Clerk.

"No, there is no need. I will tell him I need his men here to help the citizens. He is to assess the state of the mines. We cannot cover all the ground on the island," the Queen answered.

"What will we do if the news is not good?" asked Clerk Vivek.

"I don't know Vivek, I don't know," replied the Queen.

2

LIGHT FROM THE DARK

Queen Adriya sat and looked out across her city. People were beginning to stand up as the tremors faded, hugging whoever was closest to them. The beautiful contrast of sandstone structures and blue cobalt-based glass windows had been replaced with a layer of grey dust that, although already two inches thick, continued to settle on any surface it could find. As the cloud thinned, the Queen was able to see further, and it was now visible to her that the districts closest to the mountain had been completely demolished. Piles of rock now stood where buildings once were.

A navy-blue banner embroidered with gold writing reading "The Queen's Table" lay across the ground, pinned down by a number of fallen books. Usually a room full of discussion, debate and decision making was now the scene for a sombre, thoughtful, and somewhat oppressive silence as the Queen and Clerk listened to the sounds of the streets below with no interest in resolving the mess strewn upon the floor.

Time seemed to stand still for the moments the Queen and the Clerk waited for Adriya's Uncle to arrive as the shock and daze set in and the initial rush of adrenaline waned. Before she knew it, he had arrived and was standing behind her.

"Queen Adriya! My Queen, my niece, are you okay? Can you hear me?" her uncle shouted at her whilst pulling off his gauntlet and placing a gentle hand on her shoulder as he stood behind her, with Agatha close by.

"Uncle Tarak!" announced Queen Adriya, standing up off her chair for the first time in what must have been thirty minutes to give him a welcoming hug.

"Adriya, there's panic in the streets. The people don't know what to do. There's reports of the city's Guild District being completely destroyed. We have not had a loss like this in living memory. The people need your leadership and your strength. What are we to do?" said Tarak with an urgent tone in his voice and an arm resting on the handle of his sword.

"Have your strongest soldiers and horses go to the Guild District to search the rubble for any survivors. Give them horses and carts to move the wounded to the clinics for treatment. Direct anyone who has lost their home or is seriously injured into the castle walls. Agatha, send any maids you can spare to the streets to help the wounded. Castle Langton is still standing strong," Queen Adriya ordered.

"Right away, your Highness," replied Agatha, before scurrying away.

"Clerk Vivek, gather the other advisors and have them meet us here as soon as possible for us to discuss our recovery plans," Queen Adriya ordered again.

"At once, your Highness," replied the Clerk, managing a tame bow before slowly making his way to the exit of the room, being careful not to trip over any books or furniture on his way out.

"We will come back stronger," Tarak said to the Queen.

"Tarak, I need you to go to the mines," stated the Queen, getting straight to the reason for his summoning.

"The mines? But they're full of fugitives. We must concentrate on the citizens. We can't afford to waste valuable men on the mines," questioned Tarak, frowning with his dark, straight eyebrows.

"Not men, just you. Look out towards the mountain, Tarak. There is no red river on this side of the mountain. That must mean it's on the Northern side where the mines are and we need the mines or we will have nothing to rebuild with. I want you to go alone and scout the area, see what the destruction is like. You are the quickest horseman on the island. If you leave now, you should make it back before the moon is at its highest. Please be careful and look out for anything unusual," explained the Queen.

"Unusual?" replied Tarak.

"No one alive has ever experienced such an event before. Who knows what you might find out there? But please come back safe," she begged.

"As soon as I have organised my generals I will head out as you command," Tarak gave a gentle bow of the head before turning and leaving Queen Adriya to her thoughts, the first of which was how Agatha and Vivek failed in their own etiquette before taking their leave. Although Agatha and Vivek would be spoken to, punishment for such a minor infraction in the aftermath of such an event would not even be considered by the Queen and she soon moved onto more pressing thoughts.

Although the Queen kept to many traditions, she was known across the Island of Coryàtès for her balance and fair-

ness. She believed respect was gained through deliberation
and strong decision making, rather than shows of authority
and ruthlessness.

This is why, in her first announcement after her coronation,
that she had the spire and room she was standing in built. The
Queen's Table was not constructed out of personal vanity, but
a symbol to the people that she would listen.

The Tower of Seeds that housed The Queens Table could be
seen from anywhere within the city and for many miles
outside of it. It's spiralling, deep blue, glass windows weaved
up and around the otherwise golden sandstone structure.

Through the magnificent blue glass windows, the
armoured posture of Tarak Langton could be seen trotting
down the spiralling staircase. His upright, confident gate was
unaffected by the urgency of his descent. He reached the
bottom, without a hint of breathlessness despite the hundreds
of steps he had just traversed. A tall, grand wooden door with
elaborate metal cast hinges greeted him. Contrary to the door
of The Queen's Table, this one showed no signs of damage
from the eruption.

Tarak pushed it open with surprising ease considering its
size and proceeded into a triangular shaped hall. The room
also appeared to be unscathed from the volcano's wrath. The
slightly sloped blue glass roof was considerably dirtier and
darker than usual due to the layers of ash but the ten-foot
walls that lined each of the three sides still proudly presented
various banners, trophies and accolades. The rows of empty
seats that sat upon these imposing walls added to the eerie
echo of the room. There were two other doors in the room,
both centred in the middle of their respective walls and both
intact, much like the one Tarak had just walked through.

Just as Tarak had stepped foot into the room, both the other doors opened. Their creaking and squeaking reverberated off every surface as they did.

"Sir Langton!" sounded the deep voices of the 6 soldiers clunking into the room, adding to its ominous echoes.

"Generals," replied Tarak, authoritatively. "You," He said, pointing to the shortest of the six. "Gather any off-duty soldiers and order your battalions to go to the Guild District and search for survivors in the rubble. Inform any injured civilians to take shelter and medicine at the temple or nearby clinics."

The General nodded, before replying: "Sir Langton, I've just come past our armoury in the north. It's been toppled and the entrances blocked," the high pitch of a female General spoke. Her face bore a long, shallow, diagonal scar stretching the length of her face. Along the edges of the scar her skin tissue had contractured from the burn of whatever had caused her disfigurement.

"The Queen's focus is the people. Our soldiers are well trained in adversity, they will manage," instructed Tarak.

"But our off-duty soldiers won't have the armour and weapons to go around," the female General rebutted.

"Not all off-duty soldiers will have had their personal armour buried and they don't need chest plates and helmets to lift rubble, General," responded Tarak.

"If we don't regain our armour and weaponry, we leave ourselves open to attack whilst we are distracted by this event, Sir!" replied the female General.

"Then it's fortunate we live on an Island with no imme-diate enemies, isn't it?" Tarak replied, clearly becoming increasingly agitated at the General's questions. "Should anyone try to attack us, I'm sure Admiral Remi will inform us."

The female General backed down.

"I hope in the heat of battle you act on my orders rather than waste time cross-examining them, or you and your soldiers won't last long," warned Tarak.

The General kept her head bowed as the group headed out from the doors from which they came to see out their orders. She could feel the eyes of her colleagues silently laughing to one another as she walked behind them a few paces away.

"She's not the brightest spark in the flame is she," mocked General Omar to his counterparts as they walked ahead of her, laughing, not caring whether or not she could overhear them.

"Hey!" she shouted. "Insult me again and my spark will be the last thing you see!" getting ready to pull her longsword from its scabbard.

The group of General's ahead of her stopped. They all turned to General Omar to sense his reaction, before bursting into a roar of laughter and continued on their way.

A gentle hand fell upon the soldier's shoulder.
"Put it away Amara, now's not the time," came the calm and fragile voice of Clerk Vivek.

"Why do they treat me so?" she asked.

"Because you are different Amara, and being different often scares those who live up to their own stereotypes," Vivek said.

Vivek patted Amara's metal shoulder plating, smiled and walked away towards a group of messenger boys and their horses situated just outside the main castle gate to send the Queen's word to his advisory compatriots.

Amara turned to thank Vivek for his comfort but stopped as she caught sight of the fast, blurry figure of Tarak on horseback heading down a steep slope on the edge of the castle walls which Amara knew only led to the castle's underground sewage system.

"A strange place to be going at this time," Amara said to herself. She quickly gathered her horse and hastily followed Tarak below into the castle's foundations.

Amara headed down the slope. Fortunately, following Tarak was easy as there was only one long, dark, echoing corridor. For a while, the footsteps of Tarak's horse could be heard rebounding off the walls in front of Amara and her horse, acting as a perfect cover for her horses' own echoing footsteps. As she approached the end of the corridor Tarak's echoes stopped. Amara stopped her horse and dismounted with an impressive amount of stealth for a soldier in armour.

The end of the corridor opened into a large cavern, laden with sandstone pillars supporting the castle above. In the middle of this underground cavern ran a deep trench of water, flowing rapidly from Amara's right to her left. The flow was so heavy, splashes of water frequently spilled over the top of the trench.

Despite the natural bright colour of sandstone, the cavern was hauntingly dark as the only sources of light came from the half-moon, barred off entrance and exit of the trench.

Amara quietly hunched over and walked towards the trench using the pillars as cover to aid her stealthy move-ments. As she neared the centre of the trench, a loud, scraping noise coupled with a dart of bright light graced the cavern along the left-hand side wall. A line of pillars prevented Amara from seeing more. She had to get closer and proceeded to carefully make her way along the trench end. Her angle of sight had improved just enough to see Tarak pushing a part of the caverns wall out, like a huge, camouflaged door. His effort and grunting indicated how heavy this must have been.

When Tarak had opened the door just enough for him and his horse to pass through, multiple loud splashes echoed from behind Amara. Barrell's of faeces had come tumbling down a shoot situated above the trench entrance and landed in the water to be washed away. The volume and suddenness of the splashes startled both Tarak and Amara, causing her to slip on the wet surface. Trying her best not to voice her pain, she hit her head hard on the stone floor as her legs gave way, but she was at least thankful that she had become hidden by the long, criss-crossing shadows that the pillars cast around the basement while she lay on the floor. Tarak placed his hand readily on his scabbard and gave a quick glance at the water before seeing the barrels – which had broken on impact. Reassured, he guided his horse out the secret door.

Amara returned to her horse and untied him, still clutching the back of her head. "Ouch, this had better be worth it." she said to her horse, who was displeased at the smell in the air and lifted his nose and made noises of discontent.

"Now you know how your stables smell, hey boy!" joked Amara.

"Come now, we need to see why Tarak is leaving the city when he should be here helping like everyone else," Amara guided her companion over a small flat, barrier-less bridge across the middle of the sewage water and exited the cavern through the same secret door that Tarak had used.

Large piles of rocks lined the outside of the exit leaving only a small sandy path to traverse through.

Three horse lengths later the view opened up to a vast, sandy beach. To Amara's left towered the tall cliffs upon where Castle Langton stands. From the horizon to her right the folds of the sea could be heard toing and froing upon the fine white sand.

Amara gazed down at the footprints in the sand left behind by Tarak's horse.

"The distance between the footprints - looks like he's in a hurry," she said, talking to her horse again. "We'll be quicker without my armour,"

She moved earnestly to remove her armour. After removing her helmet, she untied the bun her long dark hair had been in and allowed it to fall down to her back. She found an opening in a pile of rocks just big enough to hide her armour in.

Amara couldn't risk anyone happening upon it and suspecting that she had fled the city. It would no doubt be deemed an act of cowardice – or indeed treason from Tarak for he would surely know she had followed him.

Amara jumped back on her stallion. "We better get going fast - Ya!" She commanded her stallion to ride at full pace, using her stirrups to enforce her command.

Soon the two were in full flow. Her long hair was flying behind her. Her dark brown shirt, and dark blue trousers tightly gripping the front of her battle toned body as the light material trailed and flapped behind loosely in the wind. The vast sandy beach was a playground for speed. If only the sun was not blocked out by the grey ash cloud above, thought Amara.

It was some time before the two stopped, but it wasn't tiredness that caused them to halt. Rising in front of them at the foot of the easterly face of the mountain was a churning, vertical cloud of white smoke. Amara checked the ground and Tarak's tracks veered inland into a wooded area towards the smoke. She had no choice but to head towards the obvious danger.

This part of the island was not visited by many due to its

proximity to the mines and its inhabitants. The area was normally tightly guarded. Amara proceeded with much more caution. Judging by the overgrowth and narrowness of the track she was headed on; it was not regularly used. It was also steep as it headed up the base of the mountain.

"Woah boy!" She commanded her horse to a stop, and she dismounted. Amara paused, listening. A crackling, simmering sound could be heard, in the direction from the rising white smoke.

"Stay here, boy," she said to her horse and made her way curiously towards the noise, through the thick branches and bushes of the forest. She soon arrived at a cliff ledge and could go no further.

"Oh no..!" she exclaimed as she gazed out in horror, covering her mouth with the top of her shirt as the toxins in the air caused her to cough uncontrollably.

Below her was a scorching hot, red river of lava flowing down the mountain side caused by the eruption. The billowing white smoke was caused by the meeting of the river with the coolness of the sea. A few rocky islands were dotted amongst the lava pool, still slowly melting into the burning liquid. Burnt bodies lined the banks of the river flow. Fallen bricks and bent melted metal lay upon a black, scorched land the other side of the red river.

"The river has destroyed the mines. It destroyed it all. Everything in its path. It's all gone," Amara said to herself in disbelief.

Amara was still taking in the magnificence and horror of the view when the figure of Tarak appeared through the gaps in the smoke and began jumping from rock to rock.

Amara moved closer to the edge of the cliff and lay down and looked over the edge to get a closer look. The thick white smoke made it difficult to see. Suddenly a strong gust of wind briefly parted it for long enough for her to see what he was trying to move towards. What she saw made her question herself, briefly even her own sanity. Maybe the toxins were playing tricks with her mind?

Tarak was standing upon a rock where half of its surface was still covered in grass. The only grassy rock amongst the scorching lava and heat. He was also not the only living thing on this half-covered rock. He carefully knelt down and gently picked up a small bundle of light blue clothes that was wriggling and screaming. Tarak was cradling a living baby amongst all of this destruction. He paused, glancing his head towards the half of the rock that was bare from grass to examine it and stared upon a scorched black silhouette of a foetal adult figure that had been etched in its surface. In the blackened grass lay an object. Amara could not see what it was as Tarak soon scooped it up before turning to jump back to safety.

As soon as he had made his jump off the rock and back towards the stable ground beneath Amara, the grass from the rock was incinerated and began to slowly melt like all the other rocks in the river of lava.

Amara leapt up and ran towards her stallion. As she arrived at him, she could hear Tarak and his horse hastily heading towards her position.

She knew he would see her on the open beach if she were to leave now, so she took her horse into the dense forest and hid behind a large cluster of fallen trees. She watched from behind them as he soon sped past, focussed on returning to Castle Langton without any sense of Amara being nearby.

"I've just seen the strangest thing," Amara said to her horse, in awe of what she had just witnessed. "But how did he

know to come here? And the way he looked at that silhouette... he had a look on his face I've never seen before. He actually looked... scared..." Amara stroked her horse's neck for
reassurance, more for her than for her horse.

She straddled her steed again and took off towards the
direction of the beach.

As the hoofs made their first imprints in the sand, Amara
squinted and raised her hands to shield her eyes from the
bright daggers of a setting sun that were beginning to penetrate the thick moody greys of volcanic dust cloud that were
moving quickly across the skyline as the coastal wind moved
them on. The combination of yellows, reds and greys taking
their turns in reflecting off the white sandy beach were a truly
beautiful and breath-taking vision to behold.

The strong wind across the weightless, fine sand had
come as a welcome piece of luck to Amara, whose previous
hoof tracks had been covered up, alleviating potential
suspicion.

Amara darted back across the blowing, cartwheeling sand
through the streaks of sunlight that periodically hit the ground
and made her way as quickly as possible back to the rock pile
entrance of the sewer house.

"That's a relief, it's still here!" Amara declared to her horse
as she began to retrieve and redress her armour from the rock
pile where she had hidden it.

Darkness had now fallen upon the landscape as they made
their way back inside the castle walls. The pair, tired from the
long ride and now breathing heavily, made their way through
the underground corridors and up the slope to the castle's
deserted courtyard entrance.

Amara caught sight of Agatha coming out of a building on
the other side of the courtyard carrying a pile of linen.

"Agatha!" shouted Amara running across to greet her "Have you seen Sir Langton recently?"

"Oh yes Ma'am, he's in the Triunity Hall speaking to the Queen. If I were you I wouldn't disturb them. They're discussing something very, very important," said Agatha before hurriedly departing.

'I know exactly what they're discussing,' thought Amara to herself.

Amara made her way to the large triangular building at the foot of the courtyard. She peered through the keyhole of the left-hand wall's pair of doors. The vague outlines of the Queen and Sir Langton stood in the middle of the hall; however, she couldn't make out what they were saying through the thick door.

'I'll have to try and sneak into the seating area. I have to know what this is all about.'

Turning to her left, she began climbing the wide steps that lined the wall and crouched as she traversed them to maintain a stealthy approach.

Amara's luck continued as she found the doors at the peak unlocked and slightly ajar. Her slender and slight figure squeezed through the tiny gap without the doors moving so much to be noticeable by the pair below her.

She edged her way down the rows of empty seating and peered over the cusp of the 10ft wall and listened quietly and intently to the whispering conversation taking place.

"You knew this baby was there, didn't you Iya?" Tarak questioned the Queen.

"I, I wasn't sure for certain Uncle. I had to be sure," replied Queen Adriya.

"So does this mean the ancient story is true?" questioned Tarak again.

"I suppose it does," replied the Queen.

"And you sent me out there. On my own? I could have been killed. If not at the hands of the red river or the toxic smoke, but by the hand of..."

"I'm sorry!" Queen Adriya cut Tarak off. "But I couldn't leave this child there and I couldn't risk anyone else finding out! Please, Uncle, you have to understand."

"I don't question your decision, I question why you didn't confide in me before I left, unprepared. How long have you known?" responded Sir Langton.

"We received word from the mines just two days ago. We hadn't even had a chance to confirm the report, that's why you had to go, to make sure," the Queen replied, emotionally.

"So, what does this mean?" Tarak continued his interrogation.

"Everyone knows the ancient story. But that's all we thought it was, a story. A story told by the Visendi to scare us and make us follow their teachings. But we've been wrong Uncle, it's always been a warning. We have to begin preparing the rebuilding of our city and the religion. We cannot let more devastation befall us. No one knows how long we have, but we must do what we can," urged the Queen.

"This is beyond doubt a dreadful state we find ourselves in, and it will certainly not be easy, but I will always be at your side, Iya," said Tarak.

"Thank you, Uncle. Thank you," She hugged him with one arm as her other cradled the sleeping baby.

Amara quickly ducked behind the ledge as Tarak turned and exited through the door beneath her.

Just a few moments after he had left, the door behind the Queen that led to The Tower of Seeds opened and Clerk Vivek appeared.

"The child is certainly a pretty one, your highness," Vivek complimented the baby in the Queen's arms.

"Look at her sweet smile, emerging through the day's dust, like a spark of light from the depths of darkness," replied the Queen.

"What are we to do with the child? Should we look to home it with a family where we can keep a close eye on it?" Vivek asked.

"Absolutely not, I will keep the baby as my own," the Queen replied.

"And how do you propose we manage that without arousing suspicion?" Vivek continued to enquire further.

"You will put an announcement out tomorrow that I was injured in the quake, and I needed to recover in private due to the extent of my injuries. In two months', I will emerge claiming this child as my new born baby and announce that at the time of the quake I was nearly six months pregnant," said Queen Adriya.

"With all due compliments, Your Highness, you don't look six months pregnant. That may take some convincing," Clerk Vivek replied.

"I'm sure you can find a physician who can claim to be a witness to such an occurrence," The Queen said, looking down her nose at Clerk Vivek with an obvious hint that someone can be bribed, at the very least.

"And who would be the father?" asked the Clerk.

"I am the Queen, Vivek, and the people will need to know who I spend my time with is my choice and I do not need to explain everything to them. Unlike many other monarchs I invite them into my home and give them the opportunity to be involved in decisions of the city, but they do not need to be involved in the beginning and ends of my private matters. The people do not need a false father for this child so I will not give them one. They will accept her as mine," replied the Queen assertively.

"As you wish my Queen," said Vivek, turning away, before turning back to ask one final question. "One final thing, Your Highness. Have you thought of a name for the child yet?"

"Indeed, I have. I will call her, Liana."

3

PEER PRESSURE

"**G**o on Liana, I dare you!" encouraged a scrawny, curly blonde-haired boy.

"Do you know how much trouble I'd be in with my mother?!" Liana exclaimed to the boy sitting beside her as she peered down over the ledge of the rooftop.

"Someone's got to teach her a lesson, might as well be you, you're the only one who can get away with it," said a girl with tightly braided brunette hair, crouching the other side of Liana.

"Look at her down there, commanding everyone using fear and threats. It goes against everything your mother stands for, Liana," continued the boy.

"He's right, you're only doing your Royal duty," confirmed the girl.

"I suppose so…" Liana replied nervously "Ok, give it here, if I duck down quick enough, she won't see me."

"Awesome!" replied the boy, with a huge smile spanning his face as he passed a heavy bucket to Liana.

Liana slowly lifted the bucket onto the rooftop ledge. She peered over, being sure to get a good aim.

"Ok. 3.. 2.. 1.." she tipped over the bucket and its contents went plummeting towards its target.

Liana was quick to duck back down behind the ledge.

"AAARRRGGGHHH! It's so sticky, and it smells... it smells really bad!" shrieked the voice from below, amongst a chorus of laughing onlookers.

"Result!" said the boy chuckling with the two girls beside him. "I'm guessing some of those eggs must have been off!"

The trio's giggles didn't last long, not one moment later, a voice thundered up towards their direction.

"LIANA!"

The trio gasped and gazed at each other.

"How does she know it was me?!" panicked Liana.

"Liana, your hair..." said her female accomplice, pointing to Liana's long, vibrant electric blue hair, half dangling over the ledge. "Since there's no one else with hair like yours, it doesn't take much working out!"

"You'd better run!" urged the boy.

Liana jolted up before hesitating to turn back to the motionless duo.

"Joel, Saffina, aren't you coming with me?" Liana questioned.

"Well, she doesn't know *we're* here," replied Joel.

"You have got to be joking Joel. You're the one who egged me on!"

"Ha-ha, egged, nice pun!" laughed Joel.

"Seriously Joel?!" Liana's face scrunched in anger. "Saffina, you're with me, right?"

"Well... I didn't even encourage you to do it, so..."

"You two are unbelievable! Urgh! You know if I just stayed here all three of us would get caught."

"No, no, no, no, no, no, no!" Saffina and Joel begged before Liana cut them off.

"You two had better remember this," she said, pointing her finger at both her friends, before spinning around and accelerating away from them towards the opposite side of the flat roof.

"Get her! Get. Her!" instructed the angry voice from below.

Liana, running at her full pace over the rooftops, jumped effortlessly over the small gaps separating several neighbouring buildings.

Onlookers below, who had stopped in their daily business to witness the developing chase, could clearly see flashes of Liana's vibrant blue hair racing above their heads. Not a moment sooner than seeing the flash of blue, the smell of rotten egg would waft past them.

Liana approached the last building on the terrace. A taller building, with a spire.

'This will be tricky,' Liana thought to herself. She took a moment to peer down and check that her victim was still on her trail. She was. Liana could see the stern and straight edged jawline of her pursuer shaking in anger at her. Their eyes met and locked on to each other for an unusually long time, which seemed to only intensify the situation.

"You're mine Liana! You're going to pay for this!" the girl from below bellowed towards Liana.

"You deserved it, Yasmin!" replied Liana.

Liana then broke the everlasting staring contest so she could assess her options.

She couldn't go back. It was hard enough making good

friends being the Queen's daughter, even if they were faint-of-heart. To her right was the road where Yasmin stood, and to her left was a pile of rubble, full of broken stone and split wood.

Liana had only one option, she had to make the jump to the spire. If she could make the jump and shimmy around to the other side and slide down the butcher's awning, then she would be clear to make a run for her horse that was tied up on the opposite side of the city square.

But it was difficult as the gap and elevation was as high and wide as Liana herself. Not to mention the fact that the spire was made, as most things in the city, of smooth shining blue cobalt which would be too slippery to hold on to. She would have to jump far enough and high enough to grab the weathervane sitting atop of the spire.

She stepped back ten paces, took a deep breath, and ran towards the ledge. She planted her right foot with perfect timing and pushed with every ounce of energy up the length of her body. The setting sun glistened off Liana's bronze skin as she rose through the air. All she could see as she flew was the spire and the mixture of oranges, purples and blue of the evening sky as it's backdrop.

She made it… sort of… with a bit of a rough slap-like land-ing. Winded and with her body sprawled out in the shape of a star on the side of the spire, she was surprised to discover she wasn't slipping down the smooth, blue translucent surface. But as the winded feeling in her stomach faded, came another pain from on top of her head.

The force of her impact dislodged part of the weathervane from its mount and it was now flopping down lopsidedly with Liana's blue hair entwined around it. This is what was stop-ping Liana from sliding down the spire and was also the cause of the pain on her head, as her hair was being held taut between the weathervane and its roots.

Despite the immense pain of her hair being pulled from her head, Liana still managed to shimmy around the spire and position herself above the butcher's awning.

With her hair still tangled, Liana quickly had to come to terms with what she must do next. She reached to her leather waistband and pulled out a beautifully crafted dagger from its scabbard. Its unique design bore a hole through the middle of its black grip. The black cross-guard had a dragonfly intricately detailed on it. Liana took to her hair with it. The sharp blade, which glistened red in the sunlight, made easy work of freeing her from the weathervanes grasp and she slid down the spire, bounced on a sun-bleached brown awning and tumbled onto the floor in front of the butcher, dropping her dagger in the process.

"Liana, I'm coming for you!" Liana flashed her head in the direction of another cry from Yasmin as she came hurtling around the street corner.

Quickly pushing her small and slight body up off the floor, Liana accelerated across the square, dodging the crowds of traders and the bustle of consumers to get to her horse she'd tied up against some wooden scaffolding.

"Where is she?!" Yasmin shouted at the blood-covered butcher as he stood outside his shop, investigating the noise Liana had made a few seconds prior. The butcher shrugged his shoulders. "No! I've lost her! I'll get her, my father's going to hear about this!" Yasmin threatened. "What's this?" she continued muttering to herself, as she bent down picking up the dagger that Liana had dropped. "Ha! This proves it was her. *Her Majesty* won't be able to defend her precious daughter this time," Yasmin smirked.

"Pew!" exclaimed the butcher, holding his nose. "An' I know where me unsold bucket o' eggs went that were waitin' to be collected from the refuse collector outside me shop this mornin'!"

Yasmin scowled at the butcher, and marched off down another street, presumably to her home to wash off.

Liana could just about make out her horse through the moving legs and bodies of the crowded city square. A figure in a full-length hooded brown robe moved in front, blocking her view, but she had seen enough to plot her path. A quick check behind her indicated that she'd finally lost Yasmin. A few more strides and she'd be safe for sure, until she turned back around and immediately hit something hard and solid, knocking her back onto the ground.

Casting a long-sweeping shadow over Liana stood a large, well-armoured man whose metalwork glinted all over in the setting of the sun.

"In a hurry, Liana?" beckoned the man.

A guilty stare at the imposing figure was all Liana could conjure in response.

"Let's see. Your hair is in shreds, your clothes are covered in dirt, you were running as if you were being chased, your dagger is missing and you have that guilty look on your face," said the imposing man, looking at Liana's empty scabbard. "What have you done now?"

"Nothing, Great Uncle Tarak!" insisted Liana.

"Really, well your mother and I won't be happy if you've lost the dagger I gifted to you when you were five. It'd be sold off in no time, an object like that would be worth a small fortune to many of our citizens."

"I know it is, I'll find it, I swear," urged Liana.

"A unique and valuable item like that won't stay lost for

long. How many times have I covered up for you now Liana? There comes a time when you have to take responsibility for your actions, Princess," said Tarak softly, suggesting he wasn't wholly angry at her.

"What are you going to do?" asked Liana, worriedly. "Well for a start, it will look better for you if you go to the Queen yourself," advised Tarak.

Liana gave a shallow nod.

"I can't imagine she'll be best pleased about the state of your hair either. What were you thinking? The day before your birthday celebrations!" Tarak said, shaking his head.

Liana gently pulled the longest strands of hair, holding it between her thumb and forefinger in front of her matching blue eyes in an attempt to try and analyse how bad it was. She let go and let it dangle in front of her slightly elvish looking face.

Tarak gazed around at the three horses tied up to the scaffolding.

"I'm assuming you've been with Joel and Saffina in your recent... adventure?"

"What? No, um..." stuttered Liana, still attempting to protect her friends.

"Perhaps it would also be best for them to also go with you," suggested Tarak.

Liana bowed her head "I'll go and find them," she said quietly to the floor.

"Well, up you get then. Don't leave it too long, the Queen will need enough time to get over your misendeavours before your birthday," Tarak smiled with raised eyebrows and an understanding demeanour.

Ever since he had rescued Liana from the small, isolated, lava-engulfed rock, he had always been uncharacteristically

lenient with her. He saw many traits of himself in her,
including the mischievous ones when he was her age. None of
which were ever intentionally amoral, more trying to, in fact,
be moral but just never quite working out that way in his
youth. Something that infantry training had ironed out in him.

Sir Tarak mounted his horse and trotted off in the direction
of Castle Langton.

Liana once again picked herself up off the sandy floor and
half-heartedly attempted to dust off her black, short-sleeved
top which had become untucked from her clay-coloured
trousers. As she was tucking her top back in, someone from
behind her whipped it out again.

"That was incredible!" said an excitable Saffina, spinning
around in front of Liana as she released the top from her
grasp.

"I can't believe you got away with it, that was awesome!"
laughed Joel, breathlessly.

"Come on, you've got to admit that was funny. She
deserved it! Who does she think she is, pretending to be her
father? Ordering those tiny kids to fetch her this and that,
running her errands, threatening them to be sent to the mines,
that's cruel!" said Joel.

"Just because she's the daughter of the Master of the Mines
doesn't mean she should use it to her advantage. You're so
much better than her, Liana," said Saffina, supportingly.

Liana's smile gradually reappeared, and she nodded in
agreement. "She's one of those people who you just walk by
and can feel she's bad. Like, you don't even have to speak to
her, she just gives off... mean vibes."

"I know what you mean. She makes the hairs on your body
stand on edge just by being near her," agreed Joel.

"She must get it from her dad." Saffina hugged herself as

his image in her mind sent a chill down her spine. "He really gives me bad vibes."

"I have got some bad news though, guys. We kind of... didn't really get away with it," said Liana.

"What do you mean?" asked Joel.

"And what do you mean, 'we'?" asked Saffina.

"My Great Uncle caught me, just as I was about to ride off," Liana explained. "He said we need to visit my mother and tell her what we've been up to, before he does."

"You mean you stitched us up as well?!" accused Joel.

"No, it wasn't like that. Didn't take him much to work out. After all, he has been the Commanding Knight of the Langton Army for as long as anyone can remember."

"Do you think she'll punish us?" panicked Saffina. Liana shrugged her shoulders. "My family is already in enough trouble with her as it is."

"Only one way to find out. Hey, did either of you see my dagger?"

Joel and Saffina shook their heads. The trio untied their horses and walked them by their harnesses over to the butchers.

"You lookin' for summin' Princess?" said the ever-jolly butcher as the trio half-heartedly searched the front of his shop for the blade.

"I think I dropped my dagger near your shop, Benji," replied Liana.

"Ah, I ain't seen it exactly, but I did see Yasmin pick summin' up. Maybe she knew it were yours and wan'ed to keep it safe for ya. You should go 'n' ask her."

"Great..." Liana said sarcastically under her breath.

"What was that Princess, didn't quite 'ear ya?" Benji said.

"Great!" Liana said louder, pretending to sound genuinely

thankful at the situation. "Thanks for your help, Benji, and you know I'm not a proper Princess."

"Aye but t'morrow ya will be!" he replied.

"Just because I'm turning thirteen and I can officially hold the title doesn't make me a real Princess. It's like I walk around knowing that behind my back everyone is just saying 'Why her?' and 'She doesn't deserve to be next in line' or 'She won't make a very good Queen,'" a doubting Liana said.

"Now you listen t' me. Bein' a good King or Queen is nothin' to do with anyone else 'part from you and your mother knows it. A great leader is raised, not born," encouraged Benji, who was pointing his blood-covered meat cleaver towards Liana as if to ensure the point he was making really sunk in.

Not that you'd argue with him anyway. Despite his aging years and hardened skin, Benji looked after his physique even after retiring from his years at sea as a ship's cook. Liana had always loved hearing Benji's stories of the sea when she was little and admired how nothing ever seemed to dampen his spirits. There was a reason he was the Merchants Guild Leader. Everyone loved his upbeat outlook, respected his opinions and admired his ability to listen.

"Thanks, Benji," she smiled at him before turning to her friends. "We'd better get going before my Great Uncle gets to the castle before us," instructed Liana to her friends.

4
COMING OF AGE

The three friends mounted their horses and trotted their ways through the streets of the city.

The strong, all-black steeds of Saffina and Joel were brothers and would have been nearing retirement among the royal herd and ready for selling at the Annual Royal Auction, but Liana had convinced her mother to allow them to be sold to Saffina and Joel's families for a reduced price. If it was up to Liana, she would have gifted them to her friends for free, but Queen Adriya always made a point to Liana that as a Royal you are not to give away your assets for free, or you risk being taken advantage of or accused of unfairness, bribery or corruption.

Liana's steed was, just like her, unmistakable. It's unique, golden pearl coat shimmered in the sun and glistened in the moonlight. It never seemed to tire and could outrun any horse in the city.

According to her mother, the breed was called Akhal-Teke. A small team of them had been sent as gifts to the Island of

Coryàtès from an ally of Liana's Grandfather to celebrate the birth of Queen Adriya.

With her shining horse, intense blue hair and being heir-to-the-throne, the public's eyes were always on Liana. This made her feel quite uncomfortable and self-conscious.

Unlike many lands, the sole city of the Island of Coryàtès, Swyre, was predominantly a safe place meaning Liana didn't need a guard or escort around her. She enjoyed this freedom but would also often find herself dangling her feet over the cliffs behind Castle Langton, looking out to sea procrastinating alone to the sound of the crashing waves against the rock formations when the pressures and expectations of her position became too much.

The trio pulled up to the Tower of Seeds and dismounted before their horses were led away by an on-hand stable boy.

"I'm not sure what's worse. Having to see the Queen or walk up all these steps," complained Joel as they began their climb up the spiralling staircase. "Does she really do this every day?"

"Looking over the city whilst she works reminds her of her duty," Liana replied.

"It's not like you're going to forget being Queen, is it? She must have the legs of an army General!" Joel continued to complain.

"I don't know why you're complaining Joel, you're the reason we're here in the first place," replied Saffina. Despite being last in line of the ascending trio, she sensed Joel's eyes rolling as he walked. "You're right though, climbing these is punishment enough. Maybe that's another reason she works up here. Double punishment for troublemakers like you and Liana,"

"Just me and Liana? You better not be thinking of blaming

this all on us, Saffina," Joel stopped and turned to accuse Saffina.

"Well, you came up with the plan and pressured Liana into it, then she actually did it," Saffina pointed her finger at the Princess "I didn't do anything, why should I be punished." argued Saffina.

"You didn't have to come up to the roof with us and I didn't hear you trying to stop us either," continued Joel.

"How was I meant to stop you, 2 against 1?"

"You wouldn't have any way!"

"You don't know that!"

"STOP IT!" Liana ordered. "None of that will matter to my mother. If we were there together, we take the blame together. Now come on, we're only halfway there."

Joel and Saffina scowled at each other before the trio continued their rise up the tower without any more conversation and only the echoing sound of their footsteps on the hard stone floor to be heard.

Finally, the door to the Queen's Table greeted them.

"Maybe if we knock quietly, she won't hear us and we can tell Commander Tarak that at least we tried and then let this all blow over," suggested Joel.

"I think we've had enough of your bright ideas today, Joel," replied Liana. "Here goes."

Liana raised her hand to the door, knocking three times against the wood.

"Enter," came the Queen's voice from within.

Pushing the door open without a hint of creak or strain, Liana and her accomplices sidled their way into the Queen's Table.

Queen Adriya was standing over the large triangular table that took up most of the circular room, assessing papers and materials of designs and decorations that were ready for tomorrow's birthday celebrations.

"Hello Liana, Joel and Saffina how are you all?" asked the Queen, before looking up from the table and laying her eyes upon the trio. "Liana! What's happened to your hair?!" asked the Queen.

"Hello, Your Majesty," chorused Joel and Saffina in a monotone fashion.

"Hello mother," Liana replied, sheepishly.

"I'm assuming the state of your hair has something to do with why you three are all the way up here?" enquired the Queen inquisitively.

"Erm, well..." stuttered Liana.

Queen Adriya stared intently at Liana who quickly realised their visit wasn't going to bring any sort of good news to her.

Liana's gaze quickly dropped to her feet.

"Well, we saw Yasmin being horrible and mean to some of the city's orphans," started Liana.

"Yeh, she was threatening them with the mines and everything!" interrupted Joel, before Saffina gave him an elbow to the ribs to shut him up before he inevitably said something that would only make this worse for them.

"Liana, please continue," the Queen ordered.

"Well, we thought she shouldn't be ordering them about as her personal slaves just because her father is Master of the Mines so we thought we should do something about it. I mean I am your daughter so it's my responsibility to be fair and punish people who are doing bad things and you're always telling me how I should take my position more seriously and..."

The Queen sat down on a neighbouring chair, finally

breaking her stare from Liana, and put her head in her hands. "Get to the point Liana. What did you do?" she sighed.

"We…" Liana started, before changing her mind. "I tipped a bucket of rotten eggs onto Yasmin's head, and she saw us."

"We, or I?" enquired the Queen.

Liana turned around and looked at her friends. Their heads were bowed, hands behind their back. Saffina was shaking with nerves and Joel had his eyes closed tight in fear. Liana turned back towards her mother.

"I. Just me. Joel and Saffina were around, but it was me, mother. It was my decision," Liana declared. "As I was running away, my hair got caught. That's why its half shredded. I had to cut it with my dagger." At this point, Liana decided to omit the fact she had lost her blade.

The Queen paused and looked towards Liana's friends. "Joel, Saffina, you may leave. Liana, sit," the Queen ordered, gesturing a hand to a chair sitting directly next to her.

The two friends' heads shot up in surprise. The pair were so startled that they would not be punished; they both made eye contact with Liana telepathically asking her 'Are we actually free to go?' and 'Will you be okay?' Liana darted her eyes to the door and back, as if to say, 'Just go, I'll be fine.'

Saffina and Joel gave a nod to Queen Adriya and hastily left the room, closing the door behind them.

Liana gingerly walked towards the chair that her mother had gestured towards. The closer she got, the more the atmosphere felt increasingly awkward, like two ends of a magnet pushing each other away.

She sat down and purchased herself on the edge of the chair furthest from her mother, doing her best to avoid making eye contact.

"Liana, sit properly and look at me," instructed her mother.

Liana did as she was told.

"I expect you think I'm going to shout at you and come up with some imaginative punishment," said Queen Adriya. "Well, we've been down that route before, haven't we Liana? It's worked for a time and then you end up getting in trouble again. I can't help but think your two friends are not completely innocent."

"No, please don't blame them, I've no idea what I'd do if I lost them as friends. We didn't mean to get seen by Yasmin."

"Whether you meant to be seen or not isn't the point. The action you took was inappropriate and short-sighted. What do you think the consequences, which I will now have to resolve, are?" said Queen Adriya, calmly.

"Yasmin will tell her father, who will be mad," said Liana.

"Yes, he absolutely will be, but it's much more than that Liana. We know he is not a pleasant man. Men like Yasmin's father like having power over people and have a way of gathering support from those easily influenced, which can lead to uprising or revolutions. I gave him control of the mines to satisfy his needs for power, but we also wronged him and his family. Someday this power won't be enough, and he will seek more and all he will need is the smallest of reasons. I don't want that reason to be you."

"You think he'll start a revolution because I poured some eggs over Yasmin?" Liana asked.

The Queen smiled and shook her head at Liana's naive and innocent question.

"Tomorrow afternoon is your birthday and inauguration to be my heir. The last thing you or I need are people to question your decisions. Poor decisions now will only plant seeds of doubt in citizens on how good a Queen you will become. Actions are remembered and will be used as reasons by people like Yasmin's father to manipulate others into believing they are a better option," said the Queen.

"If you're that worried about Yasmin's father, can't you do something about him now?"

"I've built my reputation on trying to be fair, Liana. That's how this city is so peaceful. He hasn't yet done anything for me to punish him. If I act in an unjust way, others will follow my lead, and then Swyre will fall into chaos. As Queen I am the role model to all others."

"You would think a Queen could do what she wanted, when she wanted and how she wanted. It's not like that though, is it? We're not free to do what we want are we?" Liana said despondently, beginning to understand how her life would evolve.

The Queen put a reassuring hand on her daughter's shoulder, before standing up and walking over to the window, where 13 years ago she stood and watched the ash cloud swallow the building below.

"It may seem restricting at first, but I get great joy in seeing the city and its people thrive. That's why I walk up and down these steps every day, so I can look out and constantly remind myself why I do what I do," said the Queen thoughtfully. "It's dark now Liana. I suggest you have an early night. Why don't you join me in the Triunity Hall in the morning? I have sentencing to carry out for those found guilty in the last round of court hearings. We can see what you've learned about from our little conversation this evening. I'll call Agatha to help you to your room. Hopefully she can do something with your hair too."

The Queen walked over to the opposite side of the circular

room. Hanging on the wall were a series of golden bells. Below each bell was a tube that disappeared into the ground. Queen Adriya rang a bell underneath a plaque which read 'Maid's Quarters'. Other plaques read 'Military Quarters', 'Kitchen', 'Stables', 'Portcullis' and 'Maintenance'. Clerk Vivek also had his own plaque, bell and tube set whilst another was yet to be engraved.

Just a few moments later, the bell listed as 'Maid's Quarters' sounded. The Queen lifted the flap covering the smooth, sandstone tube that was situated directly below the bell and spoke loudly into it.

"Agatha. Could you escort my daughter to her room please? She'll meet you at the bottom of the tower," requested the Queen, politely.

"On my way, Your Majesty," came the echoed response from the tube.

She closed the flap, making sure it was locked tight with its latch before turning to speak to Liana. "What you did today was wrong Liana, but your reasons for doing so were understandable. I will appease Yasmin and her father. Off you go, I'll see you in the morning."

Liana quietly left the room and made her way down the Tower of Seeds.

"Oh, my darling, what happened to your hair? And you look like you've had all your energy sucked right out of you!" The gentle soft tones of Agatha's reassuring voice instantly made her feel better.

"Do you think you'll be able to sort my hair out?" Liana responded.

"Well, let's get you to your room. We'll give it a proper trim and then get you tucked up nice and tightly before your big day. Would you like me to get the kitchen to bring you anything?" Agatha asked.

"Just some water please," replied Liana, as the pair made their way through the long, tall, intricately designed, and decorated corridors of Castle Langton.

Liana's room was up a single flight of stairs to the south of the castle. It wasn't her mother's choice. She used to have a room in the western tower near her mother's room which overlooked the city, but she insisted on a view of the cliffs and sea to look out upon. The brushes of the waves onto the cliffs and beach below helped her fall asleep. This particular room also had a covered balcony large enough for her Chaise Lounge, where she would sit and read. Liana enjoyed adventure novels where she could escape into a fantasy away from her responsibilities. Clerk Vivek tried to get her to read educational books on history and finance, but Liana could never get past more than 3 or 4 pages at a time.

The Queen acknowledged the importance of Liana being amongst the citizens and building relationships despite Clerk Vivek's greater intelligence both in knowledge and teaching abilities and so her education time was split between attending one of the city's schools (where she first met Joel and Saffina) and personal tutoring from Clerk Vivek in the castle in his large study.

Having been an advisor to the Langton family for over 50 years, he had built up quite a collection of materials and scientific instruments that filled his studies shelves from floor to ceiling. Books, ancient scrolls, golden telescopes, framed maps, clamps, timepieces, petri dishes, ornaments from other lands – Vivek had everything.

Liana spent as much time browsing the artifacts as she did studying. Her favourite section was the collection of valuable and colourful gems and stones. One item in particular always drew her attention, almost like it was calling to her. A small yet perfectly smooth red sphere that Vivek kept in a clear cuboid box in a drawer along with all his other gems. She'd once opened the box and was adamant that the sphere's vivid red shades pulsed as she stared into it, but Vivek had caught her as she held it and warned her never to touch anything without his permission. She abided by his wishes; such was her respect for him.

Clerk Vivek's skills ranged from finance to chemistry, and he was one of the main reasons that Coryàtes had become such a successful trading nation despite its miniscule size. It was his discovery into a more efficient and effective refining process of the island's famous blue cobalt glass that first brought him to the Langton family's attention. He repeated this genius not long after the Day of Darkness had occurred when the mountain's eruption caused cobalt and quartz to melt together. After a short period of theorising and testing, he had found a refining process to make a more translucent blue shaded element. He called it Quartaltium and soon every land wanted a piece of this unique substance.

For the last couple of years, he had been working on a unique piece of armour for Liana's mother. Apparently, only the Queen and the castle's metallurgist knew anything about this commission. Liana had only found out after barging into his study in tears following a particularly fraught coming together with Yasmin at school. Vivek had ushered her out quickly and called for Agatha to console her. Liana didn't see much through her tears, but Vivek had been wearing a pair of magnifying eyeglasses so the work must have been intricate. She nagged the metallurgist for details, but he could not provide much information on the design, only the pieces of metal he'd created. Although she did get out of him that rather than standard hinges for the moving parts, Vivek had strangely requested them to be ball shaped. Liana was curious but did not pursue anymore as she knew how privileged she was to have such an esteemed teacher and did not want to cause any tension between them.

Soon Agatha and Liana entered the bedroom. "Into your bathroom, dear. We'll trim your hair and then we'll get some nice new soft bedding ready for a good night's sleep." said Agatha, opening a grand, wooden wardrobe as she hunted for the bedding and handed the Princess her night clothes.

Liana made her way to her en-suite and sat on a chair in front of her dressing table. She looked into the mirror in front of her, reflecting on the day, as Agatha stood behind her evening out the jagged and split hairs. Once Agatha had finished, she quickly got changed and returned to her room where the maid was already making the final adjustments to the bed.

She got in and wrapped the soft new sheets around herself tightly.

"I'll be right back sweet, I'm just going to get you that jug of water you wanted," said Agatha, as she turned off the oil-fuelled lamps hung around the room before leaving.

Liana's eyes were already heavy and despite her dry throat she could feel herself drifting off to sleep almost as soon as the last lamp was turned off.

But she awoke for what seemed to her to be no more than 30 seconds after putting her head down on her duck-feather pillow.

The source of her awakening emanated from the small gap surrounding her bedroom door as magnificent bright, white light rays penetrated the room. Squinting, both from the light and tiredness, Liana briefly thought she was dreaming, before the door opened...and into the room entered Agatha. The bright, white light surrounded and moved with Agatha like a baby in a blanket. Strangely, the light didn't interfere with the image of Agatha herself, merely bordering her outline.

"Sorry I was a little longer than I thought I would be, dear. Darling, what's wrong? You look like you've seen a ghost!" laughed Agatha, placing the water jug and a glass onto the bedside table.

"The light. Can't you see the light Agatha?"

"The light? Whatever are you talking about. I think somebody fell asleep already and is all confused. I'll leave you in peace now darling. I'd best be off to bed too, I'm very much looking forward to tomorrow's celebrations!" and with that Agatha left the room, closing the door behind her.

Liana fixated on Agatha and her glow the whole way out and watched as the light from the corridor dimmed as she moved further away.

Convincing herself Agatha was right, Liana lay her head back down and drifted back to sleep.

5

THE TRIUNITY INJUSTICE

"Why is it taking so long? We're running out of time."

"I've told you already, we cannot rush such big projects. Nothing has changed since the last Queen's Table meeting. Clerk Vivek has reviewed it's progress and he is not happy to open it yet."

"Clerk Vivek will never be happy since it's not his project!"

"He is a busy man, I couldn't afford to let him have this project, it would have taken too much of his time, but I need his assessment."

Liana, stood awaiting her mother at the foot of the Tower of Seeds, heard her disgruntled voice descending down the spiralling staircase and darted to the other side of the grand wooden door into the large triangular auditorium. She pressed her ear gently to the door, curious to hear more of her discussion.

"There is nowhere for our people to learn, train and pray. I don't understand why we couldn't have continued using the old temple."

"The old, underground temple was a symbol of rebellion and then became a symbol of death on the Day of Darkness. We had to abandon it and begin afresh. The new temple is almost ready. Just a little more patience, Priestess," replied the defiant Queen.

"13 years ago, you announced we were no longer the 'Forbidden Religion'. That our teachings and prophecies were to be believed and that we should be welcomed back with open arms," said the Priestess. "Yet we have not been allowed to open our doors to anyone. Have you forgotten what our books have written in them?"

"They are not prophecies Priestess; they are but predictions based on what we now know were actual events that occurred hundreds of years ago. Predictions can be wrong, or they can be right. I did not have to welcome back the old religion, but I believe in what happened in the past and therefore the potential of the substance held in your manuscripts."

"Then how can you not tell her? She needs to know. Let me begin teaching her, with or without a temple," said the Priestess.

Liana, with her ear pressed against the door in her eagerness to hear more of the confrontation, inadvertently leaned in too hard and marginally pushed the door just enough to make it creek.

"I think someone is here," a startled Queen said, turning her head to the grand wooden door. "We'll discuss this further at the next Queen's Table meeting."

As the Queen wrapped up her argument with the Priestess, Liana made a dash to the door on the right of the triangular auditorium. Just as the Queen opened the grand wooden door through which Liana had been eavesdropping, she closed the door to which she had run to in an effort to make it appear that she had just walked into the room.

"My beautiful daughter, you're here early," beamed Queen Adriya.

"I wanted to be here at the same time as you, mother. You said I should be more responsible so I wanted to be here as early as you so I could learn," said Liana, trying to control her breathing after her short dash across the floor.

"Well, I'm glad to hear my words have had an effect," smiled Queen Adriya. "Sentencing is a very important part of a monarch's responsibilities. You have to find the right balance of punishment for the crime committed."

"Why can't we just send all the bad people away? As a small island, can't we just sail them away to the nearest beach. Then there would be no bad people," said Liana.

Smiling at Liana's naivety, the Queen walked Liana over to a wooden pedestal in the centre of the triangular auditorium.

Upon the pedestal lay an old, large, wide book. The Queen opened it at a random page, with great care to prevent any damage to its contents.

"See here," she said, pointing to the page. Liana had to stand on tiptoes to observe the writing:

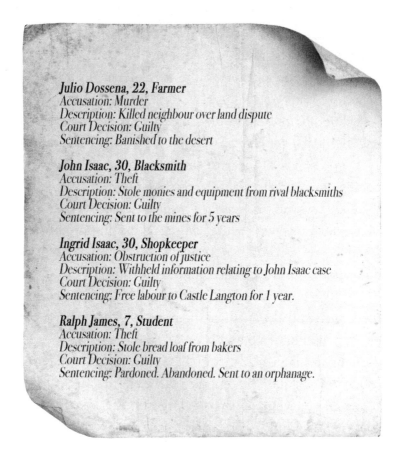

Julio Dossena, 22, Farmer
Accusation: Murder
Description: Killed neighbour over land dispute
Court Decision: Guilty
Sentencing: Banished to the desert

John Isaac, 30, Blacksmith
Accusation: Theft
Description: Stole monies and equipment from rival blacksmiths
Court Decision: Guilty
Sentencing: Sent to the mines for 5 years

Ingrid Isaac, 30, Shopkeeper
Accusation: Obstruction of justice
Description: Withheld information relating to John Isaac case
Court Decision: Guilty
Sentencing: Free labour to Castle Langton for 1 year.

Ralph James, 7, Student
Accusation: Theft
Description: Stole bread loaf from bakers
Court Decision: Guilty
Sentencing: Pardoned. Abandoned. Sent to an orphanage.

"We have many options available to us when carrying out sentencing, Liana," said the Queen. "If we just sent everyone away, we would then be asking good people to do some of the hardest work on the island and criminals wouldn't be sufficiently punished."

"Well why don't we just lock them up or kill them? Clerk Vivek has taught me we used to do that, and other lands still do," questioned Liana.

"I believe those that have committed offences against the city should repay their fellow citizens by being productive.

Our city wouldn't be this beautiful without the workforce in our Quartaltium and sandstone mines," replied the Queen. "This is why we need a good relationship with Yasmin's father. I need someone strong in charge of the mines to keep the criminals in check."

"What about this one, Julio Dossena? It says he was banished to the desert?" queried Liana.

"Murderers are the most serious, untrustworthy of criminals and we cannot have them involved in anything to do with the city. However, I cannot bring myself to order cold-blooded killing as punishment, so they are banished to the desert where there are no resources to survive. Luckily, we haven't had too many during my reign," answered the Queen.

Liana flicked through the book. The child-like curiosity in her wanted to see the details of those sentenced around the time she was born. When she finally got to the pages, which were near the start of the large ledger, one of the names and their details were smudged out, as if it had been blacked out on purpose.

"What happened to this one?" asked Liana.
"I'm not sure. It's so long ago I'm sure it doesn't matter," the Queen shuffled suspiciously as she dismissed the question.

Liana pondered over the details of the sentencing book some more. "Have you ever gotten any wrong?"

Queen Adriya paused to consider her answer, but before she could reply to her daughter, the stooping, hunchbacked figure of Clerk Vivek hobbled into the room through the grand wooden door behind the royal pair as his metallic walking stick clinked with every small step he took.

"Your Majesty," started Clerk Vivek trying, in vain, to bow as he addressed the Queen. "I think we should open the spectator doors. There's quite an audience queuing outside for this morning's sentencing."

"Thank you Vivek. Liana, I would like you to sit alongside me with the other members of the Queen's Table. Please sit, whilst I review today's cases again," said the Queen, holding out her left-hand gesturing towards a row of three leather lined chairs sitting beside the pedestal. Three identical chairs also stood on the opposite side of the pedestal. The crest of the Langton family was embroidered into the deep-blue leather covered chairs in contrasting golden thread.

The golden Langton symbol was a simple design. Four equilateral triangles fitted together to make one large triangle.

Liana made her way over to the chair closest to where her mother would soon be standing to address the audience. Gazing at the golden thread, Liana began to feel overwhelmed with the sudden expectation of responsibility that was being placed on her.

"Simple, but effective, wouldn't you say?" said Clerk Vivek to Liana, with reference to the Langton badge. "Your mother asked me to redesign the coat of arms 13 years ago when she welcomed back the forbidden religion after the Day of Darkness. Can you remember it's meaning?" asked Vivek.

"You used triangles because they are the strongest of shapes. The triangle in the middle represents the citizens. They are protected by the three triangles around them: the military, the religion, and the royal house. The four work together to form one democratic triangle. You cannot label the triangles, because if you turned the symbol around, a different triangle would be on top, therefore, not one triangle is ever more important than the other and the citizens will always remain at the centre," answered Liana.

"Perfect description, well done Liana, you have learned

something from me at least," smiled the lips of Clerk Vivek amongst his greying pointed goatee.

"But if one triangle is not ever more important than the other, how come my mother still has authority and takes on so much responsibility?" asked Liana.

"A great question Liana, one of which you did not ask when we first covered the subject in our History of Politics lessons last year! The wording is key here. It is not about authority, but importance. Let's look at each triangle.

If you took away the military, we would be vulnerable to physical attacks, so this is important to defend and protect ourselves.

The religion has yet to re-establish itself fully, but when it has it will provide many branches of important support to the mind of a citizen. The religion will listen and comfort our people, as well as give belief and hope in times of hardship.

And finally, Royalty is important for its strong vision and decision making. Without it, arguments would unfold, and progress becomes slow and foggy.

If you take one triangle away, you leave the middle triangle vulnerable and without the middle triangle, there is nothing left at all.

It is not about who holds more authority. So long as each understands that the other is equally important for their own strength, then the strength of the whole will hold" answered Clerk Vivek.

Liana and Vivek sat down next to each other.

Behind them, the grand wooden doors opened again with a loud creak and in walked Sir Tarak, in all his glorious shining armour. Liana struggled to think of a moment when she had ever seen Tarak out of his armour.

Entering the room with Sir Tarak was a large woman in an

off-white blouse and a long, unbuttoned, deep red doublet coat. In her hand she carried a brown leather tricorn hat, which usually sat on top of her short wavy hair.

"After you, Remi," said Sir Tarak to the woman he had walked in with, directing her to a seat.

"I don't need your chivalry Commander," glared the woman in an offended and direct manner to Sir Tarak, before choosing the middle option of the three empty seats.

Sir Tarak turned and smiled mischievously at Liana, knowing his chivalrous offer to Remi would annoy her. He took his seat next to Remi on the row of chairs opposite to Liana and Vivek.

Remi was the Commanding Admiral of the Navy. Together, Admiral Remi and Sir Tarak made up the Swyre military.

"I never want to get on the wrong side of Remi," whispered Liana to Clerk Vivek.

"Some would call her a harsh woman but her voice at the table is an important one. When your mother first formed the Queen's Table, just after her inauguration, the Queen and I knew that her uncle was by far the best choice of leader for our armed forces. However, having two royals at the table was bound to draw criticism of imbalance and bias, so she made Remi an Admiral of equal rank to Sir Tarak to appease any concerns.

Yes, Admiral Remi is strong, opinionated, outspoken and honest, but she also possesses a unique intelligence and viewpoint from her experiences at sea," said Vivek, responding with his usual words of wisdom.

Just then, almost as if she had glided in without her feet even touching the floor, Priestess Yi sat down next to Vivek. Liana had always admired her sense of fashion. Today she was wearing a striking dark green dress embroidered in gold phoenix's that perfectly complemented her black and green hair. The Priestess was the only other person in the city that Liana knew of who had hair that was not purely blonde, brown, ginger or black.

"Good morning, Clerk Vivek, I hope you are well," she said, before addressing Liana. "A pleasant surprise to see you sitting down here, Princess," said Priestess Yi, whose soft tone of voice was a stark contrast to that which Liana had just been overhearing and one that she sensed wasn't entirely genuine.

Liana didn't have time to respond before she saw the set of doors in front of her open. Into the auditorium strutted the tall, muscled figure of Yasmin's father. He was the only one of the Queen's Table not to enter the room through the grand wooden doors behind the pedestal.

His open, brown, sleeveless shirt exposed his trademark long thick scar that began its journey at the lump on his throat and ended at his navel. Numerous other smaller scars littered each arm amongst his tattoos.

The entire time it took him to stride across the hall to his seat next to Admiral Remi, his eyes never broke from Liana, glaring, fixated on her. Even after he had sat down, he leaned forward in front of Sir Tarak and Admiral Remi and snarled at Liana, exposing his teeth. Liana felt his eyes on her and glanced out the corner of her eyes, catching sight of his canines, which had been specially sharpened, like a wolf. It didn't take much to conclude that Yasmin must have told him about the previous day's encounter.

"Enough, Zagan," snapped Sir Tarak. Yasmin's father, Zagan, retreated and slouched back into his seat with an air of arrogance.

Liana refocussed and swallowed her nerves, looking up to the stands as the public began to flood into the auditorium.

"Eugh! What's she doing down there? I bet she's not even been punished. Why isn't my father doing something? She gets away with everything," exclaimed Yasmin to the boy next to her as they took their seats in the stand.

"Do you ever stop complaining?" replied the boy to Yasmin.

"Shut up, Eugene," said Yasmin. "Should have known you'd take her and your sister's side."

"I'm not taking anyone's side. You can hardly expect the Queen or your father to do anything publicly. How do you know she's not already been punished?" said Eugene.

"I just know," Yasmin scrunched up her face, folded her arms and scowled as she watched Liana sitting with the rest of the Queen's Table.

Eugene rolled his eyes, knowing he was in for the silent treatment for the rest of the day.

"I don't know how my brother can be friends with her," said Saffina to Joel, as they also took their seats in the stand, looking down at Yasmin and Eugene, who sat a few rows beneath them.

"Hey look, Liana's down there with the rest of the Queen's Table," said Joel to Saffina, pointing down in Liana's direction.

"Jeez Joel, she's not even been officially inaugurated as Princess yet!" replied Saffina.

"I bet it's going to be some party later though!" smiled Joel ear-to-ear, thinking about what food and festivities Liana's birthday celebration would bring. "I reckon there's going to be every type of bread and meat, cheese that the city makes. I bet they'll even have staff squeezing piles and piles of fruit to make us fresh juice. What do you think will be the entertainment? I saw some guards moving a huge wooden table before we got here. It must have been four horse-lengths long and just as wide! One of the guards dropped a pouch and some small ships and figures fell out onto the floor, so I reckon it's a new military type role-playing game that Clerk Vivek's dreamt up." Joel rambled on excitedly to Saffina.

"Sshh, the Queen's about to start," Saffina gave him a nudge in the ribs to emphasise her point. Joel promptly became quiet but there was still a shallow rumble of mumbled conversations as the audience finished their conversations.

"Citizens of Swyre," began the Queen, as the crowd quickly silenced itself, leaving nothing but the echo of the Queen's voice reverberating around the towering, triangular, blue-tinted roof and walls of the Triunity Hall.

"Welcome to this morning's sentencing. As always, it delights me to see such wonderful attendance and interest in observing what penalties will be given to those who violate our cities laws.

Today, on her 13th birthday, it also brings me great pleasure in welcoming my daughter Liana down to the rostrum as she begins her official royal journey as Princess and will start to observe the procedures of the Queen's Table.

I'm sure we are all eager to progress to this afternoon's ceremony and so, without any further delay, we will begin this morning's proceedings. Guards, please collect our first inmate for sentencing."

Two guards left through the westerly doors, the doors where Zagan had entered the hall, and returned with the first inmate. The figure of a dirty, bearded, long-haired man was escorted into the Triunity Hall. The clanking sounds of the metal handcuffs that the man was locked into vibrated around the otherwise eerily silent room. He wore nothing but the standard, knee-length cream tunic and brown clog-like shoes that all convicts were issued with.

Queen Adriya, standing tall in her long, shining blue dress and silver crown, began proceedings for the first sentencing.

"George Poulsen, 43 years of age, carriage driver. You were found guilty by the court for failing to stop after hitting and seriously injuring a fellow citizen whilst riding. Do you have anything to say?" asked the Queen to the handcuffed man. "I'm sorry, your highness, I panicked, I just panicked," the man's shaking nerves clearly apparent in his trembling hands as his chains rattled and screeched around the hall.

"Does anyone else in this hall today have any new, unheard evidence to add to this case to ensure its outcome is fitting and accurate?" boomed the Queen to the watching crowd.

A few short, silent moments passed before the Queen spoke again.

"George Poulsen, I sentence you to 2 year's community work in the city's health centre. The citizen you injured is still being cared for there and I believe this a good opportunity for you to atone for your crime by supporting hers, and others, recoveries. Clerk Vivek and Priestess Yi sit on the health centre committee." the Queen turned to look at the pair. "I trust you will both find suitable work for Mr Poulsen to partake in as part of his sentencing."

Clerk Vivek and Priestess Yi nodded back in synchronisation.

The proceedings continued in the same cycle of questioning for almost an hour as each individual was brought before the Queen. Unlike some days, today each case was straightforward, and, in her usual self-assured and balanced way, the Queen avoided any raucousness through her fair sentencing. A few of the more serious offenders were sent to the mines. Zagan joyfully commented after each judgement that saw him gain another worker, commenting how he needed as many as possible if he was to 'fulfil the demand of Quartalitium and sandstone'. Liana glanced suspiciously in his direction and a sharp snap of shivers ran down her spine as Zagan's sneering grin once again displayed his sharpened fangs.

The next criminal was ordered to serve Admiral Remi indefinitely for attempting to smuggle in banned produce, but other than these key highlights, most of those presented in front of the Queen were given various community orders relating to their offence.

Liana was trying her best to sit straight and keep attention, which was difficult for such an energetic, fidgety child. She was feeling uncomfortable just being on the floor knowing that many of these eyes had been watching her for so long, even though at present her mother was the centre of attention. She found it hard to imagine that she would one day be standing up at the pedestal. As the penultimate inmate was guided away and the inevitable murmuring of the crowd hummed in the background in the short break as everyone began discussing the previous inmate's sentence with their neighbour, Liana scanned the rows of eyes in the stands searching for the comfort of her best friends. When her eyes eventually landed on them, high up in the terraces, her cheeks dimpled with a soft smile, and she immediately felt better.

The murmuring of the audience gently softened as the westerly doors opened for the final inmate as the guards escorted in a slightly overweight male with no hair. A pair of round glasses sat upon the bridge of his nose above his soul patch beard.

"Nalan Weir, 28 years of age, Herbalist. You were found guilty by the court for the attempted murder of our cities foremost architect. Do you have anything to say?" boomed the Queen.

The man stood still and calm, staring intently back at the Queen as she questioned him. So still, not a single sound came from his chains.

"It wasn't me, your majesty," he said, without any sign of emotion.

"Mr Weir, you were caught raising a knife ready to stab the victim's back. It is only by luck that the architect's apprentice opened the door on to you causing you to miss and end up merely cutting the victim. Not to mention your less than pure record when it comes to the use and distribution of banned remedies. You have been before me in this room already. You have clearly not learned from your actions," said the Queen.

"Selling banned herbs and remedies to help those in suffering does not make me a murderer. I'm telling you this wasn't me. At least, it may have been me in body, but it wasn't me in mind," argued the inmate.

"What do you mean, Mr Weir?"

"I mean it was my physical body committing the act, but I wasn't in control of it," he said with a dead-pan expression. The Queen stared at the man, looking for any clue that he was either lying, or delusional.

"Mr Weir, you are either a very good liar or you are telling me that you were somehow possessed, that someone made you do it?" queried the Queen.

The man nodded confidently.

"Mr Weir, if I believed that excuse everyone would use it. You cannot expect me to exonerate you."

Liana, who had been watching the exchange with the most interest and concentration she'd had all morning, suddenly felt a sharp jolt in the side of head. Reacting to the piercing like pain, she shut her eyes tight and raised her hands to her temples. In an attempt to prevent embarrassment, she scrunched up her face in a bid to avoid crying out.

The pain was short and subsided quickly, but when Liana opened her eyes, she looked upon her surroundings with confusion and slight fear. All the bright colours around her disappeared into a variety of greys, whites, and blacks. The shining blue of her mother's dress, gone. The green of the Priestesses hair and dress, gone. The deep redness of Remi's doublet coat, gone. The sun's rays piercing through the roof causing a beautiful alternating of blue and white streaks, gone. The concoction of colours from the crowd, gone.

Yet no one else seemed affected. Her mother was still addressing Nalan Weir. Or at least she thought she was by her body language and waving of arms, for Liana could not hear her. She could hear nothing. But she could not dwell on either phenomenon due to the spectacle of Nalan Weir in front of her.

As with Agatha the night before, which Liana had convinced herself was a dream, Nalan was surrounded by a white light. Liana had to squint just to be able to see his body's outline. Except his glow was different. His glow was full of black speckles that were darting around, seemingly randomly, like hundreds of tiny moths to one giant lantern.

Instinctively Liana stood up without thought and walked towards Nalan. She could not hear the Queen questioning her as she walked right past her. She could only focus on the event happening before her.

The uncomfortable feeling of the crowd's eyes seemed a distant concern and instead she started to remember the feeling she had the night before. Despite her confusion, she remembered feeling calm, happy and reassured upon seeing

Agatha's light. Right now, though, she was entrenched in the feeling of caution, but did not feel threatened. She began to believe Nalan's notion that he was not himself. She began to believe he was not an inherently bad man.

"Liana! Liana! What are you doing!?" shouted the Queen once more. Liana heard her mother's cries this time, as the colours around her flickered on, off and back on again. Liana took a moment to compose herself before turning around and replying.

"I, I think he's telling the truth," she replied, with an obvious sense of wariness in her voice. The Queen leered at Liana, clearly angry at her for the disruption and taking an opposing viewpoint.

The audience seemed stunned, with the exception of Yasmin who let out a small shriek of laughter from the stands before quickly retreating to silence when no one else dared to join in, even if they might have personally agreed with Yasmin about the bizarreness of Liana's notion.

Nalan took this moment of uncertainty as an opportunity. Using his upper-body strength he shrugged off the equally stunned guards next to him, lifted his tunic and drew a familiar looking dagger, wrapped the chains connecting his cuffs around Liana's neck and held the dagger to her throat.

Liana peered down her nose to see the blade. Her blade. The one she had dropped by the butchers the day before. *'How had Nalan gotten it?'* she thought to herself, especially as he had been under lock and key.

The room drew breath together.

"No! Don't hurt my daughter!" shrieked the Queen.

Sir Tarak jumped from his seat and drew his sword, Admiral Remi was not far behind in drawing her cutlass.

"Don't. Come. Near. Me," ordered Nalan. "Or I *will* hurt

her." Nobody in the room moved. All that could be heard was Nalan's heavy breathing. Liana's heart was beating so fast and hard she was convinced it could be heard too. "Now I'm going to walk out that door and I'm taking her with me to make sure no one follows me. Understood?"

The Queen's eyes filled with water and trickled down her cheeks as she looked on to see her daughter and her captor backing out of the room.

Liana and her mother reached out a desperate hand to each as she disappeared though the Triunity Hall's eastern door.

6

AURORA VISENDUS

At least 100,000 citizens stood shoulder-to-shoulder, crammed into the city square gazing at the enormous, scaffolded structure that was being built as the new focal point on the north side. Canvas sheets hung off the wooden framework, hiding the design of the construction.

Two semi-circular ramps hugged the numerous rows of steps that led up to the building's entrance that was built in the same golden-yellow tones of sandstone as the rest of the city. The Day of Darkness had injured and maimed many residents, so the architects had been instructed by the Queen to make the temple building accessible.

At the top of the steps two guards were kneeling, fumbling with something in the ground. Clerk Vivek was hunched over the pair, waving his walking stick, and shouting profanities at their incompetence. After a few more minutes, the guards eventually pulled a podium up out of the ground. Built into the podium was the same style tube that the Queen used for communicating over distances from the Queen's Table. Clerk Vivek and the guards made their way down one of the ramps, with Vivek still having an animated conversation with them, questioning their intelligence.

A short while later, Queen Adriya made her way hastily up the centre of the steps. She eventually climbed the last step and made her way behind the podium, drawing a deep breath before speaking into the tube and addressing the onlookers below.

"Citizens of Swyre," The Queen's opening words once again enough to silence the hubbub of a crowd as her words echoed out of tubes that were protruding out of the ground around the edges of the vast square so all the tightly packed people could hear her.

"This morning my daughter was kidnapped and taken hostage by a convicted criminal," a slight murmuring hummed from the crowd as the Queen confirmed the rumour that had been spreading through the city.

"This criminal stole Liana's horse and took them away from the city, in the direction of the forest. So far, our initial searches have failed," the murmuring became louder as the crowd discussed the situation in disbelief.

"Every resource will be exhausted in finding my daughter. Please, I implore you all, do everything you can to help the search. Right now, we should be in this square celebrating her birthday and inauguration as your heir-to-be. Your futures depend on her life. Whoever finds my daughter or discovers new information will be greatly rewarded."

Yasmin and Eugene stood side-by-side at the front of the crowd in the westerly corner watching the Queen deliver her message.

"So now the city stops because the precious Princess got

herself caught," Yasmin complained to Eugene. "I'm bored of this already. I want to see what's behind the scaffolding."

"It's taken 10 years, I'm sure you can wait a few more days," said Eugene

"Ugh, sometimes you're just as boring as the Queen's speeches. I can't wait any longer, I'm going to find a way inside," said Yasmin as she peeled away from the crowd.

"Hey! I am not boring," Eugene called as he followed after Yasmin.

They entered an alleyway which was situated behind Benji's butchers and the rest of the shops that lined the City Square. Old wooden crates and barrels were untidily discarded next to the rear entrances of the various retailers and due to the height of the buildings and narrowness of the alleyway, light was unable to make its way to the dusty floor even when the sun was at its highest. The atmosphere became even more oppressive at night once the sound of the bustling City Square had disappeared and the citizens had made their way to public houses and restaurants. The pair wandered to the very end of the alleyway where a newly constructed wall stood blocking their path.

"Eugene, go back and gather a load of those crates for us to stack," he did as he was told with no objection. "If we can get into the temple's gardens, I'm sure we could find a way into the building."

The number of crates needed to make a suitable, climbable, structure was rather more than they had both anticipated. Not that Yasmin offered to help. She just stood at the foot of the wall organising the crates into position barking at Eugene to work quicker. When the makeshift structure started to ascend beyond her own height, she demanded Eugene continue building it, as well as crate gathering. "Well, I'm not risking getting injured if it all collapses," she quipped to Eugene when he questioned his extra workload. *'Alright for me to get hurt though,'* he thought to himself. He knew any open challenge would be pointless and cause an unnecessary argument, so he held onto his dissatisfaction and continued doing as he was told.

Eventually the makeshift structure was in place. Eugene tentatively climbed it first. Apart from slipping on a couple of the greasier crates, he made it to the top with surprising ease. He sat atop the temple's wall and watched Yasmin attempt her ascent.

"Watch that crate there, it's...!" Eugene tried to warn Yasmin of one of the slippery crates when she was about halfway up. Unfortunately, the lack of grip on her smooth plimsole-like shoes were of no help and Yasmin's right foot went crashing through the wood of another crate as she tried to steady herself. Eugene couldn't help but snigger and was quickly chastised by Yasmin. "Stop laughing at me and help!" she screamed. Eugene offered his hand for Yasmin to help steady herself whilst she furiously tried kicking the crate that was now wrapped around her ankle. Eventually the crate fell to the floor, but not without creating a long tear in her blue henna-style, yoga trousers. This, of course, increased Yasmin's rage as she sighed and huffed the remainder of the way to the top of the wall. Eugene briefly thought to himself that he should remind Yasmin that this was all her idea and it's her own fault but decided better of it.

The pair sat dangling their legs over the garden side of the wall admiring the scenery. In each corner, infant cherry blossom trees displayed beautiful pink petals on their branches. On each side of a pathway which ran up the middle of the garden, numerous types of plants were in flower and arranged in segments by order of colour. Perfectly topiaried, green bushes separated each colour section.

Looking over the garden at the end of the pathway stood a large fountain. The fountain sprayed its water into a large lily pond below. The water spouted from six stone-carved tulips rising one above another, each painted in a different colour, that mirrored the segments of the garden's flowers. The tulip situated at the bottom was coloured red, followed by orange, yellow, green, blue and indigo. Several wooden arbours were placed around the grounds, each painted in one of the six colours represented on the fountain.

The tranquil scene almost immediately calmed Yasmin.

Fortunately for Yasmin and Eugene, one of these wooden arbour's was directly under their dangling feet, meaning they could easily drop onto its roof and then drop onto the ground.

"It's beautiful and so peaceful. I can't even hear the crowd at the city square. It's like we've gone to another land," exclaimed Eugene, looking around with his mouth wide open in awe.

"I wonder what all the colours mean," Yasmin said as she bent over to smell one of the tulips from the orange segment of flowers.

The two friends leisurely wandered through the garden in the direction of the building. This side of the building was still under cover so they were still none-the-wiser as to what it looked like from the outside, but Yasmin was eager to sneak in and see inside. They stepped onto a wooden veranda that was protruding from the scaffolding. Yasmin peeled back one of the canvas sheets hanging from the scaffold and peered into double check nobody was around.

"Coast is clear! Let's go!" an excited Yasmin said, pushing her way past the canvas.

"I'm not sure about this Yasmin, what if we get caught?" said Eugene as he hesitated and looked behind him to check nobody had seen them so far.

"There you go again, being boorring," goaded Yasmin's voice from the other side of the canvas.

Eugene pulled back the canvas sheet and followed Yasmin. "This must be a glasshouse for growing plants," said Yasmin, staring at a few empty planters and up at the glass ceiling. The canvas was preventing any sunlight from entering the room, but it was easily noticeable that unlike most of the glass in the city this roof didn't have Coryàtès famous blue cobalt tint to it and was clear.

"Come on, this way Mr Boring," jested Yasmin.

"I'm not boring. I'm here, aren't I?" replied Eugene.

Yasmin shot a rare smile in his direction as she darted towards an archway on the opposite side of the room, dodging empty planters as she went before stopping at the entrance to the next room. She turned around to take a moment to insult Eugene's hesitancy.

"If you're too scared you can turn back now, I won't stop you. Might keep more of your hair if you play it safe," Yasmin said, laughing at Eugene's expense.

"Hey, that's out of line! My lack of hair is not my fault! Wait up!" he shouted, now feeling quite annoyed.

Yasmin knew Eugene was self-conscious about his already receding hairline despite them only being 15 years old. All the men in his family's history had lost their hair by the time they were out of their teenage years and Yasmin frequently reminded him of this hereditary trait. Eugene's rounder, oval shaped head didn't help his cause either, having often been picked on for being an 'egg-head' by his peers at school. He attached himself to Yasmin due to her fiery nature as a form of protection. Yasmin secretly liked having his consistent company. She had a tough couple of years at school after Liana joined and what happened to her. However, it was still the case that any popularity she did have was largely based on a 'better the devil you know' attitude from fellow students and anyone who got close to her often got tired of her bullying and temper which had resulted in more than one or two fallouts.

Yasmin and Eugene now stood in a bright smooth-walled corridor. To their right, the corridor sloped up in a gentle curve anti-clockwise. To their left, the corridor sloped down in a gentle curve clockwise. Directly in front of them, another archway. Yasmin tried the archway's door. Locked. "Darn," she said.

"It's like a large spiral staircase that goes around the building. well without the stairs."

"Amazing detective skills there Mr Boring. So, up or down?!" asked Yasmin.

"Down," Eugene decided.

The lack of decorations or adornments caused the corridor to echo with each footstep. The slope's downward gradient was hardly noticeable, nor was the shallow curve. It was a while before another archway and door greeted the pair.

"Damnit, this one's locked too!" said Yasmin as she tried turning the iron ring door handle. "Now I *really* want to see what's inside."

"Well Yasmin, it doesn't look like we're going to have any luck. We should head back."

"So annoying," said Yasmin, conceding defeat.

Just as the pair turned to make their way back up the corridor, they heard voices bouncing off of the walls ahead of them and they froze, listening intently trying to make out what they could hear. A muffled "See you soon," is all they could make out before the sound of footsteps began to encroach on their position.

Yasmin got a handful of Eugene's shirt to grab his attention and pointed down the slope in the hope of finding a hiding spot elsewhere, before redirecting her finger and pointing to her shoes. With her other hand she gestured to her mouth in a 'shushing' motion (as if that need wasn't obvious to Eugene already) and promptly removed her footwear in a bid to quieten her footsteps. Eugene copied and the pair moved as swiftly as they could whilst remaining as quiet as possible.

The next door they came to was at the end of the sloping corridor. Yasmin again attempted to open it... but again it was locked.

"What are we going to do now?!" panicked Eugene.

"We have to hope whoever it is doesn't come down this far..." replied Yasmin.

The pair waited anxiously for the sound of a key turning, or a door opening. None came and the footsteps got louder and louder.

"We're in so much trouble," said Eugene, who was now clinging on to Yasmin's arm like a monkey to a branch. "What if it's one of Sir Langton's guards? Or Clerk Vivek, or a hand of the Queen. We'll be in for it!"

The person's long shadow came into the friend's view as it stretched across the floor. To Eugene, it seemed like a lifetime before the actual figure of its owner began to appear round the bend of the corridor.

"Yasmin? Eugene? I thought I heard someone down here. What are you doing?" It was the Priestess and Eugene breathed a sigh of relief. If there was one person who wouldn't harm them or even report them, it was probably her.

"Well?" urged the Priestess. "How did you even get in here?"

"Priestess Yi! We're sorry, Ma'am," said Yasmin, who rarely addressed anyone with suitable decorum. "We were just eager to see what's inside. We didn't want to wait. We think if the building's ready it should be open regardless of Liana's situation."

"What's with all the 'we'?!" exclaimed Eugene. "She forced me, Priestess."

"I didn't! I just said you'd be Mr Boring if you didn't come!"

"You wouldn't have gotten in without me!"

"Oh, shut up, Baldy."

"I admire your enthusiasm for the religion," interrupted the Priestess. "Your curiosity will suit you well when we do finally open the doors to the new temple. You have a natural thirst for winning and being the first Yasmin. There's no shame in that. I will need someone with your unique traits."

"You will!" Yasmin's face brightened and another rare smile radiated from her harsh face lines.

"You will?" queried Eugene, doubtfully.

"You have great potential Yasmin, but you will need to listen carefully to all you are taught should you decide to undertake our teachings. Come with me, let me show you something."

"Potential?" queried Eugene again, as the Priestess moved the pair aside and unlocked the door behind them. She led the trio into a dark, cold room caused by the lack of windows due to the fact they were underground.

"I can't see a thing," Eugene announced, stating the obvious.

"You will," replied the Priestess, who had disappeared into the darkness.

"Yasmin, what's going on? Is this a trick? Do you think she's actually locking us up down here?" Eugene whispered into Yasmin's ear.

"Shut up, Eugene!" replied Yasmin. The pair were now standing in the room, but they could not see anything as it was pitch black. Soon, a fantastic bright red light dazzled the eyes of the two friends.

"Yasmin, where's that light coming from?"

"I think..." Yasmin paused to consider her answer. "I think it's coming from the Priestess," she continued.

"You what? You must be going mad," said Eugene, covering his eyes from the light's intensity.

"She's not wrong," said the Priestess from the other side of the room. "This is merely an example of what can be achieved if you follow the right path and teachings of the religion."

The pair, stunned, were for once speechless. Once they were able to take their eyes off the Priestess's stunning display, they glanced around the room. Rows of wooden shelves housed a variety of different items. Some shelves had boxes, jars and trinkets, others had piles of clothes and wool. It appeared to be the temple's stockroom.

"Come," said the Priestess, waving them towards her. "I want to give you each a gift as the first two students of the Tulip Temple."

"Students? You mean, you'll start teaching us now? And the temple, it's called the Tulip Temple?" asked Yasmin. The Priestess nodded.

"Take these robes," said the Priestess as Yasmin and Eugene held out their hands as she gently placed the folded garments on their outstretched arms.

Yasmin couldn't help herself and immediately unfolded them to get a closer look. The robes were made of high-quality black cloth and lined with gold decorative tramlines across the shoulders and down the button line. Yasmin twirled the garment around. Adorning the upper-back portion of the long draping robe was a crest, also sewn in beautiful gold thread. The centre of the symbol was a long, thin, upward facing arrowhead. The fold of a crashing wave wrapped itself around the lower half of the arrowhead. The bending trunks of palm trees peaked out from the upper half of the symbol. Underneath, in a twisting script style font read the words 'Tulip Clan'. Priestess Yi saw the question in Yasmin's head and answered it without waiting for her to ask it.

"The symbol is the crest the old Visendi used to represent that they were of the Coryàtès family. Our symbol represents the three main features of our island - the ocean, the tropics and Mount Indigo," Yasmin and Eugene nodded in unison to confirm their understanding, whilst still admiring the amazing detail of the stitchwork. "Each family is made up of clans. The Tulip Clan is what I am calling our faction of that family."

As she turned the robe back around, Yasmin observed an odd omittance.

"These robes have no buttons," she pointed out.

The Priestess smiled as she handed out a rectangular black box with the same golden decoration adorning its lid.

"Open them," she instructed.

They opened their boxes in synchronization and peered at the contents.

"The buttons for the robes," Eugene picked up one of the buttons and examined it. "They look like tiny glass orbs, but the silver casing is different for each button?" he asked.

"Each button - or Aura Orb as they are called - represents

the level within the religion you are at. You earn your Aura Orbs as you Ascend."

"There are six buttons here. Like the six tulips of the fountain that we saw in the garden. What is the empty domes on top of each one for?" observed Yasmin, picking each design up and examining the golden fasteners closely.

"Ah, I assume that's how you got in, over the garden walls?" the pair nodded in response to the Priestess's question. "Your correlation is correct Yasmin. You are only allowed to sew on your button once you have proven yourself at that level. You only know you have proven yourself at that level when you can fill your Aura Orb with that level's respective colour."

"Whoooooaaa," Yasmin let out an excited blurt. "How do you make it fill with colour? How do you prove yourself? How are you making that red light? I have so many questions!" Yasmin couldn't talk fast enough. She had never felt so impassioned.

"This is all I'm telling you for today. I hope I can trust you both to keep this a secret until our temple doors are open?"

The pair nodded ferociously.

"It's time for you to go. I look forward to passing on our teachings to you both. Meet me behind the Temple, on the forest edge, after dark," The Priestess was now standing on a small flight of stairs, above her, she unlocked a hatchway in the ceiling. Sunlight quickly bestowed the cellar and the Priestess's glow dissipated. Eugene spotted a stack of paper on one of the shelves beside him. He picked it up and slipped it between his garments to look at later. The trio made their way up a set of steps that led into an alleyway situated on the opposing side of the temple from which Yasmin and Eugene had originally entered the building.

All three were now drenched in sunlight again. Eugene

squinted at going from the contrast of darkness to light. Yasmin hesitated in her departure and turned back to the Priestess "Ma'am, why did you give us these robes? Anyone else would have kicked us out and reported us?"

Priestess Yi smiled shallowly "Because Yasmin, just like you, I believe we should be opening today, regardless of Liana's capture, as a symbol of strength. In fact, I believe we should have been passing on our teachings long before today. I have been holding out long enough. I need young ones with your courage today, not tomorrow," Yasmin nodded in acknowledgement. Due to the harshness of her father, it meant that in her life, she had rarely been complemented. For the first time, she felt some kind of warmth. "Yasmin and Eugene, congratulations on becoming the first official members to the reawakened religion of Aurora Visendus."

The crowds of the City Square had begun to disperse, and the roads and alleys were beginning to fill up again. Yasmin gave a further nod of respect to the Priestess before she and Eugene ran off in the direction of the residential districts. As the pair hurried away excitedly, Eugene knocked into his sister whilst turning a street corner, dropping his items from his grasp. Eugene hastily scurried to gather up his belongings.

"Damn, Eugene, be careful! Hurry up!" shouted Yasmin, before the pair ran off.

"Hmm, up to no good again, no doubt," said Joel "What were they carrying?"

"Don't know. But that's not our concern right now Joel, we have to find Liana. She could be in trouble. Hey, what's this?"

The New Order of the
AURORA VISENDUS

13 long years after our legalisation, Priestess Yi Lang is delighted to announce that the **Aurora Visendus** *is ready to accept students and believers!*

Copies of our literature have been the number one seller in Swyre for over a decade! Your c ildren have been studying our **balance of life** *principles; Security, Creativity, Strength, Love, Communication and Awareness.*

Following the devastating Day of Darkness, the monarchy recognised the need for religious belief as a sanctuary for your **body, mind and soul.**

Now that you have studied, the doors to our grand new temple are open to you all! Come and meditate, practice and learn the **beliefs and abilities** *of the God of Dawn and earn your peace in this life and for the next.*

Aurora Visendus - 'To see the God of Dawn'
'To see the beauty of the dawn, you must first see the beauty of yourself'

Saffina knelt down to pick up a leaflet that Eugene had missed picking up from his dropped belongings.

"It's a leaflet promoting the new religion. Why did Eugene have it?"

"And how did he get it?" Joel snatched the leaflet from Saffina's hands. "Don't know about you Saff, but I've always thought the books in class never really told us what actually happened."

"I know what you mean," Saffina snatched the leaflet back. "If it's always been about developing a balanced life and focussing on creating a better energy for yourself, then why ban it?" The couple stared at the propaganda for a few more seconds before Saffina folded up the leaflet and slid it into her trouser pocket.

"Staring at this isn't going to help us find Liana. We've got to start looking for her."

"How are we meant to find her if Sir Langton and his army can't even find her?"

"We're her best friends Joel, we have to try. She took the wrap for us all yesterday; we owe it to her to at least try," Joel nodded in agreement. It wasn't often his care-free nature could be dampened, but after witnessing Liana's kidnapping that morning, it had been.

"Let's quickly get our horses, head home and get some supplies, camping gear, food and water. Meet you at the forest opening closest to the Triunity Hall in an hour. We're going to find her Joel, we have to."

7

THE WHITE ROBES

After a few sluggish blinks, Liana managed to open her eyes enough for her to just about make out the glaring colours and shapes of objects in the room she found herself in. An overriding feeling of tiredness swept over her whole body before a piercing, throbbing pain emanating from each temple and around her forehead.

Instinctively, she attempted to cradle her head in hands, but her hands were unable to move from behind her back. Her blue eyes continued to find their focus. She winced through her painful headache and soon the glaring colours began to turn into objects. The floor, walls and ceiling were all crudely made from wood, the type of wood that was readily available in the forest that surrounded Swyre. To her left lay a pile of blankets and directly in front of her a small wooden table and a chair, only large enough to fit one person at. On the table was an oil lamp, a cup and a satchel hanging off the back of the chair. There was not much room for anything else.

Now that Liana had come around, she soon came to the realisation that she was sitting on the floor of this rugged wooden room, with her hands tied around her back, wrapped around a tree branch that pierced through the floor, and up through the ceiling.

Suddenly a small square trap door near her feet burst open, making her jump. She retreated her tied up ankles as much as possible in an automatic act of defence, causing her knees to press against her chest. The head of her captor poked his head up out the trap-door hole in the floor. "You're finally awake." he blandly commented, before finishing his climb, kicking the trap door shut behind him.

"What did you do to me?" Liana asked, still in tremendous pain from her headache.

"I didn't do anything. Well, anything to do with your head anyway. I told you to duck. You didn't. That's what hitting a 30-year-old tree branch feels like at full flight on your rather speedy horse," responded Nalan.

"It hurts." she complained.

"Here. I made you this." Nalan threw a tiny, corked glass jar in Liana's direction that landed beside her. She eyeballed Nalan who soon realised that she was unable to open the pot with her hands tied up. She raised an eyebrow and continued to glare at her captor. "Ah, sorry about that. Guess, I, er... should pop that on your head for you."

"Or even better you could untie me, and I could do it myself!"

"I don't think so. Not right now anyway," said Nalan as he squatted beside Liana and popped open the pot's cork before dabbing some of its contents onto the tips of his finger, gently rubbing it into the Princesses forehead.

"What is this stuff anyway?" she asked.

"Lavender Oil. Family recipe using herbs found in the forest. It should ease the pain a little."

"How come you know how to make it?"

"My grandmother was a herbalist. Taught me everything I know when it comes to herbs and nature in general. I spent more time in the forest than in the city when I was growing up."

"So, you live here, in this small wooden hut?"

"Actually, I didn't know if this cabin was still here, but it was the first place I thought of where we wouldn't be found since we're about 40 feet up in the treetops. I built it when I was about your age," he said as he pushed his circular rimmed glasses up his nose.

"You built this all the way up here when you were my age and it's still here? You did a good job," said an impressed Liana.

"Thanks," Nalan may have said the word 'Thanks' but Liana could tell it was just an automatic reaction to receiving a compliment. There was no emotion in his tone that suggested he genuinely cared about her opinion. "Look, Princess, what I said in the Triunity Hall was the truth. It's hard to explain. I mean, I was there, standing over that architect with a knife in my hand, but someone, or something, was controlling me. Well, controlling my inhibitions. I could never hurt anyone. I'm sorry I took you hostage, but someone gave me the opportunity to escape, gave me the dagger, so I took my chance."

She watched him as he sat down on the chair in front of her and necked the contents of a leather canister, before bowing his head to reflect on the situation. She could tell he was telling the truth. First, by the expressions in his face and his tone of voice as he spoke. Secondly, by the feeling inside her. Like a sixth sense. The feeling on the back of your neck you get when meeting someone. If your hairs stand up on end in anticipation of hostility, or if your muscles relax allowing someone to enter that invisible comfort space around you. She could just tell he was telling the truth. Confused, but not lying. She thought back to her episode in the Triunity Hall and the black speckled glow that had surrounded him. It must have been some clue to do with Nalan's misdemeanour. She was curious. She wanted to find out more.

"What do you remember about that night?"

"It was in the evening and the sun was just beginning to set," Nalan didn't hesitate to begin telling his story. Liana was surprised at his willingness. *'Maybe he's been holding the events inside for so long, he just needs to tell someone who will actually listen.'*

"I was walking home after collecting a variety of herbs from the forest when I saw what I thought was just a pile of old tatty discarded brown robes on some rocks. I thought it might make carrying my things easier so I went to pick them up but…" he paused, suddenly doubting if he should continue his tale. Liana nodded to encourage him through his hesitation. "But. the robes weren't empty. When I touched them, the hood turned to look at me. Except, when I looked at it, it was just a black hole. Even with the sun setting I should have at least been able to make out a face, but there was nothing. It's honestly the scariest thing I've ever witnessed," a shiver travelled down his spine.

"What happened then?" she urged him on, with great intent and interest.

"It spoke, but I can't remember what it said. I just remember the voice sounding like it was from a really, really old man. Next thing I know, I was being arrested. Everything in between is like trying to remember a dream. Bits and pieces, but doesn't actually feel like you were there, but I know I must have been."

"Creepy..." a small shiver also ran down Liana's spine. "Who do you think this Hooded Man was?" she asked, infatuated with every word.

"No idea. It's not like I've been free to roam around and look for those ghostly robes again," replied Nalan.

"You know, what happened to me in the sentencing was pretty weird too..." she thought could possibly make a connection with her captor by sharing her experience. Build enough trust to let her go. Convince him that she will protect him from punishment. Maybe investigate these phenomena together.

"Oh? Please, tell me Princess," Nalan said, running his hand over his bald head.

"When I stood up and approached you, everything slowed down. I could see that there was something different about you."

"Something... different?"

"Yeh, like you had this strange...," she couldn't finish her sentence, she was cut off as the whole room jolted and the sound of cracking wood surrounded the pair. She screamed at Nalan: "What was that? What's going on? Tell me we aren't going to fall? Let me out! Let me out, Nalan!"

He jumped up from his chair but before he could reach her, the tree branch that penetrated through the room where the Princess was tied up fell away, bringing half of the tree house down, and Liana down with it. Nalan peered over the broken, jagged edges of the floorboards and watched helplessly as she plummeted towards the ground through the trees' large leaves, and quickly out of Nalan's sight.

Horrified, Nalan quickly opened the treehouse hatch and climbed down his 18-year-old makeshift ladder as fast as he could. He descended through three layers of thick branches and leaves, hoping they may have broken the Princesses' fall. The final layer of thick leaves lay only 10 feet above the forest floor. As soon as Nalan's head perforated the final layer, he jumped off the wooden ladder to earnestly begin his search for Liana amongst the shrubs. Before he could even call out her name, someone was shouting his.

"Nalan Weir?" shouted a deep, gravelled voice. "Nalan Weir. We hear you're the criminal wanted for the kidnapping of Swyre's precious Princess Liana and attempted murder of the City's architect. You will make an excellent prisoner." A scarred-face man in a full-length tunic emerged from trees beside Nalan. The tunic clearly started off in life as pure white but contained many years' worth of staining and sun-fading. Several other men and women in similar attire emerged from the forest scene. "Tell me, where is our *glorious* heiress?" asked the scarred-face man, sarcastically.

Nalan, seeing many of the men armed with crossbows and several ropes scattered on the floor, soon realised the treehouse collapse was no accident. "You tell me. She was with me, until you ripped down half of the treehouse she was sitting in."

"Guards, search the area! She must be nearby. You -" he said, pointing towards a group of four men and women holding crossbows. "Tie Mr Weir onto a horse and take him back to Master," The women nodded and did as they were ordered.

Nalan struggled as the quartet bound his wrists and ankles with ropes. "How did you even know we were up there?"

"One of our scouts saw you tying up a gold-coloured horse not far from here. It's not often you come across an Akhal-Teke horse breed. As soon as I heard of our scout's discovery, I just had to see what the real prize was. Didn't take long to find you whilst you were picking your precious little flowers. We simply followed you back here. Definitely worth the risk venturing this far into the forest. You and the girl will be the perfect leverage we need on the City."

Nalan continued to struggle in vain as the four White Robes lobbed him across the back of a horse and tied him down.

"Put a gag on the man. I don't want to hear his voice. Now, hurry up and find that girl. She could be the key to our freedom!" The scarred-face man punched the air as his followers cheered his words of optimism.

Liana, breathing heavily, sat up against a tree and spied around the trunk as the White Robes began to spread out their search. Fortunately, her hands had been freed in the fall and she frantically began to look around for an escape route.

'I can't leave this spot without anyone seeing me, they're approaching from all sides. As soon as they reach this tree, they'll spot me. But I'm sure to be seen if I make a run for it... What do I do?' she frantically thought to herself. Her body tightened up and she closed her eyes as the crunching of branches and leaves grew louder. With her eyes squeezed shut, and the sound of a twig breaking directly beside her, she held her breath in the anticipation of being taken prisoner for the second time in as many days. The footsteps stopped, but only for a moment, before the rustling leaves resumed and moved on. Confused, she gradually opened her eyes.

To her surprise, and huge relief, she was completely covered by the large green tropical leaves that betrothed the forest skyline. Even more to her surprise was the face of a blood-red-haired boy, a few years younger than herself, she guessed. He was staring directly back at her making a shushing pose with his finger to his lips as they waited for the last of the footsteps to subside into the distance.

"Thank you," mouthed Liana silently. Once the White Robes had moved on, the boy pushed away the foliage. "Who are you?"

The boy simply smiled in response and gestured to follow him.

"You don't need to be afraid to talk to me. I'm guessing you know who I am. Please, don't feel intimidated, I'm really no different to you or anyone else," The boy's expression remained unchanged as he waited for Liana to follow his lead. "What's your name, who were those people in the White Robes?" She waited for a response but still didn't get one. The boy started to fidget impatiently. "Look, you may have saved me from being kidnapped, again, but unless you talk to me, I'm not going anywhere with you" she stamped her foot and folded her arms in an act of stubbornness, not unlike her mother.

Angrily, he took out a blade from his robes and pointed it firmly in the direction through the forest where he wanted to take Liana. She recognised the blade instantly.

"Hey, that's mine, give it back!" screamed Liana as she made a lunge for the boy. The boy slickly dodged the lunge with ease and Liana face-planted the muddy forest floor. As she lay face-down in the dusty dry mud, a familiar voice echoed in the distance.

"Lianaaa! Lianaaa!" bellowed a male voice, followed by the clickity clank of armour. The clickity clank of armour that she knew very well.

"Great Uncle Tarak! Over here, Uncle Tarak!" Liana shouted as she ran to the direction of the voice. Reunited, they embraced each other warmingly. Her short arms barely reached around her uncle's torso.

"Oh, Liana! I found you! Are you okay, are you hurt?" Sir Tarak enquired.

"Bit of a headache... and a bit dirty... but otherwise I'm fine."

"I'm so happy you're okay. Your mother's been worried sick, she'll be so relieved. Where is that fiend who took you?"

"Nalan's not a fiend. He's confused. But he's not here, some weird looking people in dirty White Robes took him. They tried to get me too but that boy over there helped hide me," Liana turned and pointed behind her into the empty depths of the forest. The boy had gone.

"Boy?" Tarak raised an eyebrow and chuckled. "I think you may have hit your head harder than you thought. You do have a miniature Mount Indigo on your head," Tarak said, gently stroking a bump on his great niece's forehead.

"No, I swear the boy was real, Uncle."

"Let's get you home, Princess," smiled Sir Tarak. "Your mother will be incredibly relieved. And now the city has so much to celebrate! Your return, your belated birthday celebrations, and the opening of the new temple. Come, let's get you back to your horse. I found it tied to a gate post half a mile back. I figured you must be nearby." Sir Tarak picked up Liana's petite figure and carried her in his arms for the half mile to her beloved golden horse. "Will you be okay to ride back? You're not gonna pass out and fall off, are you?"

"I'll be fine Uncle. I just want to get home. She doesn't need me to guide her. She'll follow you. She's a clever one," said Liana, stroking the nose of her majestic companion, before mounting her. As they strutted off, Liana felt a chill down her neck, like someone had rolled an ice cube down her spine. She looked over her shoulder and saw a hunched, hooded figure in some distant shrubbery. She briefly turned and shouted to get her uncle's attention, but when she looked back over her shoulder, the figure was gone.

8

SEEING RED

The brilliant trio of planet Mikana's silver full moons sat high in the night sky as the forest's nocturnal inhabitants rustled, hooted and hummed as they emerged from their hiding places. Gradients of tekhelet, yellow and silver, originating from the surface colours of each moon, infused the black sky where thousands of twinkling stars shone clearly through the gaps in the tree leaves and branches. The vast forest rolled over a number of peaks and troughs of hillside and flatland alike as it served as a natural border to the City of Swyre from the North-western desert land and Coryàtès' volcano - Mount Indigo - that lay to the Northeast.

Upon one of the forests' many hillside peaks, Joel and Saffina sat dangling their legs over the side of a small rock formation looking down over the forest from which they had just travelled through. The pair sat in rare silence, in awe at the beauty of the city below them. Swyre's shimmering lights offered a warm and gentle ambience against the contrast of the city's sandstone composition, it's blue polished glass and the unclouded night sky.

Silhouettes of ships masts intruded upon the meeting of sky and sea on the horizon as Swyre's navy bobbed gently on the calm sea. A gentle breeze pushed the fresh ocean air inland. It had been a tough day trekking through vines, up hills and avoiding anything 'slithery, teethy or lizardy' - as Joel put it.

"What do you want to be when you're older, Joel," asked Saffina, thoughtfully.

"Haven't a clue," responded Joel. "As long as it's not boring, gives me enough time to enjoy life, and pays enough to not have to worry, I don't care what I do, really."

"Not asking for much then," Saffina smiled.

"How 'bout you?" asked Joel.

"Well, I expect Liana would give me a job inside the castle," replied Saffina.

"That wasn't the question. What do you *want* to be?" emphasised Joel. "You don't seem like you'd be the sort of person who'd be happy at being given a job."

She smiled gently and nodded. "You're right. I obviously love Liana, otherwise I wouldn't be out here looking for her," said Saffina, keeping her gaze fixated on the landscape in front of them. "But I want to earn my way. Create my own way in life. Maybe have my own business, that sort of thing."

"If that's what you want, Saff, you'll get it. I know what you're like. Once you set out to do something, you'll do it. That's how I know we're going to find Liana," Joel's words made Saffina chuckle. "Why are you laughing?"

"That's probably the nicest and most thoughtful thing you've ever said."

"Hey, I'm not all jokes and full of carefree adventures. I'm a deep and philosophical person you know."

This made Saffina laugh even louder. Joel joined in. Their unified laughs echoed around the cave situated behind them, where they had decided to settle down for the night.

"Come on," said Joel, jumping up from the cool stone surface "Let's put our heads down. I'm sure we'll find her in the morning."

The pair made their way over to the cave where the remnants of a burned-out fire was releasing its last vapours of smoke. Joel unpacked an array of coloured, cotton blankets from their backpacks and laid them out on the floor in two piles near the smoking wood.

"Do you think she's okay?" asked Saffina as she lay down, facing her friend.

"She'll be fine. That crook probably dumped Liana as soon as he was far enough away from the city. She's probably wandering around out here trying to find her way back. We'll find her."

"I hope you're right. Thanks Joel. You know, you're a good friend."

"Let's hope Liana thinks so too when we find her. Imagine the reward!"

"Joel! And I thought you were just starting to get a bit smarter."

"I'm kidding!" sniggered Joel, staring at the damp cave ceiling. "Hey, do you remember the first time we met her?"

"How could I not?" chuckled Saffina. "The way she walked into school with her hair wrapped up in that scarf thinking no one would know who she was. If anything, it made her stand out more!"

"And the way she wrapped it up like a hermit crabs shell?

It stood so tall on her head I thought she'd have to duck through doorways!" The pair's laughs echoed around the cave as they reminisced. When they had brought their laughter under control, Saffina rolled over on her side and stared at Joel.

"What do you think life would be like if the three of us didn't become friends that day?" she asked.

Before answering, Joel also turned onto his side, so he could look back at Saffina. "I don't know, but the last six years definitely wouldn't have been as much fun. What she did on her first day, I think the whole school was grateful, not just us. We were just the lucky ones who ended up becoming friends because of it."

"You're right, Joel. We're lucky. To have each other. All three of us."

Joel smiled gently before closing his eyes. "G'night Saff."

"Night Joel."

Saffina began to stir in the early hours of the next morning as the sunrise breached the cave entrance. She was groggy from an uncomfortable and restless night. Despite the blankets, her back ached from lying on the hard stone floor. She rubbed her eyes as she wearily sat up before turning over and gently nudging Joel's arm, who groaned at her attempt to wake him. She nudged him again, forcing him to respond with actual words.

"Alright, alright, I'm getting up," he moaned.

"Don't moan Joel, your friend is missing, remember?" she chastised. "These blankets barely kept me warm, let alone doing nothing to make me more comfortable."

"Someone's grumpy in the morning," he replied, earning him his first scowl of the day from Saffina. He stretched as he cumbersomely sat up against the rock wall. "Guess I should get some wood for a fire. We've got eggs to fry."

"Seriously, thinking about your stomach? We need to get going," she said, further chastising Joel's work ethic.

"We can't go searching without eating breakfast and building our strength up. Can't have you passing out on me, can I?" he retorted.

"If anything, *you'd* pass out on me since there's no meat on you! I don't know how you stay so thin with the amount you eat," she replied. "Just hurry up will you. The longer we stay in one place the further away Liana could be moving."

Joel got up and headed towards the cave entrance, but just as he got there, he stopped.

"I said hurry up, Joel. We know how nice the view is but now's not the time to be admiring it," she shouted.

Joel ushered with his arm. "Er, Saff, come here," he shouted back, hesitantly.

She sighed as she got up and made her way towards him. "What is it?" she said, abruptly.

Against the backdrop of the rising sun was the silhouette of a child, sitting cross-legged and meditating.

"How long do you think he's been there?" whispered Joel, pointing out of the cave entrance to the same spot where the pair had been sitting the previous night. "Do you think he even knows we're here?"

"I don't know but the thought he's been here all-night creeps me out a bit," Saffina whispered back.

"Yeh... just sat there... watching you grumble in your sleep..." jibed Joel, earning him a further scowl. "Go and talk to him."

"Me? Why should I do it, you saw him first."

"Because you have more of a chance of annoying him into leaving," he smirked. Saffina grabbed Joel by the bicep and dragged him to the figure on the rock formation. The pair crept forward. Not out of stealth, but more respect that they had for the act of meditating. As their eyes adjusted to the sunlight and shadows, they soon realised the figure before them was a boy dressed in orange and red robes.

"Saff, look at his hair. It's bright red! Not like a ginger-red, but bright red! Like the red-haired version of Liana!" The boy's eyes sprung open and stared directly at Joel. "Um, sorry, I, er, didn't mean any offence. I mean, it's actually pretty cool. Well, being red coloured, it actually looks hot, not that I'm calling you hot! I just mean the colour..." rambled Joel, nervously, before receiving an elbow in the ribs from Saffina to shut him up.

"Excuse me, but what are you doing here? What's your name?" asked Saffina. The boy shifted his gaze. "I'm Saffina, this is Joel. We don't mean any harm. We're just out here looking for our friend. Have you seen her? She has bright vivid blue hair."

The expressionless boy bowed his head slightly in acknowledgement that he had seen her.

"You've seen her? Where is she? Is she okay?!" she questioned, excitedly and impatiently.

The boy offered no response.

"Saff, I don't think he can talk. I mean, he probably doesn't even understand what we're saying. For all we know he could have grown up in the forest surrounded by monkeys." The boy switched his gaze again, frowning at Joel, before reaching into his robes. He carefully pulled out Liana's dagger, holding it flat on his outstretched palms as evidence. "Hey, he's got

Liana's dagger! How did you get that? You better not have hurt her! It doesn't belong to you, give it here!" shouted Joel as he made an attempt to grab the blade. The boy effortlessly rose to his feet and evaded Joel's leap.

"Just tell us how we can find her," insisted Saffina. "Like I said, we don't want to hurt you."

The boy arrogantly leered at Saffina as he tucked the dagger back into his clothing. He remained motionless, yet alert, in his pose as he stood at the highest peak of the rock formation whilst Saffina strutted up and eyeballed him.

"Now you listen here, boy. Liana is my best friend. She is also the Princess of Swyre and next in line to be Queen. Your Queen. It is your duty to help us find her and bring her home, or else you will be acting against the will of the Langton family. Now, give me the knife, and take us to where you last saw her, or there will be consequences," Saffina glared into his eyes. Joel had never seen Saffina be so direct and assertive with anyone other than him. He kind of liked seeing this side of her, he thought to himself.

An oppressive silence surrounded the trio whilst Saffina and the boy were having their stand-off. Even the chirping of waking birds and gentle rustle of the hillside wind through the trees seemed to stop in observation, waiting for someone to make the next move.

However, the stillness was broken not by one of the three children, but the sound of breaking twigs under horse hoofs and a chortle of laughter from the forest below them.

Startled, the trio peeked over the overhang of the rock formation as they witnessed a team of white-robed men and women wading through the forest below them.

The boy, concentrating on the group below, recognised them as the same ruffians who he had rescued Liana from the previous day and did not realise that the dagger's handle was dangling out the side of his robes. Thinking quickly, Joel saw his chance to get the dagger and he made a second lunge for it. Distracted, the boy was not able to fully dodge Joel's dive, but equally, Joel was not able to wrap his hand around the knife's hilt. Instead, the blade ended up becoming dislodged. It slid out of the robes and bounced off the stone floor and plummeted down the small rocky cliff face towards the armed group below.

The blade speared itself into the ground directly in front of the group's leading horseman, who immediately raised his hand to halt his troop, believing the knife to have been purposefully thrown in his direction. He moved his gaze upwards in the direction of the three children. Despite being a 25-metre drop, the children could clearly make out the scarred-face features of the man staring back at them.

"Saffina..." said Joel, his voice trembling "Get to the horses and run!"

"GET AFTER THEM!" groups of birds that had been sitting in the treetops flapped away in earnest as the scarred-face man's voice boomed. His gravelled tone echoed around the forest as his troops took flight on their horses up towards the rock formation.

"Quick Joel!" urged Saffina, watching Joel fumble about trying to get his saddle on. "There's no time, just get on without it!"

"I can't!" said Joel "I might be tall, but I'm not tall enough to get on without the saddle!"

"They're coming!" panicked Saffina. "Come here, get on the back with me!" she suggested.

"It's fine, I've got it!" said Joel triumphantly as he hopped onto his getaway ride.

"Wait, what about the boy?" asked a concerned Saffina as she turned her horse in circles in a frantic attempt to find him.

"There, by the cave!" announced Joel. "Get going, Saff! I'll get him!"

Saffina and Joel geed up their horses. "Give me your hand!" Joel shouted as he dashed towards the boy. The boy raised his arm as instructed as the horse and rider raced towards him. Their forearms successfully coupled, and Joel whisked him up.

Despite a brisk start, the dense forest soon made a quick escape impossible.

"They're right behind us!" shouted Joel as he snuck a look behind. "Four of them!"

The chasing riders were incredibly adept in their horse-riding skills. Although their horse breeds were inferior to the two, they were chasing, the riders' anticipation and reactions to the terrain more than made up for the difference in speed.

Saffina and Joel's hearts beat faster than they've ever beaten as they ducked low-lying branches, jumped fallen logs, and clung on to their equestrian comrades for dear life. The chasing quartet matched every twist, turn, duck and jump.

"We're not losing them!" yelled Joel, still keeping an eye on their tail.

"Joel, down there, looks like a straight run, try and outrun them!" called Saffina as she pointed towards a dip in the forest floor that led onto a narrow muddy track.

They guided their horses hastily down the receding ground but being cautious enough to not slip and fall down the slope. Once at the bottom, the pair rode as fast as they could, now with clear ground in front of them.

Joel's passenger took this opportunity to bail. The boy gracefully, skilfully, and all in one move, pushed himself into a crouch position on the horse's back, before leaping onto an overhanging tree branch.

"I think we've lost them!" announced Joel, discovering his passenger was now no longer with him as he turned around to check the whereabouts of the chasing pack, when suddenly, he heard a scream from in front of him.

"STOP!" wailed Saffina, bringing her horse to an abrupt, skidding halt, forcing Joel into the same manoeuvre. "What do we do now!?"

The pair had come to a cul-de-sac, surrounded by a sheer drop on each side that was too steep to traverse. Joel's voice shook. "Hope and pray we've lost them... and they don't chuck us off the edge...?" he said as they peered over the sheer, cliffside edge that surrounded them. A drop that fell vertically into a ravine of shallow, rocky water. They were trapped.

"Hey, what happened to the boy?" questioned Saffina. Joel shrugged his shoulders, but before he could answer her with words, their pursuers had caught up.

"Now, that wasn't very clever, was it?" smirked one of the brutes, delighted at getting his catch. "Get them down and tie them up," he said, waving his hand at two of the other horsemen. "They can walk as we head back, as punishment for trying to attack us."

The pair were dragged off their saddles with little empathy for their physical well-being. Their hands were quickly tied to the reins of one of the brutes' horses, whilst two other members of the squad hooked up their black steeds as prizes.

Joel and Saffina were barely able to keep their tear ducts dry as they looked at each other and saw the fear in each other's eyes.

"I wonder what Master Thornfalcon will make of these two delights."

9
CONFLICTED EMOTIONS

Queen Adriya sat in the Queen's Table on the perch of the window that overlooked Swyre, staring absentmindedly into the distance. The same window where she sat exactly 13 years ago as clouds of smoke and ash enclosed itself around the city like a python around it's prey. The same feelings she felt exactly 13 years ago. Worry, doubt, anxiety, but also hope. Queen Adriya was never without hope. Without hope, she thought, would be to surrender. To surrender is a sign of weakness and she was anything but weak.

The infusions of purple from that evening's dusk had faded leaving only the piercing white stars as the remaining colour against the pitch black almost-midnight sky. The city below was numbingly quiet, even for this hour. Groups of citizens with experience in the forest (retired soldiers, carriage men, woodcutters, foragers, and other have-a-go citizens) had been out looking for Liana since the Queen's announcement that morning. Many had already returned when the sun began to

set. Some were still trickling back into the city's borders. Only
those who had camping equipment remained out searching.
These were the few groups of retired soldiers and a few
groups of carriage men. Carriage men knew the landscape of
Coryàtes like no one else. They were an essential service, not
just for transporting passengers around the large city itself, but
for the transport of goods and people across the whole island.
The City of Swyre was the only built-up territory, consuming
most of the quadrant on the South-Southeast sides of the
island, but other hamlets were dotted around. The fishing
villages on the northwest coast and the farmlands to the south-
west. And of course, the mines to the Northeast. The only area
of wholly unoccupied land was the desert land that stretched
from the middle of the island to the north, kissing the westerly
edge of Mount Indigo. The Queen's personal fleet of carriage
men had the responsibility of transporting prisoners after
sentencing. Most that required transporting were being sent to
work in the mines, but the most serious crimes resulted in
convicts being banished to the desert. The island's tempera-
mental tropical climate meant that carriage men often had to
deviate from planned routes in case of a sudden thunder-
storm, or a baking heatwave in the desert land. It was this
group of carriage men that the Queen held out most hope for
finding Liana. No one else possessed as much knowledge, or
even scouting ability, as the Royal Fleet when it came to the
landscape of Coryàtes.

Just as this thought lay at the forefront of Queen Adriya's
mind, she saw the Royal Fleet bounding in through the castle
gates. Hope soon turned to optimism. The fleet surely
wouldn't have returned unless they'd found Liana, she
thought. Hastily, she rose off her perch and headed towards
the pipe system on the opposite side of the room.

The Queen rang the bell under the plaque labelled 'Portcullis'. The bell immediately sounded back. She unlatched the flap to the communication tube and spoke into the opened hole.

"Guards, put Fleet Captain Munro on immediately."

"Yes, your Majesty," reverberated a deep voice a few moments later.

"Your Highness, it's Fleet Captain Munro speaking." a meeker voice soon sounded out of the pipe.

"Have you any word of my daughter's whereabouts? Do you have her?"

"I'm afraid not, not yet, your highness," the Queen sensed a tone of weariness in his voice. "Your Majesty... we were ambushed, deep into the forest."

"Ambushed?" said the Queen, shocked. "We haven't had any rebellious factions or tribes on the island for decades. The island works as one. Do you know who they were?"

"I didn't recognise them. They wore plain dirty White Robes, but they kept their hoods up. No markings on their clothing, either. I'm sure we were on Liana's trail, but a few of my men have sustained heavy injuries in the skirmish. They were skilled fighters, we are not. We are not soldiers. Some of my fleet have serious injuries. All we could do was get away, as fast as we could. I'm sorry for failing, your highness," a genuine sense of sorrow and worry emanated from the Fleet Captain's words, even though the less-than pitch perfect tube system. "We came across the kidnappers' handcuffs amongst a pile of broken wood that looked like it had been a shelter, deep into the forest, near the mines. We can only assume he still has Liana. If he doesn't, then..." The Fleet Captain hesitated.

Queen Adriya finished the sentence. "Then the ambushers may have her."

"I fear that may also be a reality, Your Highness."

"Your information is invaluable, Captain. Go and get your injuries treated."

The Queen stood motionless, contemplating the news she'd just received and the possibility that her daughter could be in even graver danger than she initially feared. She slowly lifted the flap of the tube and latched it into place. The quietness of the room, that often helped the Queen think with clarity, began to suffocate her. She could not think of anything other than the conjuring images in her mind of her precious daughter being hurt and kidnapped for a second time in the same day. Despite her hope, despite her strength, droplets of silent tears cascaded down her soft cheeks.

She felt the need to escape the smothering room and dried her wet cheeks with her hands. A cool breeze wafted up through the spiralled staircase as she opened the door. She paused to momentarily enjoy the freshness on her still damp face before she made her way down the Tower of Seeds.

As she neared the bottom of the staircase, the sound of muffled, raised voices could be heard coming from the Triunity Hall. The Queen pushed open one of the large wooden doors to the hall and saw the Fleet Captain and Agatha struggling to hold back a slightly scruffy and unkempt woman with countless piercings hanging off each ear.

"I'm sorry Ma'am, she must have followed us through the castle gate," said the Fleet Captain, using whatever strength he could muster to keep this woman restrained.

"I've told you; you can't just come barging in here," shouted Agatha, also struggling to restrain the woman.

"It's okay, let her go," instructed Queen Adriya. The Captain and Agatha released the woman immediately.

"You know her?" asked the Fleet Captain.

"This is Trisha Greymore. Saffina's mother," the Queen made her way closer to the scruffy woman, observing that she had had even more piercing in her ears than the last time they had met. "What's the matter, Trisha?"

"You! You and your daughter!" screamed the agitated woman, pointing her finger directly into the Queen's face whilst locking her raging eyes onto the Queen's. "Your daughter is nothing but trouble for my Saffina!"

"I understand she must be upset. No one is more upset than I am, she's my daughter, but I promise they'll be together soon." said the Queen, assuming the reason for Trisha's agitation was the fact that Saffina must be feeling emotional at Liana's disappearance. "You and I may have had our issues, Trisha, but I am desperate to find Liana. Please, go, and reassure Saffina we're doing all we can."

"That's it, just send me away before you've even heard me out!" Trisha continued to scream. "You did this!"

"Trisha, what's going on? Whatever do you mean? What did I do?"

"It's Saffina. My little Saff! She's gone! It's all about you isn't it! *'I implore you all, do everything you can to help the search'.* That's what you told everyone this morning wasn't it? Well, my Saff was there listening to you, as you told everyone to find *your* daughter. What about *my* poor Saff? What about those families, like ours, that are less well off? They don't care about finding your daughter, they just want your reward. How many people have you just put in danger? Just look at your carriage man! How are normal people supposed to survive out there if a trained navigator can't even get home without a scratch!"

The Fleet Captain raised his hand to a bleeding cut on his forehead and winced in pain as he touched it. Agatha untied her apron and pressed it against the captain's head before guiding him to one of the deep-blue leather covered chairs next to the hall's pedestal that had still not been packed away from the sentencing earlier in the day.

"You mean, she's gone looking for Liana?" asked the Queen, wanting confirmation from Saffina's mother.

"Yes, and she's not come home! I spoke with Joel's parents first in case she was at his house, but both are missing! They must be out looking for her together!"

"I.. I don't know what to say, Trisha," the Queen said, uncharacteristically stuttering in her response.

A sudden change in emotion overcame Saffina's mother, as she collapsed towards Queen Adriya, changing from wild rage into distraught sobbing in a split second. The Queen caught her fall and held her, subconsciously pulling her in tighter as the pair embraced without words at the shared emotions of having missing daughters.

Then, just as Saffina's mother found the strength to hold her herself up and wiped the tears from her cheeks, one of the auditorium doors flung open with resounding force and in strode the esteemed figure of Sir Tarak, clutching the hand of Liana as they entered the room.

The Queen screamed her daughter's name. She struggled to release Saffina's mother from her clinging grasp but managed to fling her sprawling arms away and dropped to her knees with outstretched arms as her daughter ran towards her. Reunited, mother and daughter held each other tighter than they ever had. Adriya pulled away to look her daughter in the eyes and check she was ok, hands cupping the side of her head. Thumbs caressing her daughter's temples affection-ately. "You're alright?" she said. Liana gave a zealous nod and smiled before the pair re-embraced for a second time.

"Thank you, Tarak. Thank you," said the Queen as she rose up from her kneeling position.

"I'm just glad she's all in one piece, Iya," he replied.

"I'm fine, mother. Nalan didn't hurt me. He's really not all that bad. I believe him when he says he didn't try to kill that architect, but the others... they would have hurt me if they found me."

"Others?" asked the Queen "What do you mean, others?"

"They wore plain dirty White Robes. No symbols on them from what I could see, and they knew I was out there. They were looking for me."

"That sounds like the group that attacked us," said the Fleet Captain, who was now sitting down on a bench along one of the Triunity's walls, still pressing Agatha's apron against his head, which was now almost completely saturated with blood.

"But how could they possibly know you were out in the forest? You were kidnapped only this morning!" remarked the Queen.

Liana shrugged in response, as Queen Adriya, Agatha, Tarak, and Munro exchanged looks of concern, realising that the kidnapping must have been set up. *'If it had been planned, then it must have been someone in the castle with access to the prisoners,'* thought the Queen.

"I can see what you're all thinking," remarked Liana, looking around the room. "The dagger that Nalan used to take me. It was mine. I dropped it yesterday outside Benji's. I'm sure Yasmin picked it up. She must have given it to him."

"Well, we can't just go accusing people, Liana," said the Queen, being diplomatic, although not disregarding the possibility that Yasmin's family was somehow involved. "We'll be sure to pick this conversation up tomorrow. For now, I think you should go to your room and rest."

"What about my girl!?" shouted Saffina's mum, having been briefly forgotten in the wake of Liana's arrival. "Her and Joel have gone out looking for you! Did you see them? Do you know where they are?!"

Liana's eyes widened. "No, I've not seen them! Why would they go looking for me on their own?!"

"Because they're your friends Liana! We have to find them, what with these horrible White Robes in the forest!"

Liana turned to her mother. "We have to find them! They could be in trouble!"

"We've had everyone out looking for you all day and night Liana. Look at Munro! We can't risk it now."

"But they're my friends. My ONLY friends!"

"Iya's right, Liana. We left the city exposed today with all of our resources out looking for you. Not only do they need to rest, but if there are unsavoury groups in the forest, we need to protect Swyre," said Sir Tarak, empathising with his great niece's situation but, as always, putting the safety of the city first.

"I can't believe it!" the Princess screamed, breaking away from her mother's reach. "My two best friends risk their lives to save me, and you won't do anything for them?"

"Liana, please, we didn't know..." pleaded Queen Adriya.

Liana interrupted with a defiant "I'm going back out there!" as she marched towards the door from whence she came, before the towering figure of Sir Tarak blocked her path. "Let me through!" she demanded, helplessly flailing her arms as she thumped her Great Uncle's metal chest plate with both fists before exhaustion set in. She couldn't remember the last time she ate.

"Come on, dear, come with me. I'm sure your mother and great uncle will come up with a solution," Agatha caringly put her arm around her. "You also need a rest and some food, my darling. You've been through a lot. Let's get you to your chambers."

Too weak to put up any more of a fight, she conceded and retreated to her room, escorted by Agatha, leaving the Queen and Sir Tarak to reassure Saffina's mother.

O n her balcony, Liana lay on her Chaise Longue, listening to the steady rhythm of waves beat against the foot of the rocky cliffside below her balustrade balcony. A sullen weight surrounded her as the cool midnight air hung as motionless as a statue. A half-eaten tray of chicken, rice and vegetables sat upon a circular-topped bedside table next to her. Only her mind's preoccupation with her friend's fates kept her awake, but she soon drifted off into a deep slumber.

10

DAGGER OF RED

I wave my arms and legs around to try and sit up, but I cannot. I open my mouth and try to call out, but I cannot. Then, in the fuzziness of my vision, a pretty woman with vivid deep blue coloured hair softly smiled as she towered over me.

"My babe," she says to me as she gently strokes my cheek. "My special little babe. You are the most important person to have ever been born. You are the perfect balance of darkness and light, of night and day, of sunrise and sunset. You are our only hope and our greatest threat. Your birth will be the beginning of the end, but to which end transpires is down to you.

It breaks my heart to know I have brought my only child into the world for a purpose other than to raise and teach you, but you are the only solution we can see that may bring about a peaceful end to this passage of time."

I notice a glow around me, looping through a sequence of colours - red, orange, yellow, green, blue and indigo before starting over again.

The woman looks up and moves out of my line of sight, leaving *me staring up helplessly at the icy glass ceiling. I can hear her voice in the distance but I'm unable to make out what she is saying, although she soon returns to my side.*

"My fellow Transcended. After much debate we have finally arrived at this important juncture of our religion. Let us not waste any time. Please, place your Spirit Orbs in their respective bases around the child."

I turn my head left and right and see six pairs of hands placing something into dipped crevices that circle my tiny body. As the hands peel away, I can see that the items are clear and translucent Orbs.

"Gilroy, the blade, please." The woman looms over me again with a familiar looking weapon. The dagger, my dagger, gifted to me by my Great Uncle when I was 5 years old. She points it at me. I sense my tiny heart beating faster and faster in fear for my life, knowing there's nothing I can do. As the blade gets closer and closer, I shout out instinctively to stop but only a high-pitched cry comes out. "It's okay my girl, I'm not going to hurt you," says the woman. 'Exactly what someone would say when they're about to hurt you' I thought.

She paused and waited, watching my light change colour in the cycle of my coloured glows. As soon as the red appeared, she pierced the light a few inches away from my body. She carefully cut the light in the shape of my tiny figure. As she circled back to the point from where she first penetrated, the red light released itself from me and became encapsulated in one of the clear orbs - turning it red. I watched as the gradients of red danced around its new prison. The woman repeated the process five more times, sending each of my coloured glows into their own orb.

"I have successfully Peeled her Aura's. The transfers to the orbs are complete. Take them and unite them with your Artifacts." The woman handed the dagger back to its original owner. I looked to my left at the Red Orb that I was so familiar with. Although I could not

make out his face, I watched the shadows of the one named Gilroy pick up the Red Orb and insert it into the circular space in the dagger's handle where it clicked into place with precision. My limited vision and movement prevented me from seeing the other Orbs become united with their Artifacts.

"I still protest," said the voice to my left.

"Everyone else is in agreement, Gilroy. Now please, proceed to your chamber," said the woman, softly but sternly. "Members of the Transcended, it's now time to make our sacrifice." I watched Gilroy's shadows again as he stepped up into an upright icy casket.

The woman stood over me once more. "Good night, sweet girl. When you awake, the world will be a different place. Your father should not find you here, but we cannot take any chances, I had to Peel your Aura Spirit's from you. The world in which you awaken will be different to this one. If by some miracle you remember this moment - remember this - seek out the coloured Spirits I have Peeled from you, little one. Use these powers for good - free of the atrocities our kind have caused this world." I watched silently as she lowered the lid to my own casket over me.

Liana opened her eyes slowly. She felt groggy as she awoke. She had to blink several times before the blurriness of her surroundings became clear. Confused, she turned around in a full circle.

'Why am I in Vivek's study?'

The last thing she remembered was falling asleep on her lounger. She had no recollection of how she got here. Had she been sleepwalking? She'd never done it before.

'Wait, what's this?'

She looked down at her hand and discovered she was holding the orb that Vivek kept stored with his collection of gemstones. The cabinet drawer was open in front of her. The orbs' smooth surface felt cold in her hands. It glowed an intense red light of dancing swirls and wispy mist.

'It's so captivating.'

She couldn't take her eyes off the magical ball of light. It drew her in, hypnotising her.

'It's like it's speaking to me.'

The sound of a door being opened echoed through the hallway outside. Liana snapped out of her trance. She frantically made her way to the door of the study and pushed it ajar. She peeked through the crack of the doorway to see Clerk Vivek coming her way. She hastily ran over to the open drawer of gemstones and shut it tight before sliding the orb into her trouser pocket. She did not want to get caught snooping, so thinking quickly, she jumped onto Vivek's desk and opened a window. The handle squeaked as she pushed it open. She clambered through the window and landed on the cool midnight grass, before gently pushing the window shut behind her and ducked down just in time before Vivek entered his study.

She ran across the lawn and turned a corner before bumping into Priestess Yi who was wearing a long brown hooded cloak over a typically vibrant dress. She fell against the wall and the orb slipped from her pocket onto the floor.

"What's this?" Priestess Yi said, picking up the sphere.

"N-nothing," stuttered Liana whilst the Priestess exchanged glances between her and the object.

"Quickly, come with me, Liana," the Priestess grabbed her hand and rushed her to a small storeroom, piled high with bags of flour and grains. "I think it's time you are told."

"Told what?" Liana raised a quizzical eyebrow.

"About you and who you might be," The Priestess had an earnest tone to her voice.

"I expect you're still angry with your mother," she started. "I also expect you think her only reason for not allowing you to search for your friends is to prevent you from getting hurt by these White Robes." the Priestess was right, but Liana sensed a further reason coming. "You see Princess, the Queen and I think you're special. Not just because you're the Queen's daughter, or the heir to the throne. But because of something far greater."

'What could be greater than being Queen of Swyre?'

The Priestess unveiled an old parchment that she'd been storing within her cloak.

"What do you know of the Aurora Visendus?" he asked.

"Only what they've taught us in school. Find your Inner Cores and the God of Dawn will provide for you in this world. If you prove yourself to the God of Dawn, she will lay the path of light for you to crossover into the afterlife. You can achieve this by studying and balancing your life in six areas; Security, Creativity, Strength, Love, Communication and Awareness."

"Excellent, you clearly listened well in your classes. Do you know why the Aurora Visendus religion was outlawed?" Liana chose to ignore the fact she had continued without answering her question.

"As war after war tore through lands in the fighting between monarchies for territory, people all over the world believed the religion should be in sole power. It was this threat of the religion gaining such support among the majority of lands that the monarchies stopped fighting each other and instead worked together to abolish the religion. As they focussed on a common threat, they united in peace," Liana responded, reciting the explanation almost like a practiced piece of scripture for a play.

"Mmmhmm," mumbled the Priestess thoughtfully,

thinking twice before continuing with her next sentence...
"What would you say if I told you that this wasn't true?"
"Honestly, I'd probably consider if you were lying to get
back at my mother for having not yet opened your temple."

"Well, you're not wrong there," The Priestess chuckled.
"But I am actually telling the truth. That spiel about the
monarchies coming together because they felt threatened. It
was made up. The fact is the truth about why the religion was
outlawed is more than just frightening."

"Why?" enquired Liana, now alert as if she'd had a full
night's sleep. "What's the truth?"

"I don't feel it's my place to tell you, and I also wouldn't do
the true story justice."

"After all that, you're seriously not going to tell me the
truth here and now? What was the point in even asking me
about it?"

"To get you questioning all that you think you know. An
open and agile mind is a valuable asset. Especially considering
what I'm about to tell you," she began to unravel the old, torn
parchment that she'd been gripping in her hands for the
entirety of the conversation.

"What is that?" asked Liana.

"As far as I'm aware, this is the last remaining scripture in
Swyre concerning the old religion of the Aurora Visendus.
All literature relating to the old ways were burned 200 years
ago when the religion was outlawed. Since then, us followers
of the religion have been worshipping in secret, with their
practices being handed down from generation to generation
within a select few families in each land. This scripture is so
important it was handed to me in person, by my predeces-
sor, and the advisor before him, and the advisor before him,
and so on, along with the whereabouts of the few families

that continue to illegally practice the old ways. This scripture was written by the last High Priestess of the Aurora Visendus."

Liana was anxious to see what was written on the old parchment. "Come on, show me what's written on it," she said impatiently.

The Priestess handed her the parchment. She carefully unravelled it and read the contents aloud, to be sure not to misread anything.

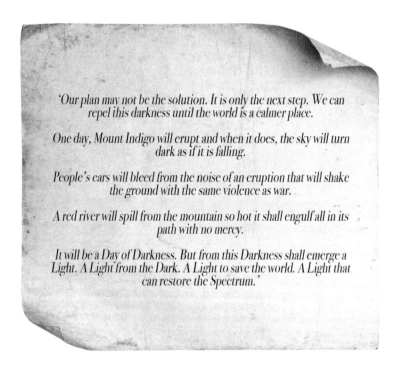

'Our plan may not be the solution. It is only the next step. We can repel this darkness until the world is a calmer place.

One day, Mount Indigo will erupt and when it does, the sky will turn dark as if it is falling.

People's ears will bleed from the noise of an eruption that will shake the ground with the same violence as war.

A red river will spill from the mountain so hot it shall engulf all in its path with no mercy.

It will be a Day of Darkness. But from this Darkness shall emerge a Light. A Light from the Dark. A Light to save the world. A Light that can restore the Spectrum.'

"I don't get it," said Liana, bluntly. "It predicts the Day of Darkness. I'm assuming this scripture is where you got the name from. But what's it got to do with me?"

"Your mother and I believe you are the Light it talks about,

Liana. The Light from the Dark. The Light that's going to restore the spectrum and save the world."

"Save the world? Me?" Liana laughed hard. "Are you joking? In the last two days I've lost my dagger, which was then used to kidnap me, then I almost got kidnapped again, and I've lost my friends! How is this about me? I'm more of a dull grey rock that's been sprinkled with a glitter of royalty."

"You lost your dagger?"

Liana thought it odd that out of all the things she listed, the Priestess chose to focus on the dagger. "Yes. Some red-haired boy has it. Saved me from the White Robes."

The Priestess pondered on Liana's words but moved the conversation on swiftly. "You are harsh on yourself, girl," she tapped Liana's knee, reaffirming her sincerity. "Let me explain some more. 13 years ago, to the day, on the Day of Darkness, you were not born from Queen Adriya. You were found. You were found by your Great Uncle, at the foot of Mount Indigo. You were a babe on a rock. The only rock on the red river that hadn't been swallowed. To quote Sir Tarak's account of that day: 'As I lifted the babe into my arms I said "How are you alive? This baby is a tiny little miracle." And then, as we jumped off that floating rock, it melted into the red river. As if this babe was the one keeping it afloat.' You see, Liana, you are not Adriya's natural born daughter. You are her rescued orphan, born out of the Day of Darkness."

The Princess sat in stunned silence. Suddenly, she wasn't concerned with how the old religion really became to be banished, or even the welfare of her friends. She'd just found out everyone close to her had lied to her whole life. Her mother, the Priestess, Sir Tarak, the whole Queen's Table probably knew, she thought. What if the whole city knew except for her? It would be a good explanation for why people always seemed to stare at her in an awkward, strange way. She felt like a fool, an idiot, for not working it out for herself.

'Of course, I'm not her daughter I have electric blue hair for starters!'

"You will probably feel even more angry and confused at your mother than you already were, but believe me when I say, everything we've done is to protect you, because we believe the fate of the world depends on the fate of you," The Priestess waited for a response, but none was forthcoming.

"There's something else," she could see Liana turning his words over and over in her head and decided to interject these thoughts with another revelation. "On the day your Great Uncle found you, there was an object with you. An object you're already familiar with. I saw it reacting to you holding it," she pointed to the red sphere in Liana's pocket. "This orb you hold was clipped into the handle of the dagger that Tarak gave you on your fifth birthday. He had Vivek remove it, saying the protruding bulges of the sphere would make it impossible to handle, and he also didn't want you being mugged as the orb looks like a precious gemstone. It's quite a unique piece."

"Why do you think it only reacts to me touching it?" she asked.

"I'm not entirely sure, but if the scripture is anything to go by, perhaps it knows that you are the one who needs to restore its contents somewhere, or to someone - 'A Light that can restore the Spectrum'." she reflected as he repeated the final sentence from the scripture.

"I still don't understand why you think I'm this light. How do you know that I wasn't just abandoned or lucky?"

"It's true, we don't know, for sure," she shrugged. "But

when you put everything together, it's the only logical explanation."

"So why tell me now? Why not keep on lying to me?" said Liana in an accusatory tone.

"Because, my dear, I've been waiting for a sign. Turning 13 seems to have activated something. You saw something unexplainable in the Triunity Hall, didn't you?" Liana nodded. "Now you need to prepare for whatever your destiny has in store for you. You need to make decisions on your own and learn from your mistakes and I believe the only way for you to do this is to understand the old ways of the Aurora Visendus and unlock the truth of your heritage. If I am right about this scripture, then I know you will not become the light that saves the world by being shielded from reality. You need to find yourself. Understand your truth. Do things on your own. Make mistakes. Find your Inner Cores. There is no better place to start than with you finding your friends."

Liana immediately perked up. Did the Priestess just advise her to break Queen's orders and seek out her friends? "Mother will go mad. You'd get in all sorts of trouble if she found out you advised me to search for them," she said, showing concern for her future. She felt less angry at the Priestess for lying to her for all these years, since she's the one who's just broken the secret and no doubt would have been under strict instruction from her mother not to say anything. "I most certainly would be, but let's deal with that at the Queen's Table, shall we?" the Priestess gave a cheeky smile.

"Where do I even begin to look for Saffina and Joel?"

"You don't, not straight away at least," she ran her fingers through the streak of green hair on her head. "If these White Robed mobs roaming the forest are as dangerous as the Fleet Captain says, then you will need some help first, and if Tarak's men cannot trace them, then they must be skilled in covering their tracks," she paused to consider her next sentence. "There is an old temple on the Northwestern side of Mount Indigo. An Old Priest and his ancestors have resided there for many generations, practicing the old ways. I have not heard from him in over a year, so I can only hope he's still alive. I don't really know him; we've never really seen eye-to-eye. He is a cautious man. Quite untrusting of any communication, but, if anyone on this island can help you understand the truth of your life, it will be him. The true Aurora Visendi possesses some quite magical skills. If you are the one this scripture refers to, you could wield some great power," she paused and looked away, as if distracted in her own thoughts... "Power that could be very... useful."

"Powers that could be useful in finding Saffina and Joel?"

"Yes... yes. That's what I mean."

"Ok, where do I find him, this Old Priest and his temple?" asked an eager Liana.

"The temple finds you. I have only travelled there once, not long after the Day of Darkness. When the Queen first laid eyes on this parchment, she instructed me to seek out those on the island that still practiced the old ways to find out more. To see if there were more writings that could verify if you were the Light from the Dark. But of course, none were found. I can help you though, but first, we must get the backing of the Queen's Table."

"Tell me more about these Powers. How are they going to help me find Saffina and Joel?"

"Your answer to that will be at the opening ceremony of the Tulip Temple."

THE RED AURA

An orange blaze of light was cast out from the rising sun as it peeked over the city's rooftops. The early morning dawn hit the face of the newest structure in Swyre before any others, revealing it's remarkable and vivid construct. The towering structure consisted of three giant sepals and three enormous petals rising high into the sky, an accurate copy of an actual tulip's design, minus the stem. Each of the sepal and petals were painted in a different colour; red, orange, yellow, green, blue, and indigo. All through the darkest hours of the night - following the Queen's orders immediately after her daughter's safe return - workmen and women had been busily deconstructing the scaffolding and canvas that had been covering the Tulip Temple, ready for its official opening that morning.

Despite her late night, Liana was already awake. She wandered down the cobbled streets between Castle Langton and the city square, taking in the hustle and bustle of the early morning traders. From butchers to grocers, she watched as they set out their stalls and shop displays and breathed in the various smells and aromas. Word had soon gotten around about the ceremony later that morning and Liana sensed a certain zest and vitality within the people.

"Glad you're okay, your Highness!" chirped a jolly baker, loading crates of bread onto a cart.

"Me too, yer Majesty!" piped a passing fisherman, carrying a barrel full of freshly caught fish. "Looks like ya'll ready for the temple's grand opening already, miss," he continued, commenting on Liana's blue sleeveless dress, embroidered in fine gold threads of her favourite creature, dragonflies, and matching gold flat shoes. Her distinctive vivid blue hair lay unmoving under an intricate and delicate golden hair piece that wrapped around the back of her head from ear to ear, embellished with a simple leaf design at each end which kept any stray wispy hairs from touching the soft skin of her face.

"Thank you both for your well wishes," Liana responded politely, keeping her response short to avoid being roped into any length of conversation about the ceremony. She was too busy reflecting on the revelations of her conversation the previous night. The words were still churning around in her head, along with the impatience of needing to speak to the Priestess about the whereabouts of this old temple and her ultimate goal of finding her friends.

As Liana approached the square, she could hear the stone trumpets begin to blare with the sound of the Queen's voice. "Citizens of Swyre, following the safe return of my daughter, Princess Liana..."

'Daughter' Liana repeated to herself. 'Not your real daughter that you led me to believe for the whole 13 years of my life. A fake daughter. A fake heir. A life you'd made me fit into even though it's always felt alien to me. A forced, fake life,' thought Liana.

"At 11am this morning, in a little under 6 hours' time..." continued the Queen's muffled voice "We will be opening the wonderfully symbolic Tulip Temple. All are welcome in the square to watch Priestess Yi unlock its doors and declare your new religion and place of respite open for practice. Your crown and your military look forward to officially welcoming the third triangle of security to its citizens, your returning religion - the Aurora Visendus." The stone trumpets that surrounded the city square retracted back into the ground as the market stall owners clapped the broadcast and the announcement soon became the topic of conversation with every passing customer.

"Princess!" shouted the loud voice of the ex-sailor, Benji the Butcher. Liana waved in the direction of the butcher's shop on the other side of the square before leisurely wandering over. "I'm so glad yer alright, Princess. You had me worried sick ya did. I remember when..." as soon as Benji started with "I remember when..." Liana knew a tale of his sea-bearing days was coming. "I remember when I was captured at sea by the fearsome Captain Stone 'n' his motley crew. O' that were a 'orrific ordeal. Me captain at the time set me up proper! As soon as he saw the flag bearin' Cap'n Stone's mark on the horizon, he made me put on his clothes so when they inevitably boarded us, they all thought I were the Cap'n! They took me 'n' held me hostage for three whole weeks. Barely givin' me enough food 'n' water to make it through each day and every so often givin' me a lashing," Benji flexed his arm muscles before continuing. "Course, that was when I decided I had to start lookin' after meslf. I wasn't always this strong ya know. Infact, ya could say I was as porky as this 'ere swine," he said, pointing over his shoulder to a rather portly sow tied up to the wall of his shop. "Most o' the crew joined Captain Stone's ranks. It were either that or walk the plank. They'd never trust another ships Cap'n to join their ranks and so I was tied up below deck. Probably thought I could be sold fer a good amount of coin I reckon."

"Wow! How did you escape? What happened to the real captain?" Liana was enjoying the distraction of a good Benji story.

"Ah, well this is the irony!" said Benji, perking up as he got to the good bit of the story. "It had been two whole days since I'd been brought any food or drink. I started to fear for the worst. Thinkin' that they'd just gone and left me and that I were no use to 'em anymore. I started shoutin' out with whatever strength I could muster... but no one replied. Thinkin' they were simply ignorin' me, I managed to swivel around the other side of the pole I was tied to where I could see up between the gaps of the wood. Now normally you'd see shadows of the crew moving about all over the place, but it were still. The few rays of sun that found its way down to me through the cracks remained unbroken. It's like they'd all vanished.

Then, the ship hit the shoreline with an almighty crash! It snapped the post I were tied to in half allowin' me to escape.

When I made my up to the ship's deck, everyone were dead! Just lyin' there with goblets in their hands. A few days beforehand I'd 'eard 'em all havin' a right ole jolly. I reckon they must've made a bad batch of spirits. Course, they wouldn't let me have even a hint o' grog for me let alone anythin' stronger. They basically wiped themselves out! If ye don't get yer brewing right, it can be fatal."

"Wouldn't have happened if you were in the kitchen!" joked Liana.

"Too right it wouldn't 'ave! Served me ole Cap'n right 'n' all! Though I did feel sorry fer me old crewmates. They didn't deserve that," Benji's jovial expressions turned to one of reflection as he reminisced about his lost sea friends. Liana's eyes also glazed over as she turned away and bowed her head. The momentary distraction was over, and she also drifted back into the thoughts of her lost friends.

"'Ere Princess, what's the matter?" asked Benji.

"Saffina and Joel are missing. They went looking for me last night and they've not come home. There's groups of thugs out in the forest and they could be in danger," not wanting to show him any sign of weakness, Liana wiped a tear from her left cheek before turning back to face Benji.

"Well, that's a couple of brave friends ye got right there. Do ya know what though, I know they're still alive."

"You don't know that," Liana stated, resigned that her friends could by now have fallen to the fate of any number of possibilities.

"Well, just like my tale I just told, if ye worth something, ye don't just get rid of it. If these people 'ave got 'em, then bein' your best friend has probably saved their life. They'll be worth somethin' to someone. And who knows, maybe they'll have the luck I did, eh?"

Even if she didn't necessarily believe it, Benji always knew how to make Liana feel better. Feeling slightly more reassured, Liana gave Benji a big hug and, seeing Clerk Vivek at the top of the staircase that led to the temple's entrance, made her way up one of the neighbouring curved ramps that also adorned the entrance of the Tulip Temple.

As Liana approached the top of the slope, she could hear Clerk Vivek's frustrated voice.

"How hard is it? You turn this knob, unlatch those hooks, grab that lever and pull!" waving his arms and stick in the air as he remonstrated with two guards. "If it wasn't for the fact I'm 80 years old I'd have this thing up on my own," he continued to tut and sigh until Liana interrupted.

"Everything alright?"

"Ah, Liana! Why don't you see if you can show these two halfwits up? Try pulling this podium up out of its nook."

"So, turn this knob here..." Liana said aloud, recalling Vivek's instructions. She knelt and twisted a handle just inside the podium's chamber. "Then, unhook these latches..." she continued, flicking two brass hooks out of their respective loops. "Grab this lever and pull!" Liana struggled with the weight of the podium, but sure enough, it began to rise out of the ground as she pulled the lever up and out, although there was a scratching sound as she did so, marking the podium with a scrape as she pulled.

"That's not meant to happen, I'll have to take a look at that... lock it into place here," said Vivek, using his foot to kick in a sliding stone block on each side which acted as a foundation and prevented the podium from falling straight back down the hole. "Wonderful, Liana!" said Vivek, again praising her efforts before turning to the two guards next to him. "See, not that hard is it. Bested by a 13-year-old girl. Not everything is about brute strength you dimwits. Now get out of here and do something useful."

The guards looked at each other sheepishly before trudging off the stage and down the stone staircase in front of them.

"You showed them! You do have potential..." Vivek

smirked, turning back to Liana. "Can't say I'm surprised to see you here this early. Must admit though, it was a bit of a struggle for me getting up after so little sleep," he rubbed his baggy, shadowy eyes. "These bones aren't what they used to be. Anyway, enough grumbling from me, do you know the order of the day?"

"No, Vivek, I have no idea."

"Well, it's very simple for you today dear. Before Priestess Yi rambles on with her speech, you are being named official heir to the throne. You know, the whole thing that was meant to happen yesterday, but didn't."

"Oh," Liana responded, feeling even less like an heir than she did the previous day. "Do I have to say anything?"

"No, no dear. We're keeping it simple. Once the usual musical ensembles and parades finish, Queen Adriya will begin proceedings by welcoming everyone, before picking up a smaller replica of her crown and asking you to join her at the podium. She'll place the crown on your head and say a few words. All you need to do is acknowledge the cheering crowd with a couple of waves, then you can retreat back to your chair. When that's all done, Priestess Yi will take over."

"Sounds simple enough."

"Yes... just make sure we don't have another Triunity Hall incident..."

"That wasn't my fault! I didn't know Nalan would kidnap me."

"I wasn't really referring to the kidnapping. I'm referring to your... episode. You know, spontaneously getting out of your chair, ignoring everyone who's trying to grab your attention and staring open jawed at who knows what whilst a room full of citizens watch on thinking you've gone insane."

"I wasn't staring into nothing! The room went black and

white and this glow..." she was unable to finish her sentence before Priestess Yi interrupted the conversation. Vivek looked slightly annoyed at Priestess Yi having cut Liana off.

"Princess Liana! How wonderful to see you!" Priestess Yi approached with open arms but her fake sounding tone and extroverted greeting made the Princess feel slightly uneasy. "I'm so glad you're safe and well. I hope you're as excited as me for today!" the Priestess grinned wide eyed from ear to ear, adding to Liana's uneasiness.

"I am," replied Liana, forcing a smile.

"Anyway, I must get on before the ceremony. Places to go, people to see. Meet you back here soon!" Liana and Vivek watched as the Priestess marched off and disappeared around the side of the temple.

"I think I'm going to tend to Sherwin until the ceremony begins," Liana said to Vivek.

"Just don't be late back, and don't ruin your outfit! Your mother had that made especially for you to wear today."

"I won't," said Liana, before making her way towards the Royal stables where her trusted golden steed, Sherwin, was being readied for Liana's ceremonial entrance.

The tuneful sounds of drums and trumpets blessed Swyre's air as the marching band headed the entrance parade down the main road from Castle Langton to the City Square. Behind the band, rows of children held aloft banners of all colours, displaying either the four triangles that made up the Langton crest or the curved AV that made up the 'eye' logo of the Aurora Visendus. Following the flag bearers, two lines of Knights and Generals bordered the Queen. A team of six white horses pulled her golden, open topped carriage. Originally, for added protection, a Quartaltium roof was installed but this proved both to be too heavy for six horses to pull and not translucent enough for the Queen who wanted to ensure that whenever an occasion was needed for the carriage, that everyone could see her, and she could see everyone. Sir Tarak objected, of course, as a close-topped carriage was much safer and the durability of Quartaltium added strong protection against all manner of weapons, but Queen Adriya insisted on her visible presence whenever possible. Years of planning and dress rehearsals ensured the short notice of the ceremony was inconsequential as dried flowers, confetti and streams of flaming arrows flickered and furnished the clear sky above.

Liana trailed the Queen's carriage, riding atop a freshly groomed Sherwin. Her barrel draped in a blue throw made to match the exact same shade of blue as Liana's hair. Golden tassels hung off the edges. On Sherwin's offside the throw displayed the Langton crest, and on his near side, the Visendi's 'eye' logo. Every effort had been made to make a very public statement that the Aurora Visendus was now, well and truly, a fully-fledged member of the Queen's Table.

The golden carriage came to a halt at the foot of the steps that led up to the podium in front of the Tulip Temple. Liana pulled up alongside. One of the Queen's guards held out a supportive hand as she made her way off the vehicle, down three steps, being careful not to trip over her long trailing dress that was made to match Liana's, but instead of dragonflies her dress was detailed with her favourite creature, butterflies.

Liana elegantly dismounted from her trusted steed herself. The trail of her dress gliding over Sherwin's back as she did.

The Queen gracefully walked up the middle of the

enveloping left hand slope of the temple entrance. Liana mirrored her mother on the opposite incline as the crowd below folded in and filled the path that had been cleared for the pair. The marching band had positioned themselves in formation on the steps, turning to face the excited onlookers, except now their pitch perfect and well-practiced songs were now accompanied by a raucous of homemade and amateur notes as the citizen's strummed guitars, crashed symbols and sang songs of celebration.

Once the Queen and Liana had simultaneously made their way to centre stage, the noisy crowd soon quickly fizzled out to an expectant silence as the Queen stepped up to the podium, where a triangular, golden crown sat, emblazoned with jewels of all six colours of the Aurora, three on each of the two front-facing sides: a red coral stone, an orange carnelian, an amber jewel, green agate, turquoise and sapphire gems. Liana looked down into the crowd and saw the angry face of Trisha Greymore staring at them. She swallowed and forced back the tears as she again thought about the fate of her friends.

"Citizens of Swyre," started the Queen with the familiar three opening words that preceded any grand speech she made. "I stand here before you all again, just one day after my desperate plea for help. I want to thank you all for your efforts and shared desire in trying to find my daughter. Words cannot express how grateful I am that my uncle, Sir Tarak Langton, found her safe and unharmed, and there is no better time for a celebration than now!" Queen Adriya paused as the crowd cheered her words. She turned to her uncle with a beaming smile. He raised his sword and bowed his head to recognise the Queen's thanks. "It is with the greatest of pleasures that I, Queen Adriya, officially announce that my daughter, Liana, has now come of age," The Queen raised her left arm in Liana's direction. Liana stood like a statue at the 100,000 pairs of eyes all focussed on her. *'I'm glad I don't have to say anything,'* she thought, knowing that her statue-like stance was out of nerves and stage-fright rather than polite and proper etiquette. "As Queen of the Island of Coryàtès, I officially announce Liana as my heir. When I pass on, there shall be no other legitimate claim to the throne," Adriya stepped out from behind the podium and picked up the crown with a claw-like grip. Liana remained rooted to the spot, staring into the faces below as the triangular crown was lowered and rested onto her head, somewhat uncomfortably, just above her hairpiece. Adriya let go and took a step back as the audience erupted into an ear-splitting roar. *'They like me. They're actually cheering for me.'* For a moment Liana forgot about her worries and concerns for her friends and revelled in the feeling of mass acceptance. She curtseyed for the crowd before turning to her mother with a beaming smile.

Her mother shared an equally blossoming smile as she gently clapped along and gestured to her daughter for her to take a chair to the side of the stage.

"Your magnificent response is truly heart-warming to Princess Liana and I," said the Queen who had made her way back to the podium. "She will make a fine leader and I know you will all support her, as you have all supported me for these past 21 years.

It is now time to handover over to Priestess Yi Lang, who has been key to the reintroduction of the Aurora Visendus in our education system and who has provided counselling and guidance to many of you already despite her limited resources. The Queen's Table thanks the Priestess for her patience and hope that she is as delighted as we are with the magnificent architecture you see before you today, which will enable her to be even more effective in delivering to you the teachings of the Visdeni and help each of you grow and find inner peace," the Queen stepped off the podium and sat down beside Liana.

An eerie lull swept over the city square, waiting for the Priestess to appear. Several minutes passed before a drone of impatient murmuring rumbled through the crowd. Adriya and Liana shared a telepathic *'What's going on?'* glance at each other. Suddenly the doors to the Tulip Temple slid open and a troop of 10 children (all younger than Liana) marched in formation of two straight lines. The lines were headed up by Yasmin and Eugene. All the children wore the same garments - black robes lined with gold decorative tramlines across the shoulders and down the button line. Yasmin and Eugene led their respective lines to flank either side of the podium as each child stood in descending height order, facing the crowd with their hands clasped together in front of their bodies, like a military parade. The Priestess then emerged from the temple, dressed in a silk dress, matching the black and gold design of her students.

She stepped up to the podium and took a moment to gather herself before addressing the thousands of people below. "My fellow citizens!" she started, welcoming the crowd before her with outstretched arms. "It's been 13 long years since we were so kindly welcomed back into your lives by our wonderful Queen."

To the audience, Priestess Yi's tone seemed genuine, but not to Liana and her mother who sensed a somewhat sarcastic undertone. Nevertheless, Queen Adriya accepted the compliment with an acknowledging nod.

"Our wonderful new Tulip Temple will enable me to step

up our teachings and help guide you on your personal jour-
neys. So far you have read and practiced the power of meditation to help you react more purposefully to events in your life
and progress through adversity with a strong and disciplined
mind.

You have learned about our origin that stretches back
10,000 years when Aurora - the God of Dawn - fought off
Tenebris - the God of Darkness - to end a 500-year ice age and
bring an abundance of flora and fauna back to this world. She
made a promise to always protect us as long as we
worshipped her and her ways. This is when she taught the few
remaining survivors about the Balance of Life principles, Security, Creativity, Strength, Love, Communication and Awareness. Aurora blessed the survivors with her presence to pass
on and teach these principles. These survivors became known
as the Aurora Visendus - those who saw the God of Dawn.
After many months of teaching, Aurora was ready to leave the
planet in their hands.

But until now, we have omitted in our teachings how
Aurora knows that we are still looking after the world that she
fought so hard to save. How she knows that we are still practising and worshipping the teachings she bestowed upon the
first group of Aurora Visendi. Well, my fellow citizens, let me
tell you this now!

Each Balance of Life principle has a corresponding colour.
Red for Security, orange for Creativity, yellow for Strength,
green for Love, blue for Communication and indigo for
Awareness." Each member of the crowd simultaneously
looked up at the colours of the Tulip Temple, now understanding it's design.

"We have 7 levels within the Temple. The ground floor
boasts an exhibition style arena where events, such as mass

services or demonstrations can be held, along with many smaller meditation spaces, such as our tranquil gardens. Each level above this is restricted until you earn your Aura."

Another low-pitched murmuring developed amongst the confused onlookers. Liana and her mother shared another *'What's going on?'* glance at each other.

"As part of Aurora's Balance of Life principles, a member of the Aurora Visdenus will be rewarded with an Aura once they have proved themself in each discipline. Each Aura grants a different power. For example, once you have proved yourself in the first principle - Security - you will be able to produce a red Aura that creates a small protective screen to help you parry a physical attack. To earn your Aura, you must not only practice the Security principle, but participate in trials to prove yourself to a Priestess or Priest, and ultimately, Aurora herself. Yasmin, Eugene, you may now show your fellow citizens."

Yasmin and Eugene reached inside their robes and pulled out a small domed object before holding them aloft high above their heads. Members of the crowd closest to the stage gasped as the sun's rays glistened off the domes. Those further back impatiently asked the rows in front of them what the object was. Liana squinted at the object being held by Eugene, who was standing directly in front of her. A spinning, wispy, whirlpooling red mist floated around inside the centre of the dome. Liana thought about the red sphere that Vivek had given her the night before and mentally compared its contents to Eugene's button. The red mist danced and glowed in the exact same way.

Priestess Yi waited a minute or two for the whispers to roll out among the rows of people before continuing. "These two bright and young prospects, Yasmin and Eugene, have already proven themselves worthy of the first Balance of Life principle. Aurora has blessed them with their Red Aura's as proved by capturing some of its essence in their button representing Security."

"HOW?!" a deep male voice shouted loudly from somewhere in the crowd.

"Find that out for yourself by joining us!" smiled the Priestess before continuing with her practiced speech. "The Security principle is about the basics of survival. For example, learning how to provide enough food and money for yourself and your family, as we have been teaching you in our schools and literature. But just think, what would be the point in being self-sufficient to then be unprepared in the event of an unsavoury attempt on your life from an evil, jealous or desperate third party? Aurora gave each level a special ability. The Red Aura's special ability helps one to defend themself. Prepare yourself for a demonstration!"

The crowd buzzed and cheered. There seemed to be an almost brainwashed anticipation amongst the people to earn their Aura's. Liana leaned over and whispered to her mother under the noise. "Did you know anything about this? How have Yasmin and Eugene already earned these... Aura's?"

"Hmm, it's not quite how we agreed to introduce the news of the Aura's. And as for Yasmin and Eugene, I had no idea." replied an annoyed Queen Adriya, showing her teeth as she faked a smile and clapped in unison with the excited crowd.

"Children of the Visendi, start distributing the leaflets," The Priestess commanded the ten children at the front of the stage. "Yasmin, Eugene, join me in demonstrating your newfound skill to your fellow citizens. Remember everyone, 'To see the beauty of the dawn, you must first see the beauty of yourself'," Priestess Yi ended with a wide, dimpled grin on her face as she signed off to the adulation of the crowd with the religion's tagline before joining Yasmin and Eugene at the front of the stage.

The five children on either side of Yasmin and Eugene descended the slopes and handed out piles and piles of leaflets advertising the Tulip Temple. The same leaflet that Saffina had picked up when her brother had bumped into her.

On the stage, Priestess Yi knelt down. The slit down the side of her black silk dress parted, allowing her to withdraw a set of Twin Sai daggers from one of her gladiator style sandals. She raised herself back up, before launching an attack on Yasmin.

Yasmin swiftly side-stepped to avoid the lunge of the Priestess. She quickly reached behind her robes and revealed a set of punching daggers. Eugene also took this moment to arm himself with a set of knuckle-dusters that covered the whole dorsal side of his hand like a shield. The Priestess faced Eugene and completed three 360-degree spins in his direction flailing her Sai daggers. Eugene parried each and every spin with the shield of his knuckle dusters before ducking under another attempted swipe from the Priestess. The crowd jumped with joy at this unexpected exhibition. Liana and Queen Adriya watched on nervously.

Clearly practiced in martial arts, the Priestess showed off her athleticism and leapt high into the air above Yasmin, ready to strike down on her pupil. Yasmin took a step back and readied her punching daggers to shield her face. Just as the Priestess descended and was about to make contact, it was clear to see that Yasmin was not quick enough. Liana and the Queen sprang from their chairs in anticipation of a disastrous scene but halted in their tracks.

The Priestess's attack was rebuffed by a thin, bright-red

glow that surrounded Yasmin's figure before slowly fading. The Priestess somersaulted backwards, landing in a crouch before she locked eyes with Yasmin in a mutual affirmation of a premeditated plan coming together.

Everyone watching fell silent at the sight of this otherworldly magic. There before them, was evidence of the Priestess's words. Yasmin had produced a Red Aura.

The sight made both Liana and the Queen feel uneasy at the potential of Yasmin already possessing such power. Now that her personal adversary had already ascended to the first level of the Aurora Visendi, Liana had even more reason to find the fabled Old Temple and seek out its Priest. Not just for the sake of finding her friends, but also for the sake of her own protection.

12
THE ZAGANITE

Red marks started to form around Saffina's left ankle as the metal cuff dug into her skin. Sweat dripped from every portion of her body as she raised the pickaxe again and again, chipping away at the line that had been marked in white painted on the mountainside for her to follow. It had only been a few days since she and Joel had been captured by the White Robed thugs, but Saffina felt like she'd been there all week. She paused to wipe some more sweat from her brow.

"How are you holding up?" Joel asked, whose metal cuff was linked to Saffina's via a thick metal chain.

"We've not even been at it for a whole week, and I feel like I'm gonna die," She responded as she wiped off even more sweat, this time from her neck. "Why would Zagan take us?" she asked. "And why does he have groups of thugs roaming the forest?"

"Beats me," Joel replied. "Someone will work out we're

missing soon enough, and we'll get rescued. I'm sure it's just a big misunderstanding."

"A misunderstanding? They know exactly who we are, Joel. They know we're Liana's best friends. This is no misunderstanding," she scowled the landscape, looking at the hundreds of workers and thinking that at some point, they must all have committed a serious enough crime at some point to warrant them being sent here. Or perhaps, they'd been captured just like her and Joel, although that seemed unlikely as people rarely went missing from Swyre.

"What I don't get is why we're chipping away at this trench in the mountainside. This is just bog-standard rock. No sandstone, no Cobalt, no Quartz. Just normal, grey rocks," Joel continued to swing his axe before a large cluster of rubble separated from the area where he was aiming and landed directly onto the top of his right foot, causing him to shriek in pain and hop up and down on his good foot. He instinctively tried to cradle his injured right foot in his hands and in doing so, forgot that his right foot was chained to Saffina's left. He lifted his leg up towards his waiting hands and as he did, pulled Saffina's left leg from underneath her and a now unbalanced Saffina fell to the floor. This in turn caused a rather comical domino reaction as everyone else chained to Saffina also tumbled. A total of 10 other miners were now lying on their backsides staring at the hot afternoon sun.

"Jeez, Joel!" shouted Saffina, rubbing her lower back. Cries of 'idiot', 'newbie' and other much harsher profanities came from the other downed miners.

"Oops..." replied Joel, who had at least managed to grab hold of his foot to examine the damage. He put his foot down and tried to put some weight on it but winced in pain as he did. "Saff, I think it's broken," he unstrapped his brown leather shoe and slid it off as carefully as he could.

"Argh Joel, it's all shades of black and blue," Saffina gagged at the sight of his injured foot. "Ugh, I can't look at it."

"Thanks for the sympathy. I need to sit down," and he perched himself on a small boulder behind him, writhing in pain. The initial adrenaline from the injury began to subside as he began to really feel the impact.

"What's going on over here?" shouted a stern, female voice from above. "Ah, newbies. Guess you don't yet know what happens when you stop swinging your axes," Saffina and Joel looked up. A female in White Robes beared down on them from above the trench. Her figure, a giant shadow against the large sun behind her. Even from the silhouette, it was easy to see that there was no ounce of fat on her muscle-clad body. Saffina didn't know whether to feel threatened or jealous. No matter how much horse riding, running, or climbing she did, Saffina never seemed to be able to shake the curvatures of her body. Then she thought about Liana and how she was always commenting on how everyone in school looked at her and it made her feel uncomfortable and self-conscious. Saffina always thought this was less to do with her royalty and more to do with her glowing good looks and it often made Saffina feel somewhat envious, although she'd never tell Liana this.

"Do I have to use this?" the woman held out a whip that dangled with intent.

"M, My foot. I, I think it's broken…" stuttered Joel. Saffina wasn't sure if his stuttering was out of fear or desire. Her and Liana were pretty much the only girls Joel could speak to without getting tongue tied.

The woman jumped down in the trench and landed with a surprising grace and ease. So graceful, the hood of her white robe remained in place. She stood with the sun facing her and Saffina could make out the shadowy figure in more detail. Under the hood, the woman wore a matching white mask that covered her nose and mouth, so only her eyes were visible. Behind the stern voice and tough body, Saffina sensed some familiarity but couldn't pinpoint why. There seemed to be a softness to her skin, a thoughtfulness to her eyes and a story behind her badly hacked cropped dark hair.

"I'll have to take you to the physician," the woman said, with directness and lack of sympathy. "I will need help to get you down the mountainside. You – "she said, pointing at Saffina. "Help me with him. There is only one other Zaganite up here and he is needed to watch over the other miners," Saffina nodded, just glad that she could stop working. "If you try anything to escape, I will strangle you with both my whip. Understand?" Saffina and Joel nodded silently in unison confirming that they would do as they were told.

The 'Zaganite' woman unclasped the cuffs before she helped Joel up off his perch. She stretched out his arm, bent herself over and flipped him onto her back into a fireman's carry before she promptly chucked his body over the rim of the trench onto the surface above and followed him by jumping and grabbing the ledge before effortlessly rising next to him as if she were exiting a river onto its bank. The Zaganite peered back over the ledge to offer her hand to Saffina, who accepted the gesture. Saffina didn't feel like she did much of the work in climbing out of the trench, due to the strength of the arm that was lifting her.

Once out, the two females took an arm each to support Joel, albeit slightly lopsided due to the disparaging heights. Naturally, the Zaganite woman took Joel's right-hand side, the side where he couldn't put any weight on.

Making the descent wasn't as tricky as Saffina thought it would be due to the crudely cut steps that had been carved into the mountainside, although there was one hairy moment when they had to cross a rickety wooden bridge over a glacier of cobalt that was only wide enough for one person at a time. They advanced by awkwardly sidestepping the length of the bridge. It was only after the trio had successfully made it across that the Zaganite decided to mention that the last time more than two people tried to cross, one of the supporting ropes had snapped and both miners fell to their deaths. Saffina let out a rebellious 'and you didn't tell us this before?!' remark before being quickly silenced by the threat of the Zaganite's free hand resting on the handle of her whip. She soon recoiled and apologised before the woman signalled for them to continue.

The three turned a left corner before the final part of their descent to ground level. As they did, Saffina spotted a large clearing in the forest directly ahead of them. In the clearing were hundreds of people wielding weapons, practice fighting each other. To her right, pockets of people sat in groups on the wide beach that stretched the distance of the Eastern side of Coryàtes. Still with her arm around supporting Joel, Saffina lightly pinched Joel on the neck to grab his attention as he was too distracted looking at the floor and where he was going. Despite a frowning 'ouch', Joel's reaction didn't catch the attention of the Zaganite woman who assumed he was complaining about his foot. Saffina nudged her head in the directions of the forest and beach for Joel to see the scene for himself.

It wasn't long before they had stepped off the last of the steps. This was the first time Joel and Saffina had seen the gaping entrance to the Mount Indigo mines as they had been taken straight to the trenches since they were captured. So much was happening it took them a few moments to take everything in.

At the huge cave entrance, wooden wheeled carts were being pulled out by miners before their loads were transferred to larger horse-drawn carts. The flow of carts coming in and out of the cave was non-stop. They churned constantly like a cog in a timepiece. Some carts were filled with magnificent deep blue Cobalt. Some were filled with glistening Quartz. The sandstone mines were a little further down the coast, past the clearing in the forest, where the Eastern beach began to transform into golden grass topped cliffs.

Joel coughed as he breathed in some of the dust being kicked out by the several refineries that lined each side of the road that led up to the cave entrance. At each refinery, one cart of Quartz, and one cart of Cobalt each tipped their loads down separate flumes. Workers were steadily shovelling fine sand into a third flume. A loud 'thump' would then repeat itself every second for about 15 minutes whilst plumes of steam emanated from a cylindrical chimney. Another worker controlled the flow of a water pipe that led into the building. The empty horse carts would then make their way to the opposite side of the building to collect their refined goods – Coryàtès' famous blue glass - Quartaltium.

On the northern outskirts of the mining district a relatively small harbour hosted half a dozen ships. The carts full of Quartaltium trotted straight onto the long, flat, shallow, wooden transporters via several ramps that were lowered from the side of the ship. The ships were owned and manned by the Swyre Navy. It was a starting position for any new cadet into the navy. There was no glorifying these ships' aesthetics. They had a job, and they did it – carry as much

material as possible to Swyre and let the numerous stone
smiths in the city purchase however many carts of Quartaltium as they needed to fulfil their purchase orders.

The escorting Zaganite signalled to an empty horse and
cart. She helped Saffina get Joel get in the back before telling
the driver where they needed to go before hopping into the
cart herself.

They soon moved out of the main mining district and into
the 'Housing' area, not that they resembled any sort of house
Joel and Saffina had ever seen. Dug out of the ground were
large square living quarters, all roughly about 30ft x 30ft and
housing roughly 20 miners. Simple wooden canopies bordered
the edges of these sunken dwellings. The canopies themselves
were only large enough to cover each of the miner's wooden
beds. Some beds only had a single blanket on to cover themselves with. In the middle of each sunken dwelling was a fire
pit and a deep hole. The deep hole, Saffina assumed, was for
excretions since there appeared to be no traditional toilet or
sewerage system. She debated with her initial reaction on how
Queen Adriya could allow this to happen in comparison to the
excellent living conditions of Swyre, before remembering these
people were making up for their crimes and this way of living
should act as a deterrent to committing more crimes if, and
when, they should return to the city.

Once they had passed the last of the square, sunken resi-
dences, the driver turned left into the forest and stopped, no
more than 20ft into the woodland.

The woman vaulted the side of the cart. "Over there," she
pointed towards a large, single storey wooden building,
surrounded by a man-made moat. The lowered drawbridge
was lined with several lit torches on either side. Between each
torch, bunting of animal bones (mostly skulls) hung

ominously. "This is where the physician will be, but we must first ask Master Thornfalcon if you are worth being attended to."

As the woman went to speak to the driver, Joel turned to Saffina. "I have a really bad feeling about this, Saff," he whispered.

"Look at the clearing over there," Saffina said, pointing to the pairs left. "It looks like Zagan's preparing a secret army."

Through the branches of the forest trees, hundreds of men and women in the same plain, dusty white robes busily trained. Some were duelling with each other whilst others practised their archery skills on straw dummies. Huts lined the edge of the clearing with blacksmiths preparing weapons and armour whilst carpenters worked on huge wooden machinery.

"He's got to be planning an attack on Swyre," said Joel.

"Looks that way. But even so, Swyre's army must be at least three time the size. Zagan wouldn't stand a chance in a head-to-head. There must be more to it," said Saffina, before silencing her words as the Zaganite returned to take her position once again under Joel's right arm.

"The driver will wait here until I say otherwise. Let's go," ordered the woman, and the trio made their way across the skull-clad, torch-lit bridge. Two other Zaganite's holding doubled-ended spears stood at the entrance's open archway.

"Guards of the almighty Master Thornfalcon," started the woman, bowing her head. "This boy has broken his foot in the trenches. I seek his permission to use his physician."

One of the white robed Zaganite's left his post without saying a word and marched inside. It wasn't long before he returned and gestured with his spear to the woman that the trio may proceed.

As they entered, another archway greeted them. This archway was completely covered in vines and leaves that acted as a curtain and prevented them from seeing in. Saffina and the female Zaganite parted the leafy curtain. Sat before them on a large, quartz, throne-like seat was Zagan, flanked by four guards also holding double-ended spears. Zagan let out a loud, evil laugh as he saw who was being brought in.

"I knew you were pathetic, but I thought you'd at least give me a full week of work," he continued to chuckle through his hoarse sounding voice, making fun of Joel's situation to the guards surrounding him. His wide mouthed Cheshire grin displaying his sharpened teeth.

"Do we have your permission to use your physician, Master Thornfalcon?" asked the female Zaganite, kneeling and bowing her head to her leader, leaving Saffina struggling to support Joel.

"Yes, yes," Zagan waved his arms casually. "No good to me injured, are they? Take them to my physician then lock them up with our other prisoner. Clearly they're not much use to our preparations so I'm sure they'll come in useful in other ways."

"Yes, Master," replied the female Zaganite.

"No wonder Yasmin's how she is!" Saffina blurted out. She was as surprised as Joel at hearing her confront the Master of the Mines.

"And just how is my daughter?" replied Zagan, immediately turning his grin into a fierce frown.

"An untrustworthy bully!" Saffina continued. "We've seen you preparing an army. You don't stand a chance if you think you're going to go to Swyre and take over our city!"

"Stop it!" warned the female Zaganite under her breath to Saffina as Zagan rose sharply out of his throne.

"Coming from a girl responsible for humiliating my daughter!" a frighteningly loud Zagan shouted angrily and directly at Saffina as he pushed over a nearby stand holding a flaming torch. She averted her eyes and cowered backwards in fear. Zagan growled before ordering his guards to take them away and ordered the escort to remain behind.

Two of the guards assumed the supporting positions under Joel's arms that the female Zaganite and Saffina previously held. The other two guards tightly grabbed the biceps of Saffina to lead her away. She caught a glimpse of the kneeling woman looking forlornly at her as they exited.

As Joel and Saffina were led away through the leafy curtain, Saffina overheard an agitated Zagan.

"Where does your loyalty lie?"

"With you of course, my Master," replied the female Zaganite, obediently. Moments later she burst out of the chamber, knocking the wobbly Joel over in the process.

"Hey!" shouted Saffina, but the woman kept on marching without turning to acknowledge the cry.

Just as the guards helped Joel back to his feet, they were almost knocked over again by a low-flying black bird that swooped into Zagan's room. "Jeez, Joel, someone's really got it in for you today!" exclaimed Saffina before her ears pricked at the sound of Zagan's voice from inside the room.

"Yes, I know you need her," he was trying his best to whisper, but his deep hoarse voice didn't give him much stealth. Zagan growled before blurting out in a rage of temper.

'No one else is in that room, is he talking to that bird?' thought Saffina.

"Does he think I'm a fool?! Of course, I haven't forgotten the agreement. I get the Princess, the dagger, and the orb in one place outside the city. In return, he helps me become King.

It's not hard to understand," the bird came swooping back out of the chamber.

Saffina and Joel were soon ushered out of earshot as the guards aggressively led them away. They shared a frightened stare. Zagan was preparing an army to take on Swyre and he was using Liana to do it, with the help of a mysterious ally.

13

OVERRULED

The Queen turned to Sir Tarak and Admiral Remi. "Any news in the search for Saffina and Joel?" she asked. Both shook their heads. "What about the White Robes?"

"They seem to have vanished too," replied Sir Tarak. "No one has seen or heard of them since Liana returned home. I can only assume they'd gotten wind of her disappearance and went searching for her but since she's made it back home safely, have since retreated to wherever they came from. She would have made a valuable asset to anyone willing to ransom for her release."

"It does mean that they must be out there still though. Keep up with your enquiries. How are the mines? I notice Zagan decided not to bless us with his presence again today," The Queen rolled her eyes, before focussing them on the seat Zagan usually sat at beside Admiral Remi. "Therefore, I decided to ask Benji to sit in on this Queen's Table instead. As the Merchant Guild Leader, I thought he could provide a different insight into the feelings of the people."

"It's a pleasure t' be 'ere yer Majesty. Many thanks fer invitin' me," Benji's ear-to-ear smile lit up the room. Liana beamed seeing her friend hold such an important position. '*At least someone here who won't treat me like a child,*' she thought.

"Let's get straight to business. Admiral Remi, in the absence of Zagan, can you provide an update on productivity at the mines?" The Queen asked.

"As productive as they've ever been." Replied Admiral Remi. "My cargo ships report nothing unusual and are constantly sailing at full capacity."

"Good. At least that's something we don't have to worry about," The Queen then swiftly adjusted her tone of voice. "Now let's discuss Priestess Yi's decision to go behind my back and tell my daughter that she was found an orphan and adopted." The unexpected and abrupt statement created an immediately oppressive atmosphere that blanketed the room like fog on a winter's morning.

The Priestess was not taken aback by the Queen's direct-ness. She held her chin defiantly.

"I can't believe you told her!" the Queen raised her voice, sharply. "That was for me to discuss with my daughter at a time when I felt it was right. I have already told her she cannot go in search of this Old Priest you have told her about."

Liana shot an angry glance towards her mother. It had been a little over a week since her conversation with the Priestess. She was incredulous that her mother refused to let her go in search of the temple and her friends, even after the show-casing of the Visendi powers at the Tulip Temple's opening ceremony. '*What if I do have that potential within me?*' she thought.

The Priestess had been so inundated with citizens wanting to earn their Red Aura that it was impossible to get a moment in private with her as her time had been taken up with mass teachings as hundreds upon hundreds of people wanted to earn their Aura's and give their thanks to the God of Dawn.

When the mass teachings or demonstrations weren't being carried out, Priestess Yi held private sessions with Yasmin and Eugene who had quickly become her trusted aides. She entrusted them to pass on these new lessons to school-aged children. The schools were more than accepting of this self-defence tutoring.

"She needed to know, Your Majesty," The Priestess spoke up, convinced her decision to speak to Liana was the right one.

"Maybe if you hadn't lied to me my whole life, I wouldn't be so keen to go and find this Old Priest," interrupted Liana, striking a verbal blow at her mother.

"I don't see why that Old Priest would know any more than we do. I exchanged a few messages with him in the years before the Day of Darkness, as I monitored the religion when it was outlawed. Never struck me as a particularly noteworthy person," replied Clerk Vivek. "I can teach you everything you need to know."

"I don't need to learn anything!" Liana shouted across the triangular table. "*My* friends are missing. Unless everyone here has forgotten that fact?"

"You know we haven't, but just how is this Old Priest going to help you find them?" the Queen asked.

"As far as I'm aware he still practices the old ways and methods the exact same way as they did hundreds of years ago, handed down through his family's generations. If Liana is the 'Light to save the world' then perhaps he can help her achieve her goal. Do you think she can be that light if she loses her best friends? If anything were to happen to them... who knows how she would react."

'They talk about me like I'm not here. Like I'm some piece of a game.'

"I know, you've told me this before, Priestess," Queen Adriya sighed before quoting her ""Without friendship she risks succumbing to darkness". But as I've always maintained, upbringing and family have as much to do with being a good person. I will not be told how to mother my child."

"We all saw her episode in the Triunity Hall. We cannot doubt now that she is the one the parchment references. We must let her explore her... beginnings."

"The importance of strong bonding friendships is written in many teachings, even outside of the Visendi. Our experiences shape us and losing such close friends so young could be extremely detrimental to Liana," continued the Priestess, throwing her arms into the air.

"But just what do we need saving from? We're not even in any kind of darkness. Look at our thriving city. Trade from the mines is at an all-time high. Crime at an all-time low. And now that word has reached the mainland's of our religious awakening, we're getting record numbers of tourists and pilgrims visiting the island," Clerk Vivek took the opportunity to try and build on his relationship with the Queen by commending her on her leadership.

"Thank you, Vivek, but we all know the state of the world outside of our island."

"I don't," Liana said bluntly.

"In time you will."

"So, how do you know that darkness isn't coming?" retorted Liana. "I'm telling you; Nalan Weir did not try to kill that architect. That day in the Triunity Hall. As I've already told you all at our last meeting, all the colours around me drained into greys. Around Nalan was a white light, like one of the Visendi's Aura's, but it seemed like it was infected with blackness. Like flies around a torch. When he took me, he told me he felt like someone else was controlling him. Controlling his inhibitions. I think it was to do with the speckled darkness I saw around him."

"Sounds to me like there's more to this religious stuff than anyone here knows about," Piped Admiral Remi. "I say we let the girl go on her adventure. And if it can help save anyone, whether it ends up just being her friend's, if not the whole world, then it's worth it."

Liana and Remi had never really spoken but hearing words of support from such a self-confident woman as the Admiral, gave her an instant feeling of connection and admiration.

"I say this can only be decided by a vote," continued the Admiral. She didn't wait for anyone to agree. Without hesitation she raised her hand to begin the vote. "Aye," she said.

The Priestess also raised her hand. Liana naturally raised her hand.

The Queen, Clerk Vivek and Sir Tarak kept theirs lowered and confirmed their position with a 'Nay'. It was 3 against 3. All eyes fell upon Benji.

As it was his first Queen's Table meeting, Benji had been largely quiet all meeting. He took a moment to look around at each person sitting at the triangular table.

Queen Adriya's eyes composed.

Tarak's eyes intense.

Priestess Yi's eyes controlled.

Vivek's eyes relaxed.

Remi's eyes assured.

Liana's blue eyes were the last he set upon. Her eyes quivered. Not out of desperation. Not out of fear. Not out of sadness. Benji saw determination and meaning that he had not seen in anyone else's eyes before. He raised his hand and confirmed the motion with an "Aye".

"That's that then. Just after my daughter return's home, *you've* voted for her to leave and put herself in danger again." The emphasised 'you've' aimed in Benji's direction.

'I hope this isn't his first... and last... Queen's Table meeting... thank you Benji.'

"Well, if she's going to go, she shouldn't go alone. She should be escorted by some of my soldiers," said Tarak.

"They wouldn't be able to find the temple," stated the Priestess. "The temple that houses the Old Priest can only be found by those who can produce an Aura. It remains hidden to anyone else. Why do you think none of your carriage men have ever come across it?"

"But Liana can't produce an Aura," Argued Tarak.

"Hopefully that shouldn't matter if she's the Light."

"Hopefully?" questioned the Queen.

"Well, I've never tried taking anyone in who hasn't been an active follower of the religion," replied Priestess Yi.

"She will also be accompanied by two members of the Visendi."

"Oh, who?"

"Yasmin and Eugene."

Liana shot a furious glance at the Priestess. No way was she going anywhere with Yasmin.

"You've seen what they can do. They will provide adequate protection."

The Queen pursed her lips. "So, we're basing this whole expedition on a scripture we know little about? All whilst there are unidentified White Robe thugs roaming this island that also no one seems to know anything about." Agitated, she looked around the room for any enlightenment from her blank-faced council. "Great!" Queen Adriya flung her arms up in the air and fell back into her chair. Liana pinched her lips to hold back a laugh at the child-like remonstration from her mother, something she had never seen before. "Imagine the reaction if I made decisions based purely on guesswork," she said, continuing her tantrum.

"How many times have you been to this temple, Priestess?" asked Sir Tarak, breaking the awkward silence following the Queen's minor outburst. "You speak of the temple like it's a living creature."

"My family and I went to seek refuge from your patrols who had been given a tip off of our whereabouts, whilst we were outlawed," The Priestess shot a sharp glance at the Queen and her uncle. "It was only for a short time and that old man wouldn't share anything about the religion with us and did his best to avoid us the entire time we took shelter there," The Priestess frowned as she recalled the time there. "The Shrouded Temple of Roots is concealed by the forest itself. Aurora taught the first Visendi that although the flora of the land cannot talk to us in traditional ways, the dawning of the sun means as much to them as you or I and that they must be equally respected. Without the sun we would not have trees to filter our air or plants to harvest. Each day when the sun rises, it serves as a reminder that Aurora ensures our basic needs - the root of our survival. The forest will decide whether one is worthy of entering one of the founding temples of Aurora. The Shrouded Temple of Roots was a foundation centre for understanding the Red Aura. Once Aurora left the world in the hands of the first Visendi, they went their separate ways to spread the word to the few remaining tribes of the world. One of them came to Coryàtès and set up the Shrouded Temple of Roots."

"The three children can take one of my jackdaw's who will be able to help assist in finding the temple. Jackdaws are very intelligent and can recognise and locate human faces. Whilst we were outlawed, the religion regularly used them to communicate between the various underground factions. It's a skill we learn when we ascend to the Yellow Aura, so that we can send the birds to specific people or locations. They don't deviate until they achieve their instruction," said a very smug Priestess.

"I agree with your suggestions, Priestess Yi, thank you," said the Queen. "Sir Tarak, please take Liana and ensure she and her counterparts are prepared for the journey."

"Can't I just go with Eugene?" Liana begged. "Yasmin hates me. I'm sure Eugene and the Jackdaw will give me enough support."

"No." the Queen said firmly. "I'd be much more comfortable knowing both Yasmin and Eugene are going with you."

"Despite her short time with me, Yasmin has made a great impression and developed an important role with me at the Tulip Temple. I will personally vouch for her behaviour." Priestess Yi smiled and nodded towards the Queen, who reciprocated.

"But she..." Liana started, before her mother raised a hand and signalled for her to stop.

"Don't push your luck, Liana," The Queen immediately put an end to any further debate. "Now that topic has concluded we still have a few other matters to tend to," The Queen shuffled a couple of papers around in front of her as she regained her usual composure.

The Queen's Table meeting continued with its agenda.

Priestess Yi's application to hire some help (such as gardeners and seamstresses) was passed. Admiral Remi's request for two new cargo ships to be built was also passed. Clerk Vivek's request to conduct a review of the city's educational programme, in light of the religion's new teachings, did not pass as it was decided this should wait until Liana had concluded her journey and returned with more information on the practices of the old religion. Tarak requested to have temporary control of the Fleet Captain and his carriage men network to aid his search for Saffina and Joel, but this was also rejected, much to Liana's objection. Her mother, the Priestess and Vivek didn't want to send out the wrong message that the army could take over anything it liked whenever it felt like it. Liana was quickly realising that she had to find this old temple as soon as she could and hoped that the old priest may be able to help her.

Tarak's motion was the last on the agenda. Before the Queen's Table council concluded and made their departures, the Queen asked the room for any requests for topics to be discussed at the following month's meeting. Only Clerk Vivek and Priestess Yi had requests.

Vivek asked for a discussion and review on the city's finances to be held at the next meeting, following the Priestess's and Remi's motions being carried. Despite the island's healthy finances due to its Quartaltium trade, the topic was unanimously agreed.

Priestess Yi wanted to discuss a proposition she had for an annual Aurora Visendus tournament. A tournament for Visendi to display their skills. She argued tournaments like this used to be commonplace and the challenge enabled followers to 'level up' and helped focus them on developing their skills throughout the year, as well as providing a spectacle for citizens and something for them to look forward to, as well as the potential for it to be monetised.

The Queen asked both Vivek and the Priestess to detail their topics ahead of the next meeting, so all members had a chance to review and form opinions on their contents.

The meeting drew to a close and all seven members that were in attendance descended the Tower of Seeds.

"Thanks for your vote, Benji. I hope you stay on the Queen's Table."

"You've a lot of determination in those eyes o' yours. I couldn't say Nay," Benji placed a hand on Liana's shoulder.

"Great Uncle Tarak, please don't stop looking. I don't know what I'd do without Saffina and Joel."

"Don't worry, either you or I will find them, Princess," said Sir Tarak as he placed a reassuring hand on the Princesses back as they headed towards Sherwin's stable to prepare Liana for her adventure.

14

FRIEND OR FOE?

Priestess Yi's jackdaw glided down onto the branch of a small dead tree that sat upon a tiny island in the middle of one of the forest's lakes. A nesting goose watched the jackdaw closely as it sat on its eggs. Liana guided Sherwin to the edge of a muddy embankment that gently sloped into the water. Yasmin and Eugene pulled their horses up either side of Liana and Sherwin, their black and gold trimmed robes gracefully draping down either side of their steeds. The trio looked at their navigator as it sat upon its perch.

"What's it doing now?" asked Liana.

"Maybe it wants a rest," answered Eugene.

"No, I think it wants us to cross the lake," said Yasmin, before looking up at the darkening sky. "That lake looks too deep to cross with the horses. We'll have to wait until morning and go around. We should set up camp here and rest for the night," and immediately dismounted her horse without putting the decision up for debate. Liana and Eugene followed suit without any argument.

"I'm not sure what's worse. You two fighting, or you two not talking," Eugene said to Liana as he began to unload bags of camping gear from his horse.

"If we can get to the old temple without saying a word, I'd consider it a successful journey," replied Liana. "You don't seem very concerned about Saff."

"She's surprisingly strong," said Eugene. "Her and Joel make a good team. Besides, when was the last time anything really bad happened on the island?"

"Well for starters, I was kidnapped last week."

"I mean, that was kind of your own fault," Liana raised an irate eyebrow at Eugene, but he carried on regardless. "I'm talking about these White Robed rogues or bandits. They're probably just a small-time group that's stowed away on one of the cargo ships from the mainland and left already. Saffina and Joel are probably just lost trying to find their way home."

"They're not just a group of small time stow-aways," Liana turned to the lake in reflection as she tied Sherwin's reins around a tree. "I almost got taken by them. They looked trained and strong… and under orders."

"If they are as organised as you say they are, then they'd better be prepared for you!" joked Eugene and he punched Liana in the chest with one of his knuckle dusters. A dull clang sounded as it connected with the chainmail that she was wearing underneath her favoured black sleeveless top. The strike was enough to unbalance the unexpecting girl and she toppled over, down the muddy embankment and she slid in slow motion into the shallow shoreline water. Eugene let out an apologetic laugh and immediately offered his hand to help Liana to her feet. She expected a callous bout of howling to come from Yasmin, but instead the pair received a chastising.

"Considering it's *your* best friend, and *your* sister that we're looking for, I seem to be the only one taking this journey seriously whilst being the only one who's here for no reason," shouted Yasmin with flailing arms.

Liana frowned in Yasmin's direction but before she could reply, Eugene interjected. "Don't even think about it," he said as he hoicked her to her feet. "Let's not turn the day's sound of silence into a sound of madness."

"Seriously Eugene, look at me," Liana looked down at her clay-coloured trousers, which were now covered in brown mud.

"I'm sorry, I'm sorry." said Eugene, still chortling. "I'll make it up to you. How about I help you get your tent up so you can change, *and* I'll wash the mud out of your clothes in the lake for you."

"Fine. But you better do a good job," warned Liana "These are my favourite."

"If only you could produce a Red Aura," bragged Eugene as he turned to walk away from Liana before turning his head back in her direction and shrugged. "Then you could have blocked me," he continued to walk towards Yasmin who was unpacking her gear in the small lakeside clearing.

"Someone seems to have found their courage," remarked Yasmin as Eugene walked past her.

"You know what Yaz, I'm actually glad you persuaded me to break into the Tulip Temple with you. If Priestess Yi hadn't caught us that day, we'd be just a number to her and not even able to cast a Red Aura," Eugene said as a thin red glow surrounded him. "Since being up on that stage at the opening ceremony, not one person at school has made fun of me."

"Well, I hope you show the same courage when we're actually in trouble," Yasmin checked her surroundings to make sure Liana wasn't within earshot. "I can't afford not to get to our destination."

"What do you mean?" asked Eugene with a confused quizzical look upon his face.

"We can't let the Priestess down, that's all," she said whilst she unhooked her tent's entrance. "She's counting on us," she said before disappearing inside.

"So's the Queen and my sister and Joel. Lots of people are counting on us to deliver Liana to the old temple so that she can find out what makes her so special. We're already Yi's number one students. Why are you so concerned about what she thinks?" Eugene waited for Yasmin to respond from inside the tent but didn't receive an answer. "Yaz, what are you not telling me?"

Yasmin poked her head out. "Sorry Gene, I shouldn't have said anything."

Eugene let out a funny, snorting kind of grunt at being called Gene. "When have you ever apologised for anything? And since when have you called me Gene? What's going on?"

"I can't tell you. If I do, I might be putting you in danger. It's better you don't know," and with that, Yasmin retreated her head back into her tent and hooked up its doorway.

"Yaz? YAZ?" shouted Eugene.

"Go away, Gene," Yasmin's voice was muffled through the tent's animal-skin material. "Make sure Liana's okay."

Eugene made his way to the opposite side of the small, muddied clearing and started on putting up his own tent.

"Eugene, I'm going to go and find some firewood. Might as well go hunting for sticks whilst I'm still covered in mud," said Liana.

"Go for it. Oh, and you can call me Gene now," Liana gave him a confused look. Gene smiled, shrugged, and nodded his head in the direction of Yasmin's tent. Liana raised her eyebrows still confused but didn't feel like enquiring any further and went in search for some dry fire-worthy twigs.

As soon as she was out of sight of the campsite, she checked her trouser pocket to make sure she hadn't lost her red sphere in the water. After a quick fumble, she pulled it out and stared once again at its mystical contents. She spun it around between her thumb and forefinger. The swirling motions didn't seem to move in tandem with the ball's shell and remained stationary as she spun it. It wasn't long before it's red centre glowed at her touch.

"Watchya got there?" Liana jumped as Gene crept up behind her and dropped the red ball. Its red light dissipated as it fell to the leafy forest floor.

"Eugene! Where did it go?!" said Liana frantically scanning the area around her feet for the object.

"Calm down. I've got it right here," Gene bent down and picked it up. "What is it?"

"I don't know. I'm hoping the Old Priest can tell me. It only lights up when I touch it" Liana attempted to snatch it back, but Gene used his height to hold it out of her reach.

"Where did you get it?" Gene closed an eye and pulled the object closer for inspection.

"Argh, give it back," Liana jumped at Gene in another effort to grab the ball.

"Calm down, Princess," Gene threw the ball back after the brief inspection. "Looks a bit like my button."

"Come to think of it, just how did you earn your Aura so quickly?"

"Priestess Yi, Yaz and I sparred all night. The Priestess

showed us a load of cool moves. Real acrobatic stuff, better than what your Great Uncle's General's teach us in cadets in school. With each new move and sparring match, our buttons began to fill more and more with the Red Aura. It was addictive, watching ourselves progress."

"Seems a bit odd that it's that easy. I thought the Visendi teachings were supposed to be about self-harmony, helping others, finding balance?"

"It is!" Gene interrupted. "But the Red Aura is about survival. How can you survive if you don't know how to defend yourself? We learned about the theory of surviving in school. How to grow and make food, make a career that suits you, social interaction and so forth, but what good is that if someone comes along and robs you of it all? That's why you need to learn to fight."

"Is that what the Priestess taught you?"

"Yes, and she has a point, don't you think?" Eugene shrugged. "I've been bullied almost my whole life Liana, until Yasmin stepped in. But what if I could have fended for myself? How much more independent I'd have been."

"You make Yasmin sound like a genuine good person. She only became friends with you because no one could tolerate her anymore."

"Charming. Thanks, Liana."

"I didn't mean it like that, Eugene."

"Then what did you mean?!" Eugene said, raising his voice. "Yasmin may have her flaws and make jokes from time to time but she's the only one who's been there for me. I don't have the luxury of being royalty to increase my popularity."

"So, what are you saying? Saffina and Joel are only friends with me because I'm a Princess?"

"Everyone knows what you did on your first day at school, and Yaz has never forgotten."

"Someone had to put her in her place."

"You made everyone hate her. She was left with no one."

"Everyone hates her anyway, I just... made her aware of it."

Gene sighed. "To me, what you did, didn't make you any different to her. Hurry up with that firewood, it's gonna get cold soon," he said, before heading back to their camp.

Liana stared at the glowing orb in her hand once more. "You're wrong!" she shouted after him, but he didn't turn around to answer her. She stared at the crested back of Gene's black robe walking away from her. Saffina and Joel wouldn't have come out searching for her if they were only her friends because she was a Princess, she thought to herself.

But what if Gene was right? What if she was no different to the bullying Yasmin?

And what if her mother was right? Maybe the scripture might not be about her or any prophecy and this sphere wasn't unique? She might just be wasting valuable time finding this priest when she could be searching for her friends.

Liana shook the doubts from her head, put the sphere back into her pocket and continued collecting firewood. She knelt down to add a final stick to the heap she already clutched. As she stood back up and balanced the last stick carefully on top, she felt hairs standing on edge on the back of her head, the same way they did when her uncle rescued her from the White Robes. She squinted through the forest's shadows of tree trunks and branches and was certain she saw the same ghostly, hunched figure. She called out to the figure, asking it to reveal itself. She accidentally dropped stick she was holding, and her eyes instinctively drew to the sound of wood-hitting-ground. When she looked up, the figure had vanished into the darkness.

The following morning, Yasmin (without any input from Liana and Gene) decided that the lake waters were too deep for the horses to swim through with all their luggage, and they must take a longer route around the shoreline.

The jackdaw remained perched on the dead tree on the island in the middle of the lake, even when the three children got to the opposite side from which they had started.

"Shouldn't that bird be moving now?" asked Liana. "I mean, we've got to go to the other side."

"You know that jokes about a chicken, right?" jested Gene. "The Priestess told me it would do this," announced Yasmin. "She said when the Jackdaw stops flying, head north-east without deviating and the temple will reveal itself."

"What? That doesn't make any sense. Why would she just tell you and not us?" questioned Liana.

Yasmin shrugged. "Dunno. Come on, let's go."

"Hold on," Liana tugged at Yasmin's arm and spun her around. "At the Queen's Table meeting the Priestess said communicating with a jackdaw is a skill learned by the Visendi and the birds can be sent to specific people or locations and will go exactly where it's instructed. It didn't sound like they would stop for no reason," argued Liana.

"Hey, I don't know, I'm not the Priestess," Yasmin argued back, raising her voice. "I'm just doing what I've been told."

"You're hiding something!" Liana squared up to Yasmin. Yasmin's taller figure looked down on Liana.

"I don't care what you think." replied Yasmin, slowly as

the pair eyeballed each other. "Don't like it? Stay here then. Do you see your precious priest and temple here?" and with that, Yasmin pushed Liana, who slipped on the wet leaves beneath her feet and tumbled backwards down into the lake.

"Liana!" Gene shouted as he watched her fall and become completely submerged by the water. He shouted her name through the sound of the splash, but she failed to emerge. "LIANA?" he shouted for a third time before turning to Yasmin. "What have you done?!" Gene hastily took off his black and gold robes and jumped into the water after her. He dived two or three times but couldn't find any sign of Liana. "She's gone. She's gone!"

15

SHROUDED TEMPLE OF ROOTS

Liana thrashed her arms under the water desperately trying to pull herself back up to the surface. The surprise of landing in the lake meant that she hadn't taken in much air before being submerged and she quickly felt the oxygen in her lungs fading fast. For each second that passed she felt like she was swallowing tiny rocks that began crushing her tightening chest. The clouded, dirty water around her began to blur as panic set in. As she continued to be drawn downwards, the sunlight faded and the rippling image of Gene calling to her disappeared. Soon she couldn't tell which way was up and which way was down. Then to add to her woes, she felt a tightening around her ankles, like a pair of hands grabbing her. Her movements became purposeful as she was dragged in one direction. She struggled to open her stinging eyes but forced herself through the pain just as she hit the lake's floor bed. She felt around with her hands desperately trying to push herself upwards, but instead of the floor bed consisting of the usual rocks, silt, and sediment, it was made up of broad entangled tree roots that entwined and overlapped one another leaving no gaps in between. The straggly ends of these tree roots were what had wrapped themselves around Liana's ankles which had now slithered their way up past her calves and thighs. As she breathed out her last few remaining bubbles of air, the scraggly tree roots yanked her towards a small vortex near the edge of the lake wall and she was flushed down the whirlpool just as she lost consciousness. Her limp body plummeted past the thick layer of entangled roots (which were as wide as she was tall) and down a small gushing waterfall onto a large lily pad which almost sank as its upturned edges folded around her. She floated on the lily pad, being gently pushed by the ripples towards the water's edge.

"Boy, Boy!" shouted a low and mature male voice. "Come here, help me. We have a visitor," he waded into the water up to his waist and pulled the lily pad the rest of the way to the shoreline. Soon, a smaller pair of hands appeared and helped lift Liana's still form onto solid ground, face up but motionless. The pair of wrinkled hands hovered over the body for a few seconds before a burst of green light pulsed out of them and against Liana's body, making her entire frame jolt. Liana immediately awoke with a startled gasp of air and spat out some water. Her eyesight was slightly fuzzy, her head slightly woozy. The man and boy sat her up against a log.

"You almost didn't make it!" the man said. "Not the usual way a guest enters the grounds of the temple!"

"The tree roots, they almost drowned me," said a panting Liana.

"Actually, I think that was the temple's way of making sure you arrived here safely."

"It couldn't do it another way?" Liana said sarcastically. "Are you the Old Priest?"

"Who are you calling old?!" replied the man.

"I'm sorry, I didn't mean to offend, it's what the Priestess called you."

The Old Priest squinted as he judged her body language and words.

"How old *are* you?" asked Liana.

"Not afraid of asking questions, are you? I'm 101 now."

"101?!" exclaimed Liana "You don't look much older than 60!"

The Old Priest chuckled with a glint in his eye as he spoke. "I look after myself."

"So, what shall I call you?"

"I am Priest Shiro Hayashi. But you can call me Master H."

"Thank you for saving me, Master H."

"Oh, I didn't save you. The temple knew what it was doing. Were you with anyone else?"

"Yes, I was with another girl and a boy."

"Then your unusual means of arrival is probably down to the temple not wanting them here," Master H. stroked his grey handle-bar moustache.

Liana shakily got to her feet and realised the boy next to her was the same boy that saved her in the forest.

"It's you! The boy with red hair who doesn't speak!"

"You know him?" asked Master H.

"He saved me from being taken prisoner by some thugs in White Robes - but stole my dagger! The boy shied away.

"Dagger? I know not of this dagger, boy? Have you kept it hidden from me?" the Old Priest questioned; the boy shook his head.

"Then it is lost?"

The boy nodded. Liana could feel her emotions building inside her. *'That was **my** dagger, for **my** sphere given to me by **my** Great Uncle,'* she thought to herself as anger and frustration began to take over.

"He's not been here long himself. Just a couple of weeks. He is but a boy, do not rage. I will deal with the matter." Master H placed a hand on Liana's shoulder. She could feel his experience and wise thoughts run through her body. *'I can trust this man. He can teach me things.'* She calmed down and let the matter go immediately.

"Oh, where are my manners? I do not often have guests; I've forgotten my social skills. Can I get you something to drink? It's rare that anyone has the privilege of visiting me these days and here I am with two younglings."

"I think I've had enough to drink, thank you," joked Liana.

The Old Priest led them past a huge field of red tulips. Liana could see no more than a dozen adults tending to the grounds.

"Where is everyone else?" asked Liana.

"Everyone else? My dear, this is everyone. Everyone that's left on Coryàtès who still practices the old and true ways of the Visendi," the Old Priest's tone lowered as he reflected on the religion's downfall.

"I thought there'd be more of you." Liana's heart sank as her optimism of finding a small army to help her find and rescue her friends couldn't even be called a hamlet.

"When Vivek came here last, there were more than six or seven times more of us, but when Queen Langton announced she would allow the religion to be taught in Swyre again, many left for the city, knowing they no longer needed to fear for their lives. I warned them that it would not be the same, but they left anyway. They believed a diluted teaching without retribution was better than a full teaching in hiding," Master H. shook his head. His tone remained sullen.

Liana felt the cavern's warm humidity on her skin. Glassy stone walls encompassed the underground temple, tropical, like Coryàtès in summer, except it shouldn't be as it was only spring. A pair of huge trees stood either side of an entrance carved into one of the walls. Liana traced the tree's trunks upward and saw them disappear into the canopy of entwined roots above, which held back the lake's water. Sunlight came from the right, where she could see the back of another, much larger, waterfall crashing against several clusters of tall, jagged rocks below. The rays of light penetrated the falling water and bounced off the glass-like stone walls giving the cavern the same brightness as if they had been standing on the surface above. She took a moment to pause, gawping at the beauty of where she was before following the Old Priest and the boy through the doorway. Infront of her, the statue of a woman sat cross-legged, cupping a tulip, above a small pond. The pond was full of life; fish, tadpoles, water-skatesmen to name a few. On the floor lay a large soft red rug. The floor creaked underneath Liana's feet as she walked over it. On the walls hung tapestries with writing of a different language that she could not understand, nor did she recognise.

"This is the meditation room. Through there..." Master H pointed to a door in the far-left corner. "Is the library and spar-ring room, and through there..." he pointed to a door in the far-right corner "Are my quarters and kitchen. If you do not wish to drink, perhaps you would like to meditate for a while and strengthen your Aura?"

"Uh..." Liana hesitated. "I don't have an Aura."

"What do you mean you don't have an Aura?" Master H

raised a quizzical eyebrow "The Shrouded Temple only let's those in who have an Aura."

"Well... I don't."

"Hmm," he stroked his moustache once again, his matching grey eyebrows frowning deep in thought before he suddenly perked up again. "Very well. It is not for me to decide who is worthy of entering. Maybe Aurora is getting desperate. At least you know about Aura's, I suppose."

"What do you mean, desperate?"

"This is one of the founding temples of the Visendi. It's connected directly to Aurora herself. Thousands of years old. She is the one who decides who shall and shall not enter."

"Okay, but desperate?"

"She used to be very particular about who she allowed to enter. At one point, she was even refusing entry to some of those who had attained their Red Aura."

"I thought if you've earned your Aura, you've proven yourself worthy to enter?"

"Not the case," he said as he waved his finger. "Not for those who choose the shortcut."

"That wouldn't happen to be gaining your Red Aura simply through fighting and sparring, would it?"

"Why, yes! You know more than what you're letting on! Are you sure you don't have your Red Aura or are you hiding it from me?" he said, leaning forward, squinting as he studied Liana's expressions.

"No. The girl and boy I was with - they shortcut. The boy, Eugene, told me they sparred all night with Priestess Yi Lang in order to gain their Red Aura."

"Bah! Yi Lang! She was always impatient." shouted Master H, throwing his arms into the air. "It seems Aurora is still rejecting those who shortcut. Although I'm still not sure why she let you in." He led Liana through to the library which preceded a large square floor space, like a dojo. It was a largish square room. Carved into the stone walls were shelves which housed the numerous and immaculately kept books and scrolls. Liana ran her finger over the edges of them and admired the many intricate details and decorations etched into the surfaces. She could tell a great amount of care and time was taken to design, create and maintain them. At the end of the room stood a wooden manikin wearing a maroon-coloured robe. Next to it, a row of wooden cabinets stood. Liana circled the manikin.

"This is the same style robe that Yasmin and Eugene were wearing," said Liana, lifting one of the sleeves. "It even has the same symbol of the arrowhead, wave and palm tree on the back. But the writing underneath is different. This says, *'Shroud Clan.'* Theirs said *'Tulip Clan'.*"

"Hmm so the Priestess has started a new clan. I suppose at least she still recognises the Coryàtès family," Master H stroked his handlebars once more. "Each land, as you know it now, used to be labelled as 'families' by the old Visendi. Each family was made up of any number of clans. A clan could be created by anyone, although usually only high-level Aura's would prevail in getting any more than just their close friends or family to join. It is...or was... natural for people to want to be part of a clan where the leader is highly ranked and could teach them much in the ways of the Visendi."

"What was the point of clans and families?"

"Competitions, mainly. Friendly, for the most part. Families would have internal clan vs clan competitions to test their Aura skills against one another. The winning clan from each family would take part in the World Visendi Tournament for a chance to be crowned as the most powerful clan and family in the world."

"That sounds amazing to watch! Have you ever seen one of these tournaments?"

"The tournaments ended long before the religion was banned and organizing such an event whilst the religion is forbidden would not have gone unnoticed, but I share your enthusiasm to be able to witness such a spectacle. I understand it was quite the entertainment."

Liana drew away from the manikin. "What's in the cabinets?" she asked.

"Various types of weapons and objects that have been used by the Visendi over the years. I'm well trained in a number of martial arts."

"So fighting is a big part of the religion?"

"Yes and no. It's not the religion's main focus, but when Aurora realised she could no longer stay and protect this world forever she had to entrust some of her power and skills to people she thought she could trust."

"*Thought* she could trust? So, they betrayed her?"

Master H hesitated before answering. "Before we go into that, what else do you know about earning your Aura?"

"Nothing," Liana answered, "I only found out less than two weeks ago that earning your Aura's were even a thing."

"When Clerk Vivek wrote to me after the Day of Darkness, he told me that Queen Langton was reintroducing the religion to their people? Did this not happen?"

"Well yes, but obviously they didn't teach us everything. Find your inner cores in Security, Creativity, Strength, Love, Communication and Awareness to prove yourself to Aurora who will help you crossover into the afterlife."

Master H shook his head vigorously, displeased at Liana's

limited knowledge. "Like making bread without flour!" He opened one of the cabinets and took out a fighting staff. With his arm fully outstretched, he balanced the 6ft pole on his middle finger. "Come, stand here, in front of me," Liana did as she was asked.

He swung the staff with a swift, one-handed spin and jab towards her. She instinctively flinched backwards. "Do not hesitate! I will not hurt you, child," he gestured a 'come hither' movement with his free hand for her to return to her previous spot - the unmoving staff less than an inch away from her intestinal area.

"Your Root - the Red Aura," he announced, before another swing, spin, and jab. Liana did her best to remain still and not flinch but couldn't help tightening up and closing her eyes. She opened them slowly to see the staff at the height of her hips.

"Sacral - The Orange Aura," he made the same swinging motion with the staff. Liana stood her ground well this time.

"Solar Plexus - The Yellow Aura,"the staff, thrusted towards her belly button.

"Heart - The Green Aura," he said as the staff retreated and thrusted once more.

"Lingual - The Blue Aura, and finally," he retreated the staff from her throat and swung it for a final time. "The Third Eye - The Indigo Aura. Strangely, the exact same colour as your hair." he held the staff firm between Liana's eyes. "These are the real names of the Six Inner Cores."

He lowered the staff. "There are many ways to earn your Aura, Liana. Each Core has its own way to shortcut, but if you earn your Aura in the right way, then that Core's special power will be stronger, longer lasting and more respected."

"That's all very interesting, but you still haven't told me what these different ways of earning your Aura are?"

"Yes, yes, we'll come to that." he said with a dismissive wave. "Tell me, have you seen an Aura Orb? Or has the wonderful Priestess omitted those from her teachings also?"

Liana thought about the Orb in her pocket. She wasn't sure she should disclose her possession until she knew more about it, especially since it seemed like Master H was about to tell her anyway. "Again, only a couple of weeks ago, when the two I travelled here with had gained their Red Aura's. Orb's mounted into buttons for their robes."

Master H nodded in approval of this knowledge. "As you perform certain tasks and practices, the Orb fills up as you start to earn your Aura and shows how you are progressing through that Core. When you achieve your Core, you attain an ability related to that Core."

"Like the screen that Yasmine and Eugene can produce, that can deflect attacks."

"Yes. Although if they had earned their Aura in a more disciplined way, they could do much more than deflect an attack."

"So, what other ways are there?" asked Liana.
"There is a whole library here for you to study and answer that question for yourself," Master H said, pointing his fighting staff around the room.

"I haven't got time to read! My two best friends have been captured and I need to find them. The Priestess said you could help me find them and rescue them. That's all I'm here for, your help," Liana raised her voice impatiently.

"You want my help and yet you haven't even told me your name! Do you have no manners, girl?"

She paused, acknowledging her rudeness. "Liana," she said softly.

"Liana... Liana... I've heard that name before..." the Old Priest stroked his grey handle-bar moustache once more. "In one of Vivek's letters. You're... you're Queen Langton's daughter!"

Liana nodded shallowly, embarrassed that even the leader of a hidden temple knows who she is. *'Isn't there anyone in the world who doesn't know who I am?'*

"I'm surprised they let you out of their sight. There must be a reason," Master H lifted Liana's bowed head up with the end of his staff and stared intently into her eyes. "Your hair. How did you get that colour?" he asked.

"This is my natural colour. I'm a freak I know. The only other person I know with such a bold hair colour like mine is the boy."

The Old Priest squinted his intense eyes even more before gesturing to her to follow him out of the temple. They stood between the two trees at the entrance and watched the boy who was tending to the fields of tulips.

"Do you know why Aurora chose the tulip to be the symbol of the religion?"

Liana shook her head. "Please, tell me."

"Firstly, they can be grown in every single colour of the Six Inner Cores. Secondly, their bloom celebrates the arrival of Aurora and longer hours of sunlight. Thirdly, they symbolise perseverance. Did you know, if you cut a tulip's stem, they will continue to grow? No matter where a tulip is, it will always point towards sunlight. So if you ever need guidance from the Goddess of Dawn, look to the tulip. On the surface, their flowers only last for a couple of weeks at most. Down here, they grow in the Shrouded Temple all year round. I believe it's why Aurora chose this place as the location for the temple of the first Inner Core."

Liana watched as the red-haired boy watered the rows of vibrant coloured flowers. "I guess tending to tulips is one way of earning a Core?"

The Priest nodded. "The very first Inner Core - your Root. The process of nurturing life from it's beginning to its end. It may not fill your Aura Orb as quickly as other means, but it develops a strong Aura. Yi Lang has reduced the Root to its very basic meaning, survival of yourself. However, Aurora's real teaching is looking after the survival of others, as well as yourself. Putting others before yourself, even endangering your own life for theirs, will earn you the strongest Aura."

"The boy, does he have any Aura's?" asked Liana.

"Not that I've witnessed, but he may be choosing not to display it," Master H shook his head. "He turned up here a few weeks ago, so judging by the rules of Aurora he should have, but since he does not seem to be able to speak, I don't know if he has an Aura. He also comes and goes from the temple as he pleases. I'm honestly not sure what to make of him, although it appears after decades of living without children, that suddenly before me I have two. Both with strangely coloured hair and both without Aura's and both allowed into the Shrouded Temple of Roots." Once again, he stroked his moustache as he pondered his thoughts. "So now that I have somewhat answered your question, what do you want from me? You said something about missing friends?"

"Yes, I want you to help me get my friends back. They're missing. I was taken hostage and they went out looking for me in the forest, but they didn't come home."

"What makes you think I can help?" The Old Priest raised

an eyebrow "I don't know who they are, where they are, or if I can rescue them."

"The Priestess told me if anyone on this island can tell me the truth about my life, it would be you. And if I know who I really am, then maybe I can help my friends."

Liana handed over the old parchment that Priestess Yi had given her. The Old Priest had barely set eyes on it as he recognised the scripture immediately. "The Priestess believes I may be the light that will save the world. There's more..." Liana reached into her other pocket and pulled out the big red Orb. As soon as she touched it with her bare hands, it glowed the brightest glow she had seen it produce.

Master's H's eyebrows raised, and mouth dropped in awe at the object. "A Spirit Orb!"

"A Spirit Orb? You mean it's different from the Aura Orbs?"

"Liana, you must tell me everything as to why the Priestess believes you are the Light from the Dark."

Master H and Liana sat cross-legged inside the temple, in front of the Aurora statue, on the meditation mat. The Old Priest listened carefully to Liana describing the story of how she was found alone on a rock surrounded by lava on the Day of Darkness and how her Great Uncle found the Spirit Orb beside her. The Old Priest pushed for as much detail as possible when she described her visions of white light from Agatha and the speckled light from Nalan. Finally, she described the dream she had of being a baby surrounded by Visendi, with the Spirit Orbs and Artifacts.

"So, do you think I'm the saviour of the world too? And can you help me save my friends?"

"Let me meditate for a little while. To clear my mind and digest this information. If you are the Light from the Dark, it is my duty to the Goddess of Dawn to serve you," with his wrists resting on his knees, Master H closed his eyes. Liana knew better to not disturb someone when they wished to meditate. Despite the countless more questions she had, she raised herself off the floor and went back outside. As she did, she saw the shadow of the boy hastily disappear from the entranceway. Liana jogged after him.

"Hey! Hey, boy! It's okay, I promise I won't be mad at you for eavesdropping," she shouted, standing on tiptoes to see if she could find where he had scurried off to hide. She looked over the rows of tulips and spotted an out-of-place shape amongst the red flowers. "I see you. Clever hiding spot."

The boy poked his head up and slowly made his way towards her. The pair sat on a nearby bench.

"Thanks again for saving me from the white robed men," the boy looked blankly back at Liana.

"This is all a bit crazy, isn't it? Cores, Aura's. Orbs. It's a lot to get your head around," the pair sat looking at the beautiful rows of tulips and streaky rays of light that bounced off the glossy cavern. "And I'm the saviour of it all," she chuckled in disbelief as she reflected on her situation. "If only I had my friends, then I'd feel a lot better about it all. Hey, you didn't happen to see my dagger, did you? I think it's important I get it back," the boy frowned. "Why the look?" she asked.

The boy picked up a stick and drew seven stick-man figures in the dirt. Four men on horses, chasing a girl, a boy, and a smaller boy. Liana quickly figured out the drawing.

"You've seen them? My friends? They were chased by the White Robed men weren't they!?" The boy nodded, then drew

a circle around his drawing of Saffina and Joel with the outline
of a dagger in the ground.

"They had it and dropped it?" the boy shook his head
violently and pointed to himself. "You had it, and they made
you drop it?" the boy nodded his head furiously.

"These men," said Liana, pointing at the drawing. "Who
are they?"

The boy drew a picture of a pickaxe and a large triangle.
'An axe and a large triangle like a mountain... the mines!'

"Are they a tribe of escaped miners?" the boy shook his
head again. He drew a face, and in the smile a series of triangles to represent teeth. *'Sharpened teeth! I knew that man was
evil!'*

"They work for Zagan?" The boy nodded. "You think
Saffina and Joel have been taken to the mines?" The boy
nodded again.

*'If Zagan has his own soldiers and my mother doesn't know, then
that's bad. Really bad... I hope Saffina and Joel are okay...'*

"Do you think they'll hurt my friends?" The boy shook his
head and pointed at Liana. "Me? That's right, they wanted me
first." She thought intently. "So, they're probably going to use
my friends to get to me?" She didn't bother to look at the boy
for confirmation and bowed her head. She knew.

"Chin up, dear." Liana looked up to see the petit round
face of a smiling, gentle young woman looking back at her.
"Before you and this boy, I was the youngest one here! It's nice
to see another new young face around here. My name's
Estrella."

Just as the young woman had finished saying her name,
Liana watched as the bright colours of the temple faded out of
existence leaving behind just a greyscale pallet. The same brilliant white light that had wrapped Agatha in Liana's very first

vision, now surrounded this Estrella woman. She did not know why, but Liana immediately felt at ease. This time, the vision lasted for only a few moments. It was a few moments of pure peacefulness and tranquillity, unlike the painful experience with Nalan in the Triunity Hall which began with a piercing headache. The temple's colourful palette soon drifted back in like a sped-up watercolour painting. She smiled sweetly at Estrella: "Hello, I'm Liana."

"Let me show you what we do here to earn our Aura's." said the young woman.

"You have an Aura? Can you show me?" asked Liana.

Estrella smiled wide, long dimples forming as she did. She flicked back her blonde hair, closed her eyes, and took a deep breath. An intense bright red light radiated around her. After a few seconds, Estrella's Aura's colour faded into orange. Moments later, changing into a less vivid yellow. "I've only just attained the Solar Plexus core, so it's still a little weak." She pointed to the twisted silver frame of the third button up on her plain, three-quarter length, black robe. A yellow, speckled light orbited gently inside the small capsule encased in the silver framed button. Liana couldn't help but stare curiously at the yellow glow. Orange and red glows emanated and danced gently in the two buttons below.

"That's amazing. Your red aura is really impressive."

"You can earn your Aura's anytime, anywhere, but this is a founding temple which focuses on the Root core. Master H. is a specialist in helping Visendi achieve their very strongest Red Aura. Come, let me show you." Estrella raised her arm in the direction of the tulip fields. Liana stood up from the bench and followed. The pair walked leisurely through the paths in the fields of the colourful flowers. A few of the temple's residents were systematically watering each row.

Estrella stopped and turned to her guest "Do you know what the Root core teaches us?" she said, still with her dimpled smile.

"Master H. just told me. He said it represents survival, of others as well as yourself. His methods involve nurturing life from its beginning to its end." She bent down and cupped the petals of a tulip in her hands. "Please tell me, how does looking after these plants help with attaining your Red Aura?" asked Liana.

"To look after yourself requires selfish discipline. To look after someone else requires selfless sacrifice. The root of life is about balance and flowers are the perfect example," Estrella knelt down beside Liana and cupped her own hands around hers. "Flowers have a selfish discipline. They need water, good earth to grow, and most of all, sunlight. If they don't get enough sunlight, they will selfishly bend towards the brightest light source to keep on surviving, trying to outgrow the flowers around it. But they are also selfless, by removing toxins from the air to make it breathable for us. By nurturing these fields of flowers, we are also helping ourselves. Surviving hand in hand."

"And you continue to do this even after you've earned your Red Aura?"

"It's not just about attaining, but also retaining. It's important we continue to practice each teaching of each core even after an Ascension, to maintain its strength."

Estrella loosened her cupped hands and guided Liana to her feet. They set off in a direction past the fields of tulips to a sandy corner of the large cavern. Three wooden poles loosely resembling human silhouettes protruded out of the sandy ground. Various types of swords, axe's, spears and tonfa's lay on an open table against the rocky cliff wall. Liana pondered why they would leave metal to rust out in the open, before suddenly realising that because the roof of the temple was constructed of the tightly entwined roots of the trees above, there could never be any rainfall. *'And this is why they must constantly water the flowers.'*

"Fighting dummies," said Liana. "I thought Master H. didn't approve of fighting to attain a Red Aura."

"Master H. doesn't disapprove of fighting. Knowing the basics of how to protect oneself is important to self-preservation. Remember, it's about balance."

"Selfish discipline, selfless sacrifice," Liana whispered to herself, repeating Estrella's teaching moments earlier. Estrella pretended she didn't hear but nodded to herself proudly at Liana's quick learning. "There's no armour here though, do you keep it somewhere else?"

"We fight with no armour. Our Aura Screens are as strong as any metal. Even when duelling. Here - try and hit me," Estrella made her way over to the table and handed Liana one of the spears. Liana noted the freshly sharpened blade at its tip.

"Go on, stop hesitating. You won't hurt me."

Liana tentatively moved her hands to point the spear at the midriff of her guide and lunged. Estrella's Red Aura lit up on impact, deflecting the spear away.

"Was that your best effort?" taunted Estrella, her smile unwavering.

Liana raised the spear again in her right hand and charged with the tip at head height. She was not a slow runner and due to her training with her Uncle, not short on strength, especially for her age. But again, Estrella's Screen deflected the spear and knocked Liana backwards, sliding along the floor like an over excited puppy on a slippery rock.

Estrella offered her hand and pulled Liana up off of the sandy floor.

"Wow, that defence is almost as powerful as an attack."

Estrella laughed. "One day, your Aura Screen might be as strong."

Liana laughed. She was engaged. She was having fun. It had been a while. "What's over there?" she said, point to the opposite corner, past the pond that she had splashed into earlier.

"The stage. We keep ourselves entertained. We often put on small shows for each other. Besides that, is the banqueting table. With all the crops and fish that we have here at our disposal, we feast every evening."

"A feast every evening?" Liana questioned with an accusatory pitch in the tone of her voice. "That sounds greedy and unbalanced."

"My, how quick you are to judge little one! We fast during the day and feast in the evening, to reap the rewards of our hard work and ensure we are energised for an early rise the next day."

"Oh," said Liana apologetically. "I'm not sure I could go all day without eating."

"You get used to it. Especially with the support of others around you," Estrella looked lovingly at her friends scattered across the temple. "Look at the state of your clothes. As our guest, I will make it my personal duty to wash, dry and fold them for you every day."

"You don't have to do that," objected Liana "Just because I'm a Princess doesn't mean I have everything done for me. That's not how I was raised."

"Until now, I had no idea you were a Princess. I was just being a good host."

Liana bowed her head apologetically, again. "Sorry, you are very kind. I look forward to hearing what you all have to teach. The old ways of the Visendi are different to what I have been taught in Swyre."

"We look forward to teaching you the ways," Estrella's smile held in her sweet face as wide as ever.

"Is there a way we can get a message to my mother, to tell her I'm ok?"

"Only Master H. has the Jackdaw ability here. I'm sure he will have no objection to you keeping in touch with your mother."

"Thank you, Estrella."

"It's my pleasure. Now, let's get you cleaned up ready for this evening's feast. I'll show you to your chamber."

As Estrella led Liana back inside, between the trees that flanked the entrance and passed the meditation room, she couldn't get one thought out of her head. *'This place feels like home. Like I belong here.'*

THE TULIP TEMPLE

The contrasting heavy footsteps of Sir Tarak and light pacing of Priestess Yi echoed through the corridor in harmony with each other as they walked the upward curving slope inside the Tulip Temple. They soon reached the entrance to the first floor. The doors were large and arched at the top. They were open and swung inwards and currently hooked invitingly into place, ready to welcome guests. Beside the door stood a tall, cuboid stand. Sitting on top of the stand was a simple wooden bowl. Priestess Yi reached into the bowl, which was deep enough for her hands to disappear from sight. When they reappeared, she was cupping a handful of dried, red tulip petals. "Now you, Sir Tarak," Sir Tarak did as he was instructed although he was careful not to take too many in his large hands and leave some petals in the bowl for others. "This floor is broken up into three disciplines. Sparring, horticulture and meditation. Around the circumference of the room, you will find dedicated space for each of these disciplines. The centre of the room is large enough for me to gather a class of up to 300 students. I usually hold two classes a day, instructing students on each of these three disciplines, although followers can come and go as they please to make use of the facilities. We can fit up to a thousand people at a time across this entire floor."

Sir Tarak raised his cupped hands. "And what do we do with these?"

"They are an offering to Aurora. Everyone who enters must do this ritual. I will show you."

They moved through the arching doorway. The image of a sun, with long wavy rays of light surrounding a large circle, was carved into angled walls either side of the entrance way. Within the large circle of the sun was the eye-like AV symbol of the Aurora Visendus. A trough ran the length of the wall underneath the carving. Large orange flames of fire flickered within the trough.

"Place your petals in the fire and wait until they have completely perished." Priestess Yi knelt down onto a singular long, red cushion that lay at the foot of the trough on her side of the entranceway. She held her hands over the trough and parted her cupped hands slowly, allowing the petals to pour gently into the flames. Sir Tarak mimicked Priestess Yi on the other angled wall. He watched as the burning petals turned black around the edges before slowly curling inwards on themselves. It didn't take long for them all to shrivel and to turn ash.

The two angled walls created an entrance-way gap. The pair walked through the gap and Sir Tarak had to refocus his eyes due to the influx of light that poured in. Clear glass windows circled the entire room's circumference sitting just below the high ceiling. On the ceiling itself were beautifully carved overlapping petals shapes. The left portion of the room was reserved for plant life. The right side of the room contained several pod-like rooms for private meditation. Straight ahead were four open-plan sparring rooms.

The Priestess took Sir Tarak over to a cabinet near the meditation pods and slid open the top drawer. "Each student gets an orb button. As you participate in each discipline, Aurora rewards you and your buttons fill up. Once you have filled your orb button, you will be able to produce an Aura. Each level gives you a different ability. The Red Aura is like a physical extension of yourself. Its most common use is to use it as a personal shield screen, just like how Yasmin and Eugene used it at the ceremony."

Sir Tarak held the button between his forefinger and thumb, studying it. "Can I have a look at one that isn't empty?" he enquired.

Priestess Yi nodded and held out her wrist. Wrapped around it was a bracelet. Hooked onto the bracelet like charms were her orb buttons. Six clasped on in total, although only five were glowing with flickering dancing light. Red, Orange, Yellow, Green and Blue.

"You have not achieved all six levels?" Sir Tarak asked.

"To achieve Transcendence is a most difficult task, Sir Tarak. It is the ultimate goal of any Visendi, but only few can achieve it, even after a lifetime of disciplined study and worship. Aurora does not willingly reward Aura's, especially to the higher echelons."

"Yet you can call yourself a Priestess and run a Temple?"

"With the religion having been forbidden for almost 200 years, Sir Tarak, it is a wonder anyone at all still has the knowledge to earn even the first level of Auras. Within my small underground faction, before your niece legalised the religion again, I was the highest ranking Visendi."

"But you think this Old Priest that Liana has gone in search of knows more?"

"Without a doubt. The Shrouded Temple of Roots has existed for centuries, if not millennia."

"Then why have you not been practising your disciplines there?"

"I did visit, once. But the Old Priest and I did not see eye to eye."

"Oh? Do tell."

"His teachings, what he believes to be the proper and only way of gaining Aura's, are slow. But we do not have time to dawdle, Sir Tarak. Our numbers have been declining rapidly over the past two centuries. Even after legalisation, your niece had such strict controls on what could or could not be shared that the religion was of no interest to ordinary folk. That's why we had to make a grand scene at the ceremony. To entice people to want to take up the religion. And my teachings are much faster than the Old Priests' methods."

"Have you heard from Liana? Has she made it to the temple yet?"

"My Jackdaw has not returned."

"Is that a bad sign?"

"I would have expected it to be back by now."

"You didn't answer my question. Is that a bad sign?"

"There could be many reasons it hasn't returned."

"None of which are good, I presume?"

"I would not like to presume anything."

Sir Tarak watched as a pair of men began sparring with each other in the room next to them.

"Can you teach my soldiers? These Aura Screens that

Yasmin and Eugene produced could be a great asset in battle. Freeing up the hand that would normally hold a heavy shield to instead clasp another weapon. It would be like having a third arm. A shield, a sword and a mace at my army's disposal would be sure to give them an advantage in any fight."

"I would not turn anyone away from the teachings of Aurora. But..."

"But what?" Sir Tarak's eyes narrowed. He did not like the tone the Priestess's voice had taken.

"But they will probably not earn their Aura."

"Why not? Because they are soldiers? Does Aurora have something against those who fight and protect their kingdom?"

"No, it's not that. They will probably not earn their Aura, because nobody here has been able to."

"Nobody? But on the way up here you told me Yasmin and Eugene had earned theirs in one night of non-stop sparring?"

"That's true."

"Then what made them special?"

"I don't believe anything made them particularly special, Sir Tarak. The way they earned their Aura's so fast does mean that they may not have the same strength as if they had earned it with all three disciplines, but it is not them who were special, more like..." Priestess Yi hesitated again.

"Come on, Priestess, spit it out," urged Sir Tarak. "It's more like there is a curse on the Temple. You see, I did not train Yasmin and Eugene here. We trained through the night in the forest and then meditated on the cliffs at dawn as the sun peaked out over the horizon of the sea. None of my students have earned their Aura yet. Some are questioning whether the ceremony was a mere trick. I am reassuring them that earning your first Aura takes time and patience. Lying to them, in fact, that I had been working with Yasmin and Eugene long before the ceremony." the usually strong-willed Priestess's head dropped, and she stared at her bracelet. "Truth is, Sir Tarak, I do not know if the temple is cursed, or if Aurora does not wish this place to be a temple of worship to her, or perhaps she is displeased with me. All I know is, I haven't seen anyone gain any Aura in their orb buttons, and that is most troubling."

"Could it be -."

The Priestess swiftly cut off Sir Tarak: "Do not say his name in this place of worship!"

"Nobody talks about the burned figure I saw when I found Liana. We have spent too long burying our heads in the sand. If she starts to show signs of..."

She interrupted him again: "We have other things to be concerned about right now."

"You've heard how bad it is in the other lands. It's only a matter of time until..."

The Priestess, now visibly agitated at the direction the conversation had taken, cut him off for a final time: "Why do you think I sent her to find the Shrouded Temple? I am no fool, Sir Tarak, if it wasn't for your niece, I would have started this process long before now."

"I do not know much about your religion, Priestess, but I can see a dejected leader when I see one." said Tarak, reading the tiredness in the Priestess's body language that came with the level of concern she held inside. "I will still send as many of my troops as you can cope with to you, in the hope they can achieve their Aura. Even if they don't, I'm sure the teachings will still be of use to them."

Sir Tarak gently let go of the Priestess's hand and turned to exit, before glancing back to her over his shoulder. "Oh, and you know what I find helps garnish people in times of discontent?" The Priestess shook her head. "A good song," he said. "Come up with a good song."

17

SHADOWS

L iana stirred. Another night of disjointed sleep. Sleep interrupted by nightmares. Re-enactments in her mind of tree roots gripping her ankles, pulling her down under cold water as she stared powerlessly up at the blurry disappearing mirage of Eugene, feeling the last ounces of usable air disappear from her lungs.

If it wasn't the images of her near-death drowning, then it was the feel of her own knife pressing on her bare neck before being taken captive by Nalan, or it was the sense of impotence as a mere babe as she watched her Aura Spirits being Peeled. All three nightmares shared one commonality: the exposing of her fear of helplessness.

'If I can't help myself, can't save myself, how am I supposed to live up to these expectations I have been burdened with?'

She sat up from her shallow bed, pondering the nightmares and her thoughts.

Every night since entering the Shrouded Temple of Roots,

she woke. Seven nights it was now. She had started to get used to the broken pattern of sleep.

She placed her bare feet on the red rug by her bed and pushed herself up, before wiping her groggy eyes and taking a sip of lukewarm water from the mug on her bedside table. She screwed up her face, expecting the water to still be cold. *'I must have woken up later than usual. Think I'll fill it up fresh.'*

She made her way out of her sleeping chambers and towards the meditation room. For a moment she considered filling her mug up with the room's fountain, but she quickly dismissed that idea once she looked at all the bugs, fish and frogs enjoying the pond, plus, she thought, it was probably sacred and frowned upon. Instead, she ventured outside and used the pumps attached to barrels in the gardens that filtered the water as it fell from the waterfall. The gentle, refreshing mist of the waterfall's light water spray helped rid her of any remaining drowsiness. She sipped the water from her refilled glass and took her time to slowly swallow, being sure to enjoy the cold sensation inside her throat as she quenched her thirst.

The murmuring of two voices near the fighting dummies disrupted her enjoyment. She hadn't noticed them earlier, either they hadn't been there, or they purposefully chose that corner as it was the area most covered in darkness.

She carefully made her way closer to the shadowy pair, staying crouched as she moved behind the boulders that lined the shallows of the waterfalls pond area. She moved close enough to make out the outline of the figures, but to her they could have been any number of people, and neither had a particularly distinctive silhouette due to the baggy, brown robes they both wore. She strained to hear what was being said.

"You made it in. I'm glad my theory worked," the voice sounded deep and hoarse, maybe of an older man.

"Yes, I'm surprised I was allowed in without my own Aura. Your Orb must carry some weight with God of Dawn." The second figure then reached into his robes and pulled out a glowing red orb. Similar to hers, thought Liana, but smaller.

"Do you think he suspects anything?"

"No, I'm being careful. I'm doing everything he asks me, which can be... difficult for me to follow," whispered the second figure, who spoke in a tone, which to Liana, sounded fake and adjusted to the quietness of their surroundings.

"I understand how hard it must be for you."

"It can be. But I understand it's necessary."

"Have you been able to learn anything new?"

"They are being trained to earn their Red Aura's, but that, of course, is not new information."

"How are their studies progressing?"

The second figure hesitated as they considered their words. "Slowly," they replied.

"Good. We must continue to monitor their progress closely. Understand any vulnerabilities they may have."

"Oh, one more thing," the silhouette shifted their stance. "I know who has the Dagger of Red."

"You could have led with that information. Who has it?"

"Zagan. One of his troops picked it up after chasing some kids in the forest. Said one of the kids threw it at them so they took them prisoner."

"What would they want with some kids?"

"Friends of the Princess, I believe. Leverage, no doubt."

"Does he know of the Dagger's capability?"

"He recognises it as the Princesses but has no clue of its history with the religion."

"This is a concern. You must get the Dagger, before he learns of its abilities."

"I doubt he will let it out of his sight, but I will do my best. I will await your next instruction," he said, before the first figure, the figure who was clearly in charge with the hoarse voice, walked away and disappeared through the curtain of falling water.

Liana, eager for answers and hedging her bets now that there was only one person, burst out from behind the wet rocks where she was crouched. The figure flinched in surprise and slipped on some wet grass, landing with a splosh in some brown, watery mud which had been dampened by the fine water sprays of the waterfall.

"You should be asleep. Have you been here the whole time, watching?"

"Long enough," said Liana, squatting to the figure's level, who had leaned himself into a sitting position against one of the wooden fighting dummies. She whipped down the hood of the figure, startled at who sat before her.

"Nalan?!"

"Please, Princess, keep your voice down," Nalan shook off and scraped the mud from his hands. "You should not have been eavesdropping."

"And you shouldn't have captured me at knife point, with my own dagger!" said Liana, lowering her voice's volume, but not the accusatory tone.

"Fair point."

"What are you doing here? Are you spying on me, on the temple?"

"The less you know, Princess, the better."

"The less I know about what?" said Liana, pushing for information. Nalan stayed silent, staring at the mini pools of brown water on the ground. "What do you know, Nalan? What do you know about my friends? What do you know about me and my Dagger?" Liana shoved his shoulder after each question, but he did not budge. "And to think I was starting to sympathise with you in your treehouse. Maybe my mother was right about you..."

"Please, Liana. You need to stay here as long as possible. You'll be safe here."

"I'm staying here only as long as I need to. Once I've trained enough, I'll be going after my friends."

"You mustn't do that. You have no chance, not alone."

"I must free them, Nalan!"

"That's not going to be possible, Liana. It's too well guarded around the mines."

"Then you can help me!"

"I can't risk that. It's not my mission."

Liana's facial expressions turned to a scowl. If there was one person who owed her, it was him.

"You're refusing to help me? After what you did to me? And here I was, thinking you weren't all bad. Believing what you said about being possessed..."

"Liana, you have to understand there is more to this. You must trust us. Please." Nalan put his palms together and begged, as if he were praying.

"I don't know who I'm supposed to be trusting," she stood up and turned her back to him. "Who was that you were just talking to?"

"I'm sorry, Liana. I can't tell you that, either."

She turned and kicked a heap of mud away in frustration. She padded toward the water, her own figure now a shadow in the darkness.

"You had better find a way to help my friends escape, Nalan. I won't just sit here in this temple."

"But..."

"I mean it, Nalan. If I'm so precious, so important, then you'll do as I ask, because otherwise, I'll just go putting myself in danger."

Nalan sighed and begrudgingly accepted the ultimatum. He stood up and brushed the dirt from his legs and backside before responding.

"I will find a way to help them, but you have to promise me that you will stay here. Stay here and learn from Master Hayashi."

Liana responded with a single nod. "I promise."

18

UNEXPECTED ALLY

Zaganite guards silently acknowledged Yasmin and Eugene as they walked past the squalid residential pits that housed the miners. The golden sand that they had just been treading was now grey and dusty. Small campfires lit up each pit as dusk set in.

Small murmurings of conversation could be heard, but the miners learned quickly that anything too raucous would be quickly punished by the guards circling the pits. Although after 12 hours of labour, they didn't have the energy for it anyway.

Eugene kept close to Yasmin, nervously checking his surroundings.

"It's okay, you're with me. No one will touch you," sighed Yasmin. "Just keep it together. Don't show any signs of weakness."

"We've probably just seen Liana drown. It's pretty hard to keep it together," replied Eugene, although his tears of sadness had long dried up in the two days of travelling since the event.

"Our choices were to come here and tell my father or go home and tell Liana's mother. What would you rather do?" snapped Yasmin.

"Honestly, that's a pretty tough choice."

"Thought you'd had enough of being a scaredy-cat? What happened to the brave new Gene Greymore of the Aurora Visendi?" Yasmin said sarcastically.

Eugene frowned at Yasmin but kept his lips tight. He knew when to keep his mouth shut, but he sensed eyes were watching. He glanced sideways into one of the pits. A group of older looking men huddled around their small fire, whispering, and lifting their heads every so often in Gene and Yasmin's direction. A sudden flurry of small rocks hurtled towards them, hitting them on the backs of their heads forcing them to duck and dive. Blasphemous shouts of 'Daughter of Tenebris!' and 'Get her! Take her hostage!' accompanied the barrage.

Six Zaganite guards quickly appeared and surrounded the pair to escort them out of danger. Eight more Zaganite guards lowered wooden ladders into the pits and took on a miner each. The old miners attempted to fight them off but their aging arms, weak from a day's labour, were no match for the armoured soldiers who quickly restrained them.

"Probably thought they had nothing to lose. Been here most of their lives, those ones," said one of the guards.

"I'm surprised the other pits didn't join in," said Gene.

"Most of the others are still holding out to join the militia. They won't risk anything." replied the guard.

"The militia?" questioned Gene, giving Yasmin a confused look. She guiltily lowered her eyes to avoid making eye contact. Before Gene could press for more information, she quickly changed the subject.

"What will happen to them now?" she asked the guard.

"They'll be separated into other pits, then be made an example of at dawn."

"Made an example of?" Gene asked. The guard didn't respond, and Gene wasn't sure if he really wanted to know anyway. He was more concerned with the secrets that Yasmin had been keeping from him.

After they had moved past the last of the pits, the guards broke off, returning to their stations, leaving Yasmin and Eugene on their own.

"So what's all this militia talk about, Yas?"

"I can't tell you," she said, picking up the pace to try and put some distance between them.

"You've been shady with me for this whole journey. What aren't you telling me?" Gene said, raising his voice.

"Just don't say a word when we get to my father okay? Let me deal with him."

"Considering his reputation, that isn't very comforting, Yaz!"

The pair marched on through the tropical trees that bordered the mines. It wasn't long before the torch-lit moat that surrounded Zagan's dwelling came into sight.

"I am *so* glad I have my Red Aura," Gene muttered to himself as he observed the series of strung-up skulls that lined the wooden bridge. "I'm not sure what's worse. Spending any amount of time with your father or telling the Queen that her daughter's probably dead."

"It's the bones floating in the moat that gets me," admitted Yasmin, looking over the side of the bridge at the murky blue-green water. Red patches surrounded the floating remains. "I'm never quite sure if they're animal bones from my father's feasting, or human ones. And it smells awful."

"Miss Thornfalcon," bowed the guards at the entryway.

Yasmin nodded at them as they passed through uninterrupted. She paused and took a deep breath before entering her father's chamber.

"Daughter!" announced Zagan, opening his arms wide as he rose from his quartz throne. He didn't acknowledge Eugene's presence.

"Father," said Yasmin with little emotion as she hugged her father.

"You have made good time! I assume you've dropped off your precious goods already?" 'Straight down to business as usual', thought Yasmin. She could sense Eugene giving her one of his quizzical looks.

"Not exactly, father," Zagan sat back down. His rare, welcoming expression was short-lived as it soon turned back to its usual fierceness. An overwhelming silence filled the room. Eugene began to focus his mind just in case he needed to call upon his Aura. Out of the corner of his eye he could see Yamin try, unsuccessfully, to hide a nervous gulp.

"The goods were lost, father," At that moment, Eugene realised that Liana was the precious goods, and Yasmin had been tasked with bringing her to Zagan.

'This must have been why she's been acting so strangely. She knew I wouldn't agree to come if she said we were going to bring Liana here. How could she lie to me? Now she's put me in danger too!' Eugene thought to himself.

"What do you mean, lost?"

"She fell into a lake. We tried to pull her out, but she didn't come back up."

Zagan menacingly leaned forward. "Are you telling me the Princess died whilst under your safekeeping?" Yasmin nodded.

Zagan rose from his throne again and ominously stood

over his cowering daughter. He slowly bent over and whispered into her ear. "Do you have any idea how serious this is?"

Yasmin stood frozen. Her eyes were tight shut. Zagan moved so close their noses were almost touching.

"I gave you one job - to bring her to me. The only job I've ever entrusted to you, and you couldn't even do that!" Zagan yelled in his loud, grizzly voice. Yasmin's hair waved at the force of his ferociousness. "She was meant to be the bait to bring out the Swyre army. She was the other half of the deal to make me King of Coryàtès..." Yasmin lowered her eyes in fright before her father's voice boomed again. "Look at me, girl!"

Yasmin looked into the cold eyes of her father.

"I guess that weakling didn't do anything to help!" Zagan turned his head towards Eugene. "Had you surrounded yourself with someone with an ounce of strength, you may actually have had a chance of succeeding!"

"It was an accident! He didn't even know about the plan!"

Eugene had always thought Yasmin was immune from her father's wrath. *'She might have lied to me'* he thought, *'but here she is also trying to protect me.'*

Zagan growled through his sharpened teeth. "Take him away. The lock-up, the mines, I don't care where, just get him out of my sight."

Yasmin protested and flailed angrily as four guards went to grab Gene. He tried to use his Red Aura, but he could only block one of the guards' approaches. He wasn't skilled or practised enough to fend off more than one. Yasmin watched helplessly as her best friend was dragged away.

"The only reason you're not joining that pathetic friend of yours is because you're my daughter," but before Zagan could continue his chastising of Yasmin, a swooping Jackdaw flew into the room and landed on the arm of Zagan's throne. "Stay here," he ordered his daughter.

He turned around and took his seat, holding out his forearm for the bird to hop onto. A thin stream of glowing blue light emanated from the Jackdaw and connected with the centre of Zagan's forehead.

"Is she now?" said Zagan. "That's a very interesting development indeed. Yes, I know that wasn't successful. No, it won't happen again," Zagan nodded a few more times, listening to what else the Jackdaw had to convey. "Come and do what you need to. We shall ready a troop."

The connection ended and the bird flew off. "Looks like you're partially off the hook. Turns out Liana's alive after all."

"She is?" asked a confused Yasmin.

"She made it to the temple," smiled Zagan, deviously.

"But how will you get to her if she's in the temple? Only Visendi can enter."

"My ally has that sorted," chortled Zagan. "Although I'll need your help too. A chance to redeem yourself."

"Release Eugene first." bargained Yasmin.

"You dare negotiate with me after your failure? Accept or I'll throw you into a pit myself. He will be reassigned to a less... hurtful department if you are successful."

Yasmin took a knee to accept the mission. She knew this was the best chance she had of helping her friend.

～

"How long have I been down here? Feels like three weeks," said Gene, rattling his chains.

"Three days," replied his sister. "Try *actually* being down here for three weeks."

"Try being down here for three weeks with a broken foot." even Joel's usual care-free and jovial spirit had been broken as he stared at the dark and empty cave. "I don't know what's worse; being hungry, bored, or in pain."

"I still can't believe she lied to me," said Gene.

"I can." replied Saffina.

Gene rolled his eyes. "I know you don't like her, but..."

"But nothing," Saffina interrupted. "She's cruel and evil, just like her father."

"No, you're wrong," Gene said, staring at his sister. "She's not all bad. Look how she's helped me over the last couple of years."

"Yeh, you're in a *really* great place now, aren't you?" Saffina said sarcastically.

An atmosphere of animosity between the siblings filled the otherwise empty cave.

"At least Liana's still alive," piped Joel, breaking the silence. Saffina and Gene nodded in unison.

"I thought I'd lost her," Gene leant his head back against the hard stone wall closing his eyes to recall the traumatic event at the lake. "When I saw her disappearing down into the water, I thought she was gone for sure."

"But why hasn't she come for us yet?" sounded a frustrated Joel.

"She has to be smart, she's on her own and she doesn't even know where you are. Swyre can't send out soldiers. The Queen doesn't know who the White Robed men are and won't leave the city unprotected. She doesn't even know where to find them," explained Gene.

"Nobody in Swyre knows that the White Robed men are in fact soldiers of Zagan and everyone who has business with the mines are far more scared of him than they are of the Queen," Saffina added.

"Tell me just how Liana spending time at this Shrouded Temple is going to help her rescue us?" Joel said, raising an eyebrow.

"Because apparently, she's the Light that will save the world," replied Gene. "That's why we were taking her to the Shrouded Temple of Roots to find this Old Priest, for her to find out more about why she's special and get the help of someone who may be able to help find and rescue you. The powers of the Visendi... they're incredible."

"Like talking birds..." Joel said sarcastically.

Gene frowned at Joel. He was beginning to get fed up with Joel and Saffina's scepticism. He had already shown them his Red Aura, but they were convinced it was some sort of trick.

The sound of footsteps then echoed around the cave. The figure, initially just a blurry shadow against the bright cave entrance, moved with speed towards them. As it got near, Saffina and Joel soon recognised who it was.

"We haven't got much time," whispered the familiar looking masked and hooded Zaganite. It was the same Zaganite who had helped Joel down from the mountain after breaking his ankle.

"We need to get you out of here before anyone notices you're gone," she bent down, took out a key from an inside pocket, and unlocked the chains restraining the three children.

"Thank you! But why are you helping us?" asked Saffina as

she rubbed her wrists, relieved at the release of pressure that had gripped them.

"I've just come out of a meeting with Zagan and some other of his highly ranked Zaganites. He knows where Liana is and how to get to her. He's planning to take her tonight. I can't let him take her," said the Zaganite.

"Why do you care?" Gene said with a suspicious tone.

"No time to explain, we've *got* to get going. You -" said the Zaganite, staring at Joel "How's your foot, can you put weight on it?"

"Some, but I can't run," Joel replied.

"Hopefully you won't need to. Now, quickly, follow me." The three children set off behind her.

"Are you sure we can trust her?" Gene whispered to his sister.

Saffina nodded. "When Joel got hurt and she led us down from the mountain I could sense something familiar about her. I'm not sure why, but I don't believe she means any harm."

"Okay, as you are my sister, I trust your instinct. As long as this doesn't turn out to be some sort of sick hunting game for Zagan to play."

The group of four neared the cave entrance. A guard stood watch on either side. The Zaganite motioned to the three children to stay hidden behind a nearby boulder. They did as they were told and watched as the Zaganite silently approached the guard on the right from behind, drew a small knife and slit his throat, before swiftly spinning across the other side to stab the other guard in the side of the neck before he even had a chance to draw his own blade. She motioned a 'come hither' gesture with her finger towards the children as indication that the area was clear.

"You have good instincts," joked Gene to his sister.

The cave entrance opened out onto the clearing where the Zaganites trained. The female Zaganite waved her hand downward to indicate to the children behind her to stay low. Fortunately, only a few Zaganites were in the clearing, facing away from the cave entrance as they practiced their archery skills. The group crouched as they walked from palm tree to palm grass around the edge of the clearing. Before long, they were clear of that danger and they made their way cautiously along a disused track, where a number of fallen branches and leaves covered the floor.

The Zaganite halted abruptly and raised her fist as an order for the children to do the same. They could hear a pair of voices approaching. The group hid behind the thick bushes that lined the old path and peered through their spikey-like leaves.

"How long since you came over?"

"About 6 months. I was one of the first."

"What's it like living here?"

"Even though Master Thornfalcon and the Zaganite I've been coupled with are pretty fierce, it's still better than back home."

"I hope that will be the case for me, too. Thanks for showing me around on my first day here."

"The pleasure's all mine, my lovely. I wish I had someone to show me around on my first day here. It's nice to come this way though. The old mines are off limits but that makes it perfect for getting away from it all, you know? Plus, you don't have to go past the horrid residential pits or the dusty refining district."

"Or the fishy smelling port. I was so glad to get off that boat."

A pair of female riders ambled along the path as they

laughed together. Saffina recognised the horses they were riding and nudged Joel with her elbow.

"Hey, Joel, they've got our horses!"

"Heeyy, you're right. We've got to get them back!"

"We can't get distracted," insisted the Zaganite.

"They were gifts from Liana. They're the most expensive things we own. We're getting them back," Saffina was stubborn and the Zaganite could tell.

"I suppose it would be better than carrying on foot," admitted the Zaganite.

"How about I distract them with my charm while you snatch them back? You know, give them some compliments, throw some wit and humour their way. Show them my Red Aura," piped Gene with a smug smile.

His three companions all looked at him and each raised a doubting eyebrow in unison.

"I know you said the Visendi could produce some amazing powers, but I don't think they're that strong," chuckled Saffina.

Gene's smug look soon disappeared. "No need to be rude."

"Like I said, just leave it to me," The Zaganite lifted up a white snood around her mouth and nose before she pounced from the bushes and halted the two horses.

"Oooh, I thought you said no one came out this way," said the younger rider to her riding partner.

"They don't. Who are you? Did you get confused on the boat over? You're meant to be *with* a Zaganite, not *be* a Zaganite." said the older rider. The pair chuckled.

"Hand over your horses," The Zaganite pulled back her white robe and gripped the leather handle of a matching white whip.

"Did you set this up to scare me? Well, I'm not falling for it.

Nice trick," the younger rider clapped sarcastically towards the older rider.

"Actually, I think she's serious," the older rider took a more serious tone.

"Oh, come on! I came over here to *avoid* this sort of thing. We're supposed to be protected here. I mean, who's stupid enough to rebel against Master Thornfalcon," the younger rider continued to believe it was some sort of initiation set up.

"Are you getting down or not?" The Zaganites gripon the whip handle strengthened.

"You know how much trouble you'll be in for this?" the older rider dismounted. "You'll be dead within a day."

"We'll see," replied the Zaganite "How about you?" turning her head to the younger rider, still on her horse. The older rider held out arms ushering for her friend to dismount.

"Oh yeah, I get down and then my new friend here has a great big laugh about how she scared me la-de-da."

"I haven't got time for this," stated the Zaganite, as she sliced the humid air with a swish of her whip and wrapped it around the wrist of the younger rider, pulling her down off of her horse. The rider squealed in pain as she landed with a thud on her back.

"Oowww!" screamed the woman.

Her friend ran over to make sure she was okay. "Are you hurt?!"

The fallen rider sat up and felt her sides. "Yes, I think I'm okay. Oh no! My ring is broken," she said, staring at her hand. "You broke my ring! That wasn't cheap, you know. My father gave it to me before I left home! Now the orange stone is all smashed!"

"You'll get over it. Now, run along before I think it'd be better to keep you silent... forever," threatened the Zaganite. The pair scrambled to their feet. "You'll pay for this. You won't survive the night! Master Thornfalcon will get you!" Their shouts fading as they ran away, holding up their dresses.

Gene, Saffina, and Joel emerged from the bushes.

"Impressive, I didn't even have to step in and use my Aura," said Gene. The Zaganite lowered her snood and looked at Saffina with disbelief at Gene's sense of self-importance. Saffina shrugged, not knowing what had gotten into her brother.

The Zaganite pointed at Joel. "I'll ride with hop-along, you two take the other horse," ordered the Zaganite.

Saffina straddled her horse. "Good to see you, old friend," she said as she leant forward, stroking its neck.

"No time for sentiment. We have to get going, the guards will be onto us quicker now," Gene said as he jumped on behind Saffina.

The group were soon on their way again, making strides into the forest. The old trail soon opened up to a wider road. A number of paths and forks split off along their route, but the Zaganite did not hesitate at each junction. She knew where they were headed.

It wasn't long before she brought the group to a stop. An unmoving river of blackened silver lay in front of them. Amongst the silver ripples, mounds of rock gave the illusion that they were folding in on themselves, like custard being poured over a cold dessert into a bowl. The silent river stretched across the wide beach to their left. To their right, Mount Indigo stretched high into the afternoon sky. Trenches of the same dark silver rock scraped down the mountainside, like a big cat's claws on human flesh.

The three children gazed at the unique landscape before them.

"Where are we?" asked Joel.

"This was the entrance to the old mines," said the Zaganite, pointing towards the base of Mount Indigo to her right. Fallen boulders had covered much of the entrance. "This is where the Red River flowed, on the Day of Darkness."

A sombre silence befell the group as they stood in silence in remembrance and respect to the hundreds who lost their lives that day.

"THERE!" a loud hoarse sounding voice pierced the silence, barking down from a ledge situated high above the group.

"Oh no, not them again!" exclaimed Joel, recognising the soldiers as the same who first captured them.

"Listen, it won't take them long to get down here. This is where we go our separate ways," said the female Zaganite.

"Great! As soon as we're in trouble you abandon us!" accused Gene.

"This was always the plan! I have freed you, don't be so ungrateful. There's no time to argue. You three need to head for the mine entrance. I'm pretty sure you'll be able to get to Liana that way," the Zaganite sensed the confusion amongst the three children. "Just trust me, okay. I think I've earned that from you. I can't say for sure, but I think you can get to the temple from here."

"You think? You broke us out on a guess?!" panicked Saffina. "Where are you going to go?"

"I'm going to ride as fast as I can to Swyre and warn Queen Adriya of Zagan's plans. He knows where Liana is and how to get to her. I have to warn the Queen."

"But she's safe. Only Visendi can enter the Shrouded

Temple," stated Gene.

"Some old Hooded Man has been helping Zagan. He has a Red Aura. Zagan doesn't want Liana, he wants Coryàtès, but this Hooded Man wants Liana. They're helping each other get each other's desires," replied the Zaganite.

"What does this Hooded Man want with Liana?" asked Saffina.

"I don't know, but it can't be good. All I know is if Zagan has Liana as bait and draws out the Swyre army, he's ready for them. He doesn't tell me much, but I know he's been building a secret fortress for years. That's why I have to warn the Queen's Table," the Zaganite sounded determined in her cause.

"Dressed like that? You won't even get to Castle Langton's gates. They're all on edge about anyone in White Robes," said Gene.

"Don't worry about me, I've got that covered. Joel, do you mind if I borrow your horse?"

"You really think I'm gonna say 'No' to you?" the Zagnite smiled at Joel's response.

"Saffina, tie your horse up behind that cluster of trees and bushes. Give him some of these berries to keep him quiet. I'll come back for him when I can." She handed some large purple fruits to Saffina. "You three had better get moving, you'll only be able to fit through the gap in those boulders at the mine entrance one at a time." The Zaganite turned her horse and headed to the beach.

"Wait!" shouted Saffina. "We don't even know your name."

The Zaganite pulled up her horse and briefly turned back to face the trio. She lowered her hood and peeled away the white mask. A long, shallow, diagonal scar embellished her face. Along the edges of the scar the skin was warped, healed from a burn. The scar reminded Saffina of the trenches they had been put to work in.

"My name is Amara. Former General in the Langton Army... and Queen Adriya's sister," said the white-robed woman. Before Saffina and Joel could speak, Amara had spun her horse back around and bounded for the shoreline.

"Nobody important then!" shrugged Joel, sarcastically. "Amara the only one who's got more questions than answers?" he joked, starting to find his jovial side once more with a rather poor pun.

"Nope, but we haven't got time to ask them, and nobody to ask them to. We gotta get going, especially with you slowing us down." replied a serious Saffina.

"Hey! Not fair!" Joel replied, as the trio headed for the boulders covering the old mining entrance.

"There's plenty of room at the top, but I don't think Joel can climb up there. The rocks all look loose too. We're better off squeezing through this gap," Gene, being the eldest, took control of the situation. "You go first Joel, then you Sis."

Saffina and Joel were in no hurry to argue. They squeezed their way into the darkness one after another. Just as Saffina got through, she heard the hoarse shouting of the lead Zaganite shouting at her brother.

"Eugene! Hurry! Quick, Eugene!" pleaded Saffina through the gap.

"I'm coming!" he shouted back, but just as his head poked through into the hole, his body jolted backwards.

Saffina peaked through the opening to see a whip wrapped around both his ankles as he was being dragged away. Eugene used his Red Aura to act as a barrier from the ground to prevent him being torn to shreds as his body was carried along the ground.

"We have to go back! We have to rescue him! Zagan's going to kill him!" Saffina poured floods of tears as she threw herself into Joel's arms.

"You know we can't do that, Saff, it'd be a suicide mission. We have to hope that Zagan has enough respect for Yasmin to not hurt him. She would never forgive her father if he killed Eugene."

"I really hope you're right, Joel," sobbed Saffina.

"The sooner we find Liana, the sooner we can help him. Come on, let's follow these tunnels."

19

TOMB OF THE TRANSCENDED

"Liana, wake up." said Master H, leaning against the bedroom doorway with his arms crossed.

She rubbed her eyes open. "What time is it?"

"Sunrise," replied Master H. *'The usual glint in his eyes seemed to be missing this morning'*, thought Liana. "You are a quick learner. Estrella has been speaking very highly of how you are learning our ways. Get dressed, I want to show you something," said the Old Priest turning away. "I'll wait for you in the meditation room."

She reached over to the rustic dresser by the side of her bed and picked up her neatly folded clothes that Estrella insisted on cleaning and laying out every day for the three weeks she'd been in the temple. Liana quickly changed into her black top and clay-coloured trousers, brushed her blue bed-head hair and made the short walk to the meditation room.

Master H was crouched at the edge of the room, holding the far corner of the rug that covered most of the room's floor.

Estrella crouched on the same edge, gripping the rug in the middle. "Help us roll this up," instructed Estrella.

Liana bent down and took the corner closest to her. The three pairs of hands rolled up the rug and uncovered a large hatch in the ground.

"So, this is what creaks every time I walk over it," said Liana as it took both of them to prise it open.

She gazed into the hole to see a staircase spiral down and quickly dim out of sight. "I can trust you, right?" Liana asked, nervously.

"Come, child. There's something I need to show you. Estrella and the residents will cover the passage up behind us."

Liana and the Old Priest descended into the darkness below the Temple of Shrouded Roots, the tapping of the Old Priest's staff creating an echoing metronome around the cave. The stone stairs widened after the first flight of steps onto a small landing. There were no banisters to prevent a potentially long and deathly fall.

She looked around and could see the stairs descend around the edges of the squarish, vertical cavern. She cautiously peered over the ledge. A form of shimmering blue light emitted from the depths that was just strong enough to reach up and show them the path ahead.

"Looks like even more parts of the staircase have fallen away," observed Master H.

"Sounds like you've not been down here in a while," said Liana.

"I first came down here in the last few days before my father passed. Despite knowing it would soon be his time to retire to the earth, he gathered his strength to show me this place. It is one the most important places in history, yet only the Priest of the Shrouded Temple ever knows of it."

Liana's mind raced. *'What could be down here?' Am I really that special that I need to know of a place only a select few in Visendi history have known about?'* she thought to herself. "Your father, he was the Priest here before you?"

"Indeed. He taught me everything he knew about Aurora and the history of the Visendi and witnessed the dramatic fall in our numbers. He was too young himself to remember the events that led to our outlawing, but he passed down to me the stories that his father had told him. None of us have really known why this place down here really exists but we have been instructed to watch over it, so that's what we do." Master H abruptly stopped talking as a small cluster of stones fell away from under his feet. He held out an arm to halt Liana and they paused for a few moments. "Come, tread carefully, but be ready to jump."

Not sooner than he had finished his sentence, the ground trembled beneath them, and large chunks of steps started to fall away in front of them. The first few breaches were small and easy to leap across as the newly formed student and teacher partnership picked up their speed, but as more and more of the staircase began to fall away, the gaps grew larger and larger.

"I can't make that next one!" shouted Liana to Master H, who despite his age was a good 10 paces ahead of her.

"Jump on my back!" he shouted back and slowed to allow Liana to catch up. Liana didn't hesitate in following his instructions and leapt onto the Old Priest.

"How are we going to make that jump!? That gap must be 3 horse lengths long!" screamed Liana.

Master H didn't reply. As they ran towards the ledge they

leapt into the air. Liana closed her eyes as they jumped, but her curiosity made her open one of them again as they began to fall. She watched as Master H called upon his Red Aura. Its glow surrounded them. Staff in hand, he planted it onto the seemingly solid Red Aura and used the long weapon to vault over to the next set of intact steps.

"That was amazing!" exclaimed Liana. "Your Aura, it was as strong as the ground itself."

"When you forge a sword, you don't just heat a bit of metal and cool it, or it will become brittle and shatter in battle. You must repeat the process, to manipulate the stresses and weak spots in the blade. Developing your Aura is no different. Your friend's Aura's will be brittle and break under pressure before long, unless they develop them in the right way," Master H threw his staff to Liana. "You try."

"But I don't have a Red Aura," said Liana.

"Doesn't matter. Try the vaulting technique. Try it on the next jump," Master H pointed down the stairwell.

Liana hesitated. She was nervous. Without an Aura she had no protection. Last time she was forced to jump by someone she ended up having to cut half her hair off.

"What have I told you about hesitating?" the Old Priest said with frustration. "Be sure in your actions. You must start trusting me and trusting yourself if you are to save the world, young one."

Master H then reached into his belt and pulled out a small tube, before flicking either end like a seesaw where it unfolded from within itself to create another staff. With a small run, he planted the bottom end into the ground once more and again performed the vault with ease.

"If it makes you feel better, I shall wait up here and catch you before you fall," The Priest, with folded arms, stood poised perfectly balanced halfway up his slanted staff. His lower foot on top of the rod pressing down, his upper foot underneath pushing up. Only his staff was touching the stone beneath him.

"How are you doing that? You should be falling over! Are you using some sort of invisible Aura?" Liana called from across the gap.

"There are no Aura's in use on this technique! Just harmony and balance. Now, come!" He waved his hand towards himself, encouraging Liana to follow.

She backed up a few paces before sprinting full speed. She planted the long staff, just as the Priest had, and pushed down to propel herself into the air. As she reached the pinnacle of her trajectory, she sensed she was falling short of her target. She desperately reached out towards the Priest who caught her, locking forearms, before pulling her onto solid ground.

"Not bad for a first attempt. But you lost focus, based on your perception of the distance. Had you not reached out for me and put yourself off balance, you would have made it. Just, but just is good enough."

"Is this really the right time to be tutoring me?" said Liana, catching her breath.

"That is the best time! We deliver our best results when under the pressure of life or death. Perhaps if I wasn't here, you would have made the jump, but instead you saw me and relied on me. Next time I shall not be so lenient. Let's go, nearly at the bottom now," Master H whisked away leaving Liana behind to try and catch up again.

She jumped the last gap. Master H's silhouette stood in the glow of a roughly dug out circular doorway before it slowly faded into the light. Liana cautiously followed.

She passed through the doorway that was situated on one

wall of an octagonal room. The ceilings, walls and floor were made with a smooth, glassy ice-like material. Glowing sparks in the colours of the six Aura's danced and flicked around within them, just like the contents of Liana's Spirit Orb.

Human sized alcoves were carved into six other walls. The wall directly opposite the entrance had largely fallen away creating a tunnel. A broken altar lay in the middle of the room, which Liana began to circle as she took in her surroundings.

"I know this room. This is the room from my dream," recalled Liana.

"Mmm." nodded Master H. "I could not ignore the description of your dream when we first met but I wanted to see your character first, your morality, before showing you this place."

"So, what is this place?" Liana jumped up into one of the recesses. "Actually, let me guess, these alcoves had statues in, that watched over the altar whilst sacrifice was made to Aurora?" she stiffened her body and posed as if holding a weapon.

"Not quite, child. This is, or was," Master H said, correcting himself. "The Tomb of the Transcended."

"Wait, I'm standing in someone's grave? Eugh!" Liana jumped down and dusted herself off frantically.

Master H chuckled. "They haven't been here for 13 years. Gone, after the Day of Darkness. I can only assume the lava got in here and melted away their bodies." Master H pointed to the hole in the wall. His light-hearted demeanour changed to a solemn one as he bowed his head. "I've felt like a failure ever since. My father entrusted me to keep them safe, and his father before him. I tried to protect them, but I was powerless. The heat was too overwhelming, even for my Aura's."

Master H sat down on the crumbled altar. Liana perched

beside him, laying a sympathetic hand on his knee. She appreciated his emotional openness.

"What did they look like?" Liana asked, softly.

"I couldn't tell you. Their resting places were covered with the same material you see around you right now. All I could make out were the outlines of their figures and the objects they held."

"Objects? Like the Artifacts described in my dream?"

"Yes. They were also blurry behind the icy stone, but some shapes were easy to make out. Like the Artifact that contained your Spirit Orb. It is called The Dagger of Red. One artifact for each colour of the Transcended."

"My Spirit Orb? You think my Orb was in this tomb?"

"It takes a powerful Visendi to create a Spirit Orb. I couldn't do it; I know that for sure. I doubt there's anyone alive who could make one now, so it seems the only logical explanation, especially since you were found with it not far from here."

"I cannot wait any longer. Tell me, what is the difference between an Aura Orb and a Spirit Orb?" Liana pulled out her glowing red sphere from her pocket.

"A Spirit Orb is the forging of a powerful fusion between an Aura and Morality. The process of removing one's Aura is called Peeling. Once a Spirit Orb is created, it can then be utilised to enhance the power and performance of a person or object. Unlike Aura's, you do not earn Morality, you are born with it. There seems to be no explanation as to how or why, but we are born with either a Bad or Good Morality. Those who have Bad Morality are naturally poor spirited. Most of us though are born with Good Morality, with good intentions for life. The strength of each can be dialled up or down, depending on various things that happen in a life, like how tough a childhood was or the loyalty of friends," explained the Old Priest.

"You mean, the Black and White glows, like what I saw with Agatha, Nalan and Estrella?"

"Yes. It's rare to have the gift of Sight though. Most people can get a sense of someone's Morality. The sixth sense it's often referred to as, but few can cross into the Morality realm. An Aura can be seen by anyone when it is called upon by its host, but not Morality. In fact, the legends I have been told state that only the Transcended had the gift to see others Morality. You are indeed a special child, Liana. If I could help you master the skill I would, but I wouldn't know where to begin."

"So, what does this all mean?" Liana asked, but she had begun to put all the pieces in her head already and was uneasy at its conclusion.

"I can see you've probably worked that out for yourself. I don't think it will surprise you when I say I believe it means that before the Day of Darkness, you were also entombed here. Right here." Master H patted the structure they were sat upon. "I no longer think this was an altar, my dear. I think this was your casket and that you weren't born 13 years ago... but closer to 213 years ago."

Liana sat, stunned as the Priest confirmed her own mind's outrageous theory. *'Am I really a girl from another time? Why was I kept here? Who were these Transcended people in the alcoves?'*

"Before you begin your next barrage of questions, some perspective and knowledge might be helpful. Let me tell you the real story behind the falling of the Visendi."

THE AURA WARS

"It started over 300 years ago. A deadly war between the most powerful people across all the lands. The religion of the Aurora Visendus was at its heights. Almost everyone practised its teachings, it was part of a citizen's life.

Some actively chose not to follow its ways. Many of those people believed that to follow meant giving themselves up to Aurora, making them submissive or dependent. This was of course their choice. Infrequent skirmishes broke out here and there, but this group largely kept to themselves. The ways of the Visendi taught its followers that all life was precious and important, so those who chose not to practice were not outcast or looked down upon but were simply rebuffed if they ever became violent.

In another land, far away from Coryàtès, the Visendi celebrated the annual marking of the Aurora Solstice - the day of the year when the sun rises at its earliest and sets at its latest, blessing us with its presence in the sky for many hours. Fields, beaches, streets, and temples would all be lined with people meditating, waiting for the first curvature of the sun's orange glow to peak its hairline over the horizon.

Once the full circle of the sun became visible, the meditation would break so the harvests and tulips could be tended to and uprooted, ready for the afternoon's offerings and feasts.

Throughout the day's celebrations, tournaments of various disciplines took place in each of the Inner Cores. Fighting contests included one versus one, two versus two and team matches. Other competitions were plenty, such as who could produce the largest and strongest Red Aura Screen, or whose Jackdaw could find and return a hidden object the quickest. Children would paint tulips and suns across the walls and streets.

In this particular year, several groups of non-followers had decided to escape the festivities of the Aurora Solstice in each of their towns and cities and hold their own celebration. They did not want to celebrate the rising sun, so they met the night before in a beautifully tranquil and largely sheltered rock formation on the coast. Stone columns bent high over their heads, as they relaxed in warm springs of crystal-clear blue pools. Ships from all over had anchored in the bay, as they drank and played music around campfires long into the night.

It was as the midday sun shone upon the non-followers, who were only just awaking from their long and exuberant night, that they were attacked. Visendi struck the columned structures from above causing them to collapse onto the people below. Less than a dozen rowboats of non-followers made it back to their ships. When they returned to their homelands, they were apprehended and put into chains.

The reason for detaining them was given as 'The future plotting of an attack against the religion'. They were arrested for something that had not happened yet. Why? Because a woman named Evelyn became the first Visendi since the original six to achieve the Inner Core of the Third Eye.

Thousands of witnesses watched as she attained her indigo button on the day of the Aurora Solstice after winning a nearby town's solo fighting tournament. Her new deep midnight blue Aura shone around her figure and within her eyes, before it slid off her like someone was peeling off a bedsheet from above. When Evelyn returned to her usual state, she announced that the power she had been gifted with for attaining her new Core was the ability to leave her body and see into the future.

This first outer-body experience, she says, was that she foresaw the non-followers in the nearby bay rising and taking arms against her town's Solstice celebrations. Her few simple words incited thousands to march to the bay and stop it before it had even happened.

Visendi called this power of attaining all six Inner Cores 'Transcendence' and it was the first domino in a series of events that would become known as The Aura Wars.

Although achieving the Sixth Inner Core was still too stretching for most Visendi, it didn't take long before another follower attained the feat. Soon, most large settlements now had at least one Visendi capable of Transcending. Belief in Aurora couldn't have been higher.

One year later, on the eve of the next Aurora Solstice, Evelyn gave birth to a child. This child was the first of its kind, born from parents who had both achieved Transcendence and more extraordinarily, was also born possessing the Aura's of all Six Inner Core's. This baby boy entered the world shining like a luminescent rainbow.

Many speculated at the time that this child was simply a gift bestowed upon Evelyn for her previous year's achievement but six months later another was born - it's parents again both Transcended. These descendants of the Transcended became known as the Spectra Children.

Due to the rarity of Visendi who possessed the Third Eye, it was a few more years before another Spectra child was born. By this time, Evelyn's son had started to manifest natural powers linked to each Inner Core. The strength of each Core was apparent. By the time the child turned 7, his Red Aura was particularly strong and bright.

The increasing abilities of the boy attracted a hysteria of attention from all the Transcended. They hastily started to pair up, yearning to have a child with such awesome capabilities. Three more Spectra children were born within the next year.

It was the birth of what was anticipated to be the seventh Spectra Child that was most significant. Its significance being that the child was not born with the expected glow of Aura's.

It had become apparent that only six Spectra Children could be born. As each of the first generation of Spectra Children grew older, each specialised in a different Inner Core. They were easily identifiable by the colour of their hair. By the time the son of Evelyn was a teenager, he could produce a Red Aura that was impenetrable. One day, to prove his Aura's strength, he even stood at the foot of a cliff as volunteers pushed a boulder off the cliff-edge above. The boulder, twice the size of any human, broke in half as it came into contact with the Aura.

However, the strength of the Spectra children caused jealousy amongst the ranks of the Visendi, especially those who had Transcended and had children of their own. They did not think it fair that there could only be six, for they had worked as hard as anyone else to please the God of Dawn, so they soon began plotting against the Spectra.

The plots began by excluding the Spectra and their parents from the religion. They were not allowed inside any of the foundation temples, nor were they invited to celebrate the Aurora Solstices in their towns. As quickly as they had become famous and idolized, had they become outcast and revered. Many lower ranked Visendi were anxious and afraid of their capabilities and the potential of their powers.

The Spectra and their families could easily have forced their way into the temples or the minds of the people, but they felt this would just be upholding the nervous feelings of the religion's followers. They decided to travel from town to town and use their abilities for good, to show people they should not be feared.

It was on one of these well intended good-natured missions where things went wrong for the Spectra. In this town, protests against them were vast and angry. The son of Evelyn was using his Aura Screen to protect a few of the Spectra who had travelled with him and his family from an array of projectiles being launched at them. The group were focussed on trying to calm the protestors down and show them they meant no harm, when a stray rock hit and injured a nearby child on the head. Blood poured from the wound, so Evelyn rushed over to help the child. In this moment, Evelyn left the safety of her son's Aura and began to use her own powers to try and heal the wound. Seeing that Evelyn - an infamous and recognisable Visendi - was alone and distracted, one lone man in a balcony above threw a blade down upon her. Evelyn died instantly, unable to switch between her Aura's in time to defend herself.

'I killed her! I killed the one who started all this! We can be free again! The first Transcendent is dead!' roared the man from the balcony as the crowd below let out a triumphant roar.

Evelyn's son rushed to his mother's side. She was already gone. No goodbye's, no embrace. Even being a Spectra couldn't bring someone back from the dead. He let out an almighty cry of pain and with it, his Red Aura shield inflated around him. It rose in a huge, raging dome of sparks. Buildings shook and crumbled to the ground. People were knocked off their feet, but within seconds they were disappearing into the earth, as the dome turned into a sphere collapsing the ground below. Mere minutes later, all that remained of a busy and thriving town was now a vast crater of rubble. Evelyn's son was the only person standing. Even his fellow Spectra hadn't survived.

Three more Spectra children were born - to replace those who had lost their lives. This confirmed what the Transcended had always theorised - that if one of the Spectra dies, the next child of two Transcended will take its place.

The Transcended couples who did not have Spectra children soon became engulfed in envy and schemes to get rid of the Spectra children. All for the intent they could replace them with their own. This scheming and jealousy caused their Core's to become unbalanced, and their Morality started to turn Bad. The Spectra lived in constant fear and suspicion of these people, who had become known as the Immorals. Immorals not only sought out and fought the Spectra, but each other too as they became single-mindedly determined to have a Spectra child.

As the years went by and battles between Immorals and Spectra became more frequent and intense, followers began to take sides. Those who were afraid and frightened of the Spectra joined the Immorals. This was mainly comprised of those people who were yet to attain an Inner Core or who had only attained their Red Aura or Orange Aura.

More experienced Visendi could see how the Immorals had lost their way and forgotten the teachings of Aurora. These higher ranked Visendi recognised their own failings and sided with the Spectra. They realised the Spectra were the product of hundreds of years of learning, sacrificing, and grafting. Symbols that the religion had peaked. They became known as the Spectra Allegiance.

The power of the Spectra Allegiance was great, much greater than what the Immorals possessed. However, the Immorals boasted greater numbers within their ranks.

The war touched every corner of our world. Over the next 70 years, the tide of who was on top changed hands more often than a ball in a game of catch. In that time, the lands' monarchies started to outlaw the practising of the religion due to the destruction it was causing, but by doing so, created a path so devastating that it is remarkable we are even sitting here today.

The Immorals went underground to recruit youth and young adults who had little to no knowledge of the Visendi ways. When the young recruits could see what the Immorals were capable of, they yearned for the same powers. They were told that they could also have these great powers. All they had to do was pass an initiation ceremony.

The ceremony was simple. The potential recruits would line up and kneel before one of the Immorals, who would place their hand on the recruit's chest. If a black light emitted from the recruit, they were accepted in. If a white light shone instead, they were sent away, although it did not end there for these rejects.

It was obvious to friends, family, and acquaintances that they had been altered in some way. They returned lacking emotion. No pride, no guilt, no sense of accomplishment, no remorse. As neutral, bland, and boring as anyone could ever be. The Spectra Allegiance soon heard of more and more of these groups and with great care not to be caught, investigated the situation with urgency, going undercover at a number of these initiation ceremonies. It was a few months before one member of the Spectra Allegiance found what had made these people devoid of life. This particular Spectra member had the ability of Sight and discovered that these people had been stripped of their Morality.

It became obvious in the next skirmish between the two sides that The Immorals had found a way of taking and utilising Morality to elevate their own powers. It was a landslide victory, a victory that shook the Spectra Allegiance to its core.

Seeing the devastating powers that the Immorals could now summon, the Allegiance and the monarchies agreed that a world ruled by the Immorals would be catastrophic, and so they joined forces. In an attempt to even up the battlefield, the monarchies asked if anyone would volunteer their Morality on the promise that it would be returned once the final battle had been won. This of course was not without risk, for if a Transcended died, the Moralities died with them.

To the surprise of the Spectra Allegiance, thousands upon thousands of non-followers were willing to give up their Morality, especially the older generations who had only ever known war and wanted an end to it, for themselves, their children, and their children's children's sakes. The Spectra Children mixed these Moralities and Peeled off bits of their Aura's to create as many Spirit Orbs as they could to distribute to their infantry.

The Battle of Grimstone was a harrowing event. Thunder-like sounds roared for miles as Aura's collided and colours of each Core lit up the sky in flashes of dazzling brilliance. The

Allegiance had the edge, not only with their vastly more powerful Aura's thanks to the Morality farming, but their ranks contained four out of the six Spectra Children. The numbers of the Immorals were strong, but once their two Spectra Children had been killed, the rest of the army soon toppled. A few of the Transcended Immorals escaped with a fraction of the infantry. The most notable was the father of one of the Spectra Children, but their number was so depleted, it could be called a glorious victory for the Spectra Allegiance.

Soon after victory was declared, a huge ceremony was arranged to celebrate and to break the Spirit Orbs. Only the Spectra Child who created them could break them. According to my father, my grandfather believed the Dagger of Red was the only object that could break a Spirit Orb, as the blade was said to be forged using the Red Aura of the Red Spectra Child, although this was only his theory.

The Moralities then returned to their non-Visendi host and the Aura's returned to their respective Spectra Child.

However, the allegiance with the monarchies came at a price for the Visendi. As part of the deal, the religion of Aurora Visendus became outlawed across all lands and books, scripts, temples, and statues were all burned and destroyed. Followers were forced to integrate into normal society and forbidden from practising or teaching the religion. Their Aura's faded away.

The monarchies did allow for the Spectra Children to continue to search out the few Immorals that had escaped. They knew they could not risk the Immorals regrouping and since the Spectra Children were born with their Aura's and could not lose them, the monarchies allowed for them to carry out their mission in secrecy. It was assumed by the monarchies that they completed their mission and passed away in peace and solitude as instructed. Since then, the majority of people have lived without ever knowing about the real history of the Aurora Visendi.

We of course know that the Spectra Children have been entombed here for the past 200 years, but there are no records to explain why or how they came to be here."

21

HOMECOMING

Amara pulled on the reins to slow her horse, kicking up a dust cloud of sand as she did. She dismounted then slapped the thigh of the horse to send it on its way back across the expansive sands that lay below Castle Langton. The salty, crisp sea air picked up its pace as she watched the horse bound out of sight against the impending sky of dark clouds that were framed by orange streaks of light of an approaching tropical storm.

She turned and strode towards the pillars of rock that concealed the hidden entrance into the Castle's sewer system. A forceful shoulder barge was required to release the bricked doorway from its moss-laden edges. As it swung open, a collection of dirt, moss and spiders fell onto her head. *'This hasn't been moved in years. Maybe I was the last person to open it.'* thought Amara as she dusted the debris off her hair and shoulders.

As Amara made her way towards the underground flowing river of stench, she cast her mind back to the last time she was there - sneaking and spying on her uncle as he ventured out towards Mount Indigo's burning embers. *'And there she was. The impossible sight of an innocent babe laying upon an unmelting rock in a river of red destruction. I've always known Liana was special. Are we soon to see just how special she is?'* She made her way around the twisting tunnel and neared the slope that led up to the Castle's courtyard.

She lowered herself to a crouch and flattened herself against the slope's wall before poking her head above the parapet to observe what activity was happening in the courtyard. To her relief, the castle grounds were quiet. A few maids moved water jugs between outbuildings and a group of four guards stood talking near the gate entrance. The approaching storm had worked in her favour. A tropical storm was easy to recognise to the citizens of Swyre and signalled a night of torrential rain and howling winds. *'The procedures of the Castle's operations have not changed. Only the essential lookouts will be outside this evening, high up in the lookout towers closest to the forest edge. No threats of opposing ships could approach from chopping sea. Fewer guards for me to worry about.'* studied Amara. *'And with a tropical storm brings a darkened night. The moons will not be shining. I shall wait an hour more before moving under the cover of darkness. The Queen's Table will surely meet in the morning to discuss what damage the storm has caused. They always do. I shall wait there for my sister. Atop the Tower of Seeds - the perfect spot to avoid being thrown out before I have had my words heard.'*

Amara waited out the hour. One watchman per tower now manned the four lookouts on the edges of the courtyard, just as she had anticipated. She crooked her neck upwards. Above, the stars and moon were not to be seen due to the layers of churning, ominous clouds rolling in from the sea behind the castle.

Under the cover of darkness, she slipped silently up the slope. Keeping close to the sandstone walls and staying in her low crouch, sleek like a prowling cat, she got to a row of stable doors, 10 entrances long. Thankfully due to the storm, both the upper and lower sections were shut tight on all the stables, so there was no risk of disturbing the horses and giving away her position. Nevertheless, she proceeded with caution and alertness.

As she passed the first door she could hear the unsettledness of the horses, anxious because of the storm. The wind was beginning to growl and whistle louder through every nook and cranny. A soft moisture in the air caressed Amara's cheeks, like the subtle touch of a caring thumb rubbing away a teardrop. The air became still and sticky.

Amara neared the fifth door, being sure to regularly check the watchtowers. The lookouts still only focussed on the affairs outside of the courtyard walls. As she advanced, the soft moisture turned to harsh rain. The night's downpour began to fall with a ferocious velocity. Puddles immediately formed. Water sloshed off the Castle's slanted roofs.

The lashing of water was quickly followed by a boom of thunder. The boom of thunder was quickly followed by a twisted fork of lighting that struck the apex of the Tower of Seeds and a stream of consecutive shattering erupted as the spiralling Quartaltium windows exploded. The broken shards of glass glistened from the Castle's lights as they fell. All four occupants of the watchtowers instinctively ducked at the frightening sound combination of breaking glass and thunder.

A gust of wind forced open the upper door to one of the stables. Amara quickly realised the guards would soon be standing to attention and look her way, towards the Tower of Seeds. With a swift hurdle, she hopped in through the opened stable door. The two horses that called this stable home both let out a loud neigh as she intruded into their space, but being the experienced handler she was, she quickly settled them. She peaked her eyes above the lower half of the stable door and saw the guards shrugging to one another whilst looking at the tower as if to say, *'nothing we can do about that'* and they quickly returned to keeping watch for anything outside of the castle's walls.

Amara hopped back into the courtyard and stealthily made her way towards the triangular structure of the Triunity Hall that joined the Tower. Still in her crouched position, she made her way to the top of one of the slopes that rose along the other two sides of the structure. She tried her chance at the auditorium doors being open but, as she expected they would be, they were locked.

'The flag poles are my best chance. The lightning breaking the windows did me a favour...' she thought to herself as she plotted her route into the tower. The route almost invited itself. Three horizontal flag poles protruded from the wall in front of her like a staircase, leading into the openings where blue glass was resetting not 5 minutes earlier.

'I may only just make the gap between the poles.' She suddenly felt the weight of her robes. The once white, now muddied, clothing was saturated from the downpour. *'Damnit! I could have ditched this in the sewer.'* She chastised herself for not thinking ahead. *'I can't afford to take it off here and leave it to be found... but can I make the jump with it on?'*

Amara pondered her predicament. She decided to keep her robes on. She could not risk the whole castle being on alert, but her approach would have to be different.

Having made her decision, she checked the guards in the watchtowers were still looking away before climbing onto the slope's ledge. Jumping from her crouched position, she reached out and grabbed the first flagpole. *'If I can't jump across them, I will have to swing between them.'* She swayed back and forth as she swung from the pole - like a child building momentum on a swing. She felt the wetness on the pole, slippery and difficult to grip. As she arched her body back and forth, her speed rose enough for her to make the second jump.

Success. *'Two more jumps to go. Same again, Amara. Same again.'*

She used the same technique. Once she felt she had built up the same pace she made the leap. Her distance was good, as her hands wrapped around the third pole, but the grip of her left hand immediately came away due to the lubrication caused by the weather. Amara's heart leapt. The drop below was the height of a two-storey house, if not more. She instinctively tightened her one-handed hold. Her whole-body weight and saturated clothes supported by just the strength of her right arm. She flung her left arm upwards and recovered. *'That was close...! One more jump. Got to make it to the window ledge.'*

She began to swing again. She neared peak momentum and let go and heard a metallic crack as she released. The pole came away from the wall and hurtled to the ground. Her body hit the ledge and she clasped her arms tightly around the bricks which bore thousands of tiny shards of broken Quartaltium. Amara pulled herself into the spiralling staircase before the clanging sound of the fallen flagpole alerted the watchtowers. She hugged her abdomen, winded from the final jump. Fortunately, her inability to foresee the issue with her sodden robe, coupled with her decision to keep it on for the jumps, meant the shards of glass did not pierce her skin.

She continued to keep her figure low to the ground as she climbed the staircase. She forced open the door to the Queen's

Table, breaking off the top hinge as she did, before taking a seat at the far side of the room. She rested her arms and head on the triangular table. After an eventful day and night, she decided she had best recover some energy and drifted off into a light sleep.

T he panting of an out of breath messenger boy echoed around the long corridors of Castle Langton. He ran into the dining hall where an early morning breakfast was being served following the stormy night. "Your majesty," he said, bowing his head and stretching out his arm. "A message. For your eyes only."

Queen Adriya reached out and took the note. Inside it read:

'Your Majesty,

I have information that your life is in danger. A traitor within your own Queen's Table. Trust no one. Tell no one of this letter. Meet me at the entrance to the old mines at noon today.

Eugene.'

"What is it, Your Majesty?" asked Clerk Vivek, seated to the Queen's right as she headed up the table.

"Just a note from my Uncle with an initial list of damages from the night."

"Why is it for your eyes only? I should read it, I may need to advise on the repair work."

"The only repair work I need you to advise on are the window repairs to the Tower of Seeds. Do not trouble yourself with this extensive list."

Clerk Vivek rose from his chair and bowed. "As you wish. I will take my leave and start dealing with the matter at once." The Queen watched as he exited the grand dining hall. Arching wooden beams supported the high-rising stone. Floor-to-ceiling portraits of the Langton monarchy adorned one wall, whilst the grandest of fireplaces lit up the room on the other. Above the fireplace hung a scene of the Queen and Liana, painted only the previous year, enjoying a picnic on the beach below the castle. Liana's vibrant blue hair the focal point as it shone out from the beige paleness of the sand.

'Eugene... I have not heard from him since they left for the temple. He must not be with Liana if he has sent this. Maybe he has information on her too. Her lack of communication is troubling me. This letter only adds to my worries. But a traitor within the Queen's Table? I am not that poor a judge of character, am I? Nonetheless I must hear what he has to say... but why not return and tell me himself? So many questions... always questions...'

Amara stirred as she heard the sound of two soft female voices approaching. She readied her concealed whip as a precaution.

"I didn't realise how cold it would get as we climbed."

"Yes! Having windows certainly makes a difference."

"I don't think they'll be fixed any time soon. Good luck to Vivek having to organize the repair."

"Indeed, but I guess that's the price you pay for having an intelligent mind."

"There's an awful lot of glass on the stairs."

"We'll need a whole team to sweep this mess up once the usual morning duties have been attended to. I'm sure the Queen will understand if the stairs aren't swept before her meeting. So long as the room is clear."

"Aren't we usually blessed with sunlight the morning after such a storm?"

"Hmm, it is strange that the rain is still falling hard. At least the thunder and lightning have stopped."

"That is one thing, but the grey clouds suggest it may not be for long."

"I'm surprised her highness still wants to carry out the meeting in the Queen's Table."

"It is not our position to question. She has always said she makes her best decisions in this room."

There was a moment's pause in the conversation.

"Strange, this door is always locked."

"Looks like the hinge is broken. Must have been the lightning."

"Yes, I expect so. At least I don't need to put these sheets down to unlock it."

Amara watched cautiously as the door opened via the pushing of a woman's plump rear end. Once the maid had edged the door open just enough for her wide frame, she turned around and immediately froze in shock.

"Everything ok, Ma'am?" said the second softly toned voice behind her.

"Yes, my dear," the woman replied after clearing her throat. The sight of Amara had twisted her tongue into a knot of anxiety. "It seems the room's not as bad as we thought it might be. Hand me that mop and bucket, I can manage this myself. There's plenty else you can be getting on with. Go and see the head housemaid, I left her to delegate the daily tasks." masking her nerves well as she spoke.

"Yes, Ma'am," Amara listened as footsteps faded away back down the tower, before the woman in the doorway turned sharply back in her direction. "Amara! What are you doing here?! I thought you were dead! Are you here for revenge? You haven't half picked your timing. I should inform Sir Tarak right away!" She headed towards the tubular communication system, lifting the cap for the tube labelled 'Military quarters.

Amara rose out her seat and intercepted, placing her hand on the flap and lowering it. "Agatha, I am no threat to you, my sister, the castle, or the city."

Agatha looked into Amara's eyes and could see only the truth in her words.

"I have risked my life coming here but I must speak with my sister."

"What could possibly be so important to you that you would return and risk your life?" Despite Agatha's gentle voice, she had the skill to also make it sound assertive. A useful trait Agatha knew many admired and even tried to replicate, but rarely succeeded. Even Vivek had told Agatha how her gentle assertiveness gave her a respect that few housekeepers could ever wish for.

"Swyre is in immense danger. Enough danger to threaten my sister's crown."

"From who? There is no chance of an attack from beyond these shores in this storm. The only threat is from these White Robes." Agatha took a step backwards, out of arm's reach, suddenly realising what Amara was wearing. She had seen many a dirtied cloth in her time, the mud did not fool her. "Robes like yours…"

Amara took a pleading step towards Agatha and placed her hands on each shoulder, as an act of reassurance.

"I promise, I am no threat to you. I am now a traitor to those who wear the White Robes. I cannot bear to see any harm come to Liana."

"Liana?! What do you know of her? Have you any news of her?! Is she in trouble?! We've all been worried sick! Almost three weeks since she left to find that damned temple and her friends."

"Her friends were in our custody. I helped them escape."

"Oh, that's so good to hear! Are they ok?"

"The boy broke his ankle but is healing. Together they are survivors, I can sense that."

"Oh, poor Joel! But why do you care about Liana? You were banished before she had even turned one year old."

"So even you don't know..."

"Know what? The fact that you abandoned the city and your post in our darkest time? Soldiers and volunteers were depending on your leadership and help."

"I didn't abandon the city. It's true, that afternoon I was not at my post. I instead followed my uncle, Sir Tarak. He slipped away on a one-man mission to the old mines. This is where I saw the miracle. A babe, on an unmelted rock, in the middle of a ferociously hot red river. Sir Tarak removed the babe from the rock and as he did, it melted, as if the babe was keeping the rock afloat. That child was Liana. I knew straight away she was special - but when I returned - my absence had already been reported. My sister, Uncle Tarak and I fought for hours. They focussed on my lack of ability to follow orders and how it meant I could not be trusted. I demanded to know about the child and how they knew she would be there. They would not tell me anything and continued to conceal the truth from me. They decided I could not be trusted with such a secret, so they banished me to the desert that night and instructed me never to return, in the knowledge that few people, if any, have survived the harshness of this island's dunes. The Triunity sentencing in my absence was just a formality. I had already been sent away." Amara bowed her head and fell into a chair as she remembered her past. Agatha could say nothing as she processed Amara's words and the out-of-character actions of the Queen.

"This doesn't sound like Queen Adriya. She has always been a fair and just leader," said Agatha after a few minutes of silence.

"You can choose what you want to believe, but the truth remains, and I know the truth. She had to be surrounded by people she could trust. She determined I was not one of them. Although this is not her only misjudgement when it comes to those close to her."

"What do you mean by that?" frowned Agatha.

Before Amara had time to answer, the crooked door, hanging off its one hinge, was pushed aside again.

"This door must be cursed. Seems like we're always..." but before the voice had time to finish, the figure in the doorway froze in the same manner Agatha had done.

"YOU!" Queen Adriya boomed. "TARAK, APPREHEND HER!" The Queen very rarely shouts, but when she does, it's fierce and penetrates straight into the chest of the recipient.

Sir Tarak hastily ran into the room, but he did not freeze in shock. Instead, the contours of his face contorted into clusters of angry wrinkles as his thick brows turned sharply downwards and his eyes glared intently. "You just can't follow orders can you," growled the Knight and he strode towards Amara.

Amara knew her homecoming would be hostile, but she had underestimated the number of raw emotions that remained even after all these years away. She had to get their attention quickly to prevent her being manhandled.

"Liana!" Amara blurted.

Sir Tarak halted, not much further than an arm's length away. "How do you know that name?" he demanded.

"She's the babe I saw you picking up at the old mines on the Day of Darkness, isn't she?" Amara glared back at her uncle. "I may have been banished but I have not been hidden from the news of the land."

Queen Adriya pushed her way between Sir Tarak and the triangular table and chairs. "Have you seen her? Is she okay?" said the Queen, anger turning to frenzy in the blink of an eye.

"To my knowledge, she is okay, for the moment," answered Amara.

"What do you mean, for the moment?" asked a concerned Agatha.

"She is the subject of much attention." Amara said, turning to Agatha.

"Attention? What has she been doing to bring attention to herself?"

"It's not what she has been doing, it's who she is."

"You mean, because she's the city's heir-apparent?"

"Heir-apparent? So you had the ceremony already" Amara turned her attention back to her sister.

Queen Adriya nodded. "She is the rightful heir to the island now. Any claim you wish to make here today is void. Presuming that's why you are really here."

"I do not care for the throne, sister. That's the truth."

"So it is just coincidence you appear merely weeks after Liana has turned thirteen and eligible to be named my heir?" said the Queen suspiciously.

"I do not care for the throne," repeated Amara.

"Yet you return and risk your life?"

"I do not care." repeated Amara sternly, pausing to emphasise the next three words. "For the throne."

"Then tell us why you're here," interrupted Sir Tarak, hand resting on the hilt of his sheathed sword, always aware and prepared for any turn of events.

Amara recognised the knife-edged atmosphere still present in the room, particularly her uncle's hardness. *'His emotions are the rawest of all. I must soften the room. Make myself vulnerable so I am not deemed a threat. Then maybe they'll listen. Maybe,'* She unbuckled her belt which held her own sheathed sword and set it down on the table alongside her whip. She pulled out a chair and sat down. *'He will recognise my actions. He holds the advantage of height, manoeuvrability and weaponry,'* Her heightened military training sensed the ever so subtle softening of her uncle's hand on his hilt. Now she could speak.

"For most of these past 13 years, I have been with Zagan at the mines. He has been using me to train the strongest of those he gets sent from your sentencing to build an army."

"The White Robes," deducted Agatha.

Amara nodded shallowly, showing regret in her hindsight. "We are known within the mines as Zaganites. He justified his actions by telling me he needed more supervisors for the miners. That they had to be trained to fend off the largest case of any mass-uprisings. That you had told him production must never ease up and that the island relies on its trade so much that he must stay in control whatever the cost. But then..." Amara swallowed as she recalled the past.

The room remained silent in anticipation before Amara continued.

"But then, a few years ago, he stepped up training, reassigned miners to areas outside of the cobalt and quartz deposits and started working the remaining miners twice as hard to prevent any loss in production. I thought he was going crazy, talking to that bird..."

"Talking to a bird?" Queen Adriya shot a telepathic-like glance at Sir Tarak. "This bird, would it have been a Jackdaw, by any chance?"

"Yes! You know about it?"

"Only recently… continue, sister."

'Sister. She called me sister.'

"He was receiving instructions for sure, but for Zagan there is only one goal. He wants your throne. He wants to be King of Swyre and Coryàtès."

Queen Adriya spun with rage at the accusation of Zagan's intent and made her way to the window where she often sat to procrastinate.

Sir Tarak let out a small burst of laughter. "Even if he had trained up every convict we've sent him in the last decade he would have no hope of overrunning our forces in the city," he turned to the Queen. "You cannot believe this traitor, your majesty! Even if what she's telling us is true, she is now a traitor to Zagan!" Sir Tarak then let out a strange, machine-gun-like laugh. "Oh, the irony. Zagan does not know how you came to be banished does he?"

Amara averted her eyes and shook her head.

"He has no idea that you caused his family's deaths? All because you went off on your own on the Day of Darkness. The other General's took advantage of their disdain for you and pulled on every resource they could find in their own assigned districts for their own gain and that included taking control of your battalions. With no battalions working in the Guilds District - the district you were assigned - people died who shouldn't have, including Zagan's parents, brother, and his sister. They could have survived if they were treated for their injuries, but no horses were available to move them to the city's clinics for treatment." explained Tarak.

"And with Zagan being the only surviving Guild Leader, we had to appease him quickly. If he influenced the new leaders of the other Guilds, we would have had a revolution on our hands. We had to remove this threat, so we decided to satisfy his craving for power. That's why I offered him control of the mines and a place on the Queen's Table, where we could still control him," the Queen finished.

"Mistrust and deviousness run through her veins. She has still not told us why she is actually here. She could be here for information, to see how we are faring after the storm. She wears the White Robes!"

"You talk of mistrust and deviousness and yet you also abandoned the city to search out this child on the Day of Darkness! You have lied to the citizens all these years! They believe Liana to be the Queen's own child, not some rescued feral!" Amara slammed her fist onto the table, making Agatha jump.

"It was the order of the Queen based on the information we had! And how dare you speak of the future Queen in such a manner - Liana is no feral child!!" Sir Tarak's hold on his hilt tightened to its max.

"Be quiet - both of you," the Queen looked out over the city and composed her feelings. "Sir Tarak is right, Amara, you need to get to your point, quickly."

"Zagan knows he cannot overrun the city. He intends to draw you out to the mines. He has prepared secret defences that will prove difficult to penetrate. Once he has depleted your forces enough, he will move for Swyre."

"And how does he intend to draw us out?"

"By capturing Liana. The kidnapping at the Triunity Hall was supposed to do this, but when the Zaganites went to collect her and Nalan, she escaped. Then when they caught her friends, Saffina, and Joel, they thought this would be enough to draw you out. That Liana would have persuaded you to mount a rescue attempt. When this didn't happen, Zagan and his bird-friend had to draw Liana back out."

"Priestess Yi," said the Queen. "She's the one who suggested using a Jackdaw to guide Liana in the forest. Who else knows or has this ability with the Jackdaw's? Surrounded by traitors...!"

"Maybe, but don't judge in haste like you did with me, sister. It was Yasmin's task to bring Liana to the mines."

"Yet if I recall, the Priestess also suggested that Yasmin be used for the task of escorting Liana to her destination," the Queen lowered her voice, to a barely audible mumble. "Zagan and the Priestess... working in unison. She has never appreciated my cautious approach to the Visendi's reintegration into society."

"Yasmin did not succeed," said Amara. "Liana is not at the mines."

"But she will not let up until she has saved her friends."

"This is why I'm here; I helped her friends escape. It's important we find Liana and you don't attack Zagans forces. Until Saffina and Joel arrived at the mines as prisoners, I did not know Liana was a specific target. Witnessing how she came into the world; I could not see her used in such a way. I feel a connection with her."

"Yet ultimately she was the cause of your banishment! Why do you possess such feelings?" said the Queen inquisitively.

"She is special. She alone kept that rock afloat on the red river. I can feel she is worth risking my life for."

The Queen pondered the information she had been given. Everyone in the room knew to remain silent whilst she thought, even Amara had not forgotten that her sister should not be interrupted whilst she was in the process of making a decision.

'This is an opportunity...'

The Queen walked over to her younger sister. Amara stood up as the pair eyeballed each other.

"It remains whether she or her words are to be trusted. I do not discard them, but I must be cautious. Lock her in one of the empty maids' rooms."

Amara understood this was probably the best outcome she could have hoped for.

"I'll have a couple of soldiers placed outside her door." said Sir Tarak.

"Don't be a fool," The Queen said as she turned to her uncle. "She could overpower even your best trained warriors, you know that. It will be a good test of her trust. If she tries to break out, we will have our answer. Besides, don't you think armed guards outside a maid's quarters would look rather suspicious?"

Sir Tarak's cheeks reddened slightly at being belittled by his niece. His emotions had clouded his thinking. Something Queen Adriya always overcame quickly in such times.

"Agatha, bring my sister some maid's clothes to change into and dispose of these robes."

Agatha nodded and immediately left to carry out her orders.

"Uncle, I want you to put the Priestess under constant surveillance. Give her one of your Generals as 'personal protection', make it seem like we've had a threat to her life made... in fact, to suppress any suspicion, have a General assigned to each member of the Queen's Table and tell them this morning's meeting is cancelled. Make it appear like a generic threat to our diplomacy. Tarak, you shall be my protection."

"Yes, your majesty," said Sir Tarak, finally releasing his hand from his sword's hilt and placing his arms by his sides as he bowed.

"When that is done, meet me at the stables. You and I have other business to attend to."

FORBIDDEN ENTRY

"So, this tomb was for the Spectra Children. The Children of the Transcended? The most powerful Visendi ever? The Visendi caused so much devastation that the religion had to be outlawed." Liana outwardly digested the story she'd just heard. Master H nodded with confirmation. "And they were born with coloured hair, like I was?" Master H nodded again. "So does that mean you think I'm a Spectra Child also?"

"If you are, then somehow, you must be a seventh. The story passed down explicitly states that there could only be six Spectra Children, but it appears your birth is the reason this chamber exists. There is much mystery about your existence indeed," said Master H.

"My existence? You make my life sound like an experiment that Vivek would work on," frowned Liana.

Master H stood up from the broken casket and circled the tomb. "Maybe back then, you were the product of an experiment."

"What do you mean?" worry and confusion flashed into Liana's eyes.

"I'm only speculating of course... but maybe the Spectra Children thought they could break the cycle and found a way for a seventh child to be born. If more than six children could be born, then perhaps the Transcended could be reunited. There would be no reason for war," he paused and once again stroked his moustache as he always did when deep in thought.

"But that obviously didn't happen. Look at the way the alcoves are surrounding the casket, like they're watching over," said Liana.

"The question is, were they watching over to protect you from the world, or to protect the world from you?" Master H stopped circling and stared intently at Liana.

'Is he debating if I could be dangerous?' Liana thought to herself before jolting up. "I don't appreciate what you're insinuating!"

"We have to consider that whatever the Spectra Children were trying to achieve didn't work and their only way to avoid devastation was to create this tomb." Master H's glare continued, unfalteringly. Liana's brows frowned angrily as they entered into a staring contest. Her opponent's stare was calm and questioning, like he was trying to enter her thoughts.

It was the sound of small rocks knocking together as they fell against each other that forced the break in their gaze towards the opening in the wall at the foot of the casket. The scrabbling sound grew louder and drew nearer before out of the hole in the wall, the heads of Joel and Saffina popped out together like a pair of meerkats.

"Liana!" the pair shouted in delight.

"Saff! Joel!" Liana rushed towards her friends and planted a big, wet kiss on each of their foreheads.

"You're alive!" they all said in unison, before breaking into a spell of laughter.

"Any chance of a helping hand?" Joel asked. Liana reached down and Joel grabbed her forearm. His injury caused him to pull hard on her arm as he struggled to climb out, almost dragging her down.

"Jeez, Joel! Careful, you almost pulled me to the floor." Liana steadied herself.

"Sorry, Liana. I broke my ankle in the mines. It's still quite painful," he explained.

"He did it, Nalan broke you out!" Liana joyously exclaimed.

"Nalan?" Saffina and Joel questioned, perplexed.

"He promised me he'd break you out."

"No, not Nalan, he's still the bad guy, right?" Saffina and Joel both raised a questioning eyebrow. "We went out into the forest to search for you, after you were taken by him in the Triunity Hall, but we got captured by a troop of men. They were aggressive and dressed in White Robes. They took us to the mines. The White Robed men - they're trained by Zagan. He's been secretly building an army for years. He wants to dethrone your mother and take control of the island! He wants you as a hostage, to draw your uncle's army out and into the mines." Saffina spoke fast and frantically.

"The White Robed men, they came after me too," Liana replied. "But I hid, and they only took Nalan. I guess when they saw who you were, they took you both knowing I'd come back out to search for you." Saffina nodded in agreement. "How did you escape?"

But before Saffina and Joel had time to answer, Master H moved next to Liana and reached out a welcoming hand to Saffina, who shook it without hesitation. "I am Master Shiro

Hayashi, Priest of the Shrouded Temple of Roots. You can call me Master H."

"Pretty small temple," said Joel, looking around the tomb.

"This isn't the temple," Liana rolled her eyes. "This is the Tomb of the Transcended. We're under the temple."

"What's a... Transcended?" enquired Joel.

"It's a long story. I'll explain on the way back home," replied Liana.

"Home? We can't go home, we have to save Eugene, he never escaped!" exclaimed Saffina.

"It'll be okay, we'll get home and tell my mother about Zagan's plans and the Swyre army will come and take control of the mines and save him," said Liana, in a very matter-of-fact tone.

"They could have killed him by then! Zagan hates him!" Saffina raised her voice to Liana. "If we don't rescue him straight away, he'll be the victim of our escape! Zagan will want to take it out on someone, and Eugene will be the one in the firing line," Saffina squared up to Liana.

"How am I meant to do that? He has more chances of escaping than I do of freeing him. I thought by coming here I would gain the same powers as he has. Hell, I thought by coming here I'd get better powers since I'm supposed to be *so* special. But guess what - I haven't," Liana straightened herself and eyeballed Saffina.

"You could at least try. You're not even considering helping him. You're just doubting yourself like you always do," Saffina screamed back.

"Oh, look at you! Few weeks away from mummy and now you're Little Miss Brave and independent," Liana didn't blink or hesitate in her response.

"He's my brother!"

"Who was taking me to be imprisoned!"

"He didn't know that!"

"I wouldn't bet on it! Yasmin's like a sister to him. She probably told him everything."

"Never! You take that back!"

"ENOUGH!" a thunderous loud voice echoed around the tomb. Master H slammed down his staff with such force that the already fractured casket completely broke apart. A short silence followed as the three friends looked toward their elder, held in suspense, expecting a chastising speech. Instead, he put his finger to his lips and whispered - "Listen."

Liana, Saffina, and Joel all strained to listen.

"I don't hear anything," said Joel. Liana and Saffina shook their heads in agreement with his assessment.

"There's a disturbance in the temple. I can feel it in my Aura. There are people here who are not meant to be. I must investigate," he turned to Liana. "Don't leave this tomb. There's a likelihood you are the target. Be it Visendi, or otherwise. I will deal with this."

"Why the concern? I thought you said I could be dangerous," replied Liana.

"Yes, you could be... but I never told you what I believed to be true. If you are the Light from the Dark, then I would not be a very good Priest if you were killed under my supervision, would I?" The corner of his mouth lifted with a cheeky and wry smile before he swiftly turned and exited through the door.

"What the... where did he go? He literally just walked through a wall!" Joel ran in the priest's direction, studying the doorway.

"Now's not the time for games Joel."

"Liana, Joel's not lying. That old man just shimmered with

a red glow and walked right through that wall." Saffina stood next to Joel.

"Oh, come on you two. There's a great big archway right there, stop pretending and let's figure things out. Stop kidding around."

"We're not kidding, there's no archway here."

"Ugh! Fine!" Liana marched over to her friends and grabbed their hands. "Come on," she pulled the three of them forward together.

"See." said Liana, throwing her arms in the air of the deep damp cavern. She gazed upwards. Master H was nowhere to be seen. Not only had he already ascended to the hatchway at the top of the staircase, but somehow organised lengths of stone to bridge the gaps left by the previously fallen steps. *'Wow, he really is fast,'* she thought to herself, before doing a full circle to check where her friends were.

She turned to see Joel and Saffina holding their noses, still beyond the archway and in the tomb, almost as if they'd just walked straight into a wall. *'They've got to be faking. They've probably practised this prank a million times,'* thought Liana. That was until Saffina lifted her hand away from her nose. Liana saw a trickle of blood flowing out of her nostrils. *'No way could she have faked that!'* and she dashed back into the tomb.

"You did it too! You went all red and walked right through that wall! I thought you said you had no powers!" Saffina winced in pain as she spoke whilst clutching her nose tightly.

"I... I don't," and then she remembered that the Shrouded Temple only let in Visendi who were worthy of Aurora. "I don't understand. The Temple only let's in Visendi. Not even all Visendi, it didn't even present itself to Eugene and Yasmin. I've not even been practising the religion, yet it's let me in. I guess this tomb is outside of the temple's boundary."

"But that means we have no way out," observed Saffina. "What are we going to do? If we go back the way we came we'll be sure to run into some of Zagan's thugs."

The three friends fell into silence once more, deep in thought to find some options. Liana was also concerned with what trouble could be occurring overhead.

A few minutes later, a Jackdaw flew in from the hole in the wall.

"The Priestess's bird," said Liana. "It guided me here, to the temple."

"The Priestess's bird?" Saffina and Joel spoke in unison once again before Saffina continued. "Are you sure this is the same bird... it's just... we've seen a Jackdaw communicating with Zagan."

"Communicating with Zagan?" a concerned look fell over Liana. "The Priestess, she took Yasmin in and showed her how to earn her Aura overnight. She's the one who suggested Yasmin escort me here... and when the Jackdaw stopped, Yasmin told us to walk Northeast."

"Northeast? We've just come from the Northeast... that would have taken you straight into the mines!" said Joel.

"That can only mean... Zagan and the Priestess must be working together. And if the Priestess has been helping Zagan... She could have taught them the powers of the Visendi! Did either of you see any of his troops produce Aura's whilst you were at the mines?"

Saffina and Joel shook their heads.

"Good, but just because you didn't see it doesn't mean they didn't have them."

"Oh no," Saffina swivelled to face Joel. "Amara. She's going to warn the Queen about Zagan! But if the Priestess is working on the inside, she'll do whatever she can to convince the Queen *not* to send the Swyre army to the mines to look for my brother!"

"Who's Amara?!" asked Liana.

"She's..." Saffina hesitated as she prepared for the breaking news. "She's your aunt."

"My aunt?! I don't have an aunt!"

"Hey, we were as surprised as you are. We literally know nothing else about her, except for the fact she was a Zaganite."

"Zaganite?"

"That's what Zagan's White Robes are called. Sounds like she wasn't on the best of terms with your mother... but she was desperate to protect you. She wasn't that confident of convincing the Queen either though, now she has less of a chance with Priestess Yi against her too."

The Jackdaw flew onto the shoulder of Liana.

"The bird's kinda creepy.." Joel said. The Jackdaw tilted its head sideways, as if it understood his words, before flying back out of the Tomb. "I've got a bad feeling about this."

Liana agreed. "If the bird knows I'm here, I'm not so sure staying here is a good idea. We should get out of here, before it alerts Priestess Yi."

"Or worse, Zagan," said Joel. "But how are we going to get out? For all we know, Zaganites are camped outside the cave entrance, and it's also where the bird went... which can't be good."

"We also don't know what caused the old man to rush off. Which is the lesser of two evils?" said Saffina.

'And you can't follow me up to the Shrouded Temple...' Liana thought. *'But I don't have an Aura, yet I was let in... because of the Orb! I wonder if we can use it!'*

"Guys, I have an idea," she pulled out the glowing orb once more. "This sphere contains my Red Aura, at least I think

it does. I think that's why I can get into the Shrouded Temple."
The flickering lights swam inside as intensely as Liana had
ever seen. "But it's trapped inside this Orb. It didn't glow for
Gene when he touched it... but he has his own Aura, you
don't! How about, I walk through the archway first, then
throw the orb back. Take it in turns?"

She didn't wait for an answer, she didn't want to debate.
She walked through the archway and bowled the orb along
the ground back into the Tomb. Joel picked it up. Liana
watched from the other side of the archway as his eyes opened
wide, staring towards her. *'The archway has revealed itself to
him!'*

Joel passed through and looked up at the tall spiralling,
decrepit staircase. Liana sensed him sigh to himself at the
thought of more climbing. He rolled the orb back and Saffina
soon joined them, ready to investigate the disturbance above.

C heeks wet with tears, Liana stared at the half scrubbed
out drawing of the triangle and pickaxe the boy had
drawn her. Saffina sat on the bench hunched and motionless.

"I've never seen a dead body before," said Saffina,
breaking the silence.

Liana raised her head, taking in the harrowing scene before
her once more. The fields of red tulips trampled, with not one
spared. Bodies of the Temple's last remaining Visendi lay scattered. Estrella's motionless body lay clutching the handle of a
broken katana by the fighting dummies. Charcoaled trees scattered the floor, the smell of their burning wood filled the
cavern. The pool of the waterfall was stained with a tint of red
blood. Thin streams of water flowed down from the restrained

lake above like spaghetti where roots had been cut or damaged.

Inside the temple, the hundreds of books, parchments, and scrolls had been ripped from their shelving. The weapons cabinet had been cleaned out. Even the fish, tadpoles, and waterskatesmen in the shrine had not been spared.

"I've found him! He's over here!" Joel shouted from the direction of the cavern's large waterfall which opened onto the rocks below. Liana and Saffina raced over, tasting the salty sprays of water as they approached.

"Master H! Are you okay?" Liana had only known the man for a short while but his candid, yet soft tone made her feel great affection for his wellbeing.

"He's been badly hurt," said Joel, withdrawing a bloody hand from the back of the Priests head.

Master H. grabbed Liana by the scruff of her top. "He has hidden anger. Jealousy. Resentment..."

"Who?!" exclaimed Liana, signalling for Saffina to use the clothes off one of the victims to bandage the head wound.

"The Hooded Man! He wants your Spirit Orb. He wants your Morality." Liana hesitated at his words. *"Wants my Morality". Just how many people will want me, for powers I don't yet know I possess,'* she pondered.

"What does he want with me and my Orb?"

"There could be many reasons, none of them good. All I know is that you mustn't let him Turn you. I don't have Sight, but sometimes feeling is enough. He is Immoral."

Liana paused again as those words resounded in her head again.

'"Mustn't let him Turn you." '

"They took the boy." Master H. spoke with an earnestness

that Liana had not yet seen. "I think they are working with him."

"Working with who? Zagan?"

The Old Priest nodded. "Working with Zagan to take what makes you special."

"What do they want with the boy?" she asked. Master H could only muster a slight shrug of his shoulders.

"Who's the Hooded Man?" Joel asked.

"I do not know exactly who he is, but he is dangerous and clearly of the Old Visendi. Corrupt Morality. In search of Liana. He was here, using the Dagger of Red to slash his way through..." he paused as he panted to catch his breath, but also to momentarily reflect on his next words. "To slash his way through my friends. Their Aura Screens were no match for the Dagger. We couldn't get close, the cavern was bombarded from outside, through the waterfall, with Aura Orbs of all colours, exploding around us, protecting the Hooded Man as he took one life after another..." Master H's words continued to get harder for him to say, stuttering as he spoke. "Liana, you must..."

"Master H?" Liana repeated herself louder. "Master H?!" The Old Priest's eyelids slowly opened and shut, eyes half-rolling back up into his skull. *'I must summon all the strength from my Visendi teachings,'* he thought, as he felt himself drifting into a slumber. *'She needs me. Without me she will fall... before she's reached even the first core. She is the only one who can challenge him... I must not let her succumb to him.'*

A green Aura faded into existence around Master H's body. The speckled, swirling glow culminated and moved to the trauma wound on top of his head. It pulsed as it worked its Visendi magic. Once the wet blood was clotted, the green light shifted position to the heart before dissipating into the Old Priest's body.

Joel eased Master H into a sitting position, leaning him against a moist rock, whilst gently removing the blooded garment from his crown. "Wow, what was that?!" Joel said, in awe.

"That was the working of the Fourth Inner Core - the Heart. The heart is the centre of many things, emotions, spirit and physical life. Using my Visendi teachings in the way of the Heart I was able to control my Aura to stem the bleed," explained Master H.

"Visendi can heal themselves?" Joel asked. The sight of this event had perked a particular interest in him.

"Not healed, no. You will see the wound is still there," Master H tipped his head forward, inviting Joel to view the blunt-force injury. "I have merely manipulated my body to hasten it's natural response," Joel simply sat beside Master H, gawped and open-mouthed. *'He has a curiosity for healing, this boy. Useful for a tough quest.'*

"That would have been useful for you in the mines!" joked Saffina. Joel glanced sideways to Saffina and smirked in acknowledgement of the quip, before feeling the residing pain that still remained in his ankle. Liana scolded them both with a look-that-could-kill. Now was not the time for jokes.

"So, Zagan and this Hooded Man have been working together for how long?" said Liana, turning the subject back to the task at hand with a swift shift of emotions from fear of losing her new friend to an energy of focus and determination. A shift that did not go unnoticed by the Old Priest.

"I suspect they have been working in unison for some time. Zagan's motive is obvious, the throne. The Hooded Man, his motive I'm uncertain of, but he has Visendi power," Master H squinted as he continued to reflect.

Thoughts and theories raced through Liana's head. *'Was this the Hooded Man who met here with Nalan? Did Nalan steal the Dagger of Red and cause this destruction?'*

"What about Priestess Yi?" asked Liana.

"What of her?" The Old Priests raised a curious eyebrow.

"She might be part of it too. Joel and Saff witnessed Jackdaw's sending messages to Zagan. The Priestess persuaded the Queen to let me depart on my journey only to have me accompanied by Yasmin... who was supposed to instead take me to her father before I fell into the Temple."

"Hmm." Master H. stroked his moustache in contemplation. "But for what motive? The religion in Swyre is open and she has the lead of it."

"Her and my mother don't exactly see eye-to-eye."

"Even so, from what I've heard of this Zagan, he is of an unpredictable and fiery nature. She would have much to risk in siding with him. Has your gift of Sight given you vision of the Priestess's morality? If she were to side with the Hooded Man, I would suspect her Morality to be Turning."

"It's random, I can't control my visions," Liana shook her head. "But..." she hesitated. "But I have been seeing a Hooded Man, lurking, watching me. I think Nalan might be involved."

"Nalan? Your captor?" Saffina asked.

"They were both here, about two weeks ago. I came out at night for some fresh water and saw them talking. I confronted Nalan, but he wouldn't tell me anything, but he knew that Zagan had the Dagger of Red and the Hooded Man wanted it."

"And you kept this from me?! Intruders in the temple and you failed to tell me!" Master H raised his voice in anger.

Liana had never heard him raise his voice before. She was surprised at its piercing, frightening tones which made her immediately feel like she'd made a mistake in concealing the information.

Before another word could be spoken, a Jackdaw came crashing through the nearby waterfall, barrel rolling onto the chest of the Old Priest, before recovering and flapping its way to Liana, hovering in front of her as it projected its message into her mind.

Once its message had been said, it quickly departed from whence it came.

"What did it say?" asked Joel.

"It was from Nalan. *'As soon as you receive this, come and meet me at the place you were first found. Nalan.'*"

"Nalan?" asked Saffina. "The man who kidnapped you and is the whole reason Joel and I got into this mess?"

"Yes," said Liana, "And, it's complicated."

"Complicated? How is being a criminal and a kidnapper, complicated?" Joel said, with annoyance in his voice.

"Look, he's not that bad. I saw him here in the temple, sent him to rescue you."

"Well he did a good job of that…" Saffina said, raising an eyebrow.

"I trust him, ok. He's not a bad man, not really. He's been manipulated," Liana folded her arms, stubbornly. "We should go."

Joel also raised an eyebrow, before saying: "And the place where you were first found is…"

"The entrance to the old mines," Liana said, finishing Joel's sentence for him.

"Of course it is!" Joel threw his arms up in the air. "You mean the place where Saff and I just came from and probably has Zaganites crawling all over it? That doesn't sound like a trap at all, does it?" Joel said sarcastically.

"I agree with Joel's pessimism," said Master H. stroking his moustache once again, "but I cannot ignore Liana's instinct. Tell me child, why do you think we should meet this man? What could he possibly want to tell you that's so urgent?"

"A hooded figure has been following me. I've been seeing them in the shadows. When I saw Nalan, here in the temple, he was also talking to a hooded figure. If a hooded figure did this to the temple, it might be the same person, and there's a good chance Nalan knows who's under the hood."

"That is reason enough for me," said Master H, "But before we go, let's stop by the dojo and get some fresh robes. It's time we reformed the Shroud Clan."

2 3

GRUDGES

The clearing was crowded with Zaganites, spectating as they surrounded a circular fighting ring. To the right of the fighting ring, stalls and carts of food and water provided refreshment for the tournament's participants. To the left, workshops continued crafting weapons, armour, and empty glass Orb's, ready to be filled with Visendi Aura's.

Zagan flexed his muscles and puffed out his naked chest. The scar that went from his navel to throat bulged as he stretched, like a sand snake emerging from its camouflage. He grinned, displaying his wolf-like canines as he took a low, crouching stance. His flared, baggy white ankle-length trousers rode up slightly but still offered plenty of room for movement. He put one hand on the floor to balance, posing as if he were about to start a sprint race.

His opponent was dressed in full armour on the opposite side of the fighting ring. A T-shaped slit in his helmet was the only area on his body which exposed any skin. Only his eyes, nose and mouth were visible.

"Rules of the final are simple!" shouted Nalan, who had been tasked with being the ring announcer. "First one to draw blood from their opponent wins. Auras are permitted, but no weapons allowed. If you step out of the ring, your opponent gets a free hit. Everything else is permitted."

"How can Master Thornfalcon possibly win? His opponent possesses a Red Aura and is covered head-to-toe in armour!" said a young woman in the crowd as she fiddled with a ring on her finger.

"Just watch and you'll see," said the slightly older woman next to her, who glanced down at the fidgeting fingers of the younger woman. "Why don't you just take that thing off until you get it fixed? It just looks weird," she continued, annoyed as the younger woman twisted and twiddled with the broken jewellery.

"I told you, my dad gave it to me. Even if the orange jewel is broken, it reminds me of him," she clenched her hand into a fist as she continued to try and make it feel more comfortable. "I think it's miss-shapen too. Argh, that horrible, horrible brute of a woman," She finally took off the ring and threw it on the ground. "Fine!" she said, folding her arms with a pout.

"Fighters, are you ready?" Nalan looked at each fighter, who in turn nodded back to confirm. "Fight!"

Zagan raced out of his crouched position. His legs sprang to action like a leaping frog but bounded forward on all fours like a wild wolf. His less mobile opponent stood his ground, trusting their armour and Screen to rebound the frenzied attack.

"I think this one will be quick," Nalan said to the two young women as he retreated into the edge of the crowd. "Hey, I think you dropped this." he bent down and picked up the discarded ring.

"Actually, I threw it away. It's broken and uncomfortable," replied the young woman.

"I think I know someone who can fix it." said Nalan. "It would be a shame to throw away something that matched your orange hair so perfectly." he flirted. The young woman blushed. "They would need to know the name of their customer, of course," he raised up her hand and moved to put the ring back on.

"My name's Myra," she said, watching willingly as he slid on the piece of jewellery. "And this is Dimitra."

"Pleasure," replied the slighter older Dimitra, puffing up the sides of her short bobbed brunette hair.

"I'd better get back to my job. I'll find you later to get that ring fixed," Nalan winked as he turned back to face the fight.

Zagan had bounded the diameter of the circle. He was now within jumping range of his opponent. He moved into a frog-like crouch as he wound up his quad muscles and sprang upon his armoured foe. As he did, he grabbed a fistful of grass.

The Zaganite opponent braced himself as he put one foot, and one shoulder forward and lit up his Aura Screen, ready for his master's impact.

The impact was a heavy one. The Red Aura of Zagan's opponent flashed on impact and absorbed some of the force, but the sheer ferocity of Zagan's lunge still knocked his opponent off his feet. Surprised, unfocussed, and off-guard, Zagan's opponent momentarily dropped his concentration and his Screen dispersed. As the pair crashed into the ground, Zagan shoved the fistful of grass into the only bit of exposed flesh available - his opponent's mouth. As his opponent gagged, Zagan moved quickly to remove his helmet. The grass stuffed hamster-cheeked face stared terrified as his Master wasted no time in breaking his nose, spraying a fan of blood across the floor. The fight lasted mere seconds.

"And the winner is Master Zagan Thornfalcon! Congratulations Master," announced Nalan.

Zagan grunted and smiled menacingly, shaking his arms and shoulders in a chauvinistic arrogance.

His opponent was helped up by members of the crowd, groggy with concussion.

"I thought the rules said no weapons," said Myra to Nalan.

"Would you really call grass a weapon?" he replied. "I call that being resourceful."

"Incredible," Dimitra whispered to herself in awe as Zagan started to walk towards them. "Master Thornfalcon, you were..." she started, but did not finish, as he pushed his way between the women and away from the fighting area without saying a word.

Zagan heard Nalan announce the start of the next fight but soon moved out of earshot and the announcer's words faded. He made his way over to a nearby detached cart and picked up one of the large watermelons piled upon it and smashed the green fruit onto a rock in such a way that it folded out into segments. He leaned casually against a tree whilst he ate.

"Pathetic." he talked aloud to himself, not caring about the fruit's red innards that dribbled down his chin as he spoke. "With idiots like that in battle it only proves why we cannot be the ones to launch an assault." he bit into another segment.

"The ambush on the temple better prove worthwhile. I need some reason for them to attack us here. Clearly that Eugene child isn't worth their risk..." more fruit dribbled over his bottom lip. "At least he's an extra pair of arms we can control."

"I still don't see what Yasmin sees in him. She will do

anything for that Eugene boy... at least she's proving useful... If my Visendi friend is right, there won't be much left of that temple once they are done," he grabbed another handful of juicy melon.

"They should be back soon..." he gobbled up the last of the watermelon and haphazardly wiped the juice from his hairless chin and chest. As he did, his fingers slowed, tracing the ridges of his long scar. "And then soon I shall have my revenge against the Langton's after 13 long years..."

The sound of hoofs approached Zagan as he leaned on the inward curve of a palm tree. He looked towards the small dust cloud that was formed by the galloping horses on the sandy road.

Two horses skidded to a halt in front of him. The cloud of dust hung in the air as if it were a golden-coloured fog. Only the rider of the first horse dismounted.

"Father," said Yasmin as she climbed down. "The plan worked. We were able to sabotage the temple."

Zagan smiled an evil smile, turning up one corner of his mouth.

"We used the dagger just like he said we could. He Peeled my Red Aura and infused the empty Aura Orbs with it. It was like the power of a ship's cannon, in my hand. It provided useful cover for your ally to go in and do his thing."

Zagan looked up at the figure who had not dismounted. The dark brown robes the rider wore seemed to melt into the dark brown coat of his horse as if they were one and the same. No matter what angle he looked at him, Zagan had never been able to see the face of the Hooded Man. Just a menacing black, oval hole looked back at him.

"So where is she?" said Zagan, looking between Yasmin and the Hooded Man.

A deep, haggard voice replied. "She could not be found. My Jackdaw searched the whole area and returned with no information of her whereabouts."

"You don't seem concerned."

"Wherever she is, she will return to the temple. She has built up an affinity with the clan there. When she sees the bodies and devastation, there will only be two choices for her. Come straight here for vengeance leaving her open to capture or return home for backup. Either way, we draw out the Swyre army and we both get what we want." The hood didn't even move when it spoke.

"Your confidence of defeating the Swyre army once it's here seems misplaced to me," Zagan turned his head to the fighting ring, recollecting his recent victory. "Being a convict doesn't necessarily equal a good fighter."

"The defences we have built will give us our advantage. I have told you; I know all their weaknesses." Even though it could not be seen, the pitch up in tone on the word *weaknesses* indicated the Hooded Man had a smile as evil as Zagan. "The Aura's your men are producing will give us great ammunition."

"And what about Liana? She has spent weeks in this temple, would she not have gained the same powers as my daughter?"

This time, the hood moved, side-to-side. "Her Aura is locked inside a special orb - a Spirit Orb. She cannot gain the powers without slicing it open. And she can only do that, with this dagger."

A small arm appeared out from behind the Hooded Man, holding out the shimmering red reflections off the blade of the Dagger of Red. It was only then that Zagan realised someone else was riding with the Hooded Man. The second hood had given the appearance of a hunchback on the Hooded Man, until the hunch moved, and a flash of spiky red hair protruded out.

"I still say that should be mine," Yasmin piped. "It was me that found it after Liana had dropped it running away from me." she pouted as she remembered the smell of egg in her hair. "Finders keepers…"

"And I thank you for giving it to your father, who in turn gave it to Nalan. It gave us the opening we needed," said the coarse voice of the hood. "And it will remain in *our* hands to do the deeds we require it to do." The slight turn of the hood to the figure sat behind him indicated who *our* meant. "It is a Visendi Artifact."

"I am a Visendi," replied Yasmin.

The Hooded Man let out a deep, cackling laugh. "The product of a desperate Priestess. She set out the game and gave you a weighted dice to play it. You could not lose." Yasmin scowled at the insult to her skills. "When this is over and Zagan is King, I will teach you properly. At least the Priestesses' view of your potential was not misplaced."

Yasmin glared at the empty looking hood, but his assertiveness and authority prevented her from pursuing the subject. If her father was cautious around the figure, she should be too, she thought.

"You seem to possess all this knowledge of the workings of Swyre and the Visendi. Tell me, is it through your Visendi powers, or do you have special training in espionage?" Zagan said suspiciously.

"Neither."

"Then how can you know so much? I have sat on the Queen's Table for 13 years and still cannot give you the depth of detail regarding those around the table. Yet you seem to know the particulars of Tarak's army, the Priestesses' faults, the Queen's motivations, Liana's movements *very* well?"

The Hooded Man stared (Zagan assumed) back and did not respond. A few moments of awkward silence passed. Zagan did not trust just anyone willingly, and if he were to fight alongside this thing, he wanted reassurances. It did not take long for Zagan to snap. "We are allies! For me to fully trust you, reveal yourself! I must know who lies behind the hood!" he shouted. Anxiety grew within him as he could feel the time of battle fast approaching.

The Hooded Man continued to stare, refusing to speak.

Zagan squinted in resentment at the Hooded Man's display of arrogance. "Then answer me this, what do you intend to do with Liana, kill her?" asked Zagan.

"I'm sure with your grudges you do not care what her end is." Zagan and his daughter nodded shallowly in agreement to the dark statement of intent.

"Yasmin - she has battled you her whole life, never getting into trouble for your feuds, always making you look like the bad egg."

Yasmin's upper lip twitched at the words 'bad egg', almost like the Hooded Man was trying to incite her. "Zagan - the loss of your whole family on the Day of Darkness, when your parents and siblings could have been saved, if only the Langton's had sent help to your district. It was like they wanted to be rid of you as The Merchant Guild Leader." Zagan growled as the memories flashed in his head. "And then there's the boy here, who has been trapped for 200 years against his will. We all have our reasons." The second hood lowered after the old voice finished and revealed the red hair of the 10-year-old Visendi boy, the Spectra Child, Gilroy.

"You do not need to remind us of our reasons for

vengeance," growled Zagan. "But there is still the small matter of luring them to our fortress."

"I have a new plan," replied the Hooded man.

"I am running out of patience with your failing plan's."

"This one will force the Queen's hand. We will hit Swyre from within. She will be sure to act if she believes her innocent citizens are under threat."

"And how do you propose to hit Swyre from within?" said Zagan.

"With a single saboteur," the Hooded man paused as Zagan's facial expression screwed up with doubt. "It relies on the Aura Orbs, which are now able to harvest thanks to you men."

"Do you not think my army would be better off keeping their Aura's?" Zagan scowled. "Why can't you continue to use her?" his eyes shot across to his daughter.

"She has the potential to Ascend far. I have used all the Aura I can from her if she is to realise that potential. If I take anymore then she will find it difficult to Ascend." The Hooded Man looked past the fighting ring to the crafting table on the far side of the training field. "Have someone fetch Gilroy those newly crafted Orbs. I will inform you when the Saboteur has struck the city. As soon as you receive my Jackdaw, prepare your defences. Retaliation will no doubt be swift."

"Tell me, who in the city has the access to conduct such sabotage?"

The Hooded Man lowered his hood, finally revealing his face. Zagan stepped back, surprised, and stunned, before letting out a blood-curdling laugh. Yasmin's usual straight edged jaw bones also widened as she sniggered in unison.

"To think of the arguments, we have had over the years and all along we were on the same side," Zagan chortled.

"Yes, quite the revelation, I imagine," replied the unhooded Hooded Man, with a tone of patronisation. "There's another thing we need to do before we prepare the fortress."

"Oh, and what's that?" Zagan asked, raising an eyebrow.

"We need to guarantee your troops' loyalty. Guarantee they will follow your orders. Guarantee they will not hesitate or desert the battlefield. I will need to Turn your troops into Immorals"

N alan tilted his head to the conversation behind him as he concealed himself behind a nearby tree. He closed his eyes tightly, doing his best to concentrate on positive thoughts and feelings as he listened to the Hooded Man speak. He fought the memory of his first meeting with the mysterious pile of robes, the strange encounter that led him to attempt murder. He focussed his thoughts on the people he'd helped with his herbal remedies. The tranquil days spent searching for rare forest flowers. He fought the shifting of his morality. *'I must stay strong. I must not give in to the Bad Morality. I must repent and stay at my task. Liana deserves my loyalty. She was the only one who believed me. I must believe in her.'*

24

TREACHEROUS REVELATIONS

"If this message said to trust no one, then why bring me with you?"

Adriya and Tarak Langton rode steadily through the forest that bordered their royal city.

"Uncle, if I cannot trust you, who can I trust? I have doubts on the validity of this message. If this turns out to be a trap, you are my best chance of escaping unharmed."

The tall, thick tree lines coupled with the dark clouded sky left behind from the storm created an eerie atmosphere for the time of day. It was nearly noon, so the usual vividness of the forest floor flowers should have been radiant, but they instead sat motionless and saturated without colour. The blue of the bluebells, whites of the daisies and red of the mushrooms merged into a one dour greyscale. Animals and insects that usually frequented the area for hunting and scavenging their lunchtime meals were absent. Moisture from the night's rain still dangled in the air.

'I'm worried for my daughter,' thought Queen Adriya.

Perhaps it was the oppressiveness of the strange dark-noon atmosphere, or maybe it was her motherly instinct, but she could not shake the feeling of impending dread. *'I am also afraid. Afraid for her... or afraid of her? I cannot tell. I feel many things and do my best to suppress them. I tell myself it's for the good of the Island, but it is difficult to keep these feelings suppressed. I am afraid.'*

"Uncle," said the Queen, in a low, monotone voice. "Do you believe my sister? Have I so gravely misjudged Zagan that he is now a threat to us all?"

"Perhaps it is not a case of your poor judgement, but an opportunity that the weak of mind could not resist. Having the courage to remain loyal in the wake to an offer of power, would be power in itself. We both know how much Zagan loves the idea of power."

"You sound like someone who has been taking philosophy lessons from Vivek."

"Maybe I'm just getting wiser as I get older," Tarak chuckled. "Did you know, when I promote a soldier to the rank of General, I offer all the existing Generals the chance to best me in a duel and challenge my decision."

"I can't say that I did. You've not mentioned this ritual before?" said a surprised Queen.

"It is not only a test of loyalty, but an opportunity for me to understand if my leadership continues to be proficient. Behind a leader's back, subordinates will always have cause for complaint. However, if they also cannot see reason in the rules, then they start to believe they can do things better. This is where the threat lies."

"Has anyone ever challenged you?"

"Once."

"What happened to them? I don't remember any of your Generals dying in such a way."

"You presume the duel is a fight to the death, my Queen?"

"What else would it be?"

Tarak let out a small chuckle before replying. "A battle to the death would be a waste of a good fighter."

"Then how is a winner determined?"

"It is fought with a rope in hand. The winner is the first to tie up their opponent in such a way they cannot move. A symbolic victory to show who has control over who."

"So, who was the challenger?"

Sir Tarak gave a wry smile before answering. "It was your sister, no less."

"She challenged you?! She is an unpredictable rogue." Adriya tutted angrily. "You have answered my initial question with a philosophical response where you seemingly implicate both Zagan and Amara as traitors. You haven't really answered me at all. Why don't you share with me your actual opinion?"

"Because I do not think it matters who we should believe or who is plotting against us. What matters is making the right decisions for the future of your daughter."

The Queen agreed. "Hmm... she was just on my mind, too. She's always on my mind..."

Sir Tarak raised his left arm aloft, signalling for them to slow down. "We are almost at the old mines. Wait here, I will scout the area for any sign of Zaganites. Keep the horses quiet, I will conduct a sweep of the area on foot." Queen Adriya nodded in acceptance of the instruction, as Sir Tarak dismounted and disappeared up the overgrown path ahead.

She sat atop her horse and patiently waited for her uncle to return. The silence of the forest continued to make her feel uneasy, whilst the blue-grey filter of ominous lighting gave her a sense of an inevitabile disturbance. The anxiousness of waiting and this sense of impending trouble made the passing minutes feel twice as long as reality. Her already heightened alertness rose even higher as Sir Tarak's steed snorted and jolted its head, repeatedly raising itself onto its hind legs. *'It can sense something. I must calm him before he gives me away.'* She dismounted and her own steed began stirring. She attempted to calm them with gentle strokes to their cheeks, but this did little to calm their spooks. Before she could try anything else, the bushes behind her rustled and the horses bolted into the dark forest. A man she recognised instantly appeared from the shrubbery.

"Nalan!" she exclaimed.

"We have your uncle," Nalan answered with an emotionless tone and neutral face. "Please, come with me."

Queen Adriya began remembering the hatred she held for this man, who dared kidnap her daughter from under her very nose. Every part of her wanted to strike him there. Strike him until every ounce of worry, every ounce of anger, every ounce of desired revenge was extinguished from inside her. She felt her fists tighten from emotions of the heart, but her eyes stared unblinking as her head analysed. *'I can't judge his intentions. He seems… confused. A confused soul, confused emotions…'*

After a minute of silence, and without any pressure or persistence from Nalan, the Queen decided to agree with his request. "Take me to him," she said, simply. Nalan turned and led the way, pushing aside thick shrubberies of branches and leaves.

She kept a cautious arm's length behind. It was the first time she had worn her skin-tight, all-in-one storm-grey metal bodysuit, the special construction Vivek had been working on. The Queen had protested about the intimate preparation involved in gaining her exact measurements from neck to ankle, but the Clerk insisted it was necessary to give the Queen utmost protection and manoeuvrability in the rare event she needed to be on the front line. Its flexibility was created by painstakingly hinging together over 5,000 equilateral feather-light metallic triangles. The miniscule hinges were so small they were concealed once the triangles were connected but the design meant that the segments could all work independently. It looked and behaved like a snake's skin. It had taken Vivek almost 2 years to construct and he refused to let anyone else get involved, with the exception of the castle's carpenter who was mandated to create a wooden mannequin with the Queen's exact measurements, and the metallurgist who provided the hinges and special light-weight triangle segments. The Queen's metallic black calf-high boots and mohawked helmet which covered her long ponytailed hair topped and tailed the look. The only skin showing was that from her forehead to chin.

The forestry opened up ahead and the charcoaled remains of the old mining facility lay plateaued in front of them. As she emerged from behind Nalan, Queen Adriya saw her uncle standing beside a tall figure whose entire body was concealed under a full-length, plain, muddy-brown robe. Even their bowed face was shaded by a large, overhanging hood. Queen Adriya stood there, wondering how her uncle had been captured and why he wasn't attempting to free himself. Then she noticed the streaks of red light passing over him and his captor.

"He cannot escape. He is encased in a Red Aura," Nalan said.

"Visendi, of the old ways," the Queen deduced as she mumbled to herself, staring helplessly at her uncle.

"No harm will come to him. We had to ensure a quiet assembly." Nalan continued, as he led them closer to the two figures. The Queen stood facing the hooded figure. Nalan stood facing Sir Tarak.

"Who are you? Where is Eugene?" asked the Queen.

"Eugene is a captive of Zagan." said a coarse, old-sounding voice from under the hood. "I had to lure you here somehow."

"Captive? Is he okay?"

"For the moment, but Zagan grows restless and unpredictable. He now only has a one-track mind for your throne." The figure's hood didn't even move as it spoke. It didn't even flutter in the breezy wind.

'An eerie encounter for an equally eerie day', thought the Queen, before speaking: "But he will not attack the city. I have information that he needs to draw us out in order to deplete our forces before making a move for my throne."

"Maybe. Or he could cut off the supply of your main commodity and trading asset," replied the hood. "Play the economy game. Wait for Swyre to become impoverished... hold you to ransom."

"He's had many years to try this. If he had the right contacts in the right places, he'd have attempted this already. The navy and merchants are loyal to Admiral Remi, he has no influence there. Get to the point, you did not bring me here to discuss basic politics," said the agitated Queen, already growing impatient.

"'The point, yes, the point...'" repeated the hooded figure, "Is about to appear out of that old cave." The figure pointed to the rockfall blocking the old mining entrance.

At this point Adriya expected a timely explosion, maybe a

rabble of white robes, or some spectacle of Aura's to splinter from the figure's hand. Instead, they all looked on in awkward silence, waiting.

"Ahem," coughed the hooded figure awkwardly. "They, er, must be a little behind schedule."

Adriya cast a comical and condescending eyebrow at the hooded figure.

"If this is some sort of practical joke, I do not find it funny. I am a hugely busy woman right now, show me who you are and..." Before the Queen could finish her sentence, some of the boulders at the mining entrance began to tumble and soon a hole big enough for a person had been created and out popped the head of Saffina.

"This is it!" she announced as she hauled herself up and out of the hole she'd just made. "Ow! Jeez Joel, careful!" she shouted behind her, before tumbling down the small rock pile the other side. She picked herself up and dusted herself off.

"Not gonna offer the wounded a hand then?" shouted Joel through the hole.

"Not after you just trod on me and made me fall over. I've got cuts all over my arms now because of you!"

"Boohoo! Try having a broken ankle!"

"It's not broken anymore though is it, it'll be almost fully healed by now."

"Sympathetic Saff, as always." replied Joel, sarcastically, as he also hauled himself up and out of the hole, before offering his hand to the Old Priest.

"You think I need your help boy? Have you seen me move?" came a shout from down in the darkness of the cave.

"S-Sorry, Master H." said Joel, embarrassingly.

"I don't see why you didn't just let me blast a hole with my Red Aura." said Master H as he emerged.

"You're the one who said we needed to act stealthily. Blasting a hole in these rocks wouldn't exactly be quiet, would it?" shouted another voice from the darkness. A voice that made Queen Adriya's heart skip upon hearing it.

"Liana... my dear daughter!" she whispered to herself in adulation, watching as the Princess climbed through the hole. The eerie blue-grey surroundings seemed to dissipate the moment her eyes caught sight of her daughter's vivid blue hair and matching eyes as she emerged from the cave's shadow. *"A light from the dark."* she again whispered to herself.

The re-established Shroud Clan collected themselves and scouted the area around them. The bluey-grey backdrop of the forest mixed with the fresh, blowing salty sea air made Saffina and Joel visibly shake and shiver.

"Is anyone else a little creeped out right now?" Saffina hugged herself as the chills took hold.

"A little bit more than a little," replied Joel as he also hugged himself. "I'm glad we put these robes on before we left the temple." he stretched out his arms to admire the workmanship. Unlike the gold-trimmed robes that Liana had seen Yasmin and Eugene wearing, the Shroud Clan wore robes of a solid deep maroon colour. The hexagonal honeycomb material was of the highest quality. Joel looked at the Coryàtes family emblem stitched beautifully into the back of Liana's robe, who was standing slightly in front and to the right of him. Even the gold thread used to stitch the arrowhead, the palm tree and the wave was of the highest quality. The thread itself was woven like a miniature rope, making the logo stand out and embossed against the maroon material.

"Shh," Liana put a finger to her lips and outstretched her left arm behind her as a visual indication to Joel to be quiet. "Over there, I think I see some people," she pointed towards the corner where the vast charcoaled ground met the forest and the edge of the beach. "Can you see them? I think there's three... no four of them. I can just about make out their figures against the burned ground."

"And it looks like they've seen us..." said Joel, as the four figures moved towards them. "That one looks keen - we should get out of here!" he pointed towards the silhouette of a running figure. The clan made moves to the cover of the forest, but before they could reach it, a familiar voice cried out.

"Liana - wait!"

The Princess paused in her tracks and turned around. Saffina and Joel quickly followed suit, as did Master H once he realised the others had stopped running.

"Mother... Mother?!" Liana shouted as she ran towards her. The pair embraced tightly. Weeks of uncertainty and worry flowed out of them like the gushing of a waterfall. The rest of the Clan showed their delight as they watched the long embrace. A welcome and happy relief from the devastation they'd just witnessed in the Shrouded Temple.

Queen Adriya released the grasp on her daughter, but kept her hands clasped tightly around her shoulders as she looked down on her with much love and admiration. Liana's upturned eyebrows and shaky, watery eyes reciprocated her mother's feelings.

"My darling, are you okay?" the Queen asked.

"I'm fine," said Liana, doing her best not to show her real feelings of fear and sorrow.

"You look like you've grown so much in just a few weeks," the Queen stroked a strand of Liana's hair between her fingers.

"I've not grown that much," Liana said innocently.

"I didn't mean physically, my darling." Adriya kept her eyes fixated on Liana's, as if she were trying to pry into her daughter's mind, but Liana broke off the eye contact. She knew the observation of her mental growth was an accurate one and didn't want to dwell anymore on recent events. It was then that she noticed the other three figures, who had casually ambled over to the Clan.

Liana broke off from her mother, startled. "The Hooded Man! Master H.! The Hooded Man!"

Saffina and Joel let out an audible gasp. Queen Adriya's eyes widened. "You've seen this hooded person before?" she asked.

"He just killed the entire residency in the Shrouded Temple. He's a murderer, and he's after me!" Master H, Saffina and Joel flanked Liana, alert and ready for confrontation.

Queen Adriya whipped around and glared at the fleshless figure. "Is this true? What do you want with her?"

The hooded figure did not answer and instead outstretched their arms, revealing the palms of their hands from the baggy robes, motioning for calmness.

Sir Tarak, still encased in a Red Aura, frowned quizzically as he noted the complexion of the hands.

"You shall pay for what you have done!" screamed Master H. The normally calm and considered man, awashed with anger in his voice. Even his handlebar moustache seemed to be standing on edge. He clutched his staff with both hands and made an impulsive lunge for the hooded figure, raising his Red Aura as he did so.

"Wait!" The instruction came, surprisingly, from Sir Tarak. The warning was not needed, since the figure effortlessly and successfully dodged the attack with ease, simply shifting and strafing sideways, watching the staff pass by, as if the attack was in slow motion. "I said: Wait!" shouted Sir Tarak again, as if he were commanding one of his own lieutenants.

"Listen to him, Master. That's my Great Uncle. You can trust him," shouted Liana.

The Old Priest withdrew but remained on guard. "Why should I?"

"I'm not sure this person is who you think they are, or even who they may appear to be..."

The hooded figure contemplated their next move. The salty sea breeze, the rustling of bushes in the wind and the absence of animal calls made the next few seconds feel like minutes as the tension between the groups stood teetering on a cliff edge. Eventually, the figure slowly moved their hands and pushed back the large, overhanging hood to reveal their face.

Saffina and Joel gasped at the reveal. Liana and Master H. shared a confused glance at each other. Queen Adriya physically stepped back two paces, opened her mouth to say something, before closing it without managing to say a thing. The surprise was too unexpected to put into words.

"It is nice to finally meet you in person, my daughter."

'Daughter?! As if the shock behind the hood wasn't enough!' Liana's mind raced once again.

"Who are you calling 'daughter'?" reacted Queen Adriya, finding her voice.

"I couldn't have wished for a more fortunate adoption. Being raised under the protection of royalty... perhaps our hypotheses were not wrong."

"You can't seriously be claiming to be her birth mother?"

However, on first appearance, it was difficult to argue with the claim. The figure standing before them bore the same bronze-coloured skin, same elvish shaped head, the same blue eyes, and above all, the same electric-blue coloured hair. The only differences were the three or four crow's feet lines protruding from each eye and the cosmetic touches of blue lipstick and pierced ears.

"My name is Candela and yes, I am indeed Liana's birth mother."

Liana did not know how to react and was caught in two minds. On the one hand, she was ecstatic that she would have the chance to get to know her real mother, so soon after discovering that she had been adopted by the Langton's. She had so many questions that needed answering - not least about the reason why she was frozen in time for two centuries.

On the other hand, she respected the mother who raised her into the 13-year-old she had become and did not want to be overzealous in her excitement, for risk of hurting her mother, Queen Adriya's, feelings.

She decided to control her emotions and deal with facts. She had been finding this was the best way to deal with her insecurities, so figured it would work with this unique situation. "Did you attack the Shrouded Temple?" she asked, directly and straight faced.

'Straight to the point. No emotions. Focus on the task. That's my daughter. That's how I've raised you.'

Candela shook her head, solemnly, as if the news of the deaths in the temple hurt her like she had known them personally.

"Your voice, how did you mimic an old man so well? It was hoarse and now it is feminine?" asked a still restricted Sir Tarak.

"It is a power the Visendi can use once they have attained the Lingual Core," interrupted Master H. "How can I be sure it is not you who attacked my Temple?"

"You are Master Shiro, of the Hayashi family." The Hooded Woman locked her arms by her sides and bowed forwards, before straightening up and continuing. "The Shrouded Temple of Roots has been in your family's guard for many generations. I knew your great grandfather well. His Temple was perfectly situated - underneath Mount Indigo - to carry out our plan to entomb Liana and us Spectra Children. I knew I could trust him and all his descendants."

"All that proves is you know some history of the Visendi," said the sceptical Old Priest.

"Maybe she can tell us why the tomb... why I... really exist?" Liana butted in, with an anxious tone in her voice.

Candela smiled softly before gently nodding, respecting Liana's desire... nae... necessity for questions to be answered. "Are you familiar with the history of the so-called Aura Wars?" Candela asked. Everyone but Master H and Liana shook their heads, but they too were eager to hear a supposedly real-life encounter of centuries old events.

"To put it briefly," began Candela "The Aura Wars was an Aurora Visendus Civil War. When Visendi achieved the accolade of Ascending all six Inner Core's - their Aura's - they became known as Transcended. It was discovered that when two Transcended Visendi had a child together, that child was born with one of the Inner Core's as an immensely powerful speciality. These children, such as I, were called Spectra Children. It soon became apparent that only six Spectra Children could be born, one for each Inner Core - and thus the war began. Jealousy, between the Transcended, each determined to be the bearer of a Spectra Child. The Aura Wars plunged the world into darkness. Many lives were lost over decades of fighting. Harrowing tactics were used on both sides, including the use and manipulation of people's Morality - either as weapons or recruitment to vast armies." Candela paused and bowed her head. A single tear rolled down her left cheek as nightmarish memories bubbled up within her. She raised her head back up but did not wipe the tear from her face. She did not feel embarrassment, for remembering such horrors was not a sign of weakness to her, it was a reminder to why she made the decisions she did and acted as a mark of respect to her fallen friends of the past.

"One battle, the Battle of Grimstone, essentially put an end to the Aura Wars, but also put an end to the religion of the Aurora Visendi. No monarchy felt that it could trust it's teachings and it became outlawed across the world. A few years after the Battle of Grimstone, a rare opportunity presented itself. With the birth of Gilroy, all six Spectra Children in existence were now born from Transcended Visendi of Good Morality. Except the world wasn't ready to accept the religion back.

Myself and my Spectra-powered siblings went on in life without using our abilities, a 'normal' life, so to speak. We would arrange to converse and meet up, to keep up the Visendi ways underground and in secret, hoping for the day the world would be ready to accept us back into their society.

During this time of feigning normality, I fell in love. Yonathan was eleven years my senior, approaching his fortieth birthday when we first met. Rugged features, full-bearded and incredibly self-assured. I was infatuated after our first drink together.

Now that I think about it, he didn't ever really say all that much. I guess if he did, he risked me finding out who, or what he was."

Candela breathed in deeply, the recollection of her story making her weary as she recalled it.

"What was he?" asked Joel, who was so hooked on the tale, this was probably the longest length of time he'd managed to ever concentrate quietly without getting distracted or making a bad joke.

"He was an Immoral Visendi. He had handed over his Morality in the Aura Wars and was seeking vengeance for it. I don't know how he knew I was Transcended when he first started courting me, but one night he forced himself upon me. He told me I was to keep giving him children until we had a Spectra Child of our own... and if they were not born of Spectra-ability... he would kill them. I could not use my powers, for using them on another Transcended would have required great power. I could not risk exposing myself and unsettling a world that was beginning to settle and rebuild, so I did not fight back."

The group stood in shocked silence, hanging onto every word that Candela said, trying their best to understand her pain, but knowing they could not.

"It just so happened that I went into labour one month early, while I was on my way to meet my Spectra-siblings to finally tell them about Yonathan. I had missed the last few gatherings, for Yonathan had been keeping more than a close eye on me. I took my opportunity as soon as he announced that he had to leave for two days. I can only suspect his departure was by order to meet other Immorals. Of course, he threatened me not to try anything but naturally I took advantage and sent out Jackdaw messages arranging an emergency meeting with my Spectra-siblings. The moment I arrived at our meeting place; I went into labour." Candela then made the most genuine, heart-warming smile towards her daughter. With the single tear still clinging onto the contours of her cheek, an overwhelming feeling of sadness suddenly blanketed Liana as she stared back.

"When my baby entered our world, we were all aghast

when her Aura's began cycling. Red, then Orange, Yellow, Green, Blue, Indigo, before turning Red again. Everyone in that room knew how special this child was. Somehow, a Seventh Spectra Child had been born. We debated between ourselves all through the night about my child's meaning and what we should do. I was exhausted, but I knew the fate of the world may rest on what we decided to do at this moment. And in my exhaustion, I came up with the idea of the entombing. We knew it was not a permanent solution, but a postponement, a decision that would buy us time. The plan to build a tomb under a Visendi temple that would be guarded if found or entered by an Immoral - protecting my child from her father and those he allied with. That night we set sail to Coryàtès and with the help of the Shroud Clan built the Tomb of the Transcended under the Shrouded Temple of Roots. We had known since the Aura Wars of the preservative qualities in the minerals and elements that Mount Indigo provided. We also knew it stood upon a rising red river that would one day free us of our temporary coffins. We just had to trust our Aura's would protect us.

I decided we had to provide an additional safeguard for my child, in case Yonathan found the Tomb and tried to use her for Immoral causes, so we Peeled her Aura's using the Dagger of Red and placed each of her Aura's under the guard of its respectively coloured Spectra Child inside a specially crafted orb. A Spectra Orb.

And here we are today. Except, the one thing I didn't anticipate was the Spectra Children being separated due to Mount Indigo's eruption. Thirteen years, and Gilroy is the only one I have found..."

"Wow... what a story..." Joel's mouth was wide open in awe.

"It is not a story; it is the truth," snapped Candela. "And the truth of the present is that we must reunite Liana with her Aura Spirits so that she can be the Light of the Visendi religion and deliver the teachings of Aurora as originally intended - for good." Candela replied sternly, straightening herself up. Before anyone else could speak up, she quickly moved the proceeding on.

"She possesses Sight, doesn't she?" said Candela, turning her attention to Liana.

Master H confirmed the question with a grunt. "But she cannot control it."

"Come here, child," Candela gently waved her hand, gesturing for Liana to approach her. Liana hesitated. "Even without using Sight, I think you can sense I mean you no harm." The Hooded Woman now moved her whole arms invitingly, like she was encouraging a toddler to walk for the first time. The Princess cautiously approached, but safe in the knowledge that she had the security of her friends behind her.

Candela reached out and held Liana's hands. They shared a tingling feeling as their fingers touched. A sense of connection. A natural bond. A connection and bond that Queen Adriya managed to sense telepathically. She restrained in showing her jealousy but noted the event.

"You know how to meditate, I assume?" asked Candela. Liana nodded. "To use the gift of Sight is like meditating with your eyes open. Soften your breath. Focus on each inhalation. Control each exhalation. Forget any concerns, questions, theories, worries. Just look. Look without thinking."

'Forget all these questions racing through my head? How am I meant to do that when I've just met my real (200-year-old) mother, supposed to be some Light to guide the Visendi, and have whoever else after me who wants to Turn me, or maybe even kill me!!'

"Let go, Liana! Everything you are thinking of can wait a few moments."

She took a deep breath, but her thoughts wouldn't leave her head. The same questions circling over and over. She began to get frustrated. She wanted so badly to know how to control her gift so she could reassure her friends, Master H, her Great Uncle, and her mother that this woman, and Nalan, could be trusted. Then after the questions cycled for the fifth or sixth time, she began to think of Estrella. First, of her motionless body holding the broken katana, but then of the few moments of peace and tranquillity Liana had experienced when she saw her Morality. This got her thinking about Agatha and when she saw her glowing light from outside her bedroom.

It was then that Liana realised that the oppressive, blue-grey tones of the forest had subtly faded into the now familiar greyscale of Sight. A halo of white light flickered around the profile of her birth mother. It wasn't as intense as Agatha's or Estrella's, but it was white nonetheless.

"She has entered the realm of Sight," said Candela, grinning a big smile. At least, that's what Liana lip-read since all other senses were always absent in this realm. The tingling feeling of holding her real mother's hands now felt like a numb grasp. Like trying to walk after getting pins and needles in your legs.

She turned to Nalan to see that his Morality was less speckled with darting black dots than when she had seen it in the Triunity Hall. She walked up to him and touched his cheek with her palm. She gazed curiously into his glowing white eyes. She could not see the colours in his iris, or the black circles of his pupils. Just pure whiteness emanating from his sockets. For a moment, she felt completely peaceful as she stared into the pair of oval lights.

"You did save my friends, didn't you?"

"I took a risk in trusting the Queen's sister, Amara. I didn't have the skill or opportunity to do it myself, so I had to convince someone else. She was the only one I could think of who may have felt a connection to you."

"Thank you," she said, with a soft sincerity, before turning to her friends. Every single one of them emitted a white glow, including Queen Adriya and Sir Tarak. Liana breathed a sigh of relief, before the visions ended.

"Tell them, what did you see?" said Candela.

"White glows. Around everyone. We are all good people. Everyone, except Nalan. He still has some speckling."

"Ah yes, Nalan. He was being Turned. It was fortunate I was able to intervene when I could. His infection will soon be gone."

'Infection...' For some reason, the word repeated in Liana's head.

Master H, who had been in his fighting stance the whole time, finally lowered his staff and eased his position. "If you say they are safe, my pupil, then I trust your gift."

"Now that we settled that, it's time to discuss why I really arranged for us all to meet here," said Candela. "To talk about another powerful Visendi."

"Hmm," murmured Liana out loud. "Another powerful Visendi?" she paused. "Of Bad Morality?" asked Liana tentatively. She wasn't sure she really wanted the answer, but it was a question that had to be asked.

"Indeed," said Candela, breathing deeply before her next sentence. "But what makes them more dangerous are their alliances within the Queen's Table."

"You mean, with Zagan?" asked the Queen.

"No, not just Zagan. The traitor I wrote to you about in my letter."

"The traitor who you have still not named?" frowned the Queen, impatiently.

"It's the Priestess, isn't it?" said Joel, speculating. "That's whose bird you intercepted coming out of the Tomb. Liana said the Priestess used it to guide her." but the woman shook her head. "That bird's origin was not from Priestess Yi," she replied.

"Well, if it's not the Priestess... it can't be my Great Uncle or I would have seen with my Sight, which just leaves Admiral Remi or Clerk Vivek since we already know Zagan is a traitor," Liana thought out loud as she deduced.

"But it can't be Admiral Remi or else Zagan would have gotten to her by now, used the ships, held us to ransom. But if it's not Remi, that only leaves..." Queen Adriya's eyes widened once more after realising what this meant. "I refuse to believe it!"

Just then, a series of explosions boomed through the air, causing the trees of the gloomy forest to vibrate. The group turned in the direction of Swyre, to see multiple plumes of red, churning smoke rising up in contrast against the gloomy blue greys of the treeline.

25

ARMY OF IMMORALS

"What happened?!" screamed the Queen as she bounded through the gate of Langton Castle on horseback, with Liana gripping her waist as she sat behind her. Joel rode with Tarak, Saffina with Candela, and Master H. with Nalan. Maids and guards were crossing paths in front of them running to duty and tending to the injured.

Benji came running out of the Triunity Hall. He bowed a quick shallow bow before speaking. "Yer Majesty, there's a problem with the communication pipelines. Explosion's wen' off all 'round the castle grounds 'n' the City Square."

"Vivek," said Candela. "He must have put Aura Orbs into the pipelines. The red smoke is reminiscent of it... just like the Aura Wars..." Candela closed her eyes, pushing back the tears as she remembered the troubles of her time.

"Vivek..." repeated the Queen angrily under her breath.

"Vivek? He's not' 'ere. No one 'as seen him. We've bin searchin' all over for 'im. Priestess Yi 'as been keepin' things calm o'er at the City Square and Temple. I been doing me best 'ere. I cudda really done with Vivek 'ere and 'is guidance. I'm sorry Yer Majesty. I really am." Benji bowed low this time. He hated letting anyone down, but he would also be the first to admit he was not naturally politically inclined.

The Queen put her hands on his shoulders. "It's okay Benji, this isn't your fault. None of us saw it, but Vivek is a traitor."

"A traitor, Yer Majesty? But he's served you and yer father fer years. He's developed technologies, looked after the people, 'elped raise sweet little Liana," he pointed towards the Princess and smiled.

"Yes, he's been very deceptive, and all to get close to me and Liana, waiting to see if she truly was to be the child from an old Visendi scripture. Since her episode in the Triunity Hall, he has been trying to get her away from the city. On her own, to Turn her, use her as a tool for his own ambitions." said the Queen.

Benji stood, mouth-wide open, gawping. "I guess it does kinda make sense now... the last time anyone saw 'im, was when he ordered fer the pipelines t' be flushed and cleaned. That must've been what triggered the explosions." Another horse and rider bounded in through the castle gates and immediately dismounted. "Adriya, what's going on?" said the Priestess. Her usually vibrant coloured attire dirtied from the dust cloud of the explosions.

"Priestess, how are the citizens? Is anyone hurt?" replied the Queen, typically answering a question with a question.

"There are injured, but I have not seen any fatalities. Fortunately, I was giving a lesson inside the Tulip Temple at the time of the explosions so the square itself was largely deserted."

The Queen breathed a sigh of relief and looked at Benji.

"No fatalities 'ere either Ma'am," said Benji nervously. "The pipe cleaner was injured with the kick back of the explosion. He's being tended to in the Queen's Table as we speak, but he should live."

"Do you know who's responsible for this?" asked the Priestess.

"Vivek," said Candela as she dismounted and stood next to the Queen.

Priestess Yi looked suspiciously at the blue-haired woman. "And who are you?" she said in her naturally direct tone.

"My name is Candela. I am Liana's birth mother. A Transcended Visendi and a Spectra Child."

Priestess Yi raised an eyebrow. She had always been quick to suspect anyone who claimed to be of a high ranking Visendi. "You don't believe her, do you?" She said to Queen Adriya. "She has to be an imposter. The existence of Spectra Children is a myth. We stopped talking about them in our underground factions when I was a child."

"The Queen is not wholly familiar with our history yet, Priestess," Candela interjected. "Although I have given her a pretty solid overview. Master Shiro Hayashi is very familiar with our existence and will tell you I am who I say I am."

The Priestess, who when entering the castle grounds had blanked her opposing clan leader, now decided to officially recognise his presence.

"I believe it to be the truth," said the Old Priest.

"Why would Vivek destroy his own inventions and attack the city he's advised and helped build up for so long?" asked the Priestess.

"I believe Vivek comes from a long line of Immoral Visendi," Started Candela, frustrated at her fellow Visendi for her incessant questioning. "Being the Queen's primary advisor has come with many benefits. He knows the ins-and-outs of everything in the city. He has been the one advising the Queen to keep the Visendi religion at bay, wanting to prevent you from building an army of Visendi with Good Morality. He could also get close to Liana," explained Candela.

"You seem to know a lot about what's been going on?" said the Priestess, still with a suspicious look on her face.

"I have been watching from afar since we were released on the Day of Darkness," she put her arm around Liana's shoulder, who was now standing between her two mothers.

Liana suddenly realised Candela was the hooded figure who had been following her. "You were the Hooded Man I saw in the forest after the White Robes tried to capture me from Nalan's treehouse? And the Hooded Man I saw when Yasmin, Eugene and I camped out looking for the Shrouded Temple of Roots?"

"I also saw what you did to Yasmin with those rotten eggs." said Candela, in a judging tone. Liana's cheeks turned red, embarrassed at her prior immaturity. That event seemed so long ago, she thought to herself, but in reality, it was just a couple of months.

"I believe Vivek had caught on to my incognito appearance and set out to emulate my approach."

"So, the Hooded Man we saw at the mines was Vivek? He's the one who's been communicating with the Jackdaw's to Zagan?" deducted Saffina.

Candela confirmed with a nod. "I did not know for sure until now that Vivek was the other hood. If it wasn't for Nalan spying on Zagan for me, we would still be guessing. He had to be very patient, but when Vivek finally revealed himself to Zagan, he told me as soon as possible."

Candela and Liana both smiled at Nalan as they recognised his natural Good Morality and his willingness to repent. Queen Adriya stared at them. Liana, the mini-Candela. They shared the same looks, the same features, the same facial expressions. When they smiled together, there was no denying that they were mother and daughter.

"What are his intentions?" The Priestess continued to ask question after question.

"He wants to Turn Liana into an Immoral."

"Turn?" Benji exclaimed, confused.

"There's a lot to explain, Benji, but Liana could be the one to guide the Aurora Visendi, and the world, to a whole new era of peace. I believe she will happen, so long as she remains of Good Morality" Candela swivelled dramatically to face Liana. "But there's equally a chance that she could end the world if she were to become Immoral."

"I know that girl. Nothing but good spirits, that one." Benji puffed out his chest in defiance. "But how does one become Immoral?"

"A powerful Visendi can manipulate the mind of others. They plant seeds of dark thoughts and nurture them. Usually this takes time, months usually, before someone Turns fully. Although some people are more susceptible to being Turned than others," explained Candela. "I believe this is what Vivek has been doing over a number of years with the miners. It seems that Vivek has Turned Gilroy. He was only 10 years old at the time of entombing. Myself and the other four members of the Spectra forced him into it. He never had a chance to grow up. It must have been easy for Vivek to Turn him with so much anger and resentment inside of him."

"But he still looks 10 years old? Wouldn't he look closer to 23 now?" Liana asked.

"It is curious how I and Gilroy have not aged and yet you have." Candela ran her fingers through her hair as she pondered the question. "But a question to find the answer to for another day, child." Candela stroked Liana's hair, partly reminiscing of the past, partly admiring how grown up her daughter had become. The Queen's jealousy built up inside her, but she did not show it.

"Vivek has had thirteen years to Turn me. Why wait until now?"

"Until you displayed your powers of Sight, he could not be sure you were the Seventh," said Candela. "Imagine Turning the daughter of a Queen to find out she wasn't the fabled Light from the Dark, and then have to live with her and be her tutor."

"Yeh, it was bad enough being her friend before all this Visendi stuff," piped Joel, who received a strong elbow to the ribs from Saffina.

"Once he was sure of Liana's heritage, he could finalise his plans with Zagan to help him become King of Swyre. If they take the city, they will no doubt farm everyone into Immorals. A whole island under their control."

"He set you up to look like a traitor too, Priestess," said Liana "Until you mentioned it to us at the Queen's Table, no one had heard of Jackdaw's communicating messages. He must have been hoping for the Queen to think you had been colluding with Zagan and remove you, then take over the Tulip Temple himself, but that didn't work out."

"What happens to someone who is Turned Immoral?" asked Sir Tarak to the group.

Candela answered in the most serious of tones: "An

Immoral person can be controlled unconditionally by the person who Turned them. They will act as fodder even in the most dangerous of situations. Owing to the fact they are unable to distinguish between acts of good or bad, they are deathly ruthless against anyone not on their side, even without prior training. They are human only in the way they look and move. They lack what makes us truly human - choice, self-awareness... and a soul."

"And now Vivek and Zagan control an army of them," said Nalan. "And they *are* all trained to fight."

"How do we stop them?" Tarak asked as if his question was a sincere request, but he had a feeling he already knew the answer.

"In my time, two centuries ago," started Candela "we experimented with ways to restore an Immoral to their natural Morality. All our trials failed. We have only one choice. The same choice we had during the Aura Wars. They must be killed."

Liana jolted. She hadn't heard the words *death* or *kill* as many times in her life as she had in the past two months. "You're talking about hundreds of people. People who - by your definition - don't know they have a choice. People who blindly follow orders. People..."

"People who have committed past crimes and who again threaten our innocent citizens," interrupted the Queen. "We cannot allow them to harm, or take control, of Swyre."

"But mother, you sent these people to work in the mines because you don't believe in sentencing people to death."

"We have no other choice," Queen Adriya said as she placed her hand on Liana's shoulder, stroking it reassuringly with her thumb. A small glint of water in her eyes indicated to her daughter that if there was another option, she'd take it. In this moment, she knew her mother was right. "Nalan, what can you tell us about their defences?"

Nalan shook his head. "Not a lot, I'm afraid. Vivek and Zagan have been incredibly secretive about this defence system that they've designed... I just know they've put every spare resource into it though."

"It has to be something to do with the cliffs," Joel scratched his head as he thought. "When Saff and I were there, we weren't in the mines. We were chipping at the mountainside. No Quartz, not Cobalt, not Quartaltium. Just plain old rock."

"Who knows what invention Vivek has contrived...?" the Queen mumbled, mimicking Joel's head scratching.

"There is one thing I know, Gilroy and Vivek have to be close to the Immorals to command them. If we can get close enough to them and get the Dagger of Red, we will be able to use our most powerful tool." Candela knelt in front of Liana. "Once your Spectra Orb is opened, you will have the greatest Red Aura the world has ever seen." She smiled and placed a hand on her cheek. "Queen Adriya has raised you well. You are full of Good Morality. Even in Vivek's hands you will be difficult to Turn. Don't let him take you Liana. Don't ever let him take you."

With a mixture of feeling both jealous and appreciative of the compliment, Queen Adriya interrupted this bonding moment between Candela and Liana to give her uncle instructions. "Sir Tarak, meet with Admiral Remi and prepare your forces. We will need to attack from both land and sea." Sir Tarak nodded and immediately strutted away, clanking in his armour to carry out his orders.

"Benji, please continue to manage Swyre on behalf of the Queen's Table." Benji nodded and made his way across the wet sandy stone of the Castle Langton courtyard. Liana watched Agatha greet him warmly as he issued some instructions to her. She caught Liana looking and gave her the biggest smile she'd ever received. With a cheeky wink, Agatha disappeared inside the castle.

She quickly turned her attention back to her mother who continued to dish out her orders. "Candela, Master Hayashi and Priestess Yi - it's up to you to get Liana in behind enemy lines and come up with a plan to get her dagger back."

"What about us?" Saffina and Joel said in unison.

"Do you possess Aura's?" the Queen asked. They both shook their heads. "Have you been military trained?" Again, they both shook their heads. "Then the safest place for you is behind the walls of Castle Langton. I will send for your families to join you. I owe them your safety."

"But...!" Saffina started to protest, before Liana stopped her.

"She's right, Saff. I've got you into enough mess. This fight is all about me and I won't be the cause of you getting hurt again."

"But we've always been there for you. We've only ever seen you as a friend, not a Princess. We don't care about your royalty, or power."

"Despite its perks like the horses you gave us..." joked Joel. Saffina rolled her eyes, but the comment made Liana chuckle.

"Aren't friends meant to be there for each other in the toughest of times?" Saffina's eyes started to well up at the prospect of the battle and the thought of losing her best friend.

"That's why you can't be there on this one, Saff. Because I'm protecting you. That's my way of being there for you."

Tears started to roll down Saffina's cheeks.

"Do we have to make that an order?" joked Liana. Saffina burst out into a crying laugh, and she leapt forward to hug her friend. Joel's long, gangly arms wrapped around the two girls, and he rested his cheek on the tops of their heads as the trio embraced.

"Come, Liana, we haven't much time to waste," said Master H. gently.

The trio broke off the embrace and Liana made her way inside with three Visendi masters, turning her head to grab one final look at her friends as their silhouette's disappeared around the corner.

26

BATTLE OF CORYÀTÈS

PART 1

The gloomy, cloudy sky of the storm of two nights previous had still not blown over. It seemed to be hanging with purpose over the Island of Coryàtès. The air felt close and chilling. The occasional droplet of rain threatened a larger downpour, although it was yet to come. The fleet of Swyre's navy cut through the icy water with clinical ease but the lack of wind led to an unnervingly calm sea.

Admiral Remi stood at the bow of her flagship vessel, one foot upon an upturned crate, looking through a spyglass towards Zagan's mining district.

"There's movement on the shoreline," she shouted behind her. "What are they doing?" she whispered to herself as she lowered the spyglass and squinted towards the shore with her naked eye, as if to make sure the spyglass wasn't somehow lying in what it showed her.

Queen Adriya moved up beside the Admiral. "Let me see," she reached out an upturned hand and waited for the Admiral to hand her the instrument. As soon as it was in her hand, she moved it to her right eye and peered through the circular glass before she also lowered it slowly. "Such a piece of engineering. It has the design of Vivek all over it," she touched her armour as spoke. Despite his treachery, it was impossible not to admire his intellect. His innovation with engineering was incomparable.

Admiral Remi and Queen Adriya watched as hundreds of men and women pulled on ropes tethered to the side of Mount Indigo. Slowly, but surely, four thick walls emerged from the rocky face and were being dragged on top of log-like rollers on the wide sandy beach toward each other. The four walls began to form two triangles, with the third side of each fortification being the mountainous cliff face itself.

The inner triangular fortification stood as high as the cliff itself. The outer triangular fortification stood roughly half the height of the inner walls.

"A fort formed out of the mines itself. No wonder they managed to keep it concealed all this time. Hidden in plain sight," gawped the Queen.

"That stronghold and the sandy terrain is going to make an attack difficult for Tarak and his ground troops to infiltrate." observed Admiral Remi. "The outcome of this battle may come down to us. We can besiege it from a distance with our cannons."

"You would be a fool to assume Vivek has not planned for your fleet to be involved in any encounter." The Queen handed the spyglass back to her Admiral. "Stay alert, Remi. Hold our position until we receive the signal, so we know they are in position."

"Should not be long, your Majesty." Admiral Remi raised the spyglass to her eye again, panning to the right of the enemy fortress. "The rest of my fleet are disembarking the other half of Sir Tarak's forces as we speak."

"**A**re you sure you can trust her, Sir?" Tarak rolled his tongue around in his mouth and pursed his lips as he the General stood beside him spoke the words that had been circling inside his very own head since he made the decision. "We will soon find out, General. We will soon find out."

"Pretty big risk, if you don't mind me saying, Sir."

"Liana's friends were adamant we should give her another chance. Her knowledge of the area could also prove to be invaluable." Tarak slowed his steed down and brought his half of the Langton army to a standstill.

He looked out to his right, across the sweeping, stretching beach that ran along the East coast of Coryàtès between Castle Langton and the mining district. He could just about make out the tiny dots of Admiral Remi's navy on the horizon, against the tall frothing clouds in the purple-blue sky. *'I hope these clouds move on soon. This darkness brings us no favours. We need to see the unknowns of what we are about to face. At least on a clear night sky we would have the shining of three moons.'*

Then he turned his horse to face the troops behind him. He looked around at his men and women. Well trained. Fit. Loyal. Fierce, yes, but lacking battle experience. Few in the ranks had experienced any kind of real life-threatening encounter, the result from decades of peace that his niece had embellished upon the island. He took a few more moments to look down into the eyes of as many of his soldiers as he could. *'They are afraid. Nerves and anticipation are to be expected, but fear clouds the mind. Fear brings mistakes. Mistakes bring death. Death brings defeat.'*

He then cast his gaze over his instruments of battle and felt a spiralling warmth run down his spine as he mentally commended himself. Thousands of archers, crossbowmen, swordsmen, and jousters lined up in organised, square battalions between massive machines of trebuchets, catapults and winch-drawn arbalests like a chess board. *'It would have been easy to let Vivek be involved with my machines of war or my army's gear, but there are some things a Commanding Knight should always be in charge of.'*

Sir Tarak straightened himself, making himself as tall and upright as possible. He signalled with his fingers a 'come-hither' order to a soldier on his left who held up to Sir Tarak's mouth a long, thin, flute-like instrument that flared out at its end.

"Langton Army of Swyre," he said, talking into the elongated instrument. "A threat to Swyre, Coryàtès and the Langton sovereignty has today come to a head. The Master of the Mines, Zagan Thornfalcon and Queen Adriya's aide, Clerk Vivek Tenebra have been colluding against the monarchy to overthrow it with the intention of making Zagan King of Coryàtès and Vivek an Immoral Master of the Visendi with the intention to Turn Princess Liana and bring darkness upon the whole world." Sir Tarak paused his speech, expecting the crowd to murmur amongst themselves, but to his surprise, their focus was absolute. *'Perhaps they do have it in them.'*

"We cannot let that happen! Many of you here have not fought such a battle. Many of you here have not had to worry about leaving your loved ones. Many of you here have not had to contemplate not returning home," he paused again, expecting nervous chatter, but again, the army's focus was absolute. *'They are well trained.'*

"I tell each and every one of you now, that today is the most important day you have lived so far. We must bring down Zagan and his army of convicts - and we must protect... we must believe in... Princess Liana - for she *is* the Light from the Dark. The light that will save the world."

Just as Sir Tarak finished his rousing speech to his troops, the hum of song carried through the still air. The other half of the Langton army were in position, and this was their signal.

"Your comrades are in position on the other side of the stronghold. I once knew a man, Gurney was his name, who had an inspiring song for every occasion, and it would lift those around him. He was just one man singing. Imagine what thousands of voices can do. Let us join them in song and show our enemy - we are not afraid."

When the sun doth rise ont' horizon
'N' brushes our sand-coloured walls
A new dawn is arisen'
Aurora now doth call

The God of Dawn watches over us
Giving strength to all
Victory over Tenebris
The Darkness did then fall

Her gift of enlightenment
With rewards of Aura Core's
Coryàtès passes judgement
To those who refuse her word

Cor-y-àtès
Standing tall
Cor-y-àtès
Your judgement calls

Amara looked up at the enormous fortress walls that had been hauled out of the mountainside as the troops behind her rallied together in song, galvanized by the other half of their ground forces joining in their audible signal to signify they were in position.

Zaganites took up arms along the battlements and embrasures. She scouted the ground between them and the walls. Forward and to their right would be forest clearing where the enemy's army had trained and where Zagan's own dwelling stood.

"There's a clearing in the forest up ahead where the Zaganites trained, we should check it's clear before moving or we could be ambushed."

The man standing next to Amara nodded, raised his arm, and waved two fingers to his right. Two squadrons immediately moved into the forest to scout it out. "I take your advice only because Sir Tarak ordered me to use you. If you so much as think about betraying us..."

"I tell you again, General Omar, I am on your side."

"Because you knew you would be on the losing end and decided to bail? Or because you want to worm your way back into the ranks of royalty? Or is it to try for Commanding Knight once Sir Tarak is no longer around?"

Amara felt rage building inside her. Her fire red personality had difficulty taming anyone who doubted her intentions, which seemed to be a regular occurrence. She resisted thrashing out, this time. "All I hope is that my actions here today will be enough to put to rest those who doubt my loyalty. I have no desire for power."

"Everyone has a desire for power in some form." General Omar replied, trying to incite an argument which would give him the cause to detain and be rid of her.

Amara didn't take the bait and instead took a deep breath to calm her temper. Perhaps, after all these years in the mining district, she had matured enough now to not let the rage take control. On the other hand, maybe it was the fighting instinct in her to instead focus on the impending battle. *'A focussed mind is a strong mind. A strong mind prepares the body. A prepared body means a formidable fighter.'* If her old Zaganite comrades were now fearless Immoral pawns - as her uncle had put it - she knew that once they entered into battle that the battalions behind her would need a formidable fighter to lead by example.

Afloating stream of blue light rippled between Candela and her Jackdaw.

"What's the message?" Liana asked.

"Vivek and Gilroy have taken control of one wing each. Vivek is taking the south-side forces, towards Sir Tarak. Gilroy is taking the north-side forces, towards Amara. Zagan is over-seeing from on top the battlements." Candela said, relaying the message from her Jackdaw.

"What of the Dagger of Red? Who has it, Vivek or Gilroy?"

"He did not see it."

"Then we will have to split up," said Master H. "I suggest Liana and myself go after Gilroy."

"Agreed. Priestess Yi and I will go after Vivek," Candela nodded.

The four Visendi lay prone on a patch of damp grass, high into Mount Indigo, squinting down over the two great walls that had been heaved out of rockface below them. Even at their height, the song from the Langton army on either side of their position echoed and roared around them. They looked on as the Zaganites below moved into their defensive positions and prepared their instruments of battle between the inner and outer walls of their fortification.

"I hope they don't find out that Nalan has been helping us," Liana pondered her concern aloud.

"We had to get someone back on the inside. He's making up for his actions in the Triunity Hall when he kidnapped you," explained Priestess Yi.

"But that wasn't his fault. He was Immoral, or at least Part Immoral."

"He knows that, but as he regains his Good Morality, he wants to make up for it even though he knows it wasn't really him."

"He's a good man."

A few contemplative moments later, Sir Tarak blew the War Horn to signify that the Langton army should begin it's advance. His forces started to move in, cautiously but with purpose. Mirrored on the opposite side of the beach by the forces that contained Amara.

Straight ahead, Admiral Remi moved in her ships.

"When do we go?" Liana asked her Visendi colleagues.

"Once the battle is in full flow and when our targets are

distracted and surrounded by fewer soldiers. That's when we will descend over the battlements," replied Candela.

Liana slanted her head and stared absent mindedly towards her real mother. *'She is a woman who knows the tactics and terrors of war. From a time when that was all they knew. Having her on our side is sure to give us an advantage.'*

27

BATTLE OF CORYÀTÈS

PART 2

Sir Tarak dropped the spiralled gold tubes that made up the War Horn to the floor, raised his sword-hand in the air, and let out an extended 'HE-YAH!' cry. He squeezed his legs into the side of his steed and led his forces full speed toward the first wall of the triangular fortification.

It wasn't long before they were in range of the Zaganites trebuchet weaponry. However, instead of flinging the usual ammunition of rock or flaming barrels from the equipment's long slingshot arm, they were piled full of Spirit Orbs. Their range was also impressive, with a farther reach than that of Sir Tarak's armaments.

The first barrage of Spirit Orbs exploded into the rushing troops. Their shield-like power flung troops, and even their horses 10-feet into the air as huge balls of Red Aura energy burst from the Orbs as they impacted hard onto the sandy beach.

Sir Tarak glanced back to see the damage. The troops

hauling the first row of catapults and arbalests had all been taken out.

Fortunately, most were just laying stunned or winded on the floor, but their progress had been halted abruptly. His well-drilled team organised itself so other troops took up the ropes of the equipment.

The row behind contained the first batch of trebuchet, which due to their slightly longer throwing reach than the catapults, were just about in range. Sir Tarak ordered their firing immediately. He gazed up as huge boulders flew over his head towards the wall, as he and his infantry continued their sprint.

Sir Tarak's eyes widened in shock, along with many of his onlooking comrades, as the flying boulders disintegrated through a Red Aura Screen that lit up when the boulders impacted on it. The Screen seemingly surrounded the entire wall. The Zaganites standing on the battlements shielded their eyes with the inside of their elbows as they were rained on by nothing more than pea-sized stones and dust. Watching from on top of the taller inner wall, Zagan let out a blood-curdling laugh.

The infantry neared the fortification, but 6-feet out from the wall, they were shocked backwards by the surrounding Aura Screen. The long ladders the rushing troops were carrying to raise against the battlements were useless. There was no way up to the battlements. The infantry crouched low, raising their shields to cover their body as Zaganites began to rain down arrows and rocks from above. There was no entrance to the wall. The long-range weapons of the Langton Army were proving useless against the Aura Screen. Sir Tarak could see no way of advancing and ordered a hasty retreat.

As they began to move back along the blood-stained beach,

a rush of Zaganites sprang from the forest and ambushed them, boxing them in, forcing them to fight their way backwards whilst taking a barrage from behind. Sir Tarak's forces were trapped. He looked out desperately towards Admiral Remi's ships hoping for reinforcements.

"Admiral, what's happening?!" screamed Queen Adriya, who had been sent flying to the ships deck after the ship had jolted to a blunt stop.

"I think we've...run aground!" Admiral Remi shouted as she peered over the ship's edge. "I don't know how this is possible. I know all the waters around the island. They should be plenty deep enough here. We should be able to get well within firing range of our cannons. I don't understand..."

A member of the crew helped Queen Adriya up off the wet wooden boards. She cast her eyes out to the starboard side. "The fleet flanking to the right-hand walls is still sailing."

"The mining docks are on that flank. They wouldn't have been able to build any defences which would have inhibited my merchant navy from transporting goods, to avoid suspicion. They must have built up the seabed on our side." assumed Admiral Remi. She signalled to her crew to adjust the sails and man the oars in an attempt to free themselves, but it was to no avail.

Red bursts of light lit up the shoreline ahead. Queen Adriya hastily picked up the spyglass and raised it to her eye and watched on in horror as the events of Sir Tarak's failed raid unfolded.

"We have to get to the shore! Sir Tarak and his troops are penned in!"

"Your Majesty, we only have 8 row boats, four on port-side, four on starboard-side. That's only 40 crew members. We don't have the armour to fight on land, not to mention how easy it would be for the battlements to pick off the boats before they even made land."

"I'm not going to stand on this boat watching my uncle's troops suffer."

"But, Your Majesty..."

The Queen marched over to the Port-side rowing boats and instructed the crew members there to help her with the winches. "I can't just stand here and watch my uncle and his troops get slaughtered. The act of a King or Queen moving into battle, putting their life on the line, will surely raise the soldier's spirits. If the Zaganites on the ground can be defeated, they can retreat and regroup."

Admiral Remi hesitated before jumping into the rowing boat and reaching out her hand for the Queen to join her. "Then I shall fight beside you." Queen Adriya grabbed the outstretched hand and jumped into the boat with two other crew members to row them to shore.

A mara watched, high above those around her as she sat on her horse. She positioned herself within a battalion that sat in the middle of the infantry, a number of rows back from the front. As soon as Sir Tarak's War Horn sounded, the General leading their half of the army raised his sword and ordered the charge to the wall standing before them.

The beach sloped gently upwards towards the fortification. Coupled with the fine sand, it made running hard and it slowed the charge down.

From the sea, Admiral Remi's ships began bombarding the Northern wall with cannon balls. Lights of red energy lit up as they hit the Aura Screen. The cannon balls were having more luck getting through the Visendi powers. It quickly became apparent to Amara that if two cannon balls hit in close proximity to each other, the second had a good chance of getting through and causing damage. The ships must have realised this too, as the outer wall soon became punctured in a number of places.

Amara kept her eyes ahead. She looked at the first rows of troops as they climbed the gentle slope, but soon, they began to disappear, slowly over a ridge. The slope did not continue all the way to the wall. It was an illusion, a clever trick of the eye and she realised they were, in fact, running on an elongated sandy mound. As she reached the top of the mound, she stopped.

'This should be where the worker pits are,' she thought to herself, before realising the terrible trap they were all running into. She giddied up her horse and flew as fast as she could to catch up with the leading troops. She was still the fastest horse rider on the island. She caught up to the General and pulled her horse around in front of him.

"You have to stop them! Call them back!" she screamed, pointing at the troops charging ahead towards the castle. "It's a trap!"

"I can't halt the charge now! We're just within reach of their long-range weaponry! You want us to get slaughtered? You are still with Zagan, aren't you?" the General accused, pointing the tip of sword toward Amara.

"I promise you, it's a trap, halt the charge!" she looked on in horror as the troops approached the wall. "Stop! STOP!" she screamed toward them. But it was too late.

Whole battalions of fighters were seemingly swallowed by the beach. Each pit had two doors which swung inwards. They had been layered with sand to conceal them. Collective screams and whelps rang out as the sand beneath the charging soldiers gave way and they fell into the worker pits as the doors were released. A second wave of screams rang out, but soon dissipated, and was replaced by a cackling roar of laughter and shouting. The laughter was the deathly sound of miners who had been beaten, tortured, and worked to the bone since the day of their sentencing. They began slamming the large, trap doors creating an intimidating raucous.

Amara and the General looked speechlessly at each other. The path ahead of them was scattered with pits and no easy way through to the wall.

"Fire." Amara said, finally. "We shoot flaming arrows into the pits. "There was always plenty of beer and spirits in each pit. It was the one luxury they were allowed, to keep them happy. Light them up."

The General accepted Amara's advice and gave the order.

"They're getting annihilated down there!" Liana screeched in horror as red-coloured energy illuminated the beach and sky.

"She's right. We must act now. If we can take out Vivek and Gilroy, it will at least give them a fighting chance," said Candela. "We stick to the plan though. The Priestess and I will take Vivek. You two take Gilroy."

Master H and Liana nodded in confirmation and leapt to their feet.

"Liana," Candela paused and took a moment to really look

at her daughter. The cropped, angled, vivid blue hair framing her soft eyes and cheeks. Her small, slender figure. Her innocent and fragile mind. "Good luck and may Aurora's Light guide you."

Liana smiled and nodded, sharing the emotions of the moment. She had only known her for a couple of days, but their connection was immediate and close.

The two pairs both descended the rocky mountain in silence and with a swift ease until they reached a suitable height and distance where they could vault into the space between the respective inner and outer walls. In the middle of the south-side space stood Vivek, arms raised, extending his Aura Screen. Gilroy mirrored the act on the North-side defence. Their eyes were closed with a wrinkled frown. The effort of expanding their Aura's was clear to see in their expressions and tensing of all their muscles.

Recognising this, Candela called for her Jackdaw by softly mimicking the bird's chattering sound. She raised her arm for it to land on as it glided down, before transmitting her message. The bird then flew the short distance over to Liana and Master H.

"Candela believes that if the Admirals' ships on this north-side all fire their cannons at Gilroy's Screen at the same time, it will collapse long enough for us to get through." said Master H. relaying the Jackdaws message before it flew away across the sky towards the ships to deliver the same message. He pulled out a small tube from inside a pocket of his black Shroud Clan robe and flicked the ends up and down. 4-foot poles shot out each end, creating a staff. He reached inside his robe again to another pocket and pulled out a slightly smaller tube and handed it to Liana, who repeated the flicking action, revealing a staff about half the size of her teachers.

Master H knelt on one knee. "Place your staff around my chest like a horse's reins and stand crouched on my back, ready to jump off. Don't stray too far from me, or my Screen around us will weaken." Liana did as she was instructed, and the pair watched and waited.

There was a momentary pause of the bombardment from the ships as they prepared to synchronize their attack. In the lull from the booming cannons, the sounds of screaming men and women screeched even more prominently through the air as the armies fought each other.

Over twenty cannonballs whistled through the air, hitting along the Aura Screen at almost the exact same time. Although each cannonball still disintegrated on impact, Candela's theory was right, the Screen flickered and phased out of sight. 'The knowledge of war,' Liana thought to herself.

Master H. leaped forward with Liana clinging on. He used his staff to bounce off his Red Aura below him in the same way when they had descended to the Tomb of the Tran-scended. This made sure they landed in the middle of the opening, next to Gilroy.

Gilroy took a startled step backwards as the Old Priest landed in front of him, creating a cloud of sand which temporarily blinded the Zaganite guards in the immediate vicinity.

"You have something that belongs to me," said a childlike, but commanding voice. Gilroy whipped around to see the battle-ready stance of Liana.

"And you have something that belongs to me," Gilroy snapped out of his initial surprise before smiling an evil smile.

"So, you can talk," Liana observed.

"Words are overrated," he laughed. "Too many people talk, not enough people listen. If they did, I wouldn't be here today." his laugh turned to anger. "I know you have no Aura, Princess. It's all locked up in your little Spectra Orb, isn't it?"

The boy pulled aside his white robe and reached for the Dagger of Red. "The Dagger of Red belonged to me first. It's the Artifact of my land," he snarled and scrunched up his nose in anger. "Do you have any idea what it's like being forced to do something against your will? Being forced to leave all your friends and family behind. Not being able to grow up with those you love. Waking up in a time where everything you believed in has been forgotten. No. You have no idea."

"The Visendi in your time were destroying each other. Destroying the world," Liana argued passionately back. "Candela saw an opportunity and took it. For the past 200 years, there has been peace without the Visendi religion."

"Yet here we are. Look around you. How peaceful is this? What my Spectra Siblings and I did, to lock ourselves away, was merely a hiatus. It was inevitable the wars would resume. You cannot stop Immorals being born. You cannot stop people from becoming Immoral. The lure of power and fame will always be too great a temptation. "

"I will prove you wrong." Liana said, determined, in her own mind, that Gilroy's analysis that people could be so easily Turned, so easily persuaded by the promise of abilities and strength, was wrong. Above all, she was forcing herself to believe what so many already believed, that it was her who could put an end to the Aura Wars once and for all.

Gilroy charged forward, slashing the Dagger of Red in front of him. Liana strafed sideways and struck back at his knees as she evaded his charge with her staff. His legs crumbled beneath him. Behind her, Master H. spun and whirled his staff around in his hands so quickly, all that could be seen was a grey blur, striking any advancing Zaganite that attempted to get close to them.

Liana stood above the fallen boy, who was on his hands and knees. She shifted her staff in her hands ready to strike down onto his back. As she moved to strike, a series of cannonballs crashed through the outer wall. She had to quickly dodge the flying stone bricks. Several Zaganites were taken out by the rocky debris. Another cannonball barrage followed soon after and a section of the outer wall collapsed. The distraction gave Gilroy the chance to stagger to his feet and square up to Liana again.

He again charged forward, but this time mustered up the energy to create an Aura Screen in front of him. Liana had little time to react. She tried to straff sideways again, but she was not quick enough, and the Red Aura caught her, knocking her backwards to the ground. It reminded her of the first practice session she had with Estrella, when she skidded along the ground after attempting to pierce her Aura with a spear. *Estrella...*

The memory of Estrella resonated in Liana's mind for a brief moment. Remembering what her mother had taught her about the ability of Sight, she used this happy memory, the memory of her learnings from Estrella, to enter the Morality Realm. Sure enough, the colours faded from Liana's vision, and everything became greyscale. The sounds of shrieking soldiers and crashing walls became silent. The pain of being knocked to the ground disappeared. The taste of blood in her mouth became tasteless. The smell of sweat vanished. Her other senses had dissipated to heighten her Sight. Liana picked herself up off the sandy ground. Gilroy's dagger-wielding arm was mid-stab. The darkest of shadows surrounded his figure. *Immoral.*

She carefully watched the direction of the attack and dodged it. The boy then attempted a backhand slash aimed at her throat. Liana ducked and the dagger breezed over her head. Another cannonball hit the outer wall sending more debris flying. Gilroy had to dive out of the way, protecting his face from the flying stone. With her heightened vision, Liana evaded any threat of flying rock with ease, as if she were in slow motion, picking her path through the soaring stone shards. Gilroy lay face down in the sand, panting.

"Give me the Dagger of Red, Gilroy," demanded Liana.

"Never. It's mine." and he rolled over, arm outstretched, in another attempt to lacerate his foe. Liana, though, also had her arm outstretched, holding her Spectra Orb. The Dagger of Red sliced the edge of the Orb and it split open, as if hinged. A flurry of dancing red light burst into the air, before darting in Liana's direction. Her body absorbed the Aura and the brightest of red glows shone all around her. She somehow felt warmer and more comfortable, physically, and mentally. It was like a limb had been reattached. She was overcome with emotions of relief and satisfaction.

The Spectra Orb fell to the floor, closing itself back up. His tired panting slowed, and he looked to regain some energy, but Liana acted swiftly and struck the centre of his forehead with the end of her staff, rendering him unconscious. She took the Dagger of Red from his hand and picked up the Spectra Orb. She felt a little sad to see it empty, with no lights darting about when she picked it up.

"Liana!" a shout from the crumbled wall echoed over the heads of the fighting soldiers. Liana placed the empty orb into her robe and saw Amara standing on a pile of rubble. Streams of the Langton army began piling into the fighting area. Liana and Amara made their way towards each other, discarding any Zaganite that dared enter their path.

"Liana, are you okay?" Amara stood admiring the red glow emanating around her.

"I'm... wonderful." she said with a small burst of laughter and much relief. She looked towards the crumbled wall and noticed no more of the Langton army piling in. "Where are the rest of the troops?"

"They lay a trap. Camouflaged the miner's pits. As soon as the first battalions ran over them, they opened the hatches and our troops fell in. They didn't stand much chance. We had to wait for the tide to go out and go the long way around on the wet sand, but not before setting the enemy alight" Amara spoke in fits and starts due to her breathlessness. The flickering of flames could be seen behind her outside the Northern wall "Sorry it took so long to get here, but as soon as we saw the cannonballs getting through... let's just say morale picked up. Come on, I want to see what that Aura of yours can do."

∼

Queen Adriya and Admiral Remi ran across the wet sand left behind by the receding tide towards Sir Tarak and his troops. The large machinery had been cut off by the Zaganite forces as they closed in around the depleting Langton Army.

Sir Tarak squeezed his way through to the water's edge to greet them. "Iya, you cannot be here! We won't last much longer!"

"I couldn't watch you fall without trying to help," she replied.

The Zaganites continued to gradually press the Langton

troops. Forcing them into a smaller and smaller unit. The only way out was to run for the sea, which they all knew would be a pointless endeavour in their heavy armour.

Queen Adriya looked around the lines of Zaganite troops and noticed the heads of some at the back bobbing sideways. The sideways bobbing started to get closer and closer, until two small white robed Zaganites squeezed their way into the front line. Soon, another adult sized Zaganite appeared behind them. As if practiced for dramatic effect, all three lowered their hoods in synchronization. The faces of Saffina, Joel and Nalan appeared. They caught the Queen staring at them, and winked. Saffina and Joel reached inside their robes and took out their small tubes, flicked them side-to-side, creating themselves their own staff. Nalan was already standing armed with a long sword. Queen Adriya grabbed the forearms of Sir Tarak and Admiral Remi, guiding their gazes to match hers. They watched Saffina mouthed a countdown. *Three...two...one...*

Two Red Aura Screen's appeared around them, stunning the Zaganite troops they were standing next to. With a spin and a strike, they each took out a further nine each who were in close proximity.

"Charge!" Queen Adriya, Admiral Remi and Sir Tarak screamed from the depths of their lungs and hurtled towards the opening that Saffina, Joel and Nalan had made. Their troops followed and fought gallantly behind as they forced themselves a pathway. "Disperse into the forest!" ordered Sir Tarak as soon as the last Zaganite line had been breached, knowing that a scattered army in the cover of the forest would be difficult to pursue.

Before making her own dash into the forest, Queen Adriya turned to check on any remaining soldiers and saw Joel limping behind, still suffering from his injured ankle. His arm across the shoulders of Saffina who was struggling to support him.

A wave of Zaganites rushed toward them, spear-headed by the unmistakably harsh facial lines of Yasmin. Sprinting beside her, with an empty, expressionless complexion was her best friend, Eugene. It was not the black robes of the Tulip Clan that they wore, but the dirtied white robes of the Zaganites hung draped over their teenaged bodies, splattered with the spray of wet sand and fresh blood.

Saffina and Joel tripped over a dropped shield that had been mostly submerged by kicked-up sand. Joel screamed in pain as he landed face first. Saffina begged Joel to get up. She tugged at his arm in desperation, but he could not move his leg. Soon, a shadow swept over their horizontal bodies. Saffina rolled over and looked up at the snarling Yasmin and vacant eyes of her brother. She fumbled to find her staff, but it lay out of reach, flung aside whilst they had tumbled over the shield. Saffina trembled as Yasmin looked down on her. Joel mustered the strength to ask what was happening, but she was too frightened to answer.

"Finally, I get to see you beg again. Just like you used to before Liana showed up in your lives," Yasmin hissed through her teeth.

"You got everything you deserved at school. You were, you are, a bully Yasmin. Liana just put you in your place," Saffina yelled.

"She humiliated me."

"You were getting what you deserved. You taunted me every day. Making remarks about how poor my family was. Stealing what little I had. Food, clothes, books. I used to cry on my way home every single day. And Joel, you used to tell people not to sit next to him, saying he didn't deserve to have friends. That he was too much of a weirdo. You made our lives hell for the first two years of school. Then Liana came along and that all changed. She couldn't just sit back and watch you bully every student in the school."

"I lost my family on the Day of Darkness because of her family's incompetence! I had no one. My father spending all his time as Master of the Mines meant I spent almost all my time at the orphanage as it was the only place who would look after me. Then the few people who I spent time with abandoned me as soon as the Princess stepped foot in that school. I didn't care if their friendship was fake. At least I wasn't alone. But Liana even rid me of that. What she did to me was cruel." as she reflected on her memories, her hands clenched her sword's handle until the knuckles on her hand turned white. "A secret competition for who has the worst memory of me. She turned the thought of anyone hating me from something to be fearful of into a popular hobby." she snapped back from her memory and scrunched her face up in anger. "And here are the two winners beneath me once more."

"Eugene, Eugene, listen to me. You're better than her!" Saffina said, turning her attention to her brother in a desperate plea for help, but he just stood there, unmoving, emotionless. Saffina began to sob at the sight of her brother. "They've taken your Morality, haven't they, brother? Eugene, please, don't do this. I'm your sister. They may have taken your Morality but there must be something in your heart that tells you not to hurt me. We're family. "

"It's fun to watch you squirm and squabble before we kill you. This is what you get for being friends with that wretched Princess. Well, soon, I will be the Princess and my father will be King," her snarl turned into a shrill of manic laughing. "Do it, Gene."

With no hesitation, Eugene raised his sword and moved to thrust it into his sister's throat. But, as he thrust, a twang of metal on metal rang out and the sword was flung from his grasp and he and Yasmin were knocked to the ground, winded, with a large metal shield laying across the pair.

"Your Majesty! You saved us!" Saffina caught her breath with a sigh of relief. "That's a mighty fine throwing arm you have there!!"

"Quick, head for the forest! I'll hold them off long enough for you to escape."

"But...!"

"Don't argue, that's an order."

Joel had passed out from pain. They quickly rolled him onto an upturned shield to use as a stretcher. It was a struggle, but It meant Saffina could slide him along the ground and she soon disappeared into the forest.

Queen Adriya swung her perfectly balanced, blood laden royal sword as the swarm of Zaganites tried to follow her army into the forest to hunt them down. She would not let them pass so easily. Her swings were not of random whooshes and whips. She, too, was well trained in combat. She must have maimed a dozen Zaganites but there were too many.

"Don't kill her! Not yet!" the familiar voice of Vivek shouted from behind the cluster of Zaganites who were encroaching on her. "Bring her to the battlements. She still has worth being kept alive, for the moment." They led her through a slim, hidden opening in the outer wall, which was then closed once the last soldier had passed through. She was then ushered up the steps of the inner wall to the battlement.

"Candela, we must help the Queen, we must aim for the battlement!"

"I agree but getting close to Zagan and Vivek will not be

easy, the battlements are not wide and there are many troops up there. We do have the advantage of having many more Aura's at our disposal than just the Root Core though..."

They smiled at each other and glided down off the mountain like birds of prey. They knocked down the first lot of Zaganites as if they were merely wooden skittles.

"Hope you're not rusty. 200 years is a long time between fights."

"Don't worry, Priestess, I'll still be able to cover you. Wouldn't want one of your pretty dresses getting blood stains on it now, would we?"

"Liana Langton!" down boomed the voice of Zagan. "Your mighty Great Uncle Sir Tarak and his south-side forces have fled into the forest. And look who we managed to capture." Queen Adriya was shoved forward, her hands bound, but she still projected a dignified posture and demeanour.

Vivek stood beside the Queen and took over the speech: "Give me your Morality, Liana. A unique Spectra Child like you, and an inventor like me, we could change the world. Make it anything we want it to be."

"And what do you want the world to be like?" she shouted up.

"A world of Immorals of course! A world where I can influence anyone and everyone! A world that is under my complete control! Not in the shadows of some monarchy that only sits on their throne because of bloodline."

"That's not a world I want!"

"Then perhaps you need a little persuasion," Vivek twisted

one hand and raised his arm. His other clenching his metal stick. Queen Adriya's body began to rise in the air. He pushed his arm forward and she floated over the battlement and dangled in mid-air, 30-foot above Liana.

"Mother!" Liana screamed in panic. Hundreds of red dots covered her mother's body. It was the armour. The armour that Vivek had constructed for the Queen. The thousands of tiny triangles held together by orb like hinges, were actual orbs infused with his Aura, and he was controlling them. "Stop it! Stop it! Put her down!" Liana continued to scream.

"Put her down you say? Why, of course I can put her down." and he jolted his arm down and the Queen fell 6-foot before Vivek stopped her. "Sorry, is that not what you meant?" and cackled a cruel laugh. "So, will you join me, little one?"

Liana was trapped. She couldn't watch her mother fall to her death, but she also couldn't give her Morality up to Vivek. *'What can I do? What can I DO?'*

In a twist of fate, a stray cannon ball slammed into the wall just below where the Queen was dangling. The impact knocked Vivek off his feet, and his hold on her was lost. Liana's eyes widened in horror as her mother began to plummet.

She ran towards her falling mother and dug her staff into the sandy floor and vaulted towards her. She used the flying debris as more launching platforms, helping her rise through the air. As she approached her mother, she deflected another cannonball using her Aura Screen and it ricocheted into the same spot in the wall as the previous cannonball. The second cannonball caused that portion of the wall to become unstable and it trembled as it tried to stay standing, but it did not hold. The ground fell away beneath the feet of Zagan and Vivek and they tumbled down with the crumbling rubble. Liana grabbed onto her mother in mid-air and the two fell together, watching as the rubble headed down with them and impacted onto the ground below, causing a huge mushroom cloud of sand and dust to rise up. A quiet lull swept through both armies as they looked on in anticipation. A streak of sunlight broke through the grey clouds above and lit up the fortification like a spotlight.

Amara and Master H stared at the pile of rubble, speechless. Amara's eyes became watery. She couldn't remember the last time she had cried. Candela and Priestess Yi had only just managed to break through the forces on the battlements and now looked down from above.

"What's... what's going on?" shouted a voice from the opening in the outer wall. "Why's everyone stopped fighting?" Saffina, Joel, Sir Tarak and Nalan clambered into the fighting space.

"It's Liana... and my sister..." Amara swallowed as she fought to find the words to say. "They've been buried with Vivek and Zagan. In there." she slowly pointed to the devastation.

"No... NO!!" Saffina screeched. An ear-piercing screech of pain. She ran to the mound of rubble. Joel followed as quickly as he could, hobbling behind. When he had caught up, Saffina was already down on her knees, sobbing. He felt his own knees go weak and he soon followed suit. Tears streamed down his cheeks.

As their tears landed on the white sand, turning it brown, the boulders began to vibrate. Softly at first, but the intensity increased. Joel reached for Saffina and tried to drag her back from the vibrations. Her eyes were too wet to see, and her heart had become so hollow it clouded her senses. She fought with Joel to get him off her, but more hands grabbed her robe as they pulled her away. Her feet dragged in the ground leaving behind parallel trenches in the sand.

The vibrations from the rocks intensified. A low, muted rumble stirred from within the pile which grew in volume with the increased shaking of the rocks. Boulders the size of horses visibly shook, before an explosion erupted from the centre of the mound. Rocks flew in all directions as an incredible dome of vivid red light burst across the battlefield and into the surrounding forest and sea causing the trees to sway and water to churn as if they'd been hit by the hurricane of a tropical storm. The brilliant red light penetrated everything that stood its way. After the domed light had faded into the horizon, a second dome of light burst from the rock mound. A light so bright that it forced every soldier to cover their eyes, or risk being blinded. A light that not only penetrated through every tangible object, but one that could be felt within a person. Felt within the place between a person's heart and mind. Felt within the place where the decision to be selfless or selfish lies. After the white light had also faded into the horizon, the soldiers of the Langton Army withdrew their hands and arms that had protected their eyes and found themselves looking down upon the Zaganites whilst they remained standing, and in place of the rocky mound, stood the glowing red figure of Liana, holding her mother's hand. Vivek lay motionless on the floor. Zagan was bloodied and bruised but alive. Liana looked down on him and spoke in a confident address.

"My name is Liana Langton. I am the Seventh Spectra Child. A descendant of the Transcended of the Aurora Visendus. Princess of Coryàtès and heir to the throne. I command you to release these prisoners, relinquish your title and surrender yourselves to your Queen." Zagan mustered a laboured nod before collapsing. Liana turned to the crowd.

"Followers of Zagan. I have gifted you part of my Morality. You are no longer Immorals. It will be at my mother's will to decide how to judge your actions." The Langton Army, led by Sir Tarak, roared in a rousing cheer of victory.

Master H. and Amara hurried to Liana's side.

"You have learned a lot in a short space of time. You have made the clan proud." bowed Master H.

"The clan? She has done the whole island proud." beamed Amara as she wrapped her arms around her.

When Amara finally released her grasp, Joel and Saffina stood waiting their turn. Liana opened her arms wide and felt the wetness of their cheeks against hers. "What are you doing here?"

"Well, as soon as we earned these, we knew we had to come and help." Joel and Saffina held up their Root Core buttons which glowed with their Red Aura.

"Wow! That's awesome! You've earned them. Well done guys."

"Not quite a match for yours, though," joked Joel. The three laughed together for the first time in what seemed like a lifetime. As they pulled away from their embrace, a sudden bolt of light appeared to their right.

"Useless child. I thought you Spectra Children were supposed to be strong! At least I'll have your complete Aura now." Vivek had pulled his body along the floor next to the still unconscious Gilroy. In his hand, an open Orb which was sucking the special Red Aura from Gilroy's body.

Liana ran towards Vivek, determined to stop his thievery. She didn't realise he was concealing a discarded sword in his other hand, and he pointed it to the sky as she neared him.

But she did not get injured, for the figure of Nalan appeared between them.

Liana shrieked Nalan's name as the pointed end of the sword protruded through his ribcage. His mouth dropped and eyebrows raised as the immense pain shook his body and he fell to the floor. Vivek sealed the Orb. She attacked with the Dagger of Red, but he called out a Jackdaw caw and a rain of birds descended onto his position. The rapid fluttering of their hundreds of wings made Liana withdraw and she could only watch as they carried the small old man away into the sky as he offered words of warning to her. "Aurora will side with me. You'll see little one. You'll see!"

Liana knelt beside Nalan. She could see life evaporating from his eyes.

"Did I make up for what I did to you, Princess?"

Full of tears, Liana mumbled "Yes. Yes, Nalan. I forgive you. We all forgive you."

"Do I die a good man?"

Liana could not concentrate enough to enter the Realm of Morality, but she knew she didn't need to go there. "You have always been a good man, Nalan."

Just before he drew his final breath, a peaceful smile stretched across his face. His muscles loosened and his face drooped solemnly. Liana cradled his head to hers and sobbed until there were no more tears left inside her.

2 8

FRIENDSHIPS

Liana and Queen Adriya sat contentedly as Zagan was escorted out of the Triunity Hall. It was the first time the Queen had banished someone completely off the island. The rest of the Queen's Table had met earlier in the day, and she had informed them of what her judgement was going to be. They fiercely disagreed, saying he should be put to death, but the Queen argued if she committed the man to death, she would be no better than he or Vivek. Sir Tarak raged that they had killed many soldiers, that they should not get mercy for their actions, but she did not believe it to be moral to kill in cold blood. As soon as she had even so much as hinted that her Morality would be in question, the Queen's Table soon backed down.

The Queen wrapped up the sentencing, announcing that all the Zaganites who fought in the Battle of Coryàtès would return to the mines and to make it functional again. The Queen had decided that Zagan and Vivek were solely to blame, that their actions meant that the miners were helpless to obey, so they would not be punished further for their participation. However, many of the former miners remained missing, having run off into the forest during and after the battle. It also transpired that just like Nalan's encounter with the architect, none of the soldiers could remember their actions. In fact, many couldn't remember where they had been for over a year, such was the effect of losing their Good Morality, and the evidence to the extent of which Vivek and Zagan had been plotting against the monarchy.

The jostling crowd made their way down the slopes of the Triunity Hall back to Swyre's golden city streets. Liana exited through one of the side doors and immediately heard her name being called. It was Saffina and Master H, with Joel in tow as he struggled to keep up as he hopped along on crutches.

"We've barely seen you since the battle," stated Saffina.

"I'm sorry," Liana apologised, sincerely "I didn't realise how much work there was to being on the Queen's Table. It's been non-stop meetings, checking in on people, interviewing..."

"It will all calm down soon enough." Master H said in his usual tone of wisdom.

"Have you any word of my brother?" Saffina asked, swallowing as she held back her tears. "My mum is going crazy."

Liana shook her head. "Eugene and Yasmin were not found on the beach. I'm sorry Saffina. We still have soldiers searching the forest for any stray Zaganites, but nothing on your brother. I'm sorry, Saff."

"He'll turn up. I just know it," said Joel, as he put a comforting arm around his friend.

"And when... if... he does, how will he be? Will it even be him? Neither of you saw him when he tried to kill me. It was like he had no idea who I was." A single tear drop fell onto the dusty ground. The wet speck formed a sun-like pattern.

"Well, if it isn't the pride of the Shroud Clan," a jovial voice penetrated the sombre atmosphere.

Master H. bowed respectively: "Priestess Yi."

"Master Hayashi," Priestess Yi tilted her head and reciprocated the gesture. "Liana, I wanted to thank you again for using your Sight to identify the cause of why my students have been unable to achieve their Aura's."

"That's quite alright, Priestess. I'm glad I was able to use my ability to help."

"I still can't believe the paints used for the Temple's petals were infused with Bad Morality. No wonder Aurora didn't gift us her rewards. Only Vivek would have been able to conjure up such an inventive way of halting our progress. It's been him in your mother's ears all these years, trying to hold us back, stop us from rebuilding the religion. He knew fighting against an army with Aura's would have been futile."

"It still was," piped Joel.

"Yes, but only thanks to this one though," Priestess Yi beamed a smile at Liana. "He probably tried to have that architect killed so he could take over the project. He knew the Queen would have entrusted it to him if he'd have asked, but when his attempt to use Nalan failed, he must have come up with a different plan. That's why he was so keen to delay the project, until he had had his extra layer of special paint coated on."

"I still can't believe he's so evil. The hours I've spent alone with him, learning from him as my tutor, trusting him. I don't know what to believe anymore," Liana sighed.

"I expect he only lied to you about the religion... and anything relating to his plans of conquering the island. Any other general knowledge he imparted to you would likely have been genuine.I expect he sees you as an essential tool to carry out his plans for power. It wouldn't make sense for you to be ignorant of things like science, technology and sociology." more wise words from Master H.

"He's still out there, though. And he probably still wants me. Or at least, wants my powers."

"This battle will have weakened him, so at least now we have some time, little one," Master H. stroked his moustache. "Although it may not be long before he gets his strength back. Men like Vivek feed off the Morality of others. The more he feeds, the stronger he becomes."

"I must be getting back to the Temple," said Priestess Yi. "Are you sure you can't recreate that white dome, Liana? It certainly would save a lot of time. It's going to take weeks to scrape that paint off and reapply."

"I have told you already, Priestess," Master H reacted sharply to the suggestion. "Liana cannot afford to go giving away her Morality at a whim."

"And I wouldn't know how anyway. It just kind of... happened." added Liana.

"Okay, Okay, very well. Liana, I shall see you after dinner?"

"After dinner?"

"This evening's Queen's Table meeting."

"Oh, right, yeh, another meeting," Liana said, rolling her eyes, before looking up at the Tower of Seeds, dreading having to ascend it yet again. "Master H how is Gilroy doing?" she said, changing the subject.

"Your mother... your birth mother... is at the Shrouded Temple caring for him. He is awake, but he has no Aura or

Morality. He is just a shell. It's like Vivek sucked out all of his energy."

"I feel sorry for him. The things he's had to endure. He's not even as old as us."

"We will make sure he is comfortable."

"Any news on the other Artifacts? My other Spirits?"

"Not yet. Candela will tell us as soon as she hears anything from her network in the other kingdoms. Until then, the safest place for you is here, Liana. Right now, though, you three should go and enjoy yourselves, whilst you can. In between your studies with me, of course."

Liana looked longingly toward her friends. "I agree. Come on guys, let's hang out, like we used to."

"And we don't even have to watch our backs for Yasmin anymore!" said an exuberant Joel, who lifted his arms in the air and forgetting he was holding a crutch, promptly smacked both Saffina and Liana square in the face.

The pair clutched their noses, blurting out in unison a cry of "Jeez, Joel!", before all three soon saw the funny side and belly-laughed, thankful that they were still together and closer than ever.

"He's in Allicalidantè. I had word fly in this morning."

"Allicalidantè? He's moving fast, faster than expected. Surely, he can't have... consumed... everything in his last known position already?"

"I wouldn't have thought so, he never moves on until he has Turned everything. He must be there for a reason."

"Another Spectra Child?"

"Possibly, there is a founding temple there, but given his

haste, I'm not totally convinced. I need to be sure of his reasons. My guess would be it has something to do with the next Artifact."

"The next Artifact?"

"Liana's Sacral Core, her Orange Aura, is in a Spirit Orb bonded with the Jewels of Orange."

"What's so special about this Artifact?"

"That's what I need you to find out."

Amara raised a quizzical eyebrow. "Thank you for confiding in me, Priestess," she said. "I won't tell Adriya of this conversation. I'm glad you finally decided to use my skills."

"If he's in Allicalidantè it'll be pointless approaching Adriya, or the Queen's Table. We haven't had any contact with their King since Liana was born, for obvious reasons."

"Don't worry, Priestess Yi. You can trust me. What do you need me to do?"

"I need you to sail to Allicalidantè and find the Jewels of Orange before anyone else."

"But I have no Visendi powers to protect me?"

"Where he is concerned, that is probably a good thing. Less attention, less suspicion, less traceability."

"How important is it to get to this Artifact before him?"

"The fate of Mikana could depend on it."

L iana will return in:
Jewels of Orange

ACKNOWLEDGMENTS

My sincerest and biggest thanks go to my wife, Sabrina, for always supporting my next crazy venture in life. Without your understanding and patience, I wouldn't have gotten close to where I am now.

My next thanks go to my dad, who was the first person to read this story cover-to-cover and provided invaluable feedback. Also, thanks to my mum, for keeping my dad on track!

Thank you also to Inessa Sage of Cauldron Press for producing such amazing cover art and formatting to turn my story into a 'proper' book!

Finally, thank you to you, the reader. I truly am grateful for every single person who has taken a punt and delved into the conjuring's of my imagination. I hope you have enjoyed these words and are looking forward to following Liana on her next adventure.

ABOUT SIMON PITTMAN

"There is something eternal about publishing a book." Says Simon, who is by trade a Learning & Development professional, and a family man who lives in Dorset, UK with his wife Sabrina and his children Jensen and Mina.

Simon didn't discover his passion for reading until his thirties. Cyberpunk, Virtual Reality and Sci-Fi genres are typically his favourite genre for reading, but as an author, it's the limitless creativity of fantasy writing.

Printed in Great Britain
by Amazon

11384740R00200